I0583457

Leave It All Behind

By: Rachel Peugh

*For my mum, Sharon. Who's always supported me
and gone above and beyond as a parent.
And for the innocent victims and survivors of gun
violence.*

Preface

This novel is a work of fiction. While it references real places, locations, and institutions, all events, characters, timelines, and operational details have been fictionalized or invented for the purposes of storytelling.

This story contains depictions of violence and trauma as part of its narrative. These moments are not intended to glorify or endorse violence in any form. Rather, they exist to explore the consequences of power, secrecy, loyalty, and the choices people make when they believe there are no good options left.

My hope in writing this book was to tell a story about survival, resilience, and the human cost of those choices—not to diminish the very real pain experienced by individuals and families affected by violence in the real world. Any harm portrayed on the page is meant to be taken seriously, with care, and with respect for those whose lives have been shaped by similar experiences.

Thank you for trusting this story and its characters.

—Rachel Peugh

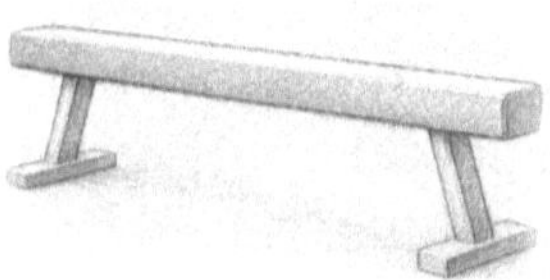

1
The Golden Girl

Early morning sun filtered through the gauzy hotel curtains as Claire laced up her purple-and-white running shoes, the same gym colors she'd worn since she was ten. Today wasn't just another meet—if she nailed this competition, she'd be one step closer to the Olympic Trials. One step closer to proving she deserved the future she'd been training for her whole life. The thought tightened in her chest. One mistake—one wobble—and everything she'd worked for could slip away.

She slipped on her matching jacket, the name of her gym—Zero Gravity—embroidered in looping purple script across the back. Her mother, Louisa, wore a nearly identical one with the word *Coach* on hers. Claire trained three days a week at a gym in Knoxville; the other four days she trained in the private gym Louisa had created in the old barn behind their home.

With less than 3,000 people in their small town, there wasn't much need for an elite gymnastics studio. On Fridays, Louisa taught beginner classes in the barn to the younger generations in their town, but she wanted Claire to be a part of a team like she had been. So three days a week, they made the ninety-minute drive to the nearest club with an elite program.

Zero Gravity had given Claire the team experience Louisa

had wanted for her, and she enjoyed their time in Knoxville. But the days training alone with her mom were her favorite. No noise, no pressure—just focus.

Ready to go, Claire slung her gym bag over her shoulder and went to the adjoining hotel door. A single knock and Louisa answered. She said nothing, just raised her finger to her lips and pointed back at the still-occupied bed. Max, Claire's dad, snored away like he had done every night since she was little. Grabbing her own small bag, Louisa stepped into Claire's room, shutting the door gently behind her.

"He had a late night. Some work emergency had him up until two. Let's go down."

Max never missed a meet, work emergencies or not. Guilt pricked at Claire—they shaped their whole lives around her dreams. She had to make it worth it.

Reaching for Claire's duffel bag, Louisa ushered them out into the hallway. "I'll take your bag to the car, while you go for your jog. Meet me in the lobby after and we will go pick up breakfast. I set an alarm and left a note for your dad already."

Getting into the elevator, Louisa reminded Claire not to push herself. Just to clear her head. She didn't want to risk an injury today of all days. Louisa's warm southern charm, coaching style and mothering instinct all seemed to roll into one caring, but firm demeanor that seemed to never turn off. More like her father, Claire wasn't very talkative this early in the morning. She preferred to have a cup of coffee or a run before talking too much. Today the jog would have to do, as Claire didn't drink coffee on competition mornings. Water only—until after the meet was done.

Waving goodbye to her mom, Claire picked up the pace jogging lightly around the Chicago streets. Her long, straight auburn hair bounced in the ponytail that she had haphazardly tossed it into. She would redo her hair once they left for the meet.

There was a park not too far away, but when in the city Claire preferred to stay in the most populated areas. Her father's self-defense lessons had been drilled into her head from a very young age. Always keeping an eye out. Never running with earbuds in. Never running in an unpopulated area where there weren't any witnesses.

She scanned faces out of habit. It was second nature now, baked into her bones. Her dad called it vigilance. Most people didn't grow up being taught how to spot danger before it spotted you. Sometimes she wondered if her dad was overprotective or if he knew something she didn't. The thought always left a pit in her stomach.

Claire bounced on her toes at a stoplight, waiting for the crossing signal to change. She watched cars drive past while she thought about everything that had led up to today. When she was young, she had been a rambunctious toddler always climbing and jumping off everything and anything. When she was little, Louisa started coaching and would take Claire with her. She'd sneak out of the daycare room and into the gym, mimicking the older kids with every chance she got. She was a natural and lived for the feeling of flying, tumbling, and twisting. Realizing she'd been twisting her braided leather bracelet, she stopped and twisted it around so the knot was on the bottom again. The light changed and the flashing hand turned to the little white walk signal.

The city came to life around Claire as she ran, forgetting to take it easy. The city sounds surrounded her; taxi drivers honking, women laughing as they gossiped on their way to work, and then the sudden scream of sirens in the distance. They made her skin prickle; they always had. Her dad seemed to tense the same way. She shook it off, but the unease of nearby danger lingered longer than it should have.

Returning to the hotel, Claire spotted her father first and then her mother. Her father held a *large* cup of hotel coffee in his hands, while her mother tucked a spare banana and water bottle into her crossbody bag, a Kate Spade satchel her dad had gifted her last Christmas.

After a breakfast of more coffee for Max and a healthy fruit-filled Greek yogurt and granola bowl for Claire and Louisa, the trio climbed into the rental car and set out for the arena. Many gymnasts and their families stayed within walking distance to the arena; however, Max always insisted on being further away. He used price gouging as his excuse, but Claire suspected there was more to it than that.

The buzz in the air was electric as they drove to the arena. Her dad began whistling an old tune from the driver's seat, while Claire fixed her hair into a neat and secure bun. Rules only stated that hair was neat and pulled back to keep from "infringing on your performance." However, Claire found that her long hair would whip around too much in a ponytail—often smacking her in the face.

She had just finished her hair when Max pulled into the arena's parking lot. He stopped whistling and started loudly complaining about parking lot etiquette—or the lack thereof—when he was cut off by another driver. Claire barely noticed; she was too preoccupied mentally going over her routines. If she failed today, it would be another four years before she could make it to the Olympic Trials.

Inside the stadium, she soaked in the energy, nerves bubbling beneath her skin. As they passed the familiar faces of gymnasts and coaches in the corridors, Claire did her best to ignore their gazes. She knew what they were thinking, she was the one to beat—the one they'd all love to see fall. One of her competitors, Ruby, gave Claire a fake smile that didn't reach her eyes. She had left Zero Gravity for a more "elite" club two years ago and hadn't spoken to Claire since. She simply nodded in return and turned away, focusing on Louisa's calm, grounding presence. She refused to let Ruby's petty elitist attitude affect her today.

While Louisa checked in at the table for coaches, Claire checked in at the athlete table. Showing the QR code on her phone, a volunteer handed her a laminated badge with her photo and "Zero Gravity" printed beneath her name. A purple wristband was secured around her wrist—training hall access—and a branded folder containing her rotation schedule and venue map was slipped into her hands.

Entering the locker room, Claire kept to herself as she passed by several other competitors. She hadn't made close friendships with any of the girls, but she recognized most of them by reputation alone. Sasha, a young woman from California, was in the corner of the room fixing her hair in the mirrors. Then there was a girl called Gigi, from Portland. Claire knew very little about her but she seemed nice enough. Finally, there was Destiny from Boston—older, powerful, and one of the top contenders—she was Claire's real competition.

Finding a free spot on the benches, she dropped her duffel bag. Claire slipped into her competition leotard, a deep purple leo with sheer long sleeves, white geometric diamonds, and rhinestones cascading around the shoulders and down her arms. Slipping her warmup pants on top, they made a crinkling swishing sound as she pulled them over her hips, thinking about how this polyester sport fabric basically defined 90's fashion. Finally, Claire carefully removed the leather band around her wrist. The worn band was held together with a tight knot that had almost fused together from age, friction, and body heat. Getting the knot to give way she was able to tuck it into the zippered pocket of her warmup bag. She had worn it daily since he had given it to her. A braided piece of leather from inside his thrift shop leather jacket.

Verifying her bag was securely zipped shut she slung the strap over her shoulder and went to meet her mom on the competition floor. The rhinestones on her leotard sparkled beneath the lights as she walked out to the training hall for warm-ups.

Claire met Louisa in the hall, a mini gym with all of the apparatus used for warming up before stepping onto the competition floor. She had thirty minutes to stretch, do some basic skills and then do a few light passes on each of the four rotations.

The training hall buzzed with a low thrum of activity and chalk dust hung in the air like a fine mist, settling on mats, grips, and the low beams that lined along one wall. Only eight girls were assigned to Claire's warm-up session. Sixteen competitors in total—every one of them razor-focused, all capable of getting on the podium if she slipped up today.

Destiny was already on a low beam, snapping into a back handspring with the kind of precision that made her coach smile proudly. Gigi marked her floor choreography in the corner, earbuds in, body loose and fluid.

Claire stretched her calves near the vault runway, trying to pretend she wasn't watching everyone else. But that was impossible in the close-quartered training hall. You couldn't help but see—and measure—your competition.

Farther down, Sasha adjusted her grips and hopped onto the uneven low bar. Claire watched from the corner of her eye. Sasha had been clean last season but inconsistent... nothing too threatening. But today she moved differently—sharper, confident, almost buoyant.

She cast into a handstand, then released into a Ray—high, clean, and caught with barely a wobble.
Louisa inhaled softly beside Claire.
That was new.

And it was good—good enough to bump Claire out of the top rankings on bars if Sasha hit it in competition.
Claire forced her gaze away, rolling her shoulders back as she started her general warm-up. She wasn't supposed to watch others, not this closely. But this was the nature of elite gymnastics—one new skill from a competitor could shove you from the podium to the middle of the pack.

Destiny stuck a crisp double layout on the soft tumbling strip, her feet thudding against the floor with authority. Ruby stood staring at Destiny, her hands planted firmly on her hips, like she was cataloging every flaw. Claire tried to pay her no attention, it wasn't worth her energy.

Claire swallowed. Everyone had come prepared. Hungry. This wasn't Nationals when she was twelve; this was the big leagues. And the girls around her weren't just familiar faces—they were the people standing between her and the Olympic Trials.
"Eyes on your own path," Louisa murmured, looping an arm gently around Claire's shoulders. "You've worked hard for today. Trust in your own skills."

Claire nodded, letting out a breath as she jogged toward the vault runway to begin warming up her legs. But even as she moved through the motions—lunges, kicks, hurdles—her mind kept drifting back to that Ray release. To the way Sasha had caught the bar like she was born to do it.

Sixteen competitors—and only one shot to prove she deserved to stand among them. Today, everyone looked ready to fight for it.

Twenty minutes later the loudspeaker called for the competitors to report to the floor. Claire and Louisa exchanged nods, a silent understanding passing between them. "You've got this, love," Louisa whispered, brushing a stray hair behind Claire's ear.

After all of the gymnasts were in the competition arena, the judges called for the "Four-Minute Touch" to begin—a brief window before each rotation where gymnasts tested a skill or two on the apparatus ahead. Claire's first event was the vault. She would compete moving from one apparatus to the next with her group of eight gymnasts from the training hall. When she was done with her final vault warm-up she retreated to her chair and finished stretching. While sitting in the middle splits she looked up and found her dad in the stands. She gave him a smile, receiving a wink in response. His presence always made her feel more calm.

She was the third gymnast to compete within her group of eight. Destiny competed first, landing her vault perfectly, but surprisingly she threw one that wasn't worth as many points as she had in the past. There had been rumors she was retiring after this year, maybe it was true. Sasha was next, with a simple but clean vault. Most gymnasts only threw one vault, unless they were trying to medal in that apparatus specifically.

When it was Claire's turn she took a deep breath as she approached the raised platform. Despite it being one of her favorite events she knew the risks. Last year one of the older gymnasts had landed just slightly wrong and destroyed her career in less than 30 seconds. Ever since, the potential ways to fall flooded Claire's head every time she stepped up to the track. One wrong angle and she could shatter her ankles. She pushed the thought down—fear had no place here, not today.

Claire chalked her hands and approached the runway with laser focus. Her first vault was a Cheng: a round-off onto the springboard, a half-twist onto the vaulting table, then one and a half twists in the air. With a difficulty value of 5.6, it was one of the more difficult vaults. Raising up on her toes she took a deep breath before launching down the runway. Her body hummed with focus as her feet pounded the mat moving at full speed toward the stationary vault. If anyone blinked they'd have missed it. She landed, two feet planted, no step back. Perfect.

Her second vault was much riskier, the Produnova—the infamous vault of death. With a high risk of spinal injury if done wrong it had a starting value of 6.0. Connecting her hands to the ground she pushed both feet into a round-off, front handspring onto the vault. Then rotating into two and a half somersaults before landing, she stuck it. The arena roared.

A smile and water bottle greeted Claire as she descended the apparatus platform to Louisa. Quickly peeking over at her competitors, a mix of glares, open mouths and worried faces stared back at her.

Claire sat down with her gear to begin prepping for the next rotation, the uneven bars. Twisting around them was her happy place, the one place she felt truly weightless and free. It was one of the only places the world went silent. If only life outside the bars felt as simple.

Ruby descended from the platform having just finished her own vault. Claire hadn't even seen it. She wasn't concerned about her old friend's performance. The girl's voice oozed faux concern when she spoke. "Nervous, Claire? Your vaults looked… ambitious."

Claire smiled without warmth. "See you from the podium."

Louisa ripped off a piece of tape for her wrist and gave her the look—ignore it, she's not worth the distraction. No drama, not today. Louisa had also competed against girls like Ruby. They cared more about the prestige than the sport and spent more time flirting with the male athletes instead of training. She had been happy when Ruby left; Claire could, and did, do better in the friend department. Ruby was only holding her daughter back.

Bars came next. Waiting for her turn, Claire stayed in her own zone and focused on mentally going over her routine. It wasn't long before Louisa was tapping her shoulder to indicate it was her turn. She hadn't even noticed how the two before her had done.

On the platform with her wrists taped and her leather grips securely strapped to her hands, Claire turned to the judges to salute and begin her routine.

Claire took to the bars with flair, launching into her routine with speed and confidence. The moment her hands found the wood, everything else faded—the crowd, the pressure, the weight of expectation. She moved through her releases and transitions in a seamless rush of motion, swinging higher and faster until the world narrowed to timing and trust.

When she let go for the final time and landed, chest high, the feeling was familiar and electric. Controlled. Confident.

The exhilaration Claire felt every time she flew through the air, jumping from bar to bar, was what made the bars her favorite. But in this moment after completing her salute, Claire didn't know how she hadn't exploded from the adrenaline that flooded her system.

Returning to her mother she heard the announcer read off her scores. Full points. Claire often tried to tune out the scores, she didn't need a numerical value to tell her how she had done. She was aware of every tiny mistake or unpointed toe that the judges would also catch. But hearing them now boosted her confidence for the next round.

Removing her grips she prepared herself mentally to move onto the hardest apparatus next, beam. As a child she was fearless on the beam but the 4-inch-wide block of wood was a lot closer to the ground back then. When she was twelve she got a case of the "twisties," a mental block that made her unable to complete previously mastered skills. It only affected her on the beam but even after overcoming it she still felt a tiny fear that remained, trying to break free.

As Claire sat waiting to be called she felt her mother's hand on her shoulder.

"You've got this. Just stick it."

Nodding to Louisa's favorite mantra, Claire looked up into the crowd, scanning until she found her dad's gaze again. He smiled, and Claire felt the warmth of a bear hug only her father could give, spanning the vast arena from a hundred feet away.

Before she knew it, she was stepping into the chalk bin, covering her feet in a layer of the white powder. Louisa placed the springboard just right for her daughter's mount onto the beam. Saluting the judges, Claire was ready.

Her mount was a back handspring onto the springboard landing firmly on the beam. She moved through the sequence with confidence and flair—tight landings, sharp arms, the kind of control that made it look easy. When she got to her combo jumps she bobbled, small and barely noticeable, but it was there. That could be a .1 deduction. She moved on as best she could, trying not to tense up her muscles. A few artistic elements and jumps and she was almost done. Claire's body floated with each element into a leap combo. Then came her dismount, a double Arabian known as the Patterson, with her knees tucked up, she held them to the side as she rotated forward, soaring through the air. Landing it, solid and precise.

She let out a breath. It was done.

Her final challenge was the floor. A twelve-meter square with springs. If she steps outside of the square—deduction. Going over her ninety-second allotted time slot—deduction. Failing to jump high enough on leaps, jumps or flips, also a deduction. And yet Claire loved the floor almost as much as the bars. The musical element added so much to a performance, allowing gymnasts to experiment and play with new movements.

Claire sat cross-legged on the floor with her headphones in, reviewing her music and steps. Her phone vibrated. Only one number was allowed through the "Do Not Disturb" setting, Mr. Leather jacket himself—Trevor.

Butterflies took flight in her stomach as she read his text, "You look amazing. That Arabian was perfect! I love you."

Claire beamed. Trevor was watching live. Her childhood best friend turned boyfriend had always been her biggest supporter, apart from her parents.

When it was time she stood, walked to the center, and saluted. Her opening pose: one fist raised, one hip popped. A nod to *The Breakfast Club*. The music hit, an upbeat, lyric-less 80s anthem. A nod to her mom's glory days.

Claire danced to the corner, her choreography precise, confident, and charming. Throwing her first tumbling pass she proved why she was the best. Her height, speed and power were unmatched. She moved into her dance sequence, clean turns, expressive arms, a joyful sassy smile. Her second tumbling pass was bold, with combinations few other gymnasts would even consider doing in competition. The final beat of the music hit as she dropped to one knee, chest heaving.

The crowd erupted. Max stood, clapping wildly. Louisa had her hand over her mouth, tears in her eyes. It didn't matter that there were still five gymnasts to go—the energy in the room said it all. Claire had beaten them.

Later, on the podium, the gold medal hung around her neck, the bouquet cradled in her arms. She had taken first in the individual All-Around.

She looked into the stands for her parents. Louisa mouthed, "You did it." Max gave a small thumbs-up, filming on his phone.

Claire had never felt so proud.

Not long after, she would also be announced as taking gold in Vault, Bars, and Floor. Her small bobble on beam downgraded her to a silver—but Claire didn't care. She'd done exactly what she came to do. Four gold medals at the U.S. Championships. Next stop: the Olympic Trials. Then the Olympic Team.

Claire had everything she had ever dreamed of—a thriving gymnastics career, Trevor, and the best parents a girl could ask for. She didn't know it yet, but everything was about to fade away like a dream that ended too soon.

2
Goodbye & Gunsmoke

After what seemed like endless press questions and fake congratulations from Claire's fellow competitors, she'd had enough and wanted desperately to go eat a real meal. Making eye contact with her mom, Claire signed that she was done and needed rescuing. Together, they had many secret signals, but this one seemed to be the most used between Claire and her mom. A little scratch behind her left ear and her mom was by her side, taking control.

Once Louisa was in control, Claire could sneak away and duck into the locker room to change. Before doing anything else, she retrieved the leather band from the zippered pocket and looped it around her wrist. She used her teeth to help pull the knot tight again. Inside her bag was a simple black halter dress. It was tradition that no matter her scores, Max would treat his hard-working girls to a nice dinner.

The dress fit her well and showed off her figure with the halter cut leading up into a wide straight band around the neck. Wrapping around her ribcage the halter neckline cut across her back at her waist and flared out into a very full circle skirt. This created a narrowing effect to her waist and added curves where she didn't have many. Adding a pair of slingback wedge heels to the look, Claire made one last adjustment, her long straight hair was let down from the bun it had been in all day. The tight twist and dried sweat had curled her hair ever so slightly, creating a soft subtle wave.

Leaving the locker room, Claire found her dad first. Max was on his phone, having a hushed argument. He paced around the empty cinderblock hallway, stopping and quickly ending his call when he saw Claire coming. "Is everything okay?" Claire asked in hush tones as she approached.

With a smile, Max slung his arm around his daughter's shoulder, "Just a small work issue. It can wait. Have you decided where we are eating? What does my gold medalist fancy?"

With a smile and a sheepish look at her dad, they said in unison, "Burger."

A typical athlete... Claire wanted red meat for a cheat meal.

Dinner was delicious, exactly what Claire had been craving. An Irish-themed pub seemed the perfect choice when searching for a burger in the big city. Louisa ended up ordering a classic Caesar salad while father and daughter both indulged in matching burgers with all the fixings.

They spoke about the day's events and how excited they were for the potential to go to the next summer Olympics in Rome. Max brought up Ruby's face when Claire had landed her "perfect" vaults. According to Louisa, Ruby's face had looked like she had just eaten a lemon. It was a serendipitous evening celebrating Claire and her accomplishments.

When it was time to leave, Max went ahead to get the car while Louisa paid. Claire sent a text to Trevor, just letting him know they could video chat soon.

Out on the humid downtown street, Max rounded the corner behind the wheel of the rental car. As they stepped out into the early summer evening, Claire thought how silly her dad looked in such a small car. She had always known him to drive larger, more imposing vehicles.

Louisa slid into the front passenger seat while Claire tucked in behind her. The car smelled of fresh flowers that had slightly wilted after an hour in the hot car. Claire buckled up and leaned her forehead against the glass window. After a long day and a filling meal, Claire was now ready to call Trevor and then go to bed.

The evening had a strange hum to it as they drove the city streets back to their hotel. Louisa was rattling off the check-in times for their return flight in the morning while Max drove, calm and in control. Despite his strange phone call earlier, Max had seemed his usual self at dinner. Claire had thought about bringing up the call at dinner, but she hadn't wanted to ruin the celebration and knew he'd just brushed it off. Max rarely talked about his security job.

As Claire watched the downtown landscape speed by, Max expertly maneuvered the city streets. Competition adrenaline had been replaced by a bone-deep tiredness that made Claire's limbs feel heavy and loose. She leaned her head back against the seat, her eyes fluttering closed, letting her thoughts drift. She didn't notice the streets had grown quiet.

The car jerked.

Not a swerve. A violent impact. Metal shrieked. Glass shattered. Claire's seatbelt caught hard across her chest as the car spun and the world flipped.

In reality, it had only been a matter of seconds but inside the car it seemed like an eternity. Claire had watched as her mother was slammed into by the once white airbag, now stained red. Her father had twisted looking back for her. He had desperately said something but Claire couldn't process what he had said.

Crashing into a cement barrier, the car finally came to a brutal, grinding halt.

Silence, but not true silence, the kind filled with broken sounds: a creaking chassis, dripping fluids, a single tire spinning uselessly, and the muffled cries Claire hadn't yet identified as her own.

Claire hung upside down in her seatbelt, the world upended and blurred. Her head ached. Blood ran into her hair as it hung limp and swayed. She reached out, instinctively, for her parents.

"Mom?" Her voice came out cracked. "Dad?"

No response.

Already tired from her day and now what she could only guess was a head wound, Claire's body fought sleep. But she had to get help. Pushing herself to wake up, she unbuckled, collapsing onto the interior roof, now the floor. She crawled toward the front seats, glass biting into her palms and knees.

She had to reach her parents. How was it that such a small car could feel so massive? Every movement felt like it took all of her strength. Reaching for her mom in the front passenger seat, Claire felt for a pulse on her neck. Louisa's arms dangled lifelessly touching the blood-soaked car ceiling. Unable to find a pulse, Claire realized her hand was covered in blood and tried wiping it on her cotton dress. Her brain refused to accept what her hands already knew. Touching her mom's neck again, she realized it was useless. She still couldn't find a pulse.

Claire felt her eyes burn white hot and her nose tingle as she fought back tears. She didn't know how her body had the strength to cry when it was all she could do to stay awake. Moving to her father, Claire's hand hovered, not wanting to know. Not ready to know if she was an orphan. But she leaned in anyway.

Nothing.

Gunshots ripped Claire out of her grief. Pinging off the top of the car consistently, the shots were precise, trained and professional.

Instincts told her to run, but slipping in the blood, she fell flat against the once beige roof of the car. The wet upholstery gushed beneath her fingers as she pushed herself up. Looking out a broken window, Claire caught a glimpse of the shooter. He was monstrously tall with tattoos covering what she could see of his arms and neck. Black hair darkened his face, his eyes were like dark lasers, focused on what Claire assumed was hitting the car's gas tank.

Adrenaline flooding her system, she reacted before she even knew what she was doing. There was no thought, only motion—the way her father had trained her. She reached between the driver's seat and the center console, grabbing the cold handle of her father's gun. Then, turning to the side window, she kicked it out the rest of the way. Hoping that the gunman hadn't heard the shattering glass she crawled out of the car. Remembering only at the last second to grab her duffel bag from the back seat. Her hands and knees screamed in pain as her body weight ground asphalt into the open wounds.

Allowing only a second to look back at the two most important people in her life, Claire whispered a goodbye and *I love you*. Using her forearm, she cleared the tears from her eyes and refocused on the task at hand. Slinging her bag over her head she looked down at the gun and turned off the safety. Getting up into a crouching position and preparing to run, Claire noticed the air was now full of the stench of gasoline pouring out from a broken tank.

Panic and fear fought with her training. But just like doing a release skill on the bars, timing was everything. She needed to time her escape with the next shot. Holding the gun between both hands, like her dad had taught her, she pointed the muzzle down at the ground. She was ready to shoot if necessary. Raising to the balls of her feet, she took a deep breath and released the bar. She ran for the darkest alley she could see.

The shooter's next shot came rapidly after the first. A tsunami of heat chased Claire as the car went up in a blaze. Only looking back when she was hidden by the shadows of the Chicago skyscrapers, Claire watched as the flames consumed the car, her family, her life, and her Olympic dreams.

Tearing her eyes away from the flames, Claire took one more look at the man walking away from the crash. His movement was calm and graceful, he didn't run or even hurry; he just strode, like he was taking a leisurely walk in the park on a Sunday morning. Claire made note of his distinct features, the dark tattoos wrapping around his body, his dark hair, a strong jaw and the vacant eyes. Pivoting away from the wreck before she could be seen, Claire dashed down the alley she had been hiding in.

Her phone was in her duffel, should she call the police? Max's voice over the years echoed in her head, "If anything ever happened to me, anything violent, you need to first get away. Get safe. Then find help, but you can't go to the police." There was more he used to say but she was struggling to remember what it was.

First she needed to find somewhere to clean up. She was covered head to toe in blood and the last thing she needed was attention. Attention could let the shooter know where she was and she didn't know if she was collateral damage or a target.

Keeping to the shadows, Claire held the gun squarely between her hands ready to shoot if necessary. She used her bag to hide the gun behind. Afraid to draw attention by running, she walked with purpose, going six blocks before she found a gas station.

Her mind raced with questions while she walked. *Why would someone shoot at their car? It was deliberate, right? Did they have the wrong car, the wrong people? Was he a crazed lunatic just murdering people because he could? Why would her dad teach her to not go to the cops?*

Some of the answers she felt she knew instantly. The shooter wasn't a lunatic, he was so calm, he walked with purpose. This had been a planned attack. It was the correct car too, she could feel it in her bones. *But why would someone want to hurt her parents?*

The ring of the bell on the metal-framed door chimed as she pushed it open. Thankfully the teller was more consumed with his small 90s TV that hid behind the counter and glass surround. Cheers came from the small tattered box, it was clearly a game, football maybe. Approaching the counter, Claire desperately tried to hide the parts of her body that were covered in semi-dried blood.

"Where's the restroom?" Claire kept her voice soft, not wanting him to look up from his game.

"In the back, left side." Unhooking a key, with a large wooden paddle attached, the cashier slid it over the counter and through the opening in the glass. He glanced up at her. He was young, in his late twenties, maybe a year or two in difference. His skin was darker, a shade of caramel with black hair. Pausing when he saw the cut on her forehead, he gestured at it with his chin, "You make a mess, you clean it up."

"I will," grabbing the key from the countertop, Claire made a dash for the bathroom. A surge of panic hitting her, she hoped she hadn't left blood from her hands on the counter. But the crowd on the TV erupted once more, catching the cashier's attention. Even if she had smeared any blood, she doubted he would have noticed.

In the back, Claire gazed at the dirty brown door that she believed hadn't been cleaned since the 1970s, when it was probably installed. The once-light-brown door was now black in several places and the metal handle was now spotty and looking more like aged bronze than the chrome it had once been. Using the end of her sleeve to touch the handle, Claire slipped the key in the opening and twisted until she heard it click. Having to use her whole body weight—one hand on the knob, and her shoulder against the wood—she pushed leaning into the door until it popped free of the frame. Slipping in, she immediately locked the door behind her.

The bathroom was just as disgusting as the door had been, maybe worse. White porcelain now a rusted cream, hand-dryer with missing parts, and a mirror cracked and broken like someone had tried to repair it after it had been punched. Feeling safer, she put the safety back on the gun. She lifted her gym bag over her head and placed it on the floor with the gun beside it, Claire rummaged through to find her warm-up gear and running shoes. Slipping out of the blood-soaked dress she wore, Claire dropped it on the floor and grabbed a towel out of her bag. The towel had been used to wipe sweat off her face but it would have to do now, she could properly clean her wounds when she got to where she was going. Wherever that might be.

Catching a glimpse of herself in the mirror, Claire didn't recognize the young woman looking back at her. She felt numb and broken. Doing her best to just function, to do what she had been told, it was like she had turned her feelings off. Let her emotions go silent.

Turning on the faucet, Claire was relieved to see that the water coming out of it was actually clean. Surprise, surprise. Moving the edge of the towel under the water, carefully holding the rest of it away from the edge of the sink, Claire wiped the dried blood from her face, hands, arms and knees. Most of the blood on her skin and clothing wasn't hers, even the dried streaks on her legs.

After cleaning her body she reached down for the warm-ups she had been wearing that morning. Bending down she grabbed her socks and as she did, she felt the cuts on her knees stretch and begin to bleed again. Pulling out the little bit of athletic tape she had left, Claire used it as bandages to wrap her wounds. Hands, knees, and a long laceration she had on her right ribcage. She hadn't realized until now that it was even there but as she pressed tape against it, she couldn't help but let out a hiss of pain.

As Claire finished tying up her running shoes she replayed the evening's events in her head. The crash unraveled in slow motion as she questioned every moment, wondering if she could have done anything different to save her parents' lives.

If they'd gone straight back to the hotel, would this not have happened? If she'd opted for dessert, would the extra twenty minutes have stopped the car from hitting them? No. Because this wasn't random, this was an attack targeting her father. She thought of his work phone call and his tensed whispers. He tried to say something in the car but what was it?

Wishing she could go back to any time before the crash, Claire went to shove her bloody clothes into her bag and saw the four gold metal boxes sitting at the base of her duffel. Tears flooded her eyes again. Just two hours ago Claire Huntington had won the U.S. Championship and was on her way to making the U.S. women's Olympic gymnastics team with her mother by her side, now... now she was leaving an old bathroom, with clothes stained in her parents' blood.

Finally, her brain processed what her father had said. She stopped in her tracks, "Run... Hugh." There might have been more, but it didn't matter. He had known—even before the gunshots—

that this wasn't an accident. She had to find Hugh.

3
The Escape

Leaving the gas station behind—along with the smell of burnt coffee and grease—Claire tried to look like just another traveler. Thankfully matching sets were in fashion, otherwise her monochromatic outfit might look out of place. With the gun hidden in her waistband, she kept checking that her warm-up jacket wasn't riding up.

The fluorescent lights above the gas pumps hummed overhead as Claire walked past the parking lot and out onto the street. Keeping her head down, she fumbled for her phone in the duffel and stuck to the shadows. The summer sun was setting and the streets were darkening quickly.

She pulled her phone from her duffel side pocket, fingers trembling as she stared at the cracked screen. Her father's voice echoed in her head—*"You know the number. If anything ever happens, call Hugh. No hesitation."*

She had memorized that number, repeating it every night until her father finally stopped quizzing her. But her thumb hovered over the keypad.

Would using her phone be safe? Or would it flag her location immediately? Was someone tracking her or did they think she was dead?

Her breath hitched when the screen lit up with an incoming video call request.

Trevor.

The photo of him smiling back at her made her chest ache. They were supposed to video chat soon. She was *supposed* to be in her PJs back at the hotel snuggled up, safe. Her parents were *supposed* to be on the other side of the door making out like teenagers. Trevor was probably wondering why she hadn't checked in.

She desperately wanted to answer his call, see his face and let him make it all better. Her thumb hovered for a second too long. If she answered, if she saw his face right now, she wouldn't be able to keep the mask on. And if anyone was already watching her...

She declined the call.

Her throat tightened as the screen went dark. The moment it did, something inside her followed.

If this was targeted—if it was because of her dad—then everything visible about her life was a liability: the Olympics, interviews, Trevor.

She couldn't afford hope. Not yet. Hugh first. Safe first. Then answers.

She slid the phone open, popped the SIM card out, and powered the phone off completely, then dropped both into her duffel.

Finding a pay phone in 2018 was like looking for a unicorn. She walked down the city street, scanning for options, when a burst of laughter drew her attention.

A group of people lined the sidewalk up ahead. Neon signs indicated the bar behind them. Many of them had drinks in their hands while others were smoking. She hated cigarette smoke but this was an emergency. One man in particular seemed just drunk enough to be willing to share his phone, but not incoherent.

Claire forced herself to smile, softening her shoulders as she approached. "Hey, sorry... my phone died. Can I borrow yours for one quick call? Promise I won't steal your data or anything."

The man blinked at her, bleary-eyed, then shrugged, pulled it from his pocket, unlocked it, and handed it over.

She turned away before dialing, punching in the number she'd never forgotten. "Don't go too far with it." He called out as she lifted it to her ear. Looking back at him she gave him a tight smile and nodded.

It rang once. Twice.

A gruff voice answered, calm and smooth. "Joe's Bar and Grill. How may I take your order?"

Claire didn't hesitate. "I'd like a medium cheese pizza with anchovies, pineapple, and alfredo sauce."

There was a pause. Then, "That'll be ready in thirty minutes. Pick up at our Charlotte location."

The line went dead.

She deleted the call log and quickly looked up the directions to the nearest train station. Then returned the phone with a quick smile. "Thanks. You just saved me."

The man gave her a quizzical look. "Anchovies and Alfredo?" he asked, raising an eyebrow.

She chuckled. "What can I say? A girl's gotta eat." She shrugged her shoulders and turned walking away from the crowd. She heard him remark to his friends that she must be stoned.

She located the cross street and worked out which way it was to Chicago Union Station. Eighteen blocks. It shouldn't take too long.

When she arrived, the station was pretty empty. Large stone columns, high ornate ceilings, and a wide-open lobby welcomed her as she entered the square building. She checked the departure board. One train left in an hour.

She walked up to a kiosk, skipping the ticket window, choosing the less memorable option. Claire searched for the most affordable private room available. She winced at the price: $575, almost every dollar she had. Her father's lessons about always carrying a prepaid credit card, the kind you could use anywhere, were the only reason she wasn't stranded. She slid the card through the reader and collected the ticket when it was printed.

She only had $25 left.

Once she boarded, she locked herself in the small cabin, tugged the curtains shut, and removed the gun from her waistband. Double-checking the safety was on, she put it on the seat next to her, easy to grab if she needed to. Sinking down into the window seat, she felt her body release a bit of tension.

Her body begged for sleep, but she couldn't let herself close her eyes. Not yet. Her fingers rubbed absently at the leather bracelet around her wrist, it was the only thing grounding her. She felt numb and wrecked all at the same time.

When the train started and pulled away from the station, slowly the city lights blurred into streaks. Rumbling forward, the lights disappeared as the train left the city and moved into the countryside.

And with the rhythm of the tracks beneath her, memories began to creep in—uninvited, familiar, and sharp enough to hurt. Memories she feared would be all she had left of the boy she loved.

* * *

The smell of sawdust and chalk filled the old barn gym behind her house. When Claire had shown so much promise and interest in Louisa's former career, she and Max decided to convert the unused barn into her private training studio. They bought lightly used equipment from a gym that was closing, they kitted it out with everything she might need: uneven bars, beam, vault, trampoline track, a springboard floor, mats, even a foam pit.

When she wasn't at school or training with the team, Claire was in the barn, Trevor often not far behind. After the two of them became such fast friends, Trevor showed up one day with an old beanbag. He said he needed somewhere to sit while she trained. Plopping it down near whatever apparatus she was on, Trevor was always nearby.

A sixteen-year-old Claire groaned in frustration and dropped down to sit on the balance beam, sweat sticking strands of hair to her cheeks.

"You've been at this for two hours," Trevor said, putting down his smartphone and standing up from his old beanbag that was worn and covered in duct tape. His brown hair was a little too long, curling against his collar, and his leather jacket looked wildly out of place in the barn.

"I almost had it," Claire shot back. "But almost isn't enough."

Trevor stepped forward, mock-serious. "Alright, fine. Let me show you how Ruby does it."

She rolled her eyes but couldn't help the laugh that bubbled up as he dramatically mimicked her old teammate's prissy posture, tiptoeing across the padded floor and flailing his arms for balance. He was strangely good at flicking his wrists and pointing his toes.

Claire laughed until her stomach hurt, leaning forward on the beam as Trevor "dismounted" with an exaggerated flourish and a flick of his imaginary ponytail.

He grinned up at her, stepping close until his hands rested on either side of her hips on the beam. "Feel better?"

The laughter faded into something heavier. Claire nodded once, trying to breathe around the tightness in her chest.

Trevor's gaze dropped to her wrist, his thumb brushing the leather bracelet, his bracelet, cut from his old jacket.

When his eyes lifted back to hers, the world seemed to still. He had chickened out so many times in the past, this time, he stopped thinking and just did it.

He rested his hand on the back of her neck and pulled her toward him gently. Slowly, he watched her for signs of disgust. When he didn't see any, he closed his eyes and kissed her. Soft and tentative at first.

Claire's heart leapt, her stomach tightened and before she could stop herself, she grabbed the front of his shirt, kissing him back with all the longing she'd buried for months. No—years. His hand slid from her bracelet to her back, pulling her closer as she wrapped her legs around his waist.

Sliding his hands down to her hips he lifted her off the beam, stepping back, only to trip over the leg of the beam. They tumbled to the floor in a tangle, laughing breathlessly before his mouth found hers again.

Claire could replay that moment a thousand times and it would never get old. Tonight it brought her comfort and pain. Pain from the fear that she would never again feel the touch of his skin.

The train jolted, dragging Claire back to the present. In a second, she was on her feet, checking the bolt. Still locked. She was still safe.

It shook again. Rapid movement thrust her mind back to the crash, like she was still there. She could feel the biting edge of glass cutting her body, the crushing absence of her moms pulse, and the blinding fear from being shot at.

Her eyes stung. She wiped at the tears before they fell. It was then that she broke, letting the tears stream down her face like a waterfall. She sobbed for her gymnastics career, for the life she might never have with Trevor, but most of all, she cried for her parents. So many people in this world have parents who don't care, or who are neglectful—but she had some of the best parents she'd ever known. Kind, supportive, non-judgmental, but still parents willing to lead, teach and educate; and they had been ripped away.

Louisa would never teach another gymnastics class to the young kids in their small town. She'd never again help Alexis, her best friend and Trevor's mom, bake 1000 cookies for a charity sale, and she'd never get a chance to become a grandparent. While Claire didn't know much about her dad's job she did know he was relied on heavily and his job, and the people he helped, would never be able to fill the hole he left. Max had always wanted to take Louisa to the Maldives, now they'd never have that chance.

Thinking of all the things they would never get to see made Claire feel guilty for all the time they had dedicated to driving her to and from practice or working to support her gymnastics career. But even when Claire had pushed them to take a few weeks off or that she would cut back on her practices, they said no. They had been where they wanted to be, with their daughter.

Hearing footsteps outside her door, Claire held her breath, afraid that she had been found. When the footsteps faded, she let out the air and wiped her eyes.

Her gaze fell to a crumpled, discarded Amtrak ticket on the

cabin floor. She picked up the self print ticket, flipped it over to the blank side, and pulled a pen from her bag.

She needed to connect with someone she loved. If she hadn't been afraid for his safety, she would've called Trevor and told him everything. Begged him to come get her and hold her until she couldn't cry anymore. So instead of calling, she wrote. Her hand shook as she wrote.

Trevor,

I don't know if I'll ever send this, but I have to write it. They're gone. Everything is. Someone killed my parents and they tried to kill me too. I'm not sure if he's still coming after me, but it wasn't an accident. I wish I could just come home to you, I know I'd feel better if you just held me. But I can't put you in danger too. I think this had something to do with my dad's job. He knew something and there was this phone call before we had dinner today. I don't know what he knew but he didn't seem surprised.

I'm on a train now. I don't know where I'll be when you get this. But just know for now I'm safe.

I need you to know.

I love you. I think I've loved you since the first day you sat in that barn, pretending to hate gymnastics just to make me laugh. I saw my future with you. A house, a dog, and a few kids with your smile and eyes. I'd go to the Olympics and teach gymnastics. You could go to medical school like you've always wanted. I think the kids would have to wait until you're at least in residency, but we could get a dog while you're still in school. A mutt, like the first one that came into your dad's vet office.

I'm scared we won't get that future together. I'm scared if I think I can have it, have you, then I'd be putting you at risk too.

Whoever came after my parents and I, he was so calculated and cold. And I worry he was just the muscle. Someone else wanted my parents gone. You deserve a future and not one in hiding.

I hope I'm wrong about all of this and we get to have the future we've dreamt about, but something just feels off. Until I know if I'm still in danger, if you'd be in danger, I have to stay away. If I could choose, I'd choose you every time. You're my best friend and I'll love you forever.

— C

Her chest ached as she folded the ticket carefully, tucking it into her duffel. She probably wouldn't send it. If she did, he'd come to find her and she couldn't have him putting himself in danger. But she felt a little better now that she had written down her feelings.

The rocking of the train lulled her. With tears still drying on her cheeks, the sound of the tracks whispering Trevor's name, she finally drifted into an uneasy sleep and despite fighting it—fearing what could happen—exhaustion won. Her eyes slid shut as the countryside blurred past.

4
The Mountain Man

Claire's chest tightened as the train hissed to a stop at the Charlotte station, the sun rising over the skyline. At 7 a.m. local time, Claire stepped off the train with her duffel slung over her shoulder, the leather bracelet warm against her wrist despite the morning chill. The air smelled of diesel exhaust and brewing coffee. A few sleepy travelers shuffled past, dragging rolling suitcases.

Walking through the small train station lobby, Claire followed the exit signs to the parking lot. She scanned the lot for any sign of Hugh. She had memorized his number and the code phrases—the rules her father drilled into her, but she had no idea what Hugh looked like. The idea that she was about to walk up to a stranger and trust him made her stomach tighten. But if her father trusted him with her life, she had to as well.

Her eyes finally caught it, drawing her up short.

A battered old American-made truck sat a few rows down, paint faded and flaking, its bumper sporting a worn sticker: a gymnast silhouette mid-leap. Her breath caught. It had to be him.

Cautiously, she approached. She scanned the lot for a getaway just in case it wasn't him and it turned out to be the shooter.

The driver's door opened, and an older man stepped out, tall and broad-shouldered, with a wiry gray beard and the kind of clothes that looked like they'd been washed a hundred times but would outlive them all. His sharp eyes met hers for a beat before he spoke.

"Anchovies from the sea and pineapple from the tree," he said, voice gravelly but even.

Claire's throat tightened, and her eyes stung. She nodded, whispering, "Medium cheese, Alfredo sauce."

Her father had been right. This man was safe. Relief flooded her to have someone else she could rely on, someone who knew her dad and could help her the way he might have. Without thinking, she closed the distance and hugged him. The hug was awkward; his arms hesitated before coming around her, giving her a quick pat on the back.

"Time to go, kid," he said simply, releasing her.
She swallowed, nodding, and climbed into the truck as he peeled the gymnast sticker from the back bumper and tossed it into the glove box.

The truck rumbled to life. Hugh handed her a bottle of water and a bag of beef jerky. "Eat. You'll need it, it's a long drive."

The city streets rolled past in silence at first, Hugh keeping his eyes on the road. Claire chewed mechanically, staring out the window, watching as the urban landscape faded into fields, then forests. By the time the highway curved into winding mountain roads, her patience cracked.

"Do you know what happened?" she blurted. "Do you know who killed them? Did my dad ever tell you what he was working on? Was it his job? Did they—"

Hugh kept his gaze on the road. "I don't have those answers yet, kid. But I'm going to find them. For him and for you."

She clenched her jaw, nodding once, and turned back to the window, gripping the leather bracelet like a lifeline. Feeling like she could cry again, Claire took some deep breaths, just like she'd trained to do before starting a difficult skill.

The truck eventually turned off onto a dirt path. Trees

pressed in thickly on both sides until they opened into a small clearing. A weathered cabin sat ahead, its wooden siding faded with age, but solid and upright despite its years. It looked like it belonged in another era.

Hugh parked on what passed as a driveway, just two worn tire tracks with no plants growing in them. "Stay in the truck," he ordered as he got out, raising his gun in both hands. Keeping it aimed at the ground but ready to shoot if necessary.

Claire watched as he moved around the perimeter, scanning the trees. He looked a little like her dad at that moment. Max had taken Claire shooting several times a year. He had called them "daddy daughter dates." Sometimes it was hand to hand combat and other times it was shooting. Hugh came back around the cabin. She could see him checking the treeline, then the dirt for tracks. She recognized the movement, yet another skill her dad had taught her. Finally, nodding to himself as he returned to open her door. "Clear. Come on."

At the front door, he waved his wrist over a small sensor above the handle. The lock clicked open. Claire raised a brow. "You have...RFID locks?"

"Embedded under the skin," Hugh replied with a shrug. "Keeps me from losing my keys."

Inside, the cabin was dim and smelled faintly of woodsmoke. It was clearly lived in by one man. The kitchen was small, cluttered but organized. Two bedrooms branched off the narrow hall: one with a large bed and a computer station surrounded by multiple monitors showing different camera feeds of the surrounding woods, and the other, a simple room with a double bed covered in plaid sheets.

"Bathroom's down the hall. That one's yours," Hugh said, nodding toward the smaller room. "Freshen up. There's clothes in the closet. I'll make breakfast."

"I, um... actually have a cut on my ribcage. It's pretty deep. I think I might need stitches." She felt awkward telling him but she knew it needed attention.

"Let's see."

She slowly lifted the edge of her warm-up set, showing Hugh the location of the wound. She was used to competing in leotards, which didn't leave much to the imagination- but showing her ribs now to someone older than her father who she barely knew felt wrong. Reminding herself that if this was her dad she'd have felt just fine, she patiently waited while he examined it.

The tape she had placed over it was hanging on by a thread. Blood and sweat made her skin too slick for it to stick. Grabbing a first-aid box from a kitchen cabinet, Hugh used an alcohol pad to sterilize the wound and the skin around it. Gently removing the tape, he pressed gauze to the wound and led her to the kitchen table.

"You're right—it needs stitches, but we should be able to get away with liquid ones. Sit down."

She dropped her bag on the floor, and nudged it out of the way with her foot as she sat down.

Before he started, Hugh handed her a bottle of acetaminophen and a glass of water, instructing her to take some. She complied. He then told her to make sure she sat straight so her skin didn't stretch. Using a tube of purple gel, he sealed the wound. The gel stung deeply for the first few seconds; she couldn't help but hiss in pain. But when it was done and dry, the wound was closed and no longer stinging. He said that as long as she taped plastic over it, she could take a shower.

Before letting her go, he took a look at her head wound as well. The cut was minimal, and explained that scalp wounds tend to bleed significantly. He told her to clean the wound over the next few days and apply antibiotic cream, which he gave her. He also explained that she should take it easy until tomorrow morning, since she probably sustained a mild concussion which, mixed with the adrenaline, had caused her sleepiness after the crash.

Claire stepped into her room, setting her duffel on the bed. The clothes she found were simple, a little big, but clean. Stepping into a hot shower felt amazing. She still felt like she was covered in her parents blood and the shower melted it and a small amount of the fear away. Getting out of the shower, she pulled on jeans and a faded sweatshirt, grateful for the comfort. She looped her long wet hair up into a messy bun, too drained to do anything else with it.

When she stepped back into the kitchen, the smell of pancakes greeted her. Hugh stood at the stove, flipping a pancake onto a plate. He looked up at her and nodded toward the table. "Perfect timing. Sit."

The pancakes were plain, but warm, and for a moment she felt almost normal as she sat at the small wooden table across from him. He placed a plate with three small pancakes in front of her along with a set of silverware and a glass of orange juice.

Sitting down with his own pancakes and orange juice, Hugh opened the maple syrup and began pouring it over his proportionally larger stack. "Do you know what your dad did for a living?" Hugh asked casually as he cut into his food.

Claire frowned, reaching for the syrup. "Security. That's what he always said. I never really knew more than that."

Hugh's gaze softened, just slightly. "Max wasn't just security. He was CIA. I was too. Retired now."

The fork froze in her hand. Her father had kept a lot from her, but this... this changed everything.

Claire sat frozen for a moment, the fork still poised halfway to her mouth. Her heart thudded as Hugh's words sank in. She stared at him, trying to read his face for any sign that he might be joking, but his eyes were steady and serious.

The acronym echoed in her head, colliding with memories of school drop-offs, burnt pancakes, and her father sitting in the stands filming every routine.

When? How? What did he do for them? Claire had so many questions.

"CIA?" she repeated slowly. "My dad... was CIA? He never said anything. Not once." Her voice cracked, a mix of anger and disbelief.

Hugh leaned back in his chair, letting her process the news. "Most don't tell their kids until they're older. It's need-to-know. And you didn't need to know, at least, not then."

Claire set her fork down, pushing the plate slightly away.

Her stomach turned, and she folded a knee up to her chest and tucked her other leg under her. Her head spun as she replayed moments with her dad still trying to understand. The way he had taught her self defense stood out the most. He hadn't taught her to fight like a father worried about scraped knees or handsy boys—he'd taught her like someone preparing her for worst-case scenarios.

"Did my mom know?"

"Yes. He was torn about when to tell you too. He and your mom decided to wait until you were done with gymnastics. They were worried about you deciding to quit because it put you in the spotlight."

"So you worked with him. You knew him. Were you friends? Or just coworkers.... Agents?" She absently began playing with her bracelet.

He gave a slow shrug. "Both. We were partners when he first started, we separated when he requested to specialize in Italy. I specialized more in Northern Europe. And we're Officers— Agents work for FBI, DIA or ATF."

When Claire was quiet for a beat too long he continued speaking. "Max was one of the best. Smart. Loyal. Stubborn as hell and unwaveringly good. The CIA often blurs the lines, so to speak, in order to see results. Your dad didn't."

She swallowed hard, glancing toward the window where morning light spilled into the cabin. For the first time, she noticed the cameras Hugh had set up outside; tiny black dots nestled in the trees, all visible from here. She thought about how many years her dad might have lived like this, always watching, always on guard.

"Was it his job that got them killed?" she whispered.

Hugh's gaze hardened, but he didn't look away. "Maybe. Probably. But I won't say for sure until I know. And I will find out, Claire. I owe him that."

A beat passed before Claire asked her next question, "Did you ever meet my mom? Did she have anything to do with this or was she just collateral damage like I would have been?"

"I met her a few times, usually in passing. I don't know what she

knew but she didn't work for the agency."
Her fingers curled tightly around the edge of the table. She wanted to ask a hundred more questions: what her dad did, who he trusted, if he'd ever been scared? But she forced herself to stop. There would be time later, and Hugh didn't look like the kind of man who shared much all at once.

After a long silence, she nodded, taking a deep breath. "Okay. Just... promise me you'll tell me everything when you find out."

He gave a short nod, no hesitation. "I promise."

Claire finally picked up her fork again, her thoughts spiraling and making it hard to focus on his words. Taking a bite of the pancakes, they weren't right, they tasted different now, like something ordinary that belonged to another life. A life Claire wasn't sure she'd ever get back.

"It's going to be difficult but when you are ready I need to know everything that happened yesterday. From the moment you got up to the time you arrived at the train station in Charlotte."

"I figured, can we eat and then maybe sit outside? I think the fresh air might help me get through it." Claire asked.

"Sure."

Hugh finished up his stack and carried his dishes over to the sink. The kitchen was small and lacked a dishwasher. Claire tried to eat, she felt hungry but also nauseous thinking of reliving everything in detail. She decided she was done after a few more bites, choosing to just get a glass of water, to sip on.

When she was ready, Claire and Hugh stepped out onto the back deck, the morning air cool and smelling faintly of pine and damp earth. Claire's pulse quickened, every creak of the deck boards making her hyper-aware of the woods stretching beyond the cabin, shadows moving like watchful eyes. Even with that, it was nicer out here than inside. A built-in barbecue stood in the corner where the railings met the house wall, while two Adirondack chairs angled toward each other sat on the other side of the deck. A small raised fire pit was added just in front of the chairs with a stone base that matched the barbecue.

Noticing her fear, Hugh reassured Claire, "You're safe here for now. If someone was nearby my system would have alerted me the second they crossed my one mile barrier."
His words sparked another memory, her dad installing various upgrades and security systems. Always the nicest ones and unlike anything her friends would ever have.

Nodding, Claire perched on the edge of one of the chairs while Hugh sat on the edge of the fire pit making sure to not turn his back on the woods. It was ingrained in him to always be vigilant of his surroundings no matter the situation, but even more so now.   Hugh suspected Claire's parents' murder had been the handiwork of the Italian mob. If it had been, Claire wasn't safe, not yet anyway. Max had sent Hugh an encrypted email the night before his death. He'd found something that suggested the mob was being funded by someone on the inside. Someone they had trusted.

Hugh gently eased Claire into the events of the prior day. He had plenty of experience questioning victims. She may have been the daughter of one of his most trusted friends, but he did his best to see her just as any other victim in this moment. He needed to keep his feelings separate, for now.

Claire took a shaky breath, staring down at her hands. "I'll tell you everything," she whispered. "But after that... what happens to me?"

Hugh's gaze flicked toward the woods, his jaw tightening. For a long moment, he didn't answer, the silence heavier than the cool mountain air. Finally, he looked back at her, eyes sharp and unwavering.

"You train," he said. "You learn to survive. You're a loose end—loose ends get removed. I'm sorry but you can't go back to being a gymnast, not publicly. Because whoever did this, they won't stop. I suspect your dad found something incriminating and you may know more than you think."

"But he didn't tell me anything."

"They don't know that, nor would they trust you saying otherwise. You're a loose end."

Claire's stomach dropped, the weight of his words sinking in. She gripped the arm of the chair, forcing herself not to flinch. Somewhere deep in her chest, anger flickered to life, pushing past the grief. Training was the one thing she understood. Discipline. Pain. Repetition until fear lost its edge. Her dad, and gymnastics, hadn't trained her to be fearless. She was trained to stay standing when fear hit—to push it away.

"Then teach me," she said quietly. "I won't be the girl who just runs."

Hugh studied her for a long beat before giving a single, firm nod. "Tomorrow morning. At dawn."

Claire exhaled, tension vibrating through her. The quiet woods around them felt suddenly alive, as if they, too, were holding their breath. Tomorrow, everything would change, and for the first time since the crash, Claire felt a spark of something fierce and unshakable waiting just beyond the trees.

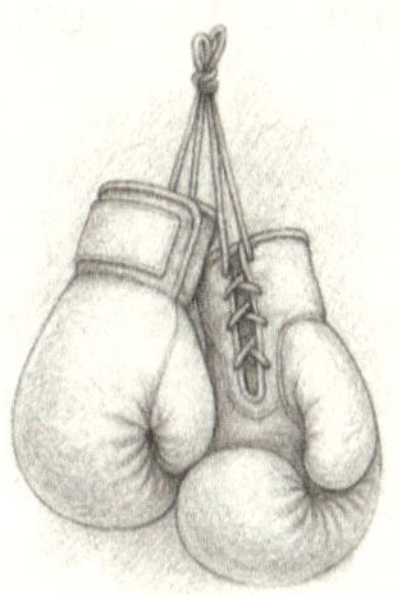

5
Training Begins

The pale gray light of dawn leaked through the thin curtains when Claire's eyes blinked open. Her body protested—sore from travel, the accident, her competition, and yesterday's emotional weight—but habits died hard and her mind was already awake. There was no room for rest now. Not now that she has made her choice.

She padded quietly into the living room to find Hugh already sitting at the kitchen table, a mug of steaming black coffee in hand. His eyebrows rose slightly when he saw her.

"You're up on time," he said, sounding almost amused. "I expected I'd have to wake you."

Claire shrugged, looking around the kitchen until she spotted the coffee. A mug sat beside the machine; she filled it to the brim. "I'm a gymnast. Early mornings are kind of my thing." That earned her a slight smirk, but it didn't last long. Hugh set his coffee down and leaned back in his chair, his expression shifting to something harder.

"Before we start, we need to talk."

Claire sat opposite him, pulse quickening. "What is it?"

He laced his fingers together, staring at them for a long moment before meeting her eyes. "I stayed up last night digging. I found security camera footage of the accident. I was able to track the man involved."

Her stomach tightened. "You... you know who did it?"

"I know who *carried it out*," he corrected. "Your dad was looking into a leak inside the Agency when he died. He'd found something. I still don't know what. That's why he was killed."

Hugh's voice stayed even, but his jaw was tight. "The people who ordered this won't stop until they're sure every loose end is tied up."

Claire's hand went instinctively to her bracelet, gripping the worn leather until her knuckles whitened.

"Claire," Hugh continued, "you told me yesterday you didn't want to run. I need to know what you mean by that. Do you want to defend yourself—learn enough to stay alive? Or do you want justice for your parents?"

She looked at him, heart hammering. "You're asking if I want revenge, aren't you?"

"I'm asking how far you're willing to go."

Her throat felt tight, but she forced the words out. "I want to be ready. Not just to survive—I want to finish what my dad started. Eventually, put it to bed so I can move on."

Hugh studied her for a moment, then gave a single sharp nod. "Then you need to know what that means." He leaned forward, elbows on his knees. "This isn't just about fighting. It's spycraft. It's infiltration. If you really want to find that leak, you're going to need to get into the CIA yourself. That doesn't mean tomorrow," Hugh added. "It means college. Background checks. Years of work. You earn your way in, or you don't get in. And that means you can't be Claire Huntington anymore."

Claire froze, her fingers curling around her bracelet so tight she worried she might rip it.

"You'll need a new identity," Hugh went on, his voice steady but not unkind. "A new name, a new life. No contact with anyone from your past. Not your hometown. Not your old friends. Not Trevor."

Her head jerked up. "How do you know about Trevor?"

Hugh's lips quirked faintly, but his eyes stayed serious. "Kid, if I can find out about him, so can the people who killed your parents. And they *will*. If you care about him, you'll keep him out of this."

Claire swallowed hard, the words sinking like stones. She had suspected this would be the case, but hearing it out loud felt like losing him all over again.

Her chest tightened; she felt like she might be sick, "Okay," she whispered. "I understand." Eyes stinging with unshed tears.

Hugh's gaze softened, almost imperceptibly. "You've got six months until you turn eighteen. You can't apply until then. And I won't send you in until you're ready. But when the time comes... you'll go under as someone new."

She nodded once, determination burning under the grief. "Then teach me. Make me ready."

With that, Hugh nodded and stood up, walking to the living room. He gestured at the sofa, "Help me with this."

The small living room smelled faintly of wood polish and old fireplace smoke as Claire helped Hugh push the sofa against the wall, clearing a small but useful space.

"Let's see what you already know," he said, tossing her a pair of training gloves, fingerless with padded knuckles.

Claire smirked faintly, pulling them on. "Easy."

He raised a brow. "We'll see."

Hugh lunged first, his left fist cutting through the air. Claire dodged, batting his arm down and away. The impact jolted through her hands, her palms stinging from the force. She blocked another punch with her left arm, then shot one of her own toward his chest.

"Better," Hugh said, circling her. "But you're pulling your punches. Hit me like you mean it, kid. You can't learn a backflip without actually rotating. Same rules apply here."

Claire adjusted instinctively, lowering her center of gravity the way she would before a beam series. Her balance came from years of knowing exactly where her body was in space—how to land without looking, how to absorb impact through her ankles and knees without locking them.

Sweat already dampened her hairline. When Hugh swung again, she struck back harder, her fist landing solidly against his forearm with a satisfying smack. Pain shot up her knuckles, but she ignored it, gritting her teeth and throwing another punch.

"Good, again. Faster," Hugh barked, stepping in closer. "If I were armed, you'd already be dead."

She moved quicker, heart hammering, the air thick with the scent of sweat. One punch slipped past his guard and connected with his ribs. He grunted, eyes glinting with approval.

When they shifted to takedowns, Hugh pressed harder, forcing her to react faster. The first attempt left her flat on her back, breathless, her hair sticking to her cheeks. Claire let out a frustrated laugh despite herself, rolling back to her feet.

"Don't think, *do*," Hugh said.

She tried again. This time, when he came at her, she feinted a punch, grabbed under his arm, and twisted. Gravity and momentum worked in her favor as she dropped low. This felt like timing a release on bars—miss it by a fraction and you crashed, hit it perfectly and the world snapped into place. Hugh hit the floor with a thud, rolling onto his back.

A grin broke across her face. "Better?"

"Not bad," he admitted, standing and dusting himself off.

They repeated it again and again. Her muscles burned from being used in a new way. Sweat soaked the collar of her sweatshirt, and her knuckles throbbed with every strike, but she kept going— jaw set with stubborn determination. Every time she hit the ground, she bounced back up, a spark of defiance in her eyes.

Finally, Hugh stepped back, lowering his hands. "Break time. Muscles need rest as much as they need exercise. Hot shower, then food."

"I can keep going," she protested, breathless, her stance still raised.

"Not if you want to be able to move tomorrow," he said flatly, already walking toward the kitchen. He snatched the tea towel off the oven door, blotted sweat from his forehead, and headed for the master bedroom.

Claire let her arms drop, chest rising and falling fast, and couldn't help the smallest victorious smile. She'd survived his first test and she was already hungry for more.

In the bathroom the shower steam surrounded her, the water washing away sweat and leaving her muscles pleasantly sore, not unlike after a grueling gymnastics training day. But these movements were different, using muscles in ways her body wasn't used to. What she would give to have one of Trevor's back rubs right now.

The thought spiraled—memories stacking on memories, a fantasy of what it would be like just to be with him for ten minutes. Claire decided she would write him another letter. Toweling off, changing and brushing her hair, she wondered if she could actually send him the letters. She knew she couldn't see him but could she at least explain?

Trevor,

I know who killed them now and why. I can't tell you, but I need you to know I'm not running. I'm staying to fight. I don't think it's what they would have wanted, but I have to do it for them. I think I have to disappear for a while. I don't know how long. Maybe years. Maybe longer. I hate this more than anything, but if I came back, I'd put you in danger. I keep telling myself you deserve peace—that I don't get to drag you into this. One day, when it's safe, if it's ever safe, maybe...

She paused, biting her lip hard.

You're going to be an amazing doctor, Trev. I believe in you. I'll be thinking about you.

—C

She folded the letter carefully and slid it into the duffel where the other one was hidden. Claire lay back on the bed, closing her eyes, willing her mind to drift where her heart already was, back home, back to him. As her body drifted into REM sleep, Trevor appeared.

* * *

She was back home, sitting on the white porch swing of the old farmhouse, its chains creaking softly with every sway. The late-afternoon sun slanted across the wraparound porch, turning the chipped white paint golden. The car sat in the dirt driveway, already packed tight with suitcases for the trip to the airport. It was the day before the Championships. In reality, it had only been a few days, but in her memory it felt like a lifetime ago, like she was watching a scene trapped in amber.

Trevor sat beside her, his arm resting over the back of the swing. Claire sat facing him with her legs draped over his. Entwined as always.

"You're going to be amazing," he said, voice warm and certain, like there was no doubt in his mind.

Claire smiled, though her chest felt tight. "I'll do well."

"No, you're going to win. Wiping the other girls off the mat," Trevor said, grinning, his blue-green eyes catching the sunlight.

"Claire!" Max's voice carried from the driveway, distant and impatient, like an echo from another life. "Are you and your mom ready? We've gotta get going!"

"Almost!" Louisa's voice floated out from inside the house where the front door stood open. "I just need to grab an extra roll of athletic tape."

Trevor's smile faltered slightly, and for a moment they just sat there, the swing rocking lazily beneath them. Claire felt like she floated on a cloud instead of her antique swing.

Louisa stepped out of the open front door, shutting and locking it behind her. She gave them a knowing look, her own grin soft. "Max, give the kids a minute. We'll wait in the car."

Max frowned but sighed, "One minute!"

Louisa winked at Claire, then disappeared down the steps to join Max in the car.

Claire turned back to Trevor, heart thudding. She leaned

closer, her hand finding his cheek, thumb brushing along his jawline. Each moment seemed drawn out, passing slower than it had actually happened.

Trevor tilted his head slightly, his smile tugging wider, but he stayed still, letting her come to him.

"Go get gold," he whispered.

Claire shook her head, her forehead resting briefly against his. "I don't need to," she murmured, her voice low and certain. "I already have it. You are my gold."

Before he could respond, she kissed him, soft at first, then deeper, passionate, trying to pour everything she couldn't say into that one moment. Trevor's hand slid to her back, pulling her closer, but they both broke apart at the sound of the car horn honking impatiently.

Claire lingered for just a heartbeat, memorizing his face, his warmth, the way his hair caught the light. Then she pulled back, slipping from the swing, and Trevor let her go, even though his hand stayed lifted like he wanted to reach for her again.

If she could control her dream, Claire would have sat back down and never stood up from that swing.

"Go get 'em," he said softly.

She gave him a smile that wavered only at the edges before jogging toward the car, her heart already aching for the moment she'd just left behind.

* * *

That evening, the cabin smelled faintly of tomato sauce as Hugh pulled a cheese-covered lasagna from the oven. He set it on the table, along with a manila folder.

"Eat," he said, pushing an empty plate and serving spoon toward her. "Then we'll talk."

Claire served herself and ate quickly, nerves buzzing as Hugh finally opened the folder. Inside were documents, a fake birth certificate, sample IDs, even mock school transcripts.

"You'll need to choose a name," Hugh said, leaning back. "We'll build the rest around it. Birthdate, background, everything. You'll need to come up with a story and stick to it. Internalize it to the point where it becomes natural to respond as her, not as Claire."

Claire swallowed. This wasn't just a disguise. It was a life. She was creating a new person entirely. She traced the blank lines of the forms with her fingers. Slowly, she looked up. "Georgia Anderson," she said finally. The name felt strange on her lips, almost like they belonged to someone else. "And my birthday... June eighteenth."

Hugh raised a brow. "Any reason for that date?"

Her fingers slipped over her bracelet, "The day I met Trevor."

He didn't comment, just gave a single approving nod. "Georgia it is."

Claire pulled the folder closer, her heart thudding with the weight of it. Georgia wasn't Claire. She would be stronger, colder— someone who could finish what her father started, even if it meant locking her heart away.

And as she sat there, staring at her photo in a mock-up drivers license, she felt the last threads of her old life slipping away.

Tomorrow, her real training would begin. Max had given her the foundation. Now it was time to expand on it. And with each lesson, Claire Huntington would fade, until only Georgia Anderson remained.

6
Goodbye Claire

The crisp morning air bit at Claire's skin as she moved through the forest. Her balance and beam work helped her move quietly without disturbing too many of the dead leaves. The ground was damp from last night's rain, still smelling faintly of dew and damp earth. Crouching down, she balanced on the balls of her feet, examining the pathway.

Hugh was somewhere up ahead. He had told her to wait five minutes before she could follow.

"Find me," was all he'd said.

She scanned for broken branches, disturbed ground cover, or anything that betrayed Hugh's path—the same way she used to check a bar that flexed too much, or a beam with tape lifting at the edges. With all his years in the CIA, he could have gone undetected but he deliberately left a few clues showing the direction he had gone. She was good but not an expert yet, though he would make her one.

Claire silently and carefully stepped around a cluster of branches and leaves. A faint sound in the distance startled a bird from its perch overhead. It had come from the left. She paused, half behind a tree, listening for more. Nothing else came. Either he'd stopped moving—or it was a distraction. Her instinct pulled her to the right. She went a few more paces before she saw it. A boot print in the damp topsoil. It was just a partial, but it was there. He was close.

Moving as silently as she could, Claire climbed up a large tree. It was fall and the maple and oak trees had dropped all of their leaves so she didn't have to worry about creating a rustling noise. She rose onto a thick branch. She moved from tree to tree the way she used to walk along on the lower bar before launching to the high one. Testing her footing, standing just long enough to launch to the next, trusting her muscle memory more than sight. Claire's heart hammered against her ribcage as she could feel him close. She was determined to get the jump on him.

There he was about fifteen feet ahead crouched behind a tree, looking in the opposite direction. Claire's muscles hummed with the familiar tension she held in her legs as she moved closer, balancing above. She kept her breath even, controlled as she moved just above him.

She didn't hesitate once she was in place, she dropped, committing the way she always had on a skill. The impact would have jarred most people's knees and thrown them off balance, but she knew how to properly land. She distributed the impact through her whole body, not just her knees—core engaged, knees bent, feet rolling from ball to heel. Using her training knife she pressed the dull flat tip into his back.

"Got you," she whispered, amused.

A slow grin spread across Hugh's face as he turned a beat later. First glancing over his shoulder up at her, then turning fully to face her and rising. "Not bad, kid. You were still too loud though. Better but you still need to be quieter."

"No, I wasn't. You didn't hear anything." Claire protested, lowering the faux knife.

"I heard you," he insisted. "I just didn't move fast enough, but you're getting close." Pride flickered in his eyes looking down at his trainee.

Hugh would never admit it, but he was enjoying this—training someone again. He had lived alone for years and though he preferred it, he was enjoying this time with his former prodigy's daughter. She reminded him so much of Max in a way that sometimes rattled him. She had more sass than Max though, she must have gotten it all from her mother.

That evening, Claire sat at the dining table, her hand cramped as she wrote quickly across her worn notebook. Her words spilled out like they always did when she thought of Trevor.

I miss you with everything in me. What I would give to be able to talk to you without risking your safety. I think I'm making progress though, it's...

She jumped slightly when Hugh's voice cut through the quiet. He entered the kitchen silently and was peering over her shoulder. His freshly washed hair was unkempt and falling in his face as he stared down at her.

"What's that?" he asked, though his eyes said he already knew. He understood her love for the boy, after all he had been there once too, but if she wasn't careful it would get her killed.

Like a kid caught stealing, Claire snapped her head up and looked back at Hugh hovering above her. His eyes said everything he needed to say, everything she knew and ultimately did her best to ignore.

Before she could answer, Hugh plucked the notebook from under her pen. "Hugh, wait..."

He scanned the page and flipped through the remnants of pages that had been torn out. His face darkened as his anger grew. It wasn't just one letter. She'd written over ten letters from the look of things.

"Claire." His voice was sharp with tension, "What the hell is this?"

"I can explain," she said in a rush, "They aren't for him. I'm not sending them." Her heart pounded so hard she swore it shook the room. "They're just for me. A way of processing, of still having a piece of him."

"That doesn't matter." Hugh sat in the seat next to Claire. He wanted to impress on her the danger she was putting herself in. He kept his voice low and dangerous, holding her gaze. "If anyone at the agency even suspects you're not who you say you are, everything is over—your new identity, your mission, your life. You can't keep these."

Claire's chest tightened. If he had caught her weeks ago her eyes would have welled up with tears, but she held them in. She had already felt herself hardening. "They help me," she did her best to keep her voice calm and level. "It's the only way I feel like I'm not losing him too. I've already lost everyone else."

"You've already lost him, you lost him when you decided to choose this path." Hugh said flatly. "Burn them, Claire. All of them." For a moment, his gaze softened, almost apologetic, before he looked away and handed her the notebook back.

Not wanting to give away her emotions, Claire stood and took her notebook from his hand, "Okay." She knew there was no arguing. He was right after all if anyone had found them, it would be over. "I'll get the others." Claire said as she walked to her room, pulling out the letters she had in her gym bag.

With the stack of letters in her hand Claire returned to the kitchen. She lifted them slightly to show Hugh she had them and wordlessly walked to the back deck.

The fire pit glowed faintly orange in the twilight. Claire stood over it, her letters in hand. All she had to do was let go, drop them into the flames. In seconds, the only way she still let herself speak to Trevor would be gone.

The heat licked her hands, urging her to let go, but her fingers tightened around the letters until the paper crumpled in her grip. She hesitated, the crackling felt like a timer counting down, daring her to drop the letters.

On a split-second decision, she tore out her latest letter from the notebook and tucked her letters into her hoodie. Then removing a few more blank pages from the notebook she dropped them into the fire. She didn't doubt Hugh would notice if there weren't paper ashes in the fire pit.

Back inside, she grabbed the new duffel bag Hugh had given her, the one without any gym logos or identifiable marks. She worked quickly, pulling a small knife from the drawer. Carefully she slit the seam along the inner lining, creating just enough space to slide the letters inside. With precise, tiny stitches, she stitched the seam, hiding the letters inside. The bag was sturdier than her old one—double-lined canvas with a foam-padded base meant to protect gear. Even empty, it held its shape, the seams thick enough to hide a lot more than paper.

No one would ever know they were there.

After that, the days fell into a pattern—training until her muscles shook, studying until her eyes burned, sleeping hard and dreamless. Weeks became months. The letters grew in numbers, staying hidden, pressed flat inside the bag, while everything else in her life sharpened into something new.

* * *

A year later.

The seasons bled together as snow gave way to spring rains, followed by summer heat, then autumn leaves again. The cabin rang out with the sharp clack of steel against steel.

Pivoting on her toes, Claire prepared for an incoming blow, the knife flashed in the dim light of the living room. Coming at her fast, Hugh swung his own blade in a tight arch. She blocked his attack, twisting her body to force his arm wide. Her movements were clean, sharp, no hesitation, just instinct.

Circling her, Hugh grinned, "Better," his breathing was heavier than usual. A slight rasp in his throat as he spoke.

Lunging forward, Claire ducked under his outstretched arm and slid behind him. She often combined the gymnastics skills she had engrained in her with the new fighting skills she had developed, creating unexpected unique movements. From behind, Claire locked her arm around his, using her leverage to force him to drop his knife. It clattered to the ground as she kicked it away and pressed her knife lightly against his back.

"Dead," she said confidently, her breathing coming quick but steady.

Hugh turned around to look at her, letting out a rough laugh. He dropped into his worn old leather sofa, coughing into his sleeve and wiping his brow before sweat dripped into his eyes.

"Your father would be proud of you, kid." He said, still catching his breath, his voice hoarse. "Every extra month we waited, was worth it."

Claire smiled faintly, furrowing her brow as he coughed again. "You okay?"

"I'm fine," Hugh reassured her, quickly waving it off. "Old man lungs, there is a reason I retired. Don't worry about me."

"Okay, but I'm getting you a refill on your water," she said, picking up his empty bottle from the side table.

"Sounds good," Hugh said as he leaned back into the sofa relaxing for the first time in hours.

After dinner, as Claire finished drying the dishes, Hugh returned to the kitchen with a heavy metal lockbox. Setting it on the table he waved her over.

"It's time to say goodbye to Claire. You have to leave behind anything that could identify you. When it's over, it'll still be here waiting for you."

Hugh lifted the lid, Claire took a deep breath before retrieving her belongings from her room. She began by placing her gold medals inside first, the heavy pendants clicking softly against the bottom of the case. Next, her old warm-up clothes with the gym logo went inside. Folded perfectly just like her mom used to do with all of her clothes. Her gym duffel was also folded and laid on top. She placed her father's gun in the case next. Of everything, she wished she could take that with her the most.

Finally, a framed photo of her parents. Claire's fingers lingered on the frame, thumb brushing over her mother's smile, before she set it inside, tucking it in against the side of the box. She had printed it from her phone a few days after arriving. They had greeted her every morning, smiling back at her from their home in Tennessee.

Hugh watched her pack the box silently, his usual gruffness giving way to something quieter, more protective. Hugh held out his hand and cleared his throat, "Your phone, too."

Despite not having a sim card in it Claire had carried it

around when not training. It was still full of texts, voicemails, and photos. She loved looking at the background photo, it was one of her and Trevor. They lay in the old beanbag from her gym, Trevor tickling her while she had tried to take a photo. It resulted in a terrible photo of her blurred from moving but she had captured the way he used to look at her, full of love and admiration. She powered it down, holding the button until the screen went black, then handed it to Hugh. He placed it in the lock box and closed the lid, locking it with a soft click.

"What's the combo?" Claire asked with a quick panic in her voice.

"It's your parents' anniversary," he said. "Something you won't forget."

Hugh pushed the box away and looked down at Claire. "Now, it's time to finish turning you into Georgia Anderson."

Twenty minutes later the cabin smelled strongly of hair bleach. Hugh stirred the mixture in a chipped ceramic bowl. Claire was surprised to hear how much he knew about hair dye but she guessed he would have had experience changing his own appearance over the years.

Claire sat at the table, a towel over her shoulders and her hair already sectioned into four quadrants using clips. Turning to her he held a full bowl of bleach. "Are you ready?" Hugh asked, looking down at her.

Claire swallowed hard. She'd never even had highlights, let alone changed her natural auburn locks to any other color. "Yeah," she said, taking a deep breath.

Hugh slid on the gloves that had come with the bleach kit, his hands stretching out the gloves so much Claire feared they'd split. He then picked up a brush and began applying the bleach to her hair, avoiding the roots and saving them for last. The sharp chemical scent burned her nose, making her eyes water as Hugh painted it through her hair. Within a few minutes her red-brown hair began to turn to a pale golden blond.

When they finished, Claire went to the bathroom and washed her hair. Catching her reflection in the mirror for the first time, she was stunned that even just changing her hair color made her look so different. But she still felt like herself, just altered.

Returning to the kitchen, Hugh sat her back down and after brushing out her wet hair he began cutting away her long locks. A sleek shoulder-length bob with face framing wispy bangs remained. Claire didn't know when the last time she had short hair was, she had always kept it long.

Finally, Hugh handed her a small case. "Contacts to change your brown eyes blue."

Returning to the bathroom Claire put the lenses in. It took her several attempts as she had never worn contacts before. Blinking, the contacts slid into place as her image in the mirror came into focus. The woman looking back at her was now a stranger. Blonde, blue eyed, and older somehow.

Staring at herself for a few moments before she whispered, "Goodbye Claire."

Hugh's reflection appeared in the mirror over her shoulder. Their eyes met and he gave a single approving nod.

The one remaining piece of the girl Claire used to be clung to her wrist: a worn leather bracelet she would never give up. Her fingers brushed over it once before she straightened, shoulders squared. Georgia Anderson had just been born and Claire Huntington had just been locked away in a metal box.

7

The Last Goodbye

The smell of the roasted chicken scented the air in the cabin. It mingled with the faint smokiness emanating from the old stone fireplace. If Hugh hadn't lit a fire outside for the evening, there was one roaring inside—even on hot summer days. He said it relaxed him. He and this old cabin had become something Claire feared had died with her parents that day: a home.

Hugh sat across from Claire at the dinner table, both eating quietly. Claire hadn't cooked much before coming to Hugh's. But while living with him, she'd learned a lot about cooking. He was good at it and used to cook often—though his recent meals had become simpler.

Hugh picked a folder up off the seat next to him and slid it toward her. "Everything you need to be Georgia Anderson."

In just a few short weeks she would be leaving to go to college. She had started online classes a year ago but she'd be joining in person next semester. Claire set down her silverware and flipped open the folder. A brand new birth certificate sat on top, followed by a passport, driver's licence and Social Security card. All with Georgia Anderson's name and birth date. A photo of her stared back, almost like she'd always looked like this. With blue eyes and a long blonde bob, this woman looked very little like the old her.

The edges of the documents were too crisp, too new—like the life inside had been vacuum-sealed. Her fingers hovered over the name *Georgia Anderson* as if touching it would make it real.

Hugh slid a new smartphone across the table. "It's already active, you'll need to memorize your new number." He began to explain when a cough hit him mid-sentence; he turned it into a casual throat-clear, but his eyes watered. When it passed, he continued. "I've also already set up a few social media accounts for you. Instagram and Facebook. Only a few posts for now. You'll need to keep posting—boring things. Coffee. Campus. A sunset. Proof you exist."

"People don't question a life that looks ordinary," he said. "They question the ones that look empty. Make sure some are of you. I also created a few photos with fake loved ones. You'll need to post them as holidays pass. Christmas, Thanksgiving, all of it. Those are in a password protected folder on the phone."

Claire gave a short nod as she took the phone, "Thank you." She tried to focus on creating a mental to do list instead of the weight behind what all of this meant. She was about to leave her protective bubble, her new life was no longer a theory but a reality. Hugh stood and picked up his plate. Taking a step toward Claire he set down one last folded piece of paper. "I think you're ready for this." He then picked up her finished plate and took both to the sink.

Unfolding the paper carefully, Claire saw that it was a newspaper article. Dated a year ago.

Family Killed in Drunk Driving Accident – Suspect Still at Large

A breath caught in her throat as Claire stared at a photo of the wrecked car. Mangled and burned to a crisp. Her eyes caught her name in the article.

"Elite gymnast, Claire Huntington, 17, died alongside her parents Max and Louisa Huntington…"

Her chest tightened as she continued to read. She knew that

the story being fed to the world was that they had all died and that it had been an "accident," but it was different to read it. To see her name next to the word *died*. It felt like a gut punch, her hands tightening around the paper.

A year ago, while she'd hidden in the mountains, the world had continued on without her. Somewhere, Alexis had read this and stopped reading for a moment. Trevor had been forced to accept a headline as truth. Claire's vision blurred—not from tears, but from rage at how easily a lie could be printed. Claire briefly wondered how many times Trevor had read about her death. She knew that she had a grave along with her parents back home. Did he visit it, or was it too painful?

"You okay?" Hugh asked quietly, pulling her away from her thoughts.

Claire folded the article back up with steady hands. Taking a deep breath she gathered everything else he had given her and rose from her seat. Putting on a fake smile she turned to him, "yeah, I'm fine." She took everything else to her room, leaving the article on the table.

In her room Claire pulled out her laptop, she had studying to do. Finals were a week away and she had to maintain good grades if she wanted to be accepted by the CIA. Majoring in Criminal Justice and minoring in Italian kept her relatively busy alongside her training schedule with Hugh.

She buried herself in homework before calling it an early night, but even with all of that studying, she still dreamt about the crash and what their funerals would have been like.

A week later, Georgia Anderson stepped into the world for the first time. Just a day trip away from the cabin but there were no wigs and no baseball caps. Just her blonde bob brushing her shoulders, soft natural makeup and a plain cream colored sweater paired with jeans and a tan jacket.

It had been a long four hour drive from the old cabin to her small town in Tennessee. She felt comforted as she drove across the town lines and to the cemetery. Hugh had argued with Claire about visiting. He thought it was too much of a risk if anyone saw her. But Claire insisted, she needed to do this – she needed to see them. She looked so different and they all believed she was dead, Claire was sure no one would recognize her. Except Trevor, he would know it was her. Thankfully, Trevor wasn't even in town, Claire had kept tabs on him over the last year. He had joined the army not long after her "death" and was currently away with his unit. If he had been here, she didn't know if she could have resisted not seeing him, at least from afar.

Parking Hugh's old truck along the street next to the back entrance of the small town's cemetery, Claire slipped her hands into her jacket pocket as she walked the path to where she knew her parents' plots were located. The autumn air was scented with rain while her boots crunched softly against the gravel walkway.

It was midday, and the cemetery was empty. Walking up to their headstones she saw there were fresh flowers laying on all three stones. A bouquet with mixed flowers was placed on Max's plaque while one with Gerber daisies was placed on Louisa's stone. Daisies were her mothers favorite, they must have been from Alexis, Trevor's mom and Louisa's best friend. To the right of her mothers headstone was her own, her flowers were a soft gathering of peonies, also her favorite. Her eyes filled, knowing her parents were being cared for and visited often.

Seeing her name carved into stone didn't feel like reading the article. This was heavier—permanent. *Claire Huntington*. Neat letters. A clean lie. She stared at the dates like they belonged to a stranger.

Kneeling down, she traced her fingers over her parents' names. "Hi Mom, Hi Dad." Her voice caught for a second but she pushed back the tears and cleared her throat. "I'm sorry I didn't come sooner."

Struggling to not cry, she changed the subject. She settled into a sitting position, crossing her legs. "So, I got a hair cut and I'm blonde now." She chuckled lightly at the slight absurdity of telling them about her hair of all things. "I'm in college, just online, but I'm getting good grades. I start in a few weeks at the University of South Florida. I'm not sure how I feel about being in Tampa of all places but it's a respected school for Criminal Justice. Oh and Hugh's great. He's a little rough around the edges but I'm glad you sent me to him. I don't know what I would do without him."

"I understand why you didn't tell me about..." she almost said the acronym, but caught herself. "Your job. I don't know how I missed it before. The training, the observant games, even how you used to wrestle with me. I guess I was just absorbed in my own life. I'm sorry for that."

Taking a deep breath she continued, "I'm doing this for you... for all of us. They took something that wasn't theirs to take. I won't be able to come back, not until it's over, but I will be back. I hope I'll make you proud. I love you."

She sat there for a long time, silent, before finally getting up. She let a few tears fall before wiping them away with her sleeve. Georgia couldn't afford for more to fall.

The sun had dipped low when she returned to the cabin, a bag of college supplies in the passenger seat. She felt oddly... lighter. Like she had actually seen her parents, maybe she had just felt their presence.

Retrieving her new belongings from the seat next to her, Claire used her RFID key to open the door. When she stepped inside, something was wrong. The cabin felt too still—no radio, no kettle, none of his usual noises. Even the air smelled flat, like the fire hadn't been tended in hours.

"Hugh?" she called, setting the bag down and instinctively pulling out her switch blade. He didn't want her to have a gun just yet, too out of place for a young woman her age to be carrying.

Hugh was slumped against the sofa, with one arm draped over the seat, his head resting on his upper arm, his face pale.

"Hugh!" Claire rushed to him, kneeling down beside the couch. She checked his neck for a carotid pulse. Her heart hammered—it was happening again. She had flashbacks to her parents' deaths and checking for Louisa's pulse after the crash. Her fingers fumbled as she searched for a beat. *Please*. Not again. Not another body that wouldn't answer her. Her mind tried to shove her back into twisted metal and smoke.

Hugh stirred, his eyes fluttering open.

"Easy, kid," he rasped, attempting a half–smile and waving her hand away. "Guess I just overdid it today."

"Overdid it?" Claire's pulse pounded in her ears. "You collapsed! What happened?"

She helped him up and onto the sofa and sat down next to him. He sighed, settling deep into the cushions. "I suppose there's no point hiding it now." He paused, it felt like minutes to Claire not seconds. "I'm sick, Claire. I have been sick for a while. It's cancer. It started in the lungs," he coughed, "turns out you don't have to be a smoker to get lung cancer."

Her throat closed, it *was* happening again. She was about to lose the only person she had left.

"I should've told you," he rasped. "I just... didn't want it to overwhelm you."

"How long?" She questioned.

"Not long." His voice softened. "A couple of weeks, maybe less. The cough. The exhaustion. The days I 'needed air.' That wasn't my age."

Claire sat frozen, her heart shattered in a way she hadn't felt since the night of the crash.

"Hey," Hugh said gently, catching her gaze and resting his hand on hers, "Don't look at me like that. I've had a good run."

With that Claire couldn't hold it back any longer. Her emotional talk with her parents and now this? She broke down into sobs leaning forward into Hugh's shoulder. He hugged her, it wasn't the first time since the day she arrived but it was the first time in a long time.

The next day Hugh pushed through training like sheer will could outpace his body. By nightfall, even his stubbornness looked tired.

Two nights later, they sat outside by the fire pit, the flames danced and fought against the cool night air. Hugh looked more tired than usual, he was fading fast. Claire firmly believed he had exaggerated the length of time he would be with her.

"I should've told you sooner," Hugh admitted, staring into

the night sky. "But I wanted to finish what we had started."
Claire absently gazed at the flames, silent, she didn't know what to
say. Then Hugh spoke again, quieter this time.

"You remind me a lot of your dad, you know that? But
you've got your mom's fire. Max used to drive me crazy in training
because he was so damn stubborn. I guess it runs in the family."
He looked at her now.

Claire gave a small, watery smile meeting his gaze.

Hugh returned the small smile and then looked into the
fire for a long moment before continuing, "I was married once. A
long time ago. Abbey—she was the most amazing and infuriating
woman I've ever met. We wanted kids, but... we couldn't have
them. She suffered a lot of miscarriages, which caused a lot
of fights. So, I buried myself in work instead of fixing things.
Eventually, she left me."

"She used to leave the porch light on when I was gone," he
said, voice rough. "Even after she stopped believing I'd come home
on time. I told myself it was duty. Truth is, it was avoidance."
His eyes softened as he looked back at Claire. "Having you here...
it's been like getting a glimpse of what being a dad might've been
like. If I would have ever had a daughter—I'd have wanted her to
be just like you."

Claire's eyes filled with tears faster than she knew was
possible. She blinked hard, trying to not let them fall. She lost the
battle and when she spoke her voice cracked, whispering, "You
would have been an amazing dad and I'm honored to be your
surrogate daughter. I don't know what I would have done without
you this last year."

They didn't say anything more after that, she just reached
out and rested her hand on his arm. With that they sat together,
staring into the flames.

After that, days became strange—measured in naps,
coughing fits, and hoarse CIA stories.

* * *

One Week Later

Claire woke early, the morning light spilling into her room

and dancing across the wooden floor. The usual scent of coffee was absent. Pulling a hoodie on she padded into the living room and saw him. Hugh hadn't moved from his favorite chair by the fireplace, head tilted slightly like he'd fallen asleep watching the flames.

But when she touched his shoulder, he didn't stir. His chest wasn't rising and she failed to find a pulse. Her chest tightened painfully as reality sank in. He looked peaceful, almost like he was smiling.

He had told her what to do. Claire couldn't call the police, she'd have been in a police report then—connecting the two of them. It was too close a link to her old life. There was a number he had given her. She called it, her voice shook when she spoke. The person on the other end didn't ask questions. They didn't offer condolences. Just instructions—calm, practiced, final. Go on a walk, it would be dealt with when she returned.

Sure enough, when Claire returned he was gone. She spent the rest of the day packing her belongings, emptying the fridge and winterizing the cabin. It would be a long time before she returned.

When she awoke the next morning a box was on the front door step.

Hugh had wanted his ashes scattered in the trees. At sunrise, Claire crouched by the fire pit, the smoke curling through the trees, carrying the scent of burning wood. She dusted Hugh's remains between the trees. The ashes drifted on the breeze, catching briefly in a shaft of sunlight before disappearing into the hills. The last proof he'd been here—gone.

Claire bit the inside of her cheek hard enough to taste blood. Georgia Anderson didn't cry, but Claire Huntington wanted to. "Thank you for taking me in and letting me be your honorary daughter," she whispered.

She stood there for a long time, her leather bracelet cool against her wrist. "I'm doing this for you too, Hugh. Thank you for everything. Tell my dad I said hi."

Before leaving, she went to gather the folder of paperwork with Georgia's papers inside. When she picked it up, a new envelope labeled with her name fell to the floor.

Inside were legal documents, two trusts, one for the cabin, one for her family's house in Tennessee. Hugh had arranged everything. *When you're ready, they'll be waiting*, his note read.

Claire closed the envelope, her fingers brushing her bracelet once before she gathered her duffel swinging it over her shoulder.

She didn't allow herself to look back as she closed the cabin door. Georgia Anderson had a new life to begin, and for now, Claire Huntington was only a name carved into stone.

8

Controlled Detonation

The soft morning light streamed through the D.C. skyline, painting streaks of pale gold across the Potomac River. Claire's sneakers struck the pavement with rhythmic precision, her body moving with a grace that still carried the remnants of a gymnast's discipline. Running was her therapy first as a gymnast, then as an orphan, and now as a CIA operative.

As she ran, Claire scanned every car window and dark shadow, always keeping an eye out, noticing the things others missed. This was something Hugh had drilled into her with every lesson.

Rounding the last corner of her five-mile loop, Claire's small ponytail bounced, snapping with every step as she pushed through the last several paces. Sweat clung to her forehead and neck, but she kept her breathing even. Hugh had always said the mind worked best after the body was exhausted. She reminded herself daily that she had to stay focused and alert at all times.

Everything she had worked for had led to this point. After getting her degrees at USF, Claire spent three years as an FBI officer in New York. A coveted assignment only given to those at the top of their game. She'd transferred to the CIA ten months ago. It had been a smooth transition—almost easy. But Langley was different. This was the lion's den, she couldn't let the ease and comfort of the job let her become complacent. While she believed most officers were good, she didn't want to forget what she was here to do: find the mole who sold out her father, resulting in the murder of both her parents.

Stopping at a familiar café, she ordered a large black coffee, no cream, no sugar. She wrapped her hands around the warm cup as she headed toward Langley. Her reflection in the glass of the CIA headquarters caught her off guard sometimes—blue eyes, sharp long bob, and a clean-cut athletic jacket. Though she'd been looking at this woman for years now, a part of her still expected to see her old auburn-haired self staring back. Of course that girl had died a long time ago.

The agency hummed with activity as Claire met up with her new partner, Colin Davenport, for a sparring session. Claire wore boxing gloves, pounding the mitts that Colin held with rhythmic thuds. She had fallen in love with boxing while in college. It was an easy way to get her mind off of the frustration she felt by having to earn a degree before she could do anything for her parents. Colin groaned as she hit with an extra hard cross hook.

"You know," Colin grunted, as he shook out his wrist, "you don't have to go that hard. We are supposed to be building trust as new partners. Right now you're just abusing me." Smirking at her. Raising her eyebrows, Claire paused and then retaliated with an extra hard punch and a roundhouse kick combination. Colin was a talented officer and good at boxing but he hadn't been expecting the roundhouse and ended up flat on his back.

Mouthing, *opps*, she removed her glove and offered him her hand. "You just need to learn to keep up."

He grinned, taking her hand, accepting the help up. "Yep, abuse." Once on his feet he chuckled and knocked his shoulder into hers as they walked to the benches to get water. "Just don't tell anyone you knocked me on my ass, deal?"

"Your secret's safe," Claire replied, smiling faintly and setting her boxing gloves down on the bench. "For now." She sipped from her water and watched for his reaction.

Colin had five years in the agency. A former NYPD detective with a background in psychology, and while he loved ribbing her, they had quickly become fast friends. Maybe it was the shared New York experience, or maybe it was because Colin had a way of making the weight of this job feel lighter. Claire often found herself thinking that he was the big brother she never had.

They were just about to head to the showers when the doors burst open. Agent Kane Bhatt strolled into the gym in a perfectly tailored suit with his tablet tucked under his arm. His long dark hair was pulled back into a loose low bun with wisps of hair floating around his head, his messy hair and circle beard was a complete contradiction to his formal attire.

"Morning, Abs, Ames," Kane nodded to Colin, then Claire. "Sorry to interrupt your little team-building exercise, but we've got a problem." He motioned for the duo to follow him as he pivoted on his leather loafers and went right back out the door.

Claire shot Colin a look. "Ames?" As they ran to catch up with Kane.

Colin rolled his eyes. "I don't know, just ignore him, eventually he gives everyone a nickname."

Kane typed away on his tablet, pulling up a file. Without looking up, he answered Claire's question. "Ames, short for Amazon. You're an amazon warrior, but Amazon is too long. It took me a while to come up with one for you."

"Whoa, she's an Amazon warrior and I'm just abs?" Colin blanched as they made it to the armory.

Kane ignored Colin's complaint as he came to a stop in front of the elevators and handed his tablet over to Claire. "Cillian O'Rourke, ring any bells? The domestic terrorism unit flagged him two months ago. CCTV just picked him up near the House of Representatives. We've intercepted chatter about a bomb threat. You two are suiting up. I'll *read you in* while you drive."

Claire was already moving before Kane finished—ten months of working with him had taught her that if he interrupted their workout, the threat was imminent.

* * *

Claire readjusted her com as Kane's voice crackled through hers and Colin's earpieces. Colin drove as the SUV sped through downtown toward the House of Representatives. "Cillian O'Rourke, code name *Blackthorn*. He is a former IRA bomb maker, one of the best in the business, or so he likes to think. He spent years perfecting his craft before going freelance. These days he blows things up for whoever writes the biggest check. So honorable." Kane's tone was laced with sarcasm. "He's forty-two, six feet, built like he spends more time hauling kegs than wiring detonators. He's got short dark hair and he's sporting a scar from his right eyebrow to his cheekbone. One of his own toys misfired back in Belfast. I guess even the great O'Rourke screws up sometimes."

Kane paused for effect. "Oh, and here's the kicker, he's got a reputation for sticking around to watch his fireworks. So bet your badges he's still close by. Probably enjoying the view and thinking he's untouchable. I've sent a photo of him to your phones."

When they arrived two police officers had already started directing traffic away from the garage. A CIA tactical team pulled up in a van behind the SUV just outside the parking garage. Walking past the lift gate, she caught the smell of oil and concrete dust. The sunlight was just beginning to filter through as people arrived for the morning session. Claire adjusted her bulletproof vest that read CIA on the back. Still in her workout gear she looked more like a fitness instructor than a trained CIA operative. If it wasn't for the bulletproof vest and her badge no one would have believed she was an officer.

Adrenaline thrummed beneath her skin as Colin directed the other officers where to start looking. Two of them had bomb dogs and took off running in the direction Colin had indicated. Claire was focused on what Kane had said. *Sticking around to watch his fireworks. He's close by.* She searched for anyone who looked out of place or fit the physical description.

She saw him at the same time Kane spoke through the comms, "I've got him, twenty yards to the west, on the walkway. Georgia... "

Claire jumped the concrete barrier like it was a vault,

landing hard; concrete didn't provide the same shock absorption as a padded floor. Her foot slipped on loose gravel, momentum carrying her forward faster than planned—but she leaned into it and drove straight into O'Rourke. Colin was right behind her, his jump over the barrier was not as graceful but he managed. Colin watched as she tackled the bomber from behind and pinned him down, preventing him from rolling over. By the time he came to a stop, Claire was pinning O'Rourke's arms behind him, he bucked violently beneath her as he tried to roll.

Without waiting for Claire to finish, Colin immediately patted the guy down looking for a detonator or any other tech.

"I didn't find anything, it's got to be on a timer." Colin told the team through the earpiece. "Has anyone found anything yet?"

Claire finished cuffing O'Rourke as she hauled him up to his feet, the guy was easily twice her size, yet she controlled him without strain, and Colin realized she wasn't overpowering him— she was outthinking him.

Embodying her new nickname she marched him toward two CIA officers arriving on scene. She didn't feel like a warrior though, Claire was just letting her body lead and relying on her training just like she used to do as a gymnast.

After handing him off, Claire reported through the comms that the suspect was in custody.

As she turned back to the garage to help search, a sharp bark echoed from behind them, and a K-9 handler shouted, "Found it!"
The dog sat, indicating an incendiary device, in front of a structural column on the ground level as Colin and Claire ran over to the bomb.

Kane's voice snapped through the headset. "The bomb squad's still three minutes out."

Claire shoved a trash can aside so they could get a better look at it. Dropping down to her knees while Colin crouched beside her. "It's got less than two minutes on it," Claire said, as the timer continued ticking down second by second.

Colin turned to the officer and his dog as Claire inspected

the device, "Get everyone out of here now."

"Kane, is there anything in his file about how he builds?" Claire questioned as she began unscrewing a cover plate. She could feel the bomb humming beneath her fingers as her pulse thrummed in her ears.

"No, he's known for using different schematics each time. Send me a pic." Kane ordered. Colin was already taking the photo with his phone. "Got it."

Kane inspected the photo in silence so long it made her uncomfortable. When he spoke, his voice didn't have its usual confidence. He guided Claire through which wires to cut. When they got to the last wire, however, he said he couldn't tell which one it was. They were the same color and both led into a black hole. "If it loops into the charge housing, it's probably the trigger... but, damn, it could be a failsafe too."

"I think it's this one," Claire said, slightly separating the wires and peering into the hole with a flashlight. She hated that mild certainty was the best she could offer, but she thought she could see one of the wires veering off to the left toward the battery.

"One wrong cut, and we're done," Colin muttered.

"Yeah, well we're done if I don't choose one." Claire said flatly, her hands were steady despite the blood pumping through her heart at a thousand miles a minute. "Maybe you should go," she said looking up at Colin.

"No, just cut it." He said with no room for negotiation as his eyes locked on hers, steady, refusing to leave her.

The timer on the device beeped signaling ten seconds... nine... eight...

Claire didn't realize she was holding her breath when she clipped the wire.

The numbers on the small digital timer continued to count down... six... five... then it blinked out.

She waited a second—just to be sure—before relaxing and feeling her body return to a normal rhythm.

"Good work, Georgia." Kane exhaled over the comms. "Davenport, were you sleeping through this one?"

"Nah, I just wanted to let the newbie have some glory." Colin said, exchanging a look with Claire before they heard the sirens of the bomb squad arriving in the distance. They would handle dismantling and removing the bomb from the scene, while Colin and Claire escorted other team members and the perp back to Langley.

Hours later, back at headquarters, Claire stood behind the interrogation glass, watching O'Rourke as he stared defiantly at his interrogators. He said nothing, just sat there with a disturbing smile on his lips.

Colin appeared by her side, leaning casually against the frame. "They're sending him to a black site. He'll talk eventually." Claire stayed quiet, her jaw tightening. Torture, she knew, was how they'd get their "eventually."

Colin glanced at her. "Look, I get it. It's ugly. But if there's another bomb, if he knows anything about other attacks... it could save lives. Sometimes ugly is what saves lives."

She didn't respond, but Claire pressed her nails into her palm, holding on to Hugh's voice like a lifeline: *Don't let this life erase who you are, Kid.*

9
Home, but Not Whole

The gravel crunched beneath the tires of Trevor's Jeep as he pulled into the long driveway, sunlight spilling across the old farmhouse. The familiar sight of the wraparound porch and fields dotted with spring wildflowers hit him harder than expected. After years of barracks and deployments, this was home.

His parents had purchased the house when he was a kid; this was the only home he remembered. While it had once been a farm, the barn out back was now used as long term housing for sick animals from his father's vet clinic. Horses, cattle, sheep, foxes, and more traditional pets—cats and dogs. If you could name it, Trevor's father, Grant had rescued or rehabilitated it.

"Trevor!"

Alexis darted out of the house, flour dusting her apron, her blonde hair pinned loosely back in a messy bun. She hugged him tightly, her cheek brushing the cold metal of his dog tags. He felt her body ease, like she could finally relax because her baby was home. Trevor knew she had been devastated when he left for the army—especially after losing Claire, Lousia, and Max. But she had understood, never saying a word that would make him second-guess his decision. She'd just hugged him goodbye, called often, and trusted him to come back.

"Mom, you're gonna crush me," Trevor laughed, hugging her back just as fiercely.

Before Alexis could respond, a blur of dirt-streaked overalls and braids collided with his legs.

"TREVOR!" Addie squealed, practically climbing him. She was grinning ear to ear, a muddy smudge across her cheek that dulled her freckles on one side, while she held a small brown rabbit tucked under one arm.

"Well, hey there, Bean," Trevor said, lifting her with one arm and petting the rabbit with the other. "And who's this little guy?"

"Mr. Fluffy," Addie said proudly. "We're fostering him until his leg heals. He broke it when he fell out of a garden box, but I found him, so I'm in charge."

Alexis sighed good-naturedly; she and Addie had gone over this a hundred times. "We're just rehabilitating him, Addie. He's not staying."

Addie gave Trevor a look like she and he were in on some unspoken secret. "That's what Mom says about *all* the animals. But we always keep them."

Trevor laughed, looking down at his mom. "She's not completely wrong."

Alexis rolled her eyes but smiled as she ushered them inside. The kitchen smelled like heaven, sugar, butter, and something citrusy.

"I've got a big order for the bakery," Alexis said, slipping on oven mitts to check the trays currently in the oven. "I needed this extra oven today. These are done. But then I have more that are about to go in. They'll need twenty-five minutes, so let's sit outside. We can talk while they bake." Alexis spoke as she removed two trays of croissants from the oven before uncovering two more and placing them in.

Going to the cupboard Alexis retrieved two glasses, filled one with ice water and another with iced tea, she then nodded to the back door and followed Trevor outside. Addie had already beaten them outside and sat in the grass with Mr. Fluffy inside a small gated pen.

A wooden dining table was surrounded by large padded armchairs, the kind you want to curl your feet up and sink back into while you have dinner and talk the night away. Lousia and Max had spent many nights in those chairs, talking with Alexis and Grant while the kids entertained themselves.

Trevor immediately caught the scent of fresh grass on the spring breeze as he and his mother sat down at the table. She passed over the glass of water to him and sipped on her own iced tea. Alexis knew her son well enough to know he was primarily a water drinker, he never did like pop or tea.

Addie chatted away to the rabbit as Alexis got right to the question she wanted to know most. "So," Alexis began with a teasing smile, "anyone special back on base? Or overseas?"

Trevor smirked. "Subtle, Mom."

"I'm just asking," Alexis said, shrugging her shoulders.

Trevor shook his head, gaze lowering to his glass of water. "No one special."

Alexis studied him for a long moment, her voice softening. "Trevor... Claire's gone. You deserve to be happy again."

His jaw tightened. The thought of being with anyone else felt like he was almost betraying her memory, cheating even. Logically he knew he wasn't and he should move on. He took a deep breath, answering, "I know."

"I know you loved her," Alexis continued gently, leaning forward and placing her hand on her son's arm as it rested on the table. "And she loved you, but... it's been seven years. She wouldn't want you to be alone forever."

He stared out at the fields wild and unmanicured, his throat tightening. "I've tried, Mom. I've gone on dates, met people... but no one is....no one is her."

Sadness flickering across Alexis's features. "I understand." She said, squeezing his arm once. "When you meet the right person, you'll know. Just... don't close yourself off, okay?"

He gave her a half-smile, though his chest felt heavier than ever. He had gone on dates, in the beginning, but even the ones that his friends had set up were pointless. The women were all nice and beautiful but there was no connection or spark. He often asked himself if he wanted to find love again—or if he was content to just remember what he had felt with Claire, even though it had been for a short time.

Alexis changed the topic to med school, his last deployment, and whether or not he was happy to be done with the army. She was happy he was done, med school was safer, but she wanted him to be happy no matter what her wishes were.

The timer chimed, pulling Alexis to her feet and sending her running into the kitchen. "Ohh, I need to get these cooled and go back over to the bakery. Can you keep an eye on Addie for me?"

"Yeah, of course," Trevor called back into the kitchen.

"Thank you, love." Alexis said, popping back out onto the deck and leaning down to kiss her only son's check before running off to work.

"Wanna see the baby goats?" Addie popped up eagerly from the pen like a little rabbit herself. Excited to have her big brother all to herself.

Trevor chuckled. "Baby goats?"

"They're so cute, and one of them keeps trying to eat my shoelaces." Addie climbed out of the pen and leaned down to get Mr. Fluffy. Placing him back in his hutch she locked the door. "Dad's keeping him close by so he can check in on him regularly. Come with me."

Trevor followed as his little sister skipped her way out to the barn. As they followed the pathway lined with old trees and a wide untamed field, the unmistakable smell of the barn grew stronger the closer they got. Hay, warm fur, and the faint sour tang of goats, all grounded by damp earth and old wood.

The old barn stood along the edge of their property, a dirt area for cars was carved out within the field to the right of the barn. Stained a deep brown, the barn felt warm and familiar. Inside the space was heated to keep the animals comfortable. Old horse stalls were being used for dogs and goats alike. Cats were kept in the old tack rooms at the back, often allowed to wander in and out.

A small paddock was set up on the shady side of the barn where a mother goat and her four babies totted around. Addie slipped through the fence, sitting cross-legged in the grass as two tiny goats clambered toward her.

"They love me," Addie said matter-of-factly, looking back at her brother and patting the ground next to her. "If you sit real still, they'll climb in your lap."

Trevor crouched down beside her, letting one sniff his hand before gently scratching its ears. The kid leaned into his hand, its ear soft and warm, twitching as he scratched just behind it. Addie grinned at him, making her green eyes dance.

"You're staying, right?" she asked suddenly. Addie was always straight to the point and never held back a question.

"For a while," Trevor said, smiling at her. "A few months; until I start med school."

"Good," Addie said, leaning into him a little. "It's not fun when you're gone. You missed *so much*. We took care of six kittens last spring, and Mom taught me how to braid bread, and.. Oh!... I beat Evan Halloway in the science fair."

Trevor laughed. "Sounds like I missed a lot of important stuff."

"You did. Don't leave for a long time again, okay?"

His chest tightened, and he put an arm around her. "I'll be here as long as I can, Bean."

After playing with the goats for a good twenty minutes, Addie insisted on showing him every animal in the barn. She knew all of their names and what had happened to each of them. Several of the dogs were being picked up by a local rescue in a few days to be rehomed now that they had recovered. Addie desperately wanted to keep one. They had lost their family dog, Scout, a few years back to old age and she was ready for another one.

As they walked back to the house to get cleaned up for dinner, Addie told her big brother and "partner in crime" all about her latest scheme, to hide Dodger, the scruffy pit bull mix they'd rescued, in her room until after the shelter folks had come and gone. If no one saw him, they couldn't take him. And if they couldn't take him, well, then he would just have to stay. She spoke with a conspiratorial grin, her arms flailing with excitement as she described the plan in great detail. Right down to how she'd stash treats in her closet and teach Dodger to be silent on command.

Trevor laughed along, nodding seriously as if she were laying out a top-secret mission. Halfway up the porch steps, Addie's boundless energy seemed to wane. Her feet dragged slightly and her shoulders drooped. She let out a small yawn that she tried to hide behind her hand.

When they stepped inside, the shift was subtle but noticeable. Addie rubbed her eyes and mumbled that she was feeling a little tired. Rather than bounding into the kitchen like usual, she turned down the hallway toward her room. "I think I'm gonna take a quick nap before dinner," she said, her voice unusually quiet. She was usually a whirlwind until bedtime, so seeing her fade this quickly made Trevor's gut twist. He told himself it was nothing, but the worry lingered.

Trevor watched Addie disappear into her room, the door clicking shut behind her with an uncharacteristic stillness. He rationalized that in combination with all the excitement, she had just overexerted herself, but the way she seemed to drain so quickly stayed with him, a stone in his gut.

Climbing the stairs he carried his duffel bag up to his old room. It felt frozen in time with baseball trophies on the shelves, an old guitar leaning in the corner, and a framed picture of him and Claire at the county fair. He used to take her every year, even before they started dating.

For a moment, it felt like he'd turn around and see her sprawled out on his bed like she used to. Trevor's fingers brushed the glass of the photo, remembering how she used to say his name. He could feel the warmth of her skin and the softness of her hair as it brushed his skin. Then suddenly he was seventeen again, Claire laughing under his hands...

* * *

She lay across his bed, laughing as he tickled her side. "Stop!" she squealed, trying to push him away.

"Not until you admit I won," Trevor teased, pinning her lightly, his body hovering slightly above and to the side of hers, his hands holding hers down.

"You didn't win anything!" she said with all the sass in the world, twisting her body beneath him, trying to wriggle free.

Going still she smiled up at him and without another word she kissed him quick at first, then deeper, hungrier. He released one of her hands, moving his to her waist and pulling her into him. She curled her hand into his white t-shirt as Trevor kissed her back, her nails grazing his skin just enough to make his chest tighten. He could have kissed her forever, it felt as if his body would just melt into hers, the two of them becoming one. She released his t-shirt and slid her hand up to his neck...

"Kids."

They froze.

Grant stood in the doorway, arms crossed, his massive six foot five frame filling the space. His face was stern, but his eyes held that patient kindness that had always defined him.

"Dad," Trevor said quickly, scrambling to sit up. Claire blushed, sitting cross-legged beside him.

Grant raised an eyebrow. "I like you both too much to be a grandfather at forty. Behave, or this door comes off its hinges. My parents did it to me— I'll happily continue the tradition."

Claire's cheeks went crimson, burying her face in Trevor's shoulder out of embarrassment. He got a whiff of her lavender scented shampoo. He wanted to disappear into a black hole, but when Grant left, Claire whispered, smiling mischievously, "Totally worth it."

Trevor grinned then kissed her forehead, and for a moment, everything felt simple.

Returning his mind to the present, Trevor sat on the bed, running a hand over his short army cut hair. He pulled out his Swiss Army knife, flipping it open and shut absently. The room was full of memories, and he needed the familiar weight of the knife to ground him. Seven years later, she was still here—in the picture frames, in the creak of the porch boards, and in the hollow ache that settled between his ribs every time he let himself remember for too long.

10
Beneath the Surface

Claire moved through the halls of Langley like a ghost in a tailored suit. Rubber soles on her practical but gorgeous heeled boots muted her steps against the polished concrete floor. Her movements were calm and practiced, her expression carefully neutral. She had just returned from a thirty-six-hour trip to Ireland, following a lead she and Colin had uncovered. A suspicious half-million-dollar transfer into O'Rourke's account. Kane had traced it to disgraced Congressman Silas Hargrave, who they had believed to be hiding in the Irish countryside.

The mission had been a success. As soon as they had Hargrave in custody he squirmed and admitted the whole thing. Claire listened as he detailed how he wanted to get back at the party and people who had betrayed him. A younger version of her would have been in disbelief, but politics and corruption went hand in hand. It no longer surprised her what people would do for re-election.

Claire and Colin had returned to D.C. late last night, hand-delivering Hargrave to the CIA's interrogation team before a quick debrief. They didn't make it to their homes until the early hours of the morning. Now, running on only a few hours of sleep and a large coffee, Claire walked through the quiet early-morning corridors to her desk. Her ID badge clipped to the navy suit jacket she wore as she focused on each person she passed, silently evaluating them as a potential suspect in her parents' deaths.

The office had a sterile energy as she sat down at her desk, sipping the too-hot coffee. She felt like a coiled snake, ready to strike at any time. The bitter taste of coffee grounded her as she scanned the people around the room. Some she had met, most she hadn't. But she was going to make it a point to know everyone. Names, faces, patterns. Observing and making mental notes of potential threats had become as natural to her as stretching was to a gymnast.

Seven years.

That was the minimum someone would have needed to be here to have played a role in her parents' deaths.

Kane was out, he had only been here two years. A street hacker with the kind of talent that made it inevitable he would either end up recruited or in jail. Colin had been here five years, not long enough either. He also didn't fit the profile. Her team was clear, but the rest of the department?

She'd started a mental list of anyone suspicious.

—Valerie Keene. She asked too many questions that went a tad too deep — and spoke fluent Italian when she thought no one was listening.

—Director James Harlow. Unreadable and impeccably diplomatic. He'd grown up vacationing in Tuscany and still kept a villa there.

—Brett Singer. Unsettling without ever saying a word. His transfer papers listed "Interpol liaison experience," but the Italian branch had no record of him.

—Mason Clark. Too efficient — no one was that precise all the time without hiding something. His most recent case files involved multiple Italian shell corporations; a few had even vanished from the database.

She kept a mental log of the names, reviewing them often

and adding details.

A notification flickered across her computer screen, reminding her that she had a meeting in two minutes.

Rising and straightening her blazer she made her way to the formal conference room. She had done an initial debriefing on her mission last night with the on duty handler. This was different, a large meeting with her whole department.

The glass-walled conference room buzzed with tension, judgement and gossip that was being masked as professionalism. Claire took a seat halfway down the table, flanked by Colin and Kane. The room was just as cold as the rest of the office, and the chairs were aggressively uncomfortable. Absently she wondered if they were designed to keep officers on edge.

Claire readjusted while noting that Kane smelled faintly of expensive cologne and espresso. Colin smelled clean and like… leather. She instinctively reached to touch her leather bracelet, the one piece of Trevor she still had. She did her best to keep the bracelet hidden under her clothing at all times but still somewhere she could feel.

Claire scanned the room, the meeting should have started a few minutes ago. She recognized most of the faces that had strolled in behind her. Some stared back at her with curiosity, while others didn't look at all. Preoccupied, indifferent or hiding something she didn't know.

Marcus Hale, Director of Operations, breezed into the room. Her direct supervisor. He was tall, overly polished, with every hair perfectly styled. He looked like someone who knew what expensive whiskey tasted like and had never had to scrub stains out of his own clothes. The suit was easily custom made from the finest of wool. Silver cufflinks and a vintage Rolex—worth at least her annual salary—adorned his wrists.

He smiled, the kind that made her skin crawl. Controlled, charming, and hungry.

"Morning," he said, eyes sweeping the room like a presidential candidate at the podium. "Let's keep this brief. Some of you have been doing excellent work. Officer Anderson," he said, nodding to Claire, "flawless infiltration in Ireland. It's nice to see someone raising the bar." She half expected him to end with a wink, but it didn't come. Director Hale moved on, "Bhatt, your hacking on the O'Rourke financials was elegant. Davenport, well... try smiling once in a while."

That drew a few polite chuckles. Claire didn't smile. Looking over at Colin instead, who gave a dry deadpan look back, eyebrows raised just slightly.

As Hale continued his rounds, asking after ongoing cases and handing out praise, like gold stars, Claire studied him. She kept a calm professional exterior but inside Hale's behavior made her ill. He was too smooth. Too clean. The kind of man who'd sell you out, then shake your hand at the funeral.

By the time the meeting ended, she had added him to her list. She had been reluctant before, he was her direct supervisor, but she couldn't deny it any longer, she didn't trust him.

Colin and Kane stood the moment the director released them, chairs scraping backward on the concrete floor. Claire followed them into the hallway as people lingered behind in the conference room.

"Coffee?" Colin asked not looking back.

"Sure." Kane was already at the elevator mashing the down arrow, like it had offended him.

The trio settled into a corner table at the café on the lower level. Colin dumped sugar into his coffee like he was trying to neutralize a poison. Claire blew on hers, then slowly sipped. Kane had ordered some complicated half foam double espresso latte served in a real mug that clashed with the paper cup aesthetic of the rest of the place.

"I got another offer last night," Kane said casually, swirling his drink like a fine wine. "Some black-hat network with an encrypted server name like a bad metal band. Payment in crypto and cursed diamonds. Very on-brand."

Claire didn't look up. "What did they want you to hack?"

Kane waved a dismissive hand. "I don't remember. Something very illegal and dramatic."

Colin leaned back in his chair sighing with relief as coffee met his lips. This was the first time he was relaxing since the meeting had started.

"You wouldn't do it though," Claire said. A statement, not a question.

Kane grinned. "I might." he said, then catching her expression, he rolled his eyes. "No, I prefer having morals more than I like having a yacht."

Colin smirked behind his cup. He wouldn't have been surprised if one day Kane retired to a yacht, living off the grid in the lap of luxury.

Claire shifted gears, "What do you two think of Hale?"

Colin didn't hesitate. "He's too polished, I don't trust people who smile that much and never blink."

Kane snorted. "I suspect he polishes his teeth with snake oil. Charisma points? Ten out of ten. Morals? TBD."

Claire laughed, brief and unexpected. Kane always had a unique way of breaking the tension without dismissing it.

Colin's phone buzzed on the table. He glanced at the screen and his expression shifted, standing abruptly. .

Kane raised an eyebrow. "Problem?"

Colin shook his head at Kane's question as he stepped away to take the call. One hand raking through his light brown hair as he turned his back to them. Claire watched him—the usually confident, grounding officer suddenly quieter, more vulnerable.

"Hey, buddy," Colin's voice softened. "No, no, I didn't forget... I know it's today. I wish I could be there too."

A pause.

"I'm sorry, my job makes it hard for me, Ethan. But, I'll call later, okay?"

He hung up and when he returned his expression was composed but his shoulders slumped, looking heavier. "My son had a science fair today."

Claire blinked. "You have a kid?"

"Yeah," he said, tone casual but tight at the edges. "Ethan. He's eleven. His mom moved him out of state a couple years ago."

"Is she your ex?" Kane asked, watching him with immense curiosity.

"High school sweetheart, we got pregnant, got married young. Things got messy after the divorce." He reached for his coffee, but the cup was empty. "Now I see him when I can. Which... isn't much."

Claire's heart ached for Ethan and Colin, she knew all too well what it was like to miss your dad and not get to see him. She already adored him as a partner but he was finally showing her a bit more of the vulnerable man behind the badge.

No one said anything for a moment. He tapped his empty paper cup on the table, rising from the table before anyone else could ask any more questions.

Then Kane chimed in with his unique timing, "You may need a new nickname now, Abs. It doesn't fit anymore."

Exiting the elevator, Kane peeled off to his lab, waving them off.

Alone with Colin, Claire quietly said, "If you ever want to talk about Ethan, I'm happy to listen. Family is complicated, kids just make it more so."

Colin gave her a half smile, "Thanks. Yeah, things were good, before Lauren decided she didn't want to be married anymore. Part of it was the job... she was just done. Now, I'm trying to get a better custody arrangement but our hours don't exactly help my case."

"No, they don't. Would you consider going back to the PD?"

They reached the bullpen where more people milled about. Colin's face shut down.

"Maybe. I'm not sure," he said, brushing it off. Claire understood, squeezing his arm gently.

At her desk, Claire glanced at the small frame, a photo of her fake family, made by Hugh. A jade plant sat next to it, in a simple white pot. Her desk was clean, clutter free. Across from her, Colin's was a mess of files and loose pens. No photos. Nothing personal. She made a mental note to fix that.

Logging onto the agency's case system, she began cross-referencing ongoing operations with international crime syndicates. Anything that was remotely tied to Italy caught her eye, as did anything filed by someone on her list.

One case stood out in particular.

Subject: Suspected money laundering through construction   fronts in Milan.
Filed by: Valerie Keene.
Current Status: Ongoing. Ties to shell corporations with Sicilian addresses.

She'd have to review the file when the office was less busy, if she lingered on it too much someone might see and get suspicious. Just the fact that Valerie was actively working on an Italian case made Claire move her to the top of her suspicions list.

The rest of the day dragged on, she wrote her formal play by play report for the Ireland mission and then moved on to a few cases she had been assigned to this morning. None of them relating to the Italian mob or her parents.

Later, as she packed up, Colin was still staring at his screen. His brow furrowed.

"Find something interesting?" Claire asked.

Colin was startled, "Oh... just an old report that isn't lining up. It's probably nothing, just a filing error." Looking away from the computer for a minute, Colin realized that the work day was over and it was time to go. He glanced at his watch, a durable tactical style, "It's the end of the day already?.... I'm going to stay a little bit longer, get this figured out. I'll see you tomorrow."

Feeling something was still off, Claire paused but ultimately chose not to push. She'd ask him what he found tomorrow, though it would continue to nag at her all the way home. "Don't work too hard."

She passed by Hale's office on the way out. The blinds were drawn and the door shut, but she could see the light still on spilling through the blinds.

Slowing to a stop, she paused and pretended to check her

bag for something. Listening for anything that might be useful.

Nothing.

Stepping into the elevator, she pressed the ground-level button with steady fingers. Through the closing doors, she watched her colleagues shut down their computers and gather their things. One of them knew what had happened to her parents. One of them had helped cover it up.

And she was going to find out who.

11
Cracks in the Glass

Claire's feet pounded against the pavement, her stride in sync with the faint music drifting from a passing cab. She still didn't run with headphones, not even one earbud. She could practically hear her dad's voice warning her it was dangerous. Sometimes, when she was really missing him, she'd consider it... just to imagine him scolding her again.

She rounded the corner, halfway through her five-mile run to work. Slowing down as the alley came into view, her breathing was still steady. Morning light filtered through the buildings, casting sharp shadows and illuminating the figure already waiting in the narrow space.

Colin.

She'd been surprised to get his text so early, but after ten months as partners, one thing was constant—if he asked her to meet, she'd show up. To strangers he looked like any other commuter—tall, handsome, coffee in hand. But Claire noticed what they couldn't; the tension in his shoulders, the sharpness in his eyes, and the exhaustion etched into his face.

This wasn't a casual meeting.

"Are you always this chipper before 7 a.m.?" Claire asked, brushing her bangs aside.

Colin cracked a smile, but it didn't reach his eyes. "I didn't want to risk talking at headquarters. Too many ears."

She nodded. "Okay, what's going on?"

Claire's mind already started to race with possibilities. It had to be the file he found yesterday, it was too big of a coincidence otherwise.

Colin pulled a flash drive from his pocket. "Last night, I went back over that case file, the one I thought was just a typo. It's worse. A lot worse." He hesitated. "I've found eight files so far. Same pattern. Missing evidence. Redacted sections that shouldn't be. Audio that doesn't match the transcripts. And surveillance footage that's been edited or scrubbed entirely."

Claire stiffened. "And who do all of these files connect to?"

"The Italian mob. Or at least someone who is adjacent to them. Some suspects vanished from custody. Others were released without explanation. A few were quietly handed over to departments that, on paper, don't even exist."

Her heart pounded, could this finally be it? "How far back does it go?"

"Six years. That's just what I've confirmed. I think there's more, but I didn't want to keep digging in the agency's servers. Not without someone watching my back."

Claire tilted her head. "You trust me that much?"

Colin didn't answer right away. Ten months of early mornings, joint ops, and near-misses flickered behind his eyes. "I do. You don't cut corners or lie to make yourself look better. I don't know what game someone's playing, but I know you're not a part of it."

She didn't know what to say, instead giving him a half smile. His words hit harder than she expected. She wasn't ready to tell him who she really was, not yet, but hearing that... it made her feel less alone—and a bit guilty. She trusted him too, he had become like a brother to her, but she couldn't tell him—not yet.

"We need Kane," Claire said finally. "He's better with digital forensics. He can check the rest of the files without being caught."

Colin gave a small nod. "I figured you'd say that. Bring him in, quietly. We can't risk alerting anyone."

Claire glanced at her watch. "He's probably getting coffee. I'll catch him before the briefing."

"I'll meet you in the old server room," Colin said. "No cameras or foot traffic in there. It's the kind of place people forget exists—plus we can't be overheard in there."

She smirked. "Perfect."

Claire took off running toward work, as if she had never stopped to talk. She arrived with twenty minutes to spare before the morning briefing.

Normally she would have joined Colin for a workout or headed to the locker room to shower and change into a suit. Instead she was looking for Kane, she stopped in the café that they had sat in the day before. Spotting a familiar sight, an empty table with a single mug still sitting on it. Kane was one of the few people who insisted on having his coffee in-house, from a real ceramic mug. She'd just missed him.

Catching the elevator just before the doors closed, Claire found herself standing shoulder to shoulder with Director Hale.

"Good morning, Georgia," he said smoothly.

"Morning, sir," she replied, matching his tone with a professional smile. She could feel his eyes on her the entire ride up.

As the elevator doors opened onto their floor, Claire calmly stepped out, heading down the hallway toward Kane's lab. Even after she turned the corner, she still felt the weight of his gaze lingering behind her.

She found Kane in his lab, but he wasn't alone. Without a word, Claire strode up to him and pulled him into the hallway.

"Well if this is a come on, I'm pretty sure HR requires a form," he quipped, letting himself be led.

Claire said nothing, keeping her pace brisk. If anyone was watching, let them assume the obvious—a workplace romance. Better that than three officers whispering about tampered files. She led him down a flight of stairs through a narrow hallway, and into an unused maintenance corridor. At the end she opened a heavy door and pushed Kane inside.

"Seriously, Ames," he deadpanned, "I had no idea you felt this way…"

"I don't."

"She doesn't."

Claire and Colin answered in unison.

Colin stepped out from the shadows, standing at the center of the room. The space was lined with old computer servers, hollow now. Their drives removed, cables stripped, and the lights dead. Only a few overhead fixtures glowed dimly above, casting long shadows against the concrete floor and walls.

"I've already swept the room," Colin said, glancing at Claire, "we're clear."

Kane looked from Colin to Claire, then back again. "Alright," he said, his usual sarcasm fading into something more serious. "Who died?"

Claire crossed her arms. Her parents—but she couldn't say that, not yet, not until she was sure. "No one that we know about yet. But Colin found something. Files. They've been edited, redacted, evidence wiped. They're connected to the Italian mob."

Kane's brows lifted. "Mob? As in, organized crime? You're saying someone here is helping the mob and trying to cover their tracks?"

"Yes," Colin said, pulling a small notebook from his back pocket, flipping it open and handing it to Kane. It listed out each of the eight case numbers. "Most of them are old cases. It was done sloppily. I've already found eight with manipulated audio or missing surveillance. One of them dates back six years."

Kane whistled low under his breath. "That's not sloppiness, that's arrogance. Whoever did this didn't think they'd get caught."

"Or they already got rid of the people who could expose them," Claire said, thinking of her dad.

That quieted the room, tension hanging in the air.

Kane ran a hand through his loose hair, pulling it back from his face. "Okay, so you want me to dig."

Claire nodded. "Carefully. If they're scrubbing these files, they're watching the system. You'll need to use a back door, so it can't be traced."

"I'll set up a ghost server through one of the old nodes, something pre-2012, before the last infrastructure overhaul," Kane said, already shifting into problem-solving mode. "It'll take time to reroute access without triggering any activity logs, but I can do it."

"How long?" Colin impatiently asked.

"Two hours to set up, maybe three to mirror the files. It depends on how deep this goes."

Claire leaned back slightly against the cold wall. "We can't afford to wait too long. Hale's watching me. He was in the elevator this morning, I could feel his eyes on me."

"Creepy," Kane muttered. "But not surprising."

"I think he suspects something," she continued. "Not everything, but something. We have to move before he shuts us down, especially if it's him. He may have noticed Colin viewed the files last night."

"You think it's the director of operations?" Kane asked, stunned.

Colin turned to Kane. "Possibly, we don't know who it is yet. Start with the eight flagged files. Look for any patterns: names, timestamps, missing footage. Anything else that links them."

"And if I find something?" Kane asked.

Claire met his eyes. "Then we follow it. Wherever it leads."

Kane gave a sharp nod, the weight of the moment settling on his shoulders. "Alright. Let's blow a hole in this thing."

* * *

Trevor

In Tennessee, the kitchen smelled of cinnamon and brown sugar as Trevor sat at the breakfast table indulging in a sweet breakfast roll Alexis had made before heading to the bakery. The mail had been collected and a letter, addressed to Trevor, had been left in the center of the round kitchen table.

He opened it before even really noticing who it was from, expecting junk as usual. It was handwritten, and Trevor's breath caught when it opened with two words: *my son*. The message was short, inviting him to Italy to meet his 'father'. The sender offered to pay for all of the expenses and said he simply wanted to get to know his son. Signed by a man named Antonio Giordano. Included at the bottom was a phone number, instructing him to call if he was interested.

He'd spent the whole day thinking about it, the letter burning a hole in his pocket until dinner was done and Addie had gone to bed.

That evening, Trevor showed his mom the letter. She didn't seem as surprised as Trevor expected her to be. He had always known that Grant was his stepfather technically and that his biological dad was out there somewhere. But Grant had always been his *dad*, he and Alexis had married when Trevor was only four and he didn't remember a time without him. Grant had been at every sporting event, driver's lesson and parent-teacher conference. Trevor had never felt like he was missing anything and, as far as he was concerned, this letter didn't change anything.

Together the three of them sat down in the living room. Alexis and Grant sat together on the sofa with Trevor in the armchair. Grant was the only one that relaxed into the padded leather set. His hand gently resting on Alexis's lower back.

The setting sun spilled through the windows, turning the dust in the air gold. Trevor barely noticed. He watched his mother's hands instead—how she fiddled with her ring, how she kept reaching for Grant like she needed to remind herself she wasn't alone in this story.

"After I graduated college," Alexis said, "I backpacked through Europe. Italy was supposed to be my first stop." Her voice hitched like she could still taste the heat of that summer. "It became my only stop."

Trevor swallowed. He'd heard pieces of this before—never the whole thing, never with this much weight.

"On my third day," she continued, "I ran into Antonio. We hit it off and spent the rest of the day together talking." Alexis reached back and took her husband's hand, needing his steadiness.

"One thing led to another and we had a bit of a romantic fling. I was only there for two weeks. When I left we decided to let what happened stay in Italy. Reality was we were from two very different worlds and I wasn't moving to Italy and he wasn't moving here. So we didn't exchange phone numbers or emails. It was 2000, so we didn't have video chat or social media."

"When I got home, I realized I was pregnant. I tried to find him then and I tried several times, until he found us when you were five." She looked at him like she was trying to read his reaction. "Your dad and I had already met and married by that point."

Letting go of Grant's hand, she reached across the distance and put her hand on Trevor's cheek, like she really wanted to impress on him what she was about to say. "I was all for you meeting Antonio, he had the right to meet you. And you had the right to meet your dad if you wanted. We were going to ask you if you wanted to. But Antonio chose not to....I don't know why... he never made that clear. He just said he would be in touch when he was ready. I figured after all these years he had decided not to reach out."

Dropping her hand she sat back and took Grant's again. Alexis was terrified of disappointing her son, she had done the best she could have. Thankfully, Grant was the calm they all needed. Just looking over at his dad gave Trevor the sense that he was taking a clean breath in a room full of smoke.

"So," Trevor said finally, clearing his throat. "He wants to meet me now? 19 years later." His stomach tied up in knots with nerves. All of this was so odd. Why now? Trevor had never really cared about meeting his biological father. But now with the letter in hand and the opportunity staring him in the face, he wasn't so sure that was still the case.

Alexis's lips parted, then closed again. "I guess... I haven't had any contact with him."

"He wants me to go to Italy," Trevor said more to himself.

"Do you want to go?" Grant spoke up for the first time.

"I don't know, it seems a little odd that he wants me to go all the way to Italy without knowing anything about me. He's even offered to pay for everything."

"Well why don't you call him and then decide," suggested Grant, he was always the pragmatist.

Trevor swallowed against the knot rising in his throat. He looked back down at the letter. It was handwritten in neat, deliberate strokes. An invitation to come to Italy.

"Mom, what do you think I should do?" he asked.

Alexis's eyes were shiny with unshed tears. "That's up to you. You deserve to know where you came from, if you want to. But don't go for me, and don't go if it feels wrong."

Trevor looked out the window. The wind was rustling the trees gently, summer still clinging to the edges of the season. His life had been moving forward, steady and safe, with medical school on the horizon. But now this... letter... *this man* had stirred something in him. Questions that wouldn't be quiet.

"I'm going to think about it," he said finally. "I might call to hear his voice. Just... talk. Then I'll decide." Looking down at the military watch he always wore, Trevor realized it was late, "It's too late to call now. If I do it, I'll do it in the morning."

Grant nodded again, his hand never leaving Alexis's back. All three of them stood, Alexis stepped forward and wrapped her arms around her son squeezing tight. When she finally released him, Grant hugged Trevor before his parents excused themselves and went to bed.

Trevor had lain awake for hours, debating what to do. Nineteen years of silence didn't disappear because he wanted a relationship now. He also had a father and didn't feel like he had a hole to fill. But he knew he might feel differently later. Maybe he owed it to himself to just talk to the man.

The next morning, with the letter in hand, he stepped out onto the porch. The phone number was jotted neatly at the bottom of the letter. He input the country code and dialed it with a strange sense of calm, waiting for the line to connect.

It rang once, twice. A nervous spike flooded Trevor's system. He debated hanging up, but didn't make up his mind in time. The line clicked and a voice answered, warm, rich, Italian-accented.

"Trevor."

Trevor's breath caught. "Yeah. Antonio?"

A pause. Then, "You sound just like your mother." Trevor didn't know what to say to that.

Antonio continued, "Thank you for calling. I wasn't sure if you would. There's so much I want to say, but mostly... I want to meet you. I don't expect anything. Just... time. A conversation. That's all."

It was a kind voice, but beneath the warmth, Trevor caught a trace of steel — like a smile that never reached the eyes. Still, he couldn't hang up. Not yet. A piece of himself he'd never known even existed was calling out from across an ocean.

"Okay," Trevor said slowly. "I'll come."

* * *

Claire

The halls of headquarters were quiet as Claire made her way down to the locker room. Fluorescent lights buzzed overhead, and the hum of the HVAC filled the stillness where conversation had once echoed. The building was nearly empty; most of the employees had gone home hours ago. Only the cleaning crew remained... along with Claire, Kane, and Colin. Director Hale had left early, throwing out some offhanded comment about a tee time and dinner—his usual swagger just a little too rehearsed.

Claire didn't believe him for a second. She had caught him looking, watching her several times today. He was clearly up to something but they hadn't figured out what just yet.

The corridor leading to the locker room was dimmer than usual, the motion sensor lights were slow to react. Claire pushed open the heavy door and found Kane already pacing near the benches, a crossbody bag at his feet. His hair was damp from a shower. He looked agitated, muttering something to himself as he tapped away on his phone.

Colin arrived moments later, dressed in all black. He looked at Claire and Kane before reaching behind to lock the door. Kane stopped pacing, instead shifting back and forth in place.

"Last place with no cameras, have you swept it?" Colin said quietly. Just because there weren't cameras didn't mean there weren't bugs that could hear every word.

Claire glanced up at the grimy ceiling tiles, then back to her teammates. Kane raised a slim black wand, a bug detector, in answer to Colin's question.

"Alright, Kane, what did you find?" Claire asked.

Kane lifted a folder from his bag and pulled out a series of printed case files, some had been dog-eared and highlighted. He laid them out on the bench between them.

"This," he said, pointing to where the lead officer's name was listed as *M. Hale*, "was supposed to be a routine surveillance op on an arms dealer in Florence, but when they got to the location, they were ambushed. Several of our guys died and the arms dealers got away unscathed. This was before Hale was promoted to director, he was on site and he got away but only with a graze. How did three officers die and he only got a graze?"

Claire leaned in, her chest tightening with anxiety.

Colin stepped closer. "And this one?" He picked up a second file, one he had reviewed the night before. "The mission objectives are redacted. But the listed officers were from our branch. Except one of them isn't in the personnel database anymore."

Claire narrowed her eyes. "Wiped?"

"Or ghosted. Either way," Kane muttered, "they don't exist on paper anymore. The oldest reports that are tampered with all have one access code used to edit them. It's Hale's access code."

The silence that followed was thick.

Claire clenched her jaw. "The director of our department has been lying, fabricating official reports, and covering up for the Italian mafia... Are we sure?" Claire asked, voice low. "Because the second we point at Hale, we either end his career—or he ends ours. Or us. We need certainty."

Kane folded his arms. "I don't have enough to prove it in court, not yet, but it's him."

Colin nodded grimly. "This isn't just betrayal. That's *treason*."

The word hung in the air like smoke and the ground felt as if it shook beneath their feet.

Claire looked at both of them. "We need to dig deeper. Everything we can get our hands on. Digital records, archived files, anything that wasn't scrubbed clean or that can prove it was him."

"I'll work from my home terminal tonight," Kane said, already pulling out a flash drive from his bag. "I can do it untraced."

Claire gave him a grateful look. "Good. Let's meet again tomorrow. We need a new place, we can't meet in the same place twice."

Colin looked from Claire to Kane and back again, "We're running out of time. If Hale gets wind we're onto him—"

"He already knows there's something going on, he's not dumb," Claire cut in. "But we can't let him figure it out, not until we have everything."

"Give me forty-eight hours. I'll pull everything I can. Then we take it up the chain, someone clean." Kane suggested.

Claire wasn't sure *anyone* in the agency was truly clean anymore, so many people bent rules. Hell the CIA is known for breaking rules to get results. But they had to try, they had to find someone who would stop Hale.

Kane zipped the files shut into his bag. "Stay off work channels and unless it's an emergency don't text or call. They can trace everything."

Claire and Colin nodded. One by one, they slipped out into the empty hallway, their footsteps echoing ominously in a building built on secrets and lies. Despite knowing he wasn't even in the building, Claire swore she could feel Hale's shadow stretching across the floor behind her, reaching for her heels.

12
The Breach

The rapid staccato of keystrokes echoed loudly through Kane's loft. He sat hunched over his custom-built desktop, four monitors casting a bluish glow across the otherwise darkened space. His fingers moved lightning-fast, navigating encrypted archives and buried case files with a practiced ease. Caffeine buzzed in his bloodstream. The remnants of wasabi peas sat beside a half-drunk matcha tea.

He'd already found six more tampered operations. The problem was, Hale had gotten smarter—using new access codes each time, sometimes even codes belonging to recently deceased officers. The earlier cases were minor. But the more recent they got, the more egregious the cover-ups became. Hale was clearly willing to do anything for a paycheck.

"Come on," he muttered, dragging lines of code into a separate window. He was close to finding Hale's offshore account. Domestic bank records were spotless, but he had to have another stash. Kane was deep—too deep for Agency protocols, but he was on the trail.

Then, the synthetic ping of his security system snapped him upright.

PERIMETER BREACH flashed across his far-left

monitor.

Kane's blood chilled. He tapped a key and pulled up his exterior cameras. Grainy black-and-white footage loaded: two men in dark clothing, moving with trained, military precision. One carried an assault rifle, the other a suppressed handgun. Both wore gloves with no identifying features visible.

Hale's guys or the Italians. Kane didn't need to know which. He just had to get out. Hale had moved faster than he'd expected.

Kane grabbed his phone and dialed Claire. No time for pleasantries. No questions.

"Move. Now," he said, "They're here. Armed. I'm leaving. You've got maybe two minutes. *Find me where kings take root and leaves command loyalty.*"

He didn't wait for confirmation before hanging up. Moving through his loft, he grabbed his go bag as he called Colin, repeating his words.

Then he ejected his flash drive and typed in a kill code that shut his computer down and fried the hard drives. Thankfully, his work automatically backed up to the flash drive. He swept the drive into a leather messenger bag along with his laptop and tablet. Slinging both bags over his shoulder, he then flicked a switch that killed the loft's power, plunging the loft into darkness. Moonlight filtered through the square-paned windows, casting long shadows across the loft.

Without looking back, he opened the narrow crawlspace exit behind his bookcase. An old trick from his days running black-market scripts. He nicknamed it the "rabbit hole."

His boots hit the alley pavement soundlessly as he dropped from the hidden exit. His car was a no-go, too obvious. Instead, he sprinted toward the old bike shop a block down, cutting through the shadows and pulling his hood up.

The sound of a door being kicked in echoed faintly behind him.

They were too late.

* * *

Claire

Claire was too wired to sleep. The mission might be what she'd been chasing for years, but something felt off.

She'd already triple-checked her go bag: cash in various forms, a passport, an unregistered firearm, extra ammo, hair dye, neutral clothes and a baseball cap, plus one irreplaceable thing. The stack of letters. The old duffel Hugh gave her still had the hidden lining. Every time she wrote to Trevor, she slipped the letter inside, a ritual that made her feel like he was still with her.

She sat curled in a chair at her small dining table, pen in hand.

My love,
It's been a few weeks since I last wrote to you. I told you that I really like my partner and I made a friend, Kane, he's a techie. A bit odd but he makes me laugh. Last night Colin found something, a ton of files that were compromised. I think this is it. I think we found...

Her phone buzzed in the pocket of her sweatpants.
Kane.
He spoke rapidly. "Move. Armed. Two minutes. *Kings take root, Leaves command loyalty.*"
Claire grabbed her bag and tossed the new letter in. She strapped the bag over her shoulder. She armed herself quickly with her sidearm. With a spare in the bag, she ran to the window.
Three armed men were already entering her building.
She bolted for the elevator. They'd split up—one in the elevator, two up the stairs. She had seconds.
She hit the elevator call button and raised her weapon. Keeping her back to the wall, she kept an eye on both the elevator and the stairwell. The doors opened. She had made it in time. Empty.
Going to the corner, she stepped up onto the handrail with one foot, bracing her hands against the two adjacent walls. Walking her hands up the wall, she stood up, placing her other foot on the same handrail. The elevator hatch was behind her now, she

needed to turn around. In one swift move, she turned around and stepped out to the side placing both feet on their own handrail.

The doors began to close just as she leaned forward, catching the edge of the escape hatch's lip. Pushing it open with her opposite hand she grabbed the edges and pulled her body through with pure arm strength. She had her torso and bag through—legs still dangling inside—when it began moving.

The sudden downward momentum of the elevator threw her weight forward, bringing her face within centimeters of the moving cable. She regained control and balanced her body, just in time to avoid disaster. She hauled her hips up onto the roof, she was able to pull her legs through and shut the hatch before the elevator descended too far. Keeping her body low, she braced herself against the metal edge of the elevator waiting for it to come to a stop.

Sure enough it opened on the first floor. While the gunman stepped into the elevator, Claire got up and stepped off the roof onto a thin metal edge along the cement wall. The maintenance ledge was thin, much thinner than the handrail or a balance beam. Keeping her weight on her toes, she swung her bag to the side and held it as flat as she could. The cement walls of the shaft were cold against her face as she plastered herself as flat as she could against the wall bracing her feet and hands on two vertical metal beams.

She was painfully aware of every creak and groan as she did her best to be quiet and not alert the man to her presence. A bolt creaked under her weight—soft, but deafening in the shaft. She froze. The gunman shifted below, head tipping like he'd heard something.

Claire didn't blink. Didn't breathe. Briefly, she thought of Trevor and vowed that she would not die before she got to see him again.

After a beat, he muttered to himself and the car continued upward.

As the elevator rose past her, air displaced in a rush, pulling at her hair. The metal cage passed within inches—so close she could feel the vibration through the wall. She was grateful that she was small enough that she hadn't been crushed. She'd scoped out an escape route when she moved in but she hadn't had time to test it yet.

As soon as the car had cleared her, she silently used the vertical beams to shimmy down until she was within six feet, dropping the rest of the way to the concrete slab floor. Claire moved fast, past the counterweight, under a conduit line, to a paint-chipped service door. This she'd tested before she moved in, it was locked from the hallway in, but not going out from the shaft. Now in the residents' hallway, she had one more door, an emergency exit. Down three apartments, turn left and there it was.

Stepping into the brisk night air, Claire noted how similar this felt to the night her parents were killed. The cool air did little to cool her down as the adrenaline spike continued to push her forward.

Kane had said to meet him where *kings take root and leaves command loyalty*. Claire loved a good crossword clue and knew instantly where he wanted to meet. The Royal Oak, a pub twenty minutes from her. The three of them had gone there for a drink after Claire's second day on the job.

* * *

Colin

Colin didn't remember lying down—just that exhaustion dragged him under the moment he hit the couch. The townhouse he had once shared with his wife and son was void of furniture, and what he did have he'd purchased secondhand. Lauren had taken most of the good furniture and the rest he had sold, not wanting to see her everywhere. Despite the couch being old, it was fairly comfortable—ugly but comfortable.

His phone rang loudly, buzzing in his pocket. Colin answered, groggy. It took him a moment before he realized that it was Kane on the other end. He spoke so fast that all Colin caught between the speed and exhaustion was: find me where *kings take root and leaves command loyalty*.

Thankfully, it was enough. Emergency protocol.

Colin sprang up and ran to the hall closet, grabbing his

favorite black jacket off the hanger while shoving the others aside. Behind the jackets was a safe door. He expertly typed in the code and opened the safe. Extra firepower, cash, a burner phone, and his wedding ring filled the shelves. Without thinking he grabbed a backpack from the closet floor and swept everything into the bag, wedding ring included. He couldn't leave it behind.

He was just zipping shut the bag when he heard it, the front door handle jiggled. It rang out as loud as a fire alarm in the silence.

Someone was coming in.

Colin darted into the chef's kitchen that he rarely used and ducked down behind the island. The townhouse had a large open concept living space and kitchen; he could easily see the front door from here. His only exit was that door. He knew when purchasing the house that it was a tactical nightmare but Lauren had loved it so much he'd given in. He regretted it now.

Despite the challenges, he had planned for this. A smoke bomb in the island drawer, designed to drop anyone who breathed it in. The only problem was that he had to walk through the smoke to get out. Holding his jacket over his nose and mouth he waited for the assailants to kick in his door. Launching it as soon as he could see the door open all the way.

It hit the floor hard, filling the doorway with smoke, filtering inside the house and drifting out the door. If someone was just outside they'd breathe it in but if they were a few feet away it might only make them dizzy. Colin held his breath, still covering his nose and mouth with his jacket using his left hand, and raising his firearm with his right, ready to shoot if necessary.

Three loud thuds reverberated against the high ceilings echoing through the space as the men dropped. Colin ran as fast as he could, careful not to trip on the unconscious men.

He didn't encounter or see any signs of a fourth man so he lowered the gun... slightly.

When he was sure he could breathe without inhaling the smoke he lowered his jacket, letting out the breath he held.

Colin then slipped on his jacket and used it to conceal his

gun. Still dressed in all black he blended in with the shadows as he moved away from his home on foot. Mentally repeating the phrase Kane had said, "Find me where *kings take root and leaves command loyalty.*" It took a second, then he remembered: The Royal Oak.

* * *

Claire

Arriving at The Royal Oak, Claire circled to the back of the building, staying in the shadows. She hadn't been followed and she knew she'd beaten the others there. Her loft was closest.

Entering the alley next to the pub, she found a spot behind the dumpster to hide. It was near the fire escape ladder for the building next door. Dark and hidden, it offered three escape routes: either side of the alley or up the ladder. With her weapon drawn just in case, she waited.

Kane showed up five minutes later, his messenger bag and laptop case swinging at his sides. Claire had never seen him in anything but tailored suits. Tonight he wore a matching olive green lounge set. Understated for him, but still clean-cut.

He visibly recoiled when she waved him over to the dumpster.

"Seriously?"

"Seriously," she said flatly. He sighed and joined her.

Three more minutes passed before Colin appeared, moving like he expected an ambush. Kane had fidgeted the entire three minutes, jumping up as soon as he saw Colin. He couldn't take another second next to the dumpster.

"We need somewhere safe to talk," Claire said standing up from behind the dumpster, "somewhere private."

"I've got a place. But we need a ride," Kane said, checking himself over for any unwanted residue.

"We're not stealing a car," Colin replied immediately.

"We are if you want a bed tonight and don't want to get shot in it," Kane shot back. "The Agency will pay for the car after all this, I promise."

Claire stepped out of the alley and scanned the street,

tuning them out as they continued to argue. She needed something older, mid nineties or earlier. It was less likely to have an alarm and easier to hotwire.

Two blocks down, she spotted it: a beat-up Dodge minivan that had definitely seen better days.

She pulled her baseball cap from her bag, twisted her hair up, and shoved it under the cap. To any passerby, she just looked like someone heading to her car.

Rummaging in her duffel, she palmed her window punch; one of Hugh's non-negotiable tools.

Colin and Kane fell silent, watching as she smashed the back window like it was nothing. She ducked in and started hotwiring the ignition.

They jogged toward her, not bothering to speak until they were all inside and the engine had sprung to life.

Kane gave directions from the passenger seat, leading them out of the city toward a quiet neighborhood—wide driveways, tall hedges, and no one walking their dog at midnight. Privacy was built into the architecture—tinted one-way windows.

Claire squinted over the wheel as they pulled into a wide, paved driveway. "Kane... where are we?"

"It's a safe house," he replied.

Claire raised a brow.

"Ugh, fine. It's a house the tech community uses when someone hacks into something they shouldn't have."

"So... a hacker hideout," Colin said flatly.

"Sure, do you have a better suggestion?" Kane shot back. "Because if not, we need to ditch or hide this thing—fast." He gestured to the car like it offended him.

Claire idly tapped the wheel. "Are you sure it's empty?"

"Yeah. It's a crash pad the tech community keeps off the grid—rotated keys, rotating names, utilities in a shell company. No cameras on the street-facing eaves, and the neighbors mind their own business. I pinged the group and got the green light."

Claire and Colin exchanged a look of doubt, but not disagreement.

"Alright," she muttered, pulling the minivan into the drive.

As Colin stared up at the beautiful estate, he had a thought. "How do we get in?"

"It's all electronic. Real keys'll be inside." Kane said, jumping out of the car and flipping open a keypad on the side of the garage. The door rumbled open.

Claire blinked. It seemed too simple for a "techie safehouse."

"What?" Kane asked. "Would you have preferred I hacked my way in through the house's Wi-Fi? I can close it and do that if you want to wait a minute."

Claire didn't bother to answer, she just drove the rusted minivan past Kane and inside the garage.

They stared for a beat. The minivan looked absurd parked inside the garage of a sleek, multi-million-dollar home filled with polished concrete, sharp lines, and designer lighting.

Claire snorted under her breath. "We really know how to make an entrance."

Entering the main part of the house, they walked straight into the kitchen and dropped their bags with a collective thud. The space was modern and sleek, concrete floors, marble countertops, minimalist furniture, cold and impersonal.

None of them cared.

Inside, the house smelled unused—cleaning chemicals and cold air. Kane didn't go for the couch. He went straight to the corners, checking for hidden cameras, then pulled a small device from his bag and swept the room.

'No hot mics,' he said. He reached into a drawer and tossed two black pouches onto the island. "Phones in the bags. Faraday-lined."

Colin caught one, turning it over. "Of course you have these."

Kane smirked. "What kind of hacker safe house would this be if we didn't?"

Claire was too exhausted to appreciate the convenience, but sleep had to wait. They needed answers. They needed a plan.

Kane opened his laptop on the center island, pulling a flash drive from his messenger bag and inserted it with a click. "I pulled this from the CIA server before the douche bags arrived. It was buried, encrypted three levels deep in a back-end partition labeled 'training simulations.'"

Claire leaned on the edge of the island while Colin grabbed a bottle of water from the stocked fridge. No one said anything for a few seconds. Then Kane clicked into a folder labeled 'Huntington'.

Claire froze. The breath left her lungs, her mouth parting slightly.

"You okay?" Colin noticed her sudden shift.

Claire shook her head as if to clear it, "Yeah, go on Kane."

Kane nodded and opened a series of files. The first were two more altered case files. But this time the changes were attributed to Max Huntington.

"I don't think we are the first people to suspect Hale of treason." Kane said. "Seven years ago an officer, Max Huntington, seems to have changed at least two files. But the timing doesn't add up, both times he 'changed' a file, he was out of state. But, the IP address used at the time of the change says it came from within Langley. The second one was also done on the day he died, in Chicago."

"How did he die? Did Hale do it?" Colin asked, his brows furrowed.

Claire was holding back tears now, her chest heaved quietly. Her dad had not only been murdered but Hale had tried to frame him!

Kane pulled up another file while responding, "A car accident. It killed him, his wife, and daughter." Then the screen filled with text messages, some were redacted but enough remained to paint a clear picture. The sender line was blank, but the recipient was labeled as **M.H.**—Marcus Hale.

Claire turned away, unable to look.

Kane read aloud, voice low. "*Family compromised. Tie off all loose ends. No survivors.*"

Colin's jaw clenched. "Son of a—"

Kane kept scrolling. "This one's from the day after: *Clean up confirmed. Target eliminated. Fire ruled accidental.*" He looked up. "There are more like it. Dozens. Hale ordered the hit."

The air left Claire's lungs.

She staggered backward, a hand to her ribs, the other covering her mouth. She didn't speak; just shook silently, trying not to break apart.

Colin approached her carefully, placing his hand on her arm. "Georgia? Are you-"

"Max Huntington... was my father." Claire forced the words out. "My name... isn't Georgia."

Colin didn't move for a second. His face tightened—not anger, exactly. Something like recalibration.

"You've been my partner for nearly a year," he said quietly. "And you never told me your real name."

Claire's throat bobbed. "I couldn't."

"That's not an answer," he said, then exhaled hard. "But keep going."

She looked up, eyes sharp and glassy. Colin gently guided her onto a bar stool.

Kane let out a short breath—almost a laugh. "I was wondering when that shoe would drop."

Both Claire and Colin gave Kane a quizzical look.

"I didn't know for certain," he added. "But your records were too clean. No one's that perfect."

Rolling his eyes at Kane, Colin spoke. "Go on Claire."

She didn't let her tears fall, instead she took a deep breath and began, "My name is Claire Huntington. Max and Louisa were my parents. Georgia Anderson is an alias I've been living under since I was 18."

She swallowed, "I was a gymnast. We were in Chicago for a meet. After dinner, on our way back to the hotel, we were hit by a black SUV. When I came to, the car was upside down..." Claire stared down at her bracelet, playing with it, "A man started shooting at our gas tank. I got out but my parents were already gone. Then the car went up in flames."

Colin looked stricken, he rubbed her back when the tears did fall. "You can take a minute, if you need to."

"No... I need to finish." Taking a deep breath, she went on with a steadier voice. "My Dad had always told me if anything ever went wrong, I should call his old mentor, Hugh."

Colin's eyes widened. "Hugh... You mean *Hugh McAllister*? The mountain ghost?"

Claire gave a faint, sad smile. "Yeah. He took me in. Hid me and trained me. Taught me how to survive. How to fight. He was the only one I trusted."

"What do you mean 'was?'" Kane asked.

"He died from lung cancer. Just over a year after I went to live with him."

Kane sat back, stunned. "Everything makes sense now. You were a gymnast. Your fighting style is...creative. And your—Georgia's—social media only went back to when you were eighteen. What teenage girl doesn't have social media?" Claire let out a breathy laugh, Kane seemed invigorated by how right he was.

"I changed everything. Name, background. I became someone new. I needed to find out who did it. Get justice for my parents." She looked between them. "I've always known the Italian mob carried out the hit. But I didn't know who ordered it. Hugh found CCTV of the accident. My dad suspected a mole in the agency. Apparently, it was Hale."

She paused. "I want to bring them both down."
Colin's jaw worked. "Okay. We finish this together. But is there anything else we need to know—no more surprises."

Claire's throat tightened looking up at him with surprise. "There's not."

"Good," he added.

Kane nodded. "I'll help, at least with Hale. I can keep digging, get you everything I can by morning."

Claire exhaled slowly, nodding. "Then Colin and I will go into Langley. We'll take it to the DCI in person. Show him everything and I'll come clean."

Kane was already typing. "Then you'll need hard proof.

Physical Evidence." Kane paused, looking over at Claire. "Don't admit who you are, just give them the evidence and get out. You don't deserve to go to prison for trying to get justice."

"I agree," Colin said firmly. He knew he would have done the same, especially if it had been for Ethan or Lauren. Kane worked through the night. Colin passed out, beyond exhausted from the last two days. Claire showered, changed into borrowed pajamas and finally curled into bed. Her mind was quiet for the first time in years. Tomorrow the man who murdered her parents would finally pay.

The sky was still dark as Claire and Colin pulled away from the house in the Dodge minivan. Kane hadn't found nearly enough to irrefutably prove Hale was the mole, but it was enough to start an investigation, it would have to do.

They were just turning onto the street that led to Langley when Claire's burner phone buzzed. Kane.

"Yeah?"

His voice was tight, urgent. "You need to turn on the radio. Now."

Colin reached for the dial, flipping it on. Static gave way to a news report mid-sentence:

"...three suspects wanted in connection to the explosion late last night in Arlington. Surveillance footage shows them fleeing the area shortly before the blast. Authorities are asking anyone with information on Georgia Anderson, Colin Davenport, or Kane Bhatt to come forward—"

Claire went pale.

"Some idiot blew something up," Kane said in her ear, "and they're pinning it on us."

13
New Names, Same War

Claire and Colin were on edge the entire drive back to the safe house, but they managed to do it without being seen.

"Any more news?" Colin asked as they entered the kitchen from the garage.

"Yeah," Kane said grimly. "I pulled a police report for the incident. According to Arlington PD, the bomb went off not far from the Washington Monument. It used the same schematics as the one you defused in the parking garage. O'Rourke's still in custody, so it wasn't him. Plus they've got CCTV footage that shows us planting it." He glanced up. "It's clearly faked, but it's already hit the news. And once the public sees it…"

"People think we did it." Colin muttered, dragging his hand over his face. Lauren would see that footage. There went any hope of ever getting custody of Ethan.

"Then we prove we didn't do it," Claire said, her voice hard with resolve. "We expose Hale—not just to the agency, but publicly."

"How?" Colin asked. "The case files are classified. We can't exactly post them online."

"True. So we need something bigger. Irrefutable evidence that shows Hale has been working with the Italian mob. It's going to take time," Claire said.

"We'll also need new IDs, a more permanent safe house..." Kane was already turning back to his laptop, fingers flying.

Claire touched Colin's arm gently, grounding him. "I know you're probably thinking about Ethan. I promise, we'll clear our names and get you custody. I won't let my fight for justice destroy yours."

Colin gave her a tired smile and nodded. "Thanks. But what about money? Most of mine is tied up in my house, and it's not like we can walk into a bank."

Kane and Claire answered in unison: "I have some." They both blinked, then smirked.

Kane spoke first. "I've got offshore accounts from before the agency recruited me. It's clean—enough and should last us a while."

Claire glanced at Colin, "Mine is a savings account Hugh set up for me. Completely untraceable. It's got about two hundred fifty grand in it. I've added to it over the years."

"Okay, good. Geor—" Colin stumbled on his words, correcting himself. "Claire."

"It's okay. You can still call me Georgia."

"No, Claire. You've done this before, gone into hiding. I'm guessing you're good at dyeing hair. We need to change our appearances." Colin said, running his hand through his hair.

"I am. Believe it or not, I'm not naturally blonde, and I don't have blue eyes." She popped out her blue contacts, blinked to clear her eyes and turned to Kane. "Why don't you start looking for a new place?"

"Already on it." He didn't bother looking up.

Then she turned to Colin. "Come on, I have hair dye in my go bag and I'd be surprised if this place didn't have some too. It seems to have everything."

Claire and Colin left, beginning the process to become someone else.

They raided the master bathroom, finding a stash of high-end hair dye, clippers, and even colored contacts. This place really was like an all-inclusive resort for fugitives.

When they were finished, Claire had dyed her hair a fiery red, styling it with a side part and curtain bangs. She would wear it up in public and planned to add extensions once she could get her hands on them. Her natural brown eyes stared back as she looked in the mirror, examining herself. It was nice to see a flicker of the old her returning.

Colin's light brown hair went jet black. The sharp contrast with his skin made his strong jaw look more angular and his ocean blue eyes pop. Typically clean-shaven, he decided to stop shaving for now, letting the stubble grow into a beard. His facial hair already grew in darker, so he wouldn't have to dye it too.

Kane initially refused a makeover, but relented after a little pestering. Claire gave him a modern quiff with a clean fade, shaving off his goatee and leaving him unrecognizably sharp. He groaned the whole time but didn't protest too hard. She had wanted to dye his hair but he drew the line at that.

Once they had their new looks, they took updated ID photos and printed them on the spot. Then they scavenged the mansion for everything they might need: tech gear, food, and spare clothes.

Colin expertly used paint to change a few of the license plate letters and numbers on the Dodge minivan. Then they waited for dark before hitting the road.

They drove over an hour, heading east toward the coast. The farther they got from the city, the quieter the roads became.

Galesville was barely a dot on the map. A harbor town with aging houses and a sleepy marina, it was the kind of place no one looked at twice.

The safe house Kane had secured was tucked off a back road, hidden by trees and backing up to a narrow inlet. It was an old abandoned colonial-style home that was being overtaken by weeds and ivy. It looked like it had only been deserted for a few years and would be secure enough.

Claire pulled into the gravel drive and killed the engine.

"This is it? Does it even have power?" Claire asked, skepticism lacing her tone.

"Yes, it has power and furniture. Nobody will bother us out here. Half the town's retired. The Wi-Fi's probably slow, but I'll fix that."

Claire stepped out and took a deep breath of salt-laced air. For a moment, it felt like the world stopped spinning. But it hadn't — and they couldn't rest for long.

They hid the minivan behind a cluster of red cedar trees and magnolia bushes, making it impossible to see unless looking for it. They entered the home after picking the back door's lock. It was stale and dark but with the use of their burner-phone flashlights they were able to find the breaker box and get power back on. The owners must have never had the power company shut it off completely.

Dust particles danced in the air, making Colin sneeze as they all wandered from room to room. For the most part only the valuables had been taken including silver, designer clothing, or electronics. Entering the formal dining room Claire found what must have been the point of entry, a large window that had been smashed.

She wondered if her home in Tennessee looked the same, dusty and void of life. She knew that along with the trusts, Hugh had set aside money for a cleaning crew to go in three times a year and to clean both his cabin and her parents' home. The payments were automatic, routed through an account she didn't have access to yet. She'd get access upon taking legal ownership of both houses. But the occasional clean didn't stop thieves from breaking in.

Colin joined her, his eyes on the broken window. "We'll need to board that up. I can go get more food and supplies in the morning." He scratched his jawline absently while he spoke, he wasn't used to having facial hair and was finding it itchy.

Colin and Kane moved a large bookcase in front of the broken window before heading upstairs. There were enough bedrooms that they were all able to retire to their own room for the night. Everything was covered in a layer of grime and Claire made a mental note to have Colin get some cleaning supplies when he was in town in the morning. Finding some extra sheets in the closet, each bed was remade with clean sheets. The house had a basic security system that would need some upgrades, but it would do for the night.

With both men asleep Claire needed to do one thing before she could settle her mind. She went out to the minivan and found the registration paperwork for the owner, Katy McDonald. Back inside she pulled out her burner phone and logged into her offshore account. She sent a wire transfer to Katy as payment for the stolen vehicle. Ten grand, despite knowing the minivan was only worth a few hundred at most; she wanted to make sure Katy was able to get something nicer. In the memo section she wrote: *For the minivan. Sorry for the inconvenience.* She then made sure to route the transfer through several places, making it difficult to trace.

A few days later the team had the house looking like a home, one belonging to a techie, but a home nonetheless.

Kane had been digging to find anything they could on the Italian mob. He'd uncovered the current head of the mob, a man by the name of Antonio Giordano. Recently, he had booked the finest suite at Rome's Palazzo d'Oro under his alias, Victor Leone. He wouldn't spend that kind of money unless it was for someone important. They needed to get eyes and ears inside the suite.

Now that Hale knew they had evidence against him, he would have changed his schedule but Kane doubted he was dumb enough to meet with Giordano in person. So who would be staying in that suite? They could easily tap satellites and security cameras, but without being there, they couldn't get ears or eyes inside the room.

They'd have to be on the ground in Rome. Kane pinged a dark-web contact who could slip them onto a private jet and into Europe without U.S. security. Their new passports would hold up under border control scrutiny but they didn't want to be caught on airport security cameras, not with facial recognition in play.

Colin and Claire would fly out in the morning from a private airport 30 minutes away. Kane would stay in Galesville and support them through comms, running ops from the safe house.

He preferred a night-owl schedule anyway, so the time change wouldn't matter.

Lifting the bags into the trunk of the Dodge, Colin went through his mental checklist. Weapons, check. Comms, check. Bugs, check. Passports and money, check. They had it all and if anything else was forgotten they could source it in Rome. The early morning air smelled of brine and rain from a storm that had passed through in the night.

Kane jumped into the driver's seat with Claire to his right. Colin slid into the back and pulled the door closed as Kane started the engine and drove out onto the road.

"Remember once you get into the suite I may not be able to hear you on comms. If they use a signal blocker, like I would, you'll have to return to the suite and get the bugs a few days later. It'll act like a tape recorder saving the conversations if I can't connect to it." Kane had already been over this but felt uneasy not going with the team. He was better off here, where he had the network and systems to properly help them, but they wouldn't have back up. If something went wrong their only assistance was 4,562 miles away.

* * *

Trevor

While Kane dropped Claire and Colin off at the small airport, Trevor was boarding a plane in Atlanta. Leaning back in the wide leather seat, he felt like he didn't belong there. First class felt worlds away from the cramped bench seating on military flights he was used to. Here, the air smelled like coffee instead of jet fuel. And the seats reclined to lay flat instead of being made from red netting.

He closed his eyes, letting his mind drift. Until a flight attendant passed and the scent hit him. Warm vanilla and brown sugar. Faint but unmistakable, it had been her favorite scent. Claire.

Trevor's mind went a bit hazy as it often had when he would nuzzle into her neck. The memory came heavy and fast.

She'd *dragged* him shopping—or at least that's what he would tell the guys. In reality, he would've followed her anywhere, done whatever she wanted to, without hesitation or objection. But he was fifteen, and he was already getting grief about being "whipped."

Louisa had driven them to Knoxville for a few hours. While she was two doors down picking up a bulk order of chocolate, flour, sugar, and eggs for Alexis's bakery, the kids popped into a trendy thrift store. Its brick walls were lined with vintage band tees and signed rockstar memorabilia. It smelled of old books and leather. The racks were crammed so close together that you had to turn sideways just to pass.

Claire made a beeline for a round rack of leather clothing: jackets, vests, and so many pants. He trailed behind. He flipped a price tag before even looking at the jacket itself.

Three hundred dollars. His eyes felt like they popped out—cartoon style. "I can't afford these. Did you see the prices?" he whispered as Claire inspected a black leather bomber.

"No, I–" She stopped mid sentence, spotting the $350 tag. "Okay, so let's see if they have a sale rack."

Grabbing his wrist, she pulled him toward the pierced and tattooed cashier. She looked old enough to be their grandma. But her dark hair, inked arms, and fully studded ears told another story. She smiled and nodded toward the back corner when Claire asked for a sales rack.

Claire went straight for a price tag and found some had been dropped down to fifty dollars. "See you can afford that." She said, flashing him the discounted tag.

Not waiting for Trevor to even look before she started skimming through the rack. Stopping on a worn brown leather jacket, she held it out for him to see. The color was darkest at the seams with the rest having faded into warm mid-brown tones.

Stepping closer, he caught a whiff of Claire's lotion. He couldn't recall the name but he could breathe it in for hours. A warm comforting scent that smelled like something his mom might bake.

"What do you think?" she asked.

"I like it. Do you think I can pull it off?"

She slipped the hanger out and held it open for him. "I think you could pull off anything. But yeah, I think this'll look really dapper."

Dapper? He wondered briefly if she was flirting with him. Every bone in his body ached for her to care for him the way he did for her. He was too scared to say anything though, the idea of not having her in his life was worse than never telling her how he felt.

Trevor slipped his arms in, shrugging it onto his shoulders. It was a little large especially in width but it was long enough for his lanky arms and his 5'10" frame. "It's a little big."

"Yeah but you're still growing, this way it should fit for a while. Plus it's meant to be a little baggy, like a pilot in the 1950s."

"Okay—if you think it looks good." As he spoke he looked down at the tag that hung from the wrist. It was listed at forty dollars. *That* he could afford.

The leather was soft and it needed a new lining but the zippers worked and she had picked it out. Without taking it off he walked back toward the register and the woman behind it.

On the drive back home, the kids sat in the back seat with the jacket in Trevor's lap. A hole in the lining revealed a seam where the leather had once been taken in. A long strip of the extra fabric was already cut and hanging down. Using the Swiss Army knife Grant had given him for Christmas, he cut away the rest of the loose strip and split it into three thin strips.

Louisa had been peppering him with questions about his new little sister, Addie. She had been over to see Alexis frequently over the last few months but she wanted to know how Trevor was doing with a new little sister.

He began to braid the pieces of leather as he told her about how much he adored his sister but that she could be loud at night. Knotting the ends so the braid wouldn't come untied. Reaching for Claire's wrist, he tied the bracelet without saying a word. It was a perfect fit.

Now they would both have a piece of each other. Claire looked at her wrist, and then back up at Trevor, beaming.

The pilot's voice cracked through the intercom, shattering

the spell. "Welcome aboard Flight 785 to Rome." The attendants began taking their seats as the engines began to hum louder.

Trevor tightened his seatbelt, his gaze was fixed on the window, but his thoughts lingered in the past. The jacket she had chosen for him—her jacket—hung in the first class closet. He still often wore it, and every time the worn leather brushed his skin, it was like she was there, touching him, just for a moment.

He wondered if she would have still worn the bracelet? Would she still trace over the braided leather with her thumb when she was nervous? The thought made him feel hollow.

She wasn't here, not really. He'd never actually feel her touch again. But he carried her with him, stitched into the seams of the jacket and woven into his heart. *She was so much a part of him that sometimes he didn't know where he began and she ended.*

And when he meets his biological father for the first time, she'll be there too. Not in the flesh, not in the way he ached for, but in spirit.

14
The Rome Job

The flight from Atlanta was long, but the view from the first-class window was incredible. Trevor had never been to Rome, but he'd always dreamed of going, though he had always imagined Claire would be by his side.

When the flight arrived, it pulled into a Terminal 3 gate at the large international airport. Pulling his army-style backpack from under the seat Trevor swung it onto his shoulder and collected his jacket from the flight attendant.

The walk to customs and baggage claim was long, with a tram ride to Terminal 1. Luckily, the line for foreign travelers moved quickly as they had automated machines that simply took your picture and scanned your passport.

After collecting his bag from the customs conveyor belts, Trevor stepped into the arrivals area of the airport where he spotted a man in a tailored suit holding a sign that read: TREVOR BENNETT. He had told his father he would just catch a cab, but Antonio had insisted on sending a car. Feeling painfully awkward, he approached the man, who greeted him politely and offered to take Trevor's suitcase. He let him carry the bag he had checked but kept his backpack and jacket.

Leading the way, his driver stepped out to the pickup curb

where a sleek black car waited for them. The summer sun was bright, but he had expected the air to be hotter than the pleasant warm temperature it was now. Honking drummed in his ears as he made his way to the waiting car. The driver had already loaded the trunk and was holding the door open as Trevor reached the car. Sliding in, he put his backpack on the seat next to him and laid his jacket across his lap.

The thirty-minute drive from the airport to Antonio's favorite hotel, the Palazzo d'Oro, the golden palace, was fairly silent, only filled with Trevor's thoughts. He watched out the window taking in the thousand-year-old buildings as they got closer and closer to the heart of Rome.

The car turned off the main road and pulled into the roundabout driveway of the grand and opulent hotel. Made from brick, imposing windows, marble columns and detailed moldings—the former palace was a piece of art. Trevor would have preferred the tradition and romance of a smaller bed-and-breakfast, but the Army had ingrained in him the formality of respecting your elders and being grateful for what was handed to you. So he'd enjoy his time here—but if he returned to Italy, he'd be making his travel plans, not Antonio.

Entering his suite, the splendor of the foyer and sitting room stopped him in his tracks. The high ceilings were embellished with gold and white molding and medallions that dropped down into a textured beige wall paper finally becoming a vintage parquet wood floor. Through double doors to his right, a grand wood and fabric bed frame looked like it was made for a king. To the left a small kitchen and butler's pantry had top-of-the-line appliances that he doubted any guest had ever used. A formal dining room was attached to the kitchen with enough seating to host his whole platoon. All of the historical furniture felt too expensive to use, let alone sit on, like it belonged in a museum and not in a hotel room.

Trevor had insisted on bringing up his own bags. He dropped them on the floor in the bedroom. Sitting down on a bench at the end of the bed he ran his hands through his hair, feeling unsettled and restless. He needed to get out of here.

Without unpacking, he decided it was time to explore the city.

Locking his passport in the hotel safe, he gathered his phone, wallet, key card, Swiss Army knife, and jacket. Turning to leave he stopped, feeling like he was missing something. He realized exactly what it was; the weight of his handgun was absent from his hip. He had gotten so used to carrying a gun over the years that the missing weight felt like he was about to walk out the door without his pants. But not only had he officially left the army, he was also overseas and unable to legally carry here. Putting his hand in his pocket he reminded himself he could do a lot of damage with the Swiss Army knife that he always carried, at least he had that.

Making sure the door had shut and locked behind him, Trevor walked down the hallway to the elevator. His suite was on the sixth floor at the end of a long hallway, mirrors, console tables and floral arrangements placed delicately down each side. There were only two other suite doors that he passed on his way to the gold elevator doors. Even the metal plate that surrounded the elevator call buttons was covered in filigree.

The elevator door opened, and Trevor stepped inside, pressing the button for the lobby. He watched the numbers descend, his reflection staring back at him in the mirrored elevator walls. For the first time in years, he felt unarmed—not just without his weapon, but stripped of everything familiar and comfortable.

This city wasn't his. This life wasn't his. And the "father" waiting to meet him during this trip? He wasn't sure he wanted anything to do with him anymore, it all just felt... off.

His leather jacket weighed heavily in his arms while Claire's ghost clung to him like the scent of wood and smoke. As Rome stretched out before him, Trevor couldn't shake the thought that she should've been here, holding his hand as his wife.

But she wasn't.

The elevator doors slid open, exposing him to the marble lobby buzzing with travelers and staff. Trevor squared his shoulders, forcing himself forward. Whatever came next, he'd face it head-on, just as he had since the day she had died.

Only this was different. This wasn't shooting a gun for the first time or getting into med school, it was *family*.

Trevor's footsteps carried him out into the late Roman afternoon. He gripped tightly to the idea of Claire being here with him, walking hand in hand. She would be wearing a white sundress with her auburn hair falling in soft curls. Pulling him along as they joined the throng of tourists spilling through the cobblestone streets, as he did now, alone. The city was alive in a way his hometown never was—warm, old, and humming with history. He disappeared into the crowd, unaware that only moments later a black town car slowed to a stop in front of the same hotel doors he'd just walked through.

* * *

Claire

The driver stepped out, sleek and professional, and opened the rear door for Colin. From the other side a bellman approached and with a white-gloved hand he opened the passenger-side rear door for Claire. She adjusted the hem of her pale green sundress before stepping onto the curb. Elegant sunglasses concealed the sharp sweep of her gaze as she lifted her chin toward the detailed façade of the Palazzo d'Oro. Her now long red hair caught the breeze as she waited for Colin, tucking her purse into the crook of her arm. On the other side of the car, Colin climbed out wearing a tan suit, blue-button up, and a brown tie knotted just loose enough to suggest he didn't care, a kind of rich arrogance. His hand brushed hers briefly as they together approached the revolving door. Wedding rings glinted on both their fingers.

Colin had debated just using his real wedding ring, but even just the idea of being fake-married to Claire, while wearing Lauren's ring, felt like he was cheating. So instead they both wore new rings.

"Mr. and Mrs. Mischinoff," Kane's voice teased in their ears, warm despite the static of distance. "Rome looks good on you. Don't forget to smile for the nice people at the desk." He could see them having hacked into the CCTV footage and security cameras.

Kane had organized everything from their safe house while

they were still in the air.

The driver lifted two dummy suitcases from the trunk of the car and handed them to the bellman. They were filled with belongings you'd expect a couple like the Mischinoffs to have. Their real bags were already at a private residence a mile away where Claire and Colin had stopped briefly, dropping their stuff and changing.

Claire's lips curved faintly as she entered through the impressive doors, the marble foyer felt like it swallowed them whole. Chandeliers dazzled overhead, reflecting tenfold in the polished floor. People moved in and out around them, but neither Claire nor Colin broke stride. While they were still relatively new partners, they had each done this a hundred times in a hundred places—walk in like you belonged, embodying your cover persona.

At the desk, Claire rested her faux passport lightly on the counter. "Alexandra Mischinoff," she said smoothly, letting her accent bend just slightly Russian. Colin's hand intertwined with hers, the picture of a doting husband. "And this is my husband, Jackson. We'd like a room on the east side, top floor, if possible."

The clerk's smile pinched with regret, her Italian accent thick when she said, "I'm so sorry, signora. The east wing's upper floors are fully booked tonight."

Claire's sunglasses hid the flicker of frustration in her eyes. Kane's voice cut in, "She's not lying. Antonio's suite is on the top floor east corner. There's nothing on that floor, let alone near it."

For a heartbeat, the only sound was the tapping of keys and the hum of the lobby as the clerk found them a room, "I do have something available on the third floor with the same view."

Claire's smile returned, polite as ever. "That will do," she said, sliding a credit card across the counter.

Keycards tucked safely in Colin's jacket pocket, he guided Claire toward the elevators. He let go of her hand and placed his on the small of her back. His palm was warm through the fabric of her dress, a little too convincing for comfort. Claire didn't flinch or show any indication that she was the slightest bit uncomfortable but every man's touch that wasn't Trevor's always felt wrong.

"Remember, lovebirds," Kane murmured in their ears, amused. "Security cameras are everywhere. You're supposed to look like you can't keep your hands off each other."

The elevator chimed open. Claire stepped inside first, Colin close behind. A pair of tourists joined them just before the doors closed. They were elderly and smiling, eyes lingering on the Mischinoffs' rings. It looked like the woman was about to ask questions, Claire didn't feel like answering, so she leaned in, tilting her face toward Colin's shoulder, her hand curling at his lapel. The silent cue hit him a beat late, but he bent down, brushing his lips against hers. Soft, practiced contact, careful not to linger.

The tourists chuckled fondly at the display. Claire didn't move away, pressing lightly into Colin's side, her head against his shoulder until the elevator stopped. When the couple exited, she didn't straighten. Cameras watched from every corner with red lights blinking.

"Keep smiling," she murmured without moving her lips, her voice low enough, only Colin could hear.

His arm slipped more firmly around her waist as he dipped his mouth down to her ear like he was whispering a sweet nothing. "I'm smiling on the inside."

They walked the carpeted hall in perfect step, their closeness mechanical but convincing. Colin slid the keycard into their door, holding it open so Claire could glide through first, her hand brushing his as if subtly flirting with her husband.

Only once the lock clicked shut behind them did the act collapse. Claire walked immediately to the balcony, stepping out and looking up, surveying the possibilities. The plan had been to get a room on the same floor, then use the decorative molding to scale from one balcony to another.

Colin loosened his tie, still in the entryway, his own expression flat. "Let's try and keep the kissing to a bare minimum. You're like my sister. I'm not interested in incest." he said dryly.

"She was about to start asking questions. Trust me I didn't like it any more than you did." Claire said, motioning him out onto the balcony.

Kane's chuckle crackled through the earpiece. "That was almost romantic."

Claire ignored him, "I could climb it." She said looking up at the brick walls, it would be tricky but she had climbed worse.

"No, that brick is ancient and it doesn't look in good enough condition. The handholds could crumble beneath you and you'd fall. We'll find another way. Kane?" Colin stepped back into the room waiting for Claire to follow before closing the balcony door.

"I've got the schematics pulled up but I'm not seeing many options. There are cameras everywhere." Kane typed away, the click clacking echoing through the comms.

Colin paced the room with his arms crossed. "We can't just stroll into the hallway, pick the lock, and walk in. That floor's crawling with staff."

Claire listened while she sat on the bed and removed her heels, she didn't mind them but the stilettos Kane had sourced for her cover were extremely uncomfortable.

"What about the roof?" Colin asked.

She looked up then. "Isn't there a restaurant on the roof? We'd be seen."

"Then how the hell do we get in?"

Kane yawned, it was mid-morning for him, but he had only just gotten up having worked late into the night. "Funny you should ask. I've been digging through the hotel's old schematics. You're not going to like it, but it's your best shot."

Claire glanced at Colin. "Go on."

"This place used to be a nobleman's palazzo before they turned it into a hotel. The blueprints show an old dumbwaiter system. It ran straight from the main kitchen up through service halls to the top floors. They shut it down decades ago, sealed most of the openings, but..." He paused, zooming in. "Looks like two access panels might be accessible. One in the suite's kitchen and one three floors down. Right in your corridor."

Claire's lips curved faintly. "And where is this access panel?"

"Inside a service closet behind the door. Maintenance doesn't use the dumbwaiter anymore, they've probably forgotten it's even there. Housekeeping uses the closet though, so be careful. Also, I can't guarantee what condition the shaft's in. If anyone can scale it, it's you, Ames."

Colin ran a hand down his face. "Of course. Stuff her in a dusty, vertical coffin and hope the exit is not boarded up on the other side."

Claire was already on her feet, "Sounds like a plan to me."

Their bags were delivered to the room a few minutes later and without wasting any time Claire changed into a black workout set. If anyone saw her in the hallway it would just look like she was headed to the gym for a quick session.

Kane tapped into the hotel's feed and confirmed the only guest to enter the suite today had left thirty minutes ago. It was now or never.

Wrapping her hair up into a messy bun, Claire and Colin exited their room and walked down the twenty yards to the closet. It required a keycard. Kane hacked the door lock and opened it remotely.

Inside, the opening Kane described was disguised as wood paneling behind stacked linens. Colin pushed the linens aside and wedged it open with his knife, revealing a narrow black shaft that released decades of stale dust. Metal rails lined the walls where the dumbwaiter once slid.

Claire slipped on a pair of gloves and tucked a little black pouch, the bugs, into a side pocket in her leggings. She held her hands out for Colin, he velcroed the gloves closed and strapped a headlight to her head. He turned the headlight on and with a gymnast's elegance she slipped through the shelving unit the linens had been on, and into the dark void of the metal shaft.

Before she disappeared from sight, Colin caught her wrist. "If anything goes wrong—"

"Then get out." She smirked, though her eyes betrayed a flicker of nerves. "Keep the comms clear."

She braced herself against the opposite walls of the shaft and wedged her feet between the guide rails and metal walls. They would have been used to keep the box from twisting or tilting, but for now they worked as holds for her feet. Straightening her legs she stood and then pressed her arms into the walls. The metal walls were slightly cold even through the gloves and she could hear her heart thundering in her ears. She didn't dare look down, knowing the shaft would go three more floors down to the kitchen. A fall from this height could be fatal. And no matter what, her mission would be over.

Pressing her hands and forearms into the walls as hard as she could, she removed her feet and brought them as high as she could before rewedging them. Repeating this again and again, she began to climb. Her movements were fluid, almost like she was performing a routine that she had practiced for months.

The air grew thicker as she rose, dust swirling in the light of her headlamp every time she exhaled. Claire had the top of the shaft in sight, she could even still see the pulley system that would have controlled the vintage dumbwaiter, it was very old and she wouldn't have trusted it to raise a plate of food let alone anything else.

Searching the area for the last opening, she found it on the wall to her back. She would need to turn around in order to open the panel and get out. Repeating her climbing pattern twice more she was now level with the panel. All she had to do was turn.

Claire wedged her right foot in between the rail and wall as tight as she could, then with both arms braced against the walls, she removed her left foot and placed it on top of her right. The rail was now between her legs just like a rope would have been if she were doing a rope climb at her former gym. She gripped it with her knees and prayed the rail was secure enough to take all of her weight as she removed her left hand from the wall.

She had never felt her heart beat so hard as all of her weight was now entirely supported by this one... vintage... guide... rail. All she needed to do was...

The metal groaned as bolts loosened and the rail jolted back a few inches.

The groan echoed through the shaft as she gasped in surprise.

"Claire?!" Both voices echoed in her earpiece, panic ringing out loud and clear.

She swiftly let go with her right hand and braced herself against the opposite wall, twisting her torso as she did so. Pushing as hard as she could with both hands Claire squeezed her ab muscles as she unwrapped her legs from around the tilted rail. Wedging her feet against the broken rail wasn't an option anymore as it tilted too far away from the wall. She pressed her feet out one in front and one behind her, almost like she was taking a knee.

"I'm okay." She took a deep breath calming her heart rate.

Finally, she had reached the sealed upper access, instead of a panel it looked like the original door. A thin line of light traced the door's edges—the early evening light from inside the suite. Claire tried pushing on the door to see if it would just give way. It didn't budge, so she removed her own knife from her waistband. The door would have opened into the suite so she traced around the edges of the door and then pushed as hard as she could with both hands. A soft pop sounded as the door gave way.

Claire used her back leg to push herself into a controlled forward roll, slipping inside noiselessly. She had landed in what must be a butler's pantry. The room was attached to a large dining space and sitting room.

She crouched. Listening. The suite beyond was silent, Kane was right there was no one inside.

"I'm in," she whispered into her mic.

Colin exhaled. Kane muttered, "Told you the coffin would work."

Claire turned her head lamp off and peeked around the corner double-checking for any security cameras. She didn't see any and began pulling the pouch from her pocket.

The suite was hushed, every surface immaculate in its wealth. Claire crept along the shadowed living room, the evening sky was a mix of pinks and oranges as the day was coming to an end. She focused on the job at hand and looked for three places to hide the bugs Kane had sourced.

Meetings would most likely take place in the dining room or

living room. So she quickly placed a listening device in one of the grooves of the dining table's carved wooden leg. Moving into the living room she thought how easy it would have been to hide and wait until Antonio entered the suite tomorrow.

She was so close to one of the men responsible for her parents' deaths. She could just use her knife and end it as soon as he walked in. But he would have guards with him, it would be a suicide mission and then they wouldn't have the evidence to take down Hale, and he had to be held accountable. He knew her father and *still* ordered the hit on her family.

Kneeling, she fitted the second listening device against the back of a claw foot on one of the tufted sofas. Finally she needed a third place, somewhere someone might take a private phone call. The bedroom.

She walked toward the bedroom, just two steps away when—the sharp click of a door handle turning echoed through the suite.

Her heart stopped. Kane hadn't warned her, he was supposed to be watching.

She scrambled into the bedroom, pressing herself flat against the wall just as the suite door swung open. A man's heavy footsteps crossed the decorative wood floor. The familiar mix of Cedarwood and leather wafted into the suite, growing stronger the louder the footsteps got.

Claire hadn't smelled that particular scent in ages, it was a smell she had always associated with Trevor. Her heart beat rapidly as it always had when he approached.

Steadying her breathing, she prepared for a fight. Whoever had entered the suite was coming right for the bedroom. She had the advantage, he didn't seem to know she was there. She had to get out of here as quickly as possible, without them seeing too much of her face.

He was so close now she could hear his steady breathing.

Timing was everything, she backed up running as fast as she would when he rounded the corner. She ran, pushing him into the wall, sending him to the floor. She ducked through the door back into the living room.

But he reached out and caught her ankle. His fingers clamping down like an iron shackle, he pulled her to the floor with him. Lunging on top of her as she scrambled to get up. Their bodies twisting in a heap on the floor.

With her stomach against the parquet they had yet to see one another's faces. The man reached for her arm and flipped her onto her back beneath him.

Trevor.

It was him, the scent didn't just smell like him, it was him. His shoulders were broader than she remembered. A rigidness was built into every line of him, one that hadn't been there before. His dogtags hung from his neck, catching the light as they swung.

But what was he doing here?! He was at home with his family. He was going off to medical school.

Her mind raced with questions, so much she almost forgot that he can't see her face. Thankfully she had landed with her face hidden in shadows. The light in the room was fading fast, the sun was setting.

Her focus was split—half officer, calculating strikes and leverage, half the girl who used to dream of a future with him. She could smell the bakery, hear him cheering her on from the stands, and feel the butterflies she had the first time he'd kissed her.

She couldn't let herself think about that. She twisted free of his grip, driving her elbow into his shoulder. The blow lacked her full force, not wanting to hurt him. He countered, faster than she expected, pinning her wrist again.

For a moment, they struggled in silence—his strength against her agility, neither gaining ground. Then, with a gymnast's burst of motion, she hooked her leg, shifted her weight, and flipped him onto his back.

Her knee pressed into his chest, hand at his throat. His eyes went wide as the remaining light lit up her face. He knew those eyes, the furrow of her brow, the sweeping soft jawline; he dreamed of the curve of the lips before him. But it couldn't be her. He had buried her years ago. He'd mourned her, cursed God for taking her away. And yet he was staring into her eyes.

"Claire?" He stopped fighting, his voice cracking on her name.

Her breath caught and her eyes widened. No one had said her name like that in years.

For the briefest moment, she froze taking him in. His face was older, sharper, but undeniably him. The boy she thought she'd lost.

Trevor's gaze searched hers like he was staring at a ghost. "But. You're. Dead."

She could see the pain in his eyes so clearly in that moment. The pain her absence had caused, her decision to stay away. All she wanted to do was let go, plant her lips on his and then explain everything.

Static and then Kane's voice sharp in her earpiece: "Claire, did you hear me? Get out now!"

"Claire?" Kane's voice rang out again, it dripped with urgency and fear.

She forced herself to think straight, not to get lost in Trevor. This couldn't happen. Not here. Not now.

She forced herself to spring up, even as every part of her rebelled, begging to stay with him. Bolting across the suite, her lungs burned as she darted into the butler's pantry, diving for the shadowed gap of the old dumbwaiter shaft. Metal moaned as she went headfirst into the dark hole. No time to think or turn on her light, she just had to move.

Trevor's voice rang behind her. "Claire?"

Her hands found the guide rail that was still upright, using it like a fire pole she slid into the dark void. The narrow walls scraped her shoulders as she slid down too fast. She couldn't see anything but the light up above. Feeling like she was far enough away she used her feet to slow herself down, for a more controlled descent. The old, rough guide rail had ripped holes in her gloves but had yet to cut her hands. Her shoulder however was burning, she could feel blood dripping down her back.

Above, Trevor found the open shaft door just as the pitch

black tunnel had swallowed her.

For a frozen beat he stared into the darkness, his heart drilling a hole in his chest. Listening for anything, but only the faint creak of an old metal shaft in an even older building could be heard.

Trevor pressed his palm flat against the cold antique door, his mind racing, replaying every second starting from when he had entered his suite. His rational mind screamed it wasn't possible, Claire was dead. But his heart, the endless optimist, whispered the opposite.

Maybe he'd finally lost it, or it was jet lag. Maybe he wanted her here so much his mind saw her face on someone else. Or maybe he'd just seen a ghost. But he would swear on his medical career that it was her.

15
The Alley of Answers

Claire sat at the kitchen table in the Rome safe house, fiddling with her worn bracelet while Colin pressed gauze against her right shoulder. A jagged three-inch gash from the dumbwaiter shaft still hadn't stopped bleeding. She needed stitches. Luckily, both she and Colin had completed the *Casualty Care* program and were certified to suture wounds.

Kane was connected via video chat as Colin came back to the table with a red medical bag. He pulled out everything he would need and opened a sterile cloth to lay everything on. A surgical needle, dissolvable sutures, and a syringe of lidocaine followed.

Claire couldn't wait any longer; she needed answers. Why hadn't Kane seen Trevor coming back in the building let alone the suite. "Kane, what happened back there?"

"Yeah," he paused, clearly embarrassed to have screwed up. Kane Bhatt didn't screw up... usually. "I was a little distracted, then the comms went out and I was trying to get them back when I saw him at the door."

Colin let out a low chuckle, "Bet he was ordering a pizza." He had put gloves on and was cleaning Claire's skin before injecting the local anesthetic.

"Actually, I was cracking encrypted mob files. But sure, let's go with a pizza delivery to an abandoned house that no one can know we are staying at." Kane's tone was dry and made it clear he was too stressed for bantering. "I got into Antonio's personal files, it was interesting."

"What do you mean?" Claire didn't even flinch when Colin began suturing her wound closed.

"The first folder I opened had some unexpected things: an american birth certificate and a bunch of photos. Ones of a little boy. At first I thought it was something worse — child trafficking— but the photos were only of one kid. Who got older in each set of photos. The last ones were of this guy in an Army uniform. It's the same guy who entered the suite tonight. His name is..."

"Trevor Bennett." Claire cut him off. Her mind threatened to short-circuit from all the questions she had.

"How do you know his name?" Colin was finishing her stitches and then covered them with a piece of clean gauze. Removing his gloves he sat down next to her.

Both of them were staring at her expectantly now, "He was my best friend and boyfriend from before. I've known him since I was a kid. But I don't know why Antonio would have photos of him or why he's here."

"I believe Antonio is his father." Kane said slowly. "I found these," he pulled up old photos, they featured a young pretty blonde and a handsome Italian man sitting on the Spanish Steps. They were clearly a couple with his arm around her waist while she laughed at something he said.

"Alexis," Claire breathed, the pieces clicking together, "That's Trevor's mom. She must have met Antonio during her back packing trip. Our moms were best friends and Alexis got pregnant young. She never told us who the father was. She married Trevor's step dad, Grant, when Trevor was four. He always thought of Grant as his real dad."

"There are a few more photos of them together, Antonio and Alexis. It looks like it was a short romance. She might not have known what he does—"

"Known?" Claire snapped. "No. There's no way that she

would have known or been okay with it. Alexis is the kindest person there is. She won't even kill a spider, she catches them and sets them free outside."

Colin could feel Claire's distress and put his hand on her arm, reassuring her. "We believe you."

"There is no evidence that Trevor knows anything, either. I've done a little digging on him and he's clean, like squeaky clean. From what I can find this is his first time even in Italy and he didn't speak to his father until last week." Kane said, not wanting to antagonize her again. He'd do more searching just to make sure but he wouldn't mention it unless he found something.

The team continued to discuss Antonio's personal archives. It was clear he had followed his son's life from afar and was only now reaching out. Why now, they weren't sure. When the question of whether or not Trevor could help get intel on his father came up, Claire was adamant that he was not to be involved. It was too dangerous and she hadn't disappeared from his life for seven years to put him in danger now. But now that she had seen him— touched him—every part of her ached to do it again. She wanted to tell him everything, just let him hold her, as if that could make it all go away.

But it wouldn't. Her parents would still be dead and Hale would still have framed them. Colin and Kane's lives had been turned upside down and she felt responsible.

They spoke well into the early hours of the morning, planning and scheming. Now that Trevor had caught them, would he go looking for bugs, or would he just think it was a break in. If he told Antonio about the break in, the chance of getting anything usable would be gone. He'd never show up then. But would they even get anything or would this just be an uncomfortable father son first meeting? They decided it was best to let it play out and see how it goes and for Colin to monitor and tail Trevor until he left the country, or at least until they got what they needed. A flight reservation showed he was leaving in four days.

Calling it a night at 2 am, they hadn't picked up anything on the two bugs she had placed. But Kane would continue to monitor them for anything. He'd set an alert so that his computer would wake him if there were any voices detected.

Claire awoke at 6am, still tired but the numbing shots in her shoulder had worn off and she needed pain meds. She was just taking some when she glanced at the laptop, Kane's screen was still mirrored and on it Trevor was walking down the hallway of the hotel toward the elevator.

She should wake Colin, that was the plan. In a split second, reckless decision, she slipped her shoes on and left, easing the door closed behind her so as not to make a sound.

Trevor hadn't gotten much rest. He had closed his eyes a dozen times but each time brown eyes stared back at him. Her eyes. His dreams were taunting him with half-formed memories of her that bled into reality until he jolted awake, his heart racing and his body drenched in sweat. He was still unsure if she had ever really been there. By three in the morning he had given up on sleep completely. Instead, pacing the length of the suite or staring down the empty shaft until he couldn't stand to be there anymore.

At dawn he threw on his leather jacket and slipped out. Hoping a walk through the quiet Roman streets might settle his mind.

Claire caught sight of him when she reached the hotel, he was a block away about to turn a corner. She kept a careful distance but jogged to make sure she had him insight. The lack of people at this time in the morning made it difficult to stay hidden but her quick reaction times allowed her to adjust if he moved unexpectedly.

Her shoulder was burning beneath the bandage, but the need to see him again burned hotter than the pain. Where was he going? Was he suspicious or simply restless? Either way, she told herself this was just surveillance. It was the excuse, at least.

Trevor's pace was steady. He didn't look over his shoulder or fumble with his phone. None of the nervous tells of someone who felt watched. But Claire had tailed enough people to know the difference between aimless wandering and being led. He was taking turns that didn't make sense, weaving into narrower streets, slipping into the quiet veins of Rome where tourists hadn't yet stirred.

Her gut told her he knew.

She still followed. Telling herself it was because she had to. They needed to know if he met up with Antonio and further yet, his safety could be compromised. She had to keep track of him. But her feet began moving faster than her brain could argue. She wanted—needed—to see him, like iron drawn to a magnet.

He turned down a narrow alleyway lined with doorways, any and all people were behind him now. The stone walls high and close, it was a bad idea to follow, he'd see her for sure. She hesitated only a second before desire shoved her forward after him. Every lesson screamed at her to turn back. But every piece of her said "follow." Her heart beating faster as she rounded the corner—

—strong hands closed around her arms.

Her breath caught as someone yanked her into a recessed doorway. Was it one of Antonio's men? Is this it? The man pinned her against the cool stone before she looked up into his face.

Trevor.

Her breath caught, her instincts tensed her muscles and prepared her to fight, but then he was looking her directly in the eyes. She could see the storm that waged. Confusion, exhaustion and... relief all swirling.

"I thought I was losing my mind," He said, breathless. He touched her check gently with the tips of his fingers before flattening his hand and caressing her face.

Her body betrayed her training, relaxing into his touch. She knew she should break free, disappear into the shadows again. But she stayed still, her pulse and desire growing louder than reason. As if subconsciously she had let him catch her.

Claire knew she should say something but she couldn't get her voice to work, so she just nodded. One of his hands slid down, from her upper arm where he had grabbed her, to her wrist where she had re-tied the leather bracelet. Touching it he looked down and rubbed it between his fingers.

"You still wear it." A statement not a question. His soul leaped, she still cared.

In response she reached up and touched his jacket, the one her bracelet had come from, as if to say, "you too."

For a moment they just existed together like they used to. But then his hands moved to her waist, hers to his neck and then into his hair. The need between them snapped like a live wire, and they pulled each other into a long-overdue kiss.

It may have only lasted seconds in reality but it felt like all the years they had been separated were melting away with each movement.

Claire had imagined their first kiss after being reunited so many times and it wasn't disappointing. She had craved him, not just physically, but in the way he looked at her or the way he used to tell her everything on his mind.

His hands fit perfectly on her lower back. A teenage Trevor would have been a bit more timid but this Trevor was bold moving his hands lower. His body was harder now. Toned and muscular from years of training. While keeping a hand in his hair she let the other one roam down feeling his chest and abs through his shirt. He used his body to press her back into the arched doorway, leaning flush against her. The heat radiating from his body compared to the chill of the brick wall was a good reminder that they were in public and she wasn't able to start running her hands under his shirt.

She hated his father and Hale for taking not only her parents but this. She wanted so badly to just bring him back to her safe house and tell him everything, but she couldn't. What if someone had been tailing them, someone she hadn't seen. She hadn't been on her game, what if she had just handed them over to Antonio on a silver platter? The thought festered, sobering her faster than the pain in her shoulder. She melted into one last kiss, absorbing as much of him as she could, and without giving him an option, she disappeared before his eyes were even open.

The rush of cold air where her body had been only seconds ago felt like daggers to Trevor's heart. He needed more, was desperate to never let her out of his sight again, but she had left him for a third time. Seven years he'd spent mourning a ghost, only to find she was alive—and running from him.

16
The Truth

Trevor returned to his hotel exhausted. He was still trying to wrap his head around the fact that he *wasn't* crazy—Claire was alive. Part of him longed to curl up beside her, to wrap his arms around her and never let go. The other half felt cold, confused, and betrayed. She could have spared him years of pain, but instead she'd let him believe she was dead. Why?

The lack of sleep the night before, plus the travel, was all catching up to him. When he returned to his room, he stripped down to the essentials and climbed between the silk sheets. This time it wasn't restless tossing that carried him off, but dreams of her—dreams of the life they could have now that he knew she was alive. In them, she was beside him, her laughter filling their home. Their hands were intertwined as they walked their rescue dog. All of it was a life that could be, until she disappeared into the shadows. She left him alone with the life they'd imagined in shambles.

He woke to mid-morning sunlight streaming through the curtains and an ache in his chest, the kind that came from waking up alone.

After showering and shaving, he pulled on the nicest clothes he'd packed, though nothing seemed formal enough for what was ahead. He rolled his Swiss Army knife back and forth in his palm. He'd carried it every day since Grant had given it to him but it felt almost wrong to bring with him to lunch now. Not formal enough, maybe... ignoring the odd feeling he slid the knife into its usual place in his right pocket.

His stomach was tight with nerves, but he didn't let it show, instead relying on his soldier's steadying and calm demeanor. Antonio Giordano might be his father, but none of this felt like the bond he had with Grant, the man who had raised him. It felt more like walking into a mission briefing or a business meeting rather than meeting the man who'd helped give him life.

By noon, the suite was bustling. Two men swept through first, looking like polished thugs. Their size made Trevor, who had only just left the army after seven years, feel almost scrawny. They entered without knocking, spoke in clipped tones, and visually scanned the room like they owned it. Trevor was grateful he'd closed the dumbwaiter door when they checked the butler's pantry. If they had found it open, they would've had questions he couldn't answer.

Next, a woman entered barking orders at a bewildered hotel employee pushing a cart full of covered dishes and a bottle of wine that probably cost more than Trevor made in a month. The two disappeared into the dining room, only for the waiter to reappear alone a few minutes later, exiting quickly. It all left Trevor with the uneasy feeling that this was all too much pomp for a simple lunch. He wished he could follow the waiter out.

The thugs straightened when the doors opened again. Trevor instinctively did the same, having to stop himself from saluting out of habit. The man who entered the room seemed to fill the space and demand attention. Antonio Giordano was about fifty. His thick black hair was just starting to go silver at the temples. He wore a dark suit that was perfectly tailored and his presence was magnetic. When his eyes landed on Trevor, they lit with something that might've been pride... or ownership.

"My son," Antonio said warmly, sweeping an arm out as if presenting Trevor to an audience. His voice carried the weight of command, the kind that made rooms fall silent. Clasping Trevor's shoulder in a grip that was both affectionate and unyielding, he steered him toward the dining room. "Come. Sit. We have so much to talk about."

Trevor obeyed, his heart thudding as they entered the dining room, already set with linens, crystal and polished silver. The woman from before stepped forward and pulled out the chair at the head of the table for Antonio. Trevor sat to his left where a place had been set for him.

Two plates of perfectly rare steaks were uncovered before them. A vintage red Cabernet sat in a decanter, breathing. Their glasses were expertly filled before the woman returned to the corner she had been in before, practically hiding. Trevor couldn't help but notice how anxious she was.

"To blood," Antonio declared, raising his glass, "the truest bond of all."

Raising his glass, Trevor smiled and sipped just enough to be polite, the tannins were sharp against his tongue, a taste he wasn't fond of. Antonio's toast had rubbed him the wrong way. Whether or not he meant it as a dig at Grant or not, his *blood* hadn't raised him, Grant had.

While they ate, Antonio carried the conversation, his voice warm, almost paternal. He asked about Trevor's childhood, about his time in Tennessee, and about Alexis. Trevor answered carefully, not fully comfortable, he chose not to let Antonio in on all the details.

"I want you to know something," Antonio said at last, cutting his steak with surgical precision. "You are my only child. My legacy. The business I've built, one day, it could be yours."

Trevor went still. "Your business?"

"Yes," Antonio said smoothly, nodding. "It deals with manufacturing and distribution of goods. It's not glamorous, but it is steady. Reliable. The kind of empire a man can be proud of." His smile was charming and his tone light, but his eyes flickered dark when he added, "Though it demands loyalty, and strength."

Trevor nodded slowly. Though Antonio's words were

innocent enough, something about the body guards, the lack of details, and his demeanor caused Trevor to feel uneasy, his gut twisting. "I've always wanted to be a doctor. I start med school in a few months."

"Medicine," Antonio mused, as though sampling the word, finding it distasteful. "A noble and difficult profession. I'm afraid you would be too busy. My world is… all consuming. Demanding. You would be needed here, in Italy. Full time."

The knife in Antonio's hand glinted as he gestured. Trevor couldn't shake the sense that there was a lot more to his "distribution of goods" and it was far from innocent.

The questions shifted seamlessly, as if deliberately not allowing Trevor time to think. He asked about his time in the Army—what he'd learned and seen. But some of the phrasing was too pointed. Did the military ever investigate certain shipping routes? Had Trevor heard of operations in southern Europe? Questions that could be harmless on the surface, but paired with everything else, it made him more suspicious. Trevor answered neutrally, recognizing the probing for what it was.

By the time the espresso was served, rich and bitter, Trevor's decision was clear. He not only wanted nothing to do with this man's empire but he didn't even really want him in his life. He felt the need to protect his world from Antonio. Struggling to see the man his mother had fallen for twenty six years ago.

Antonio rose from the table and placed a hand on Trevor's shoulder once more. The weight of it was heavy and the grip just a bit too tight. "You don't have to decide about taking over the company today. But I would like to see you again before you leave. Tomorrow, perhaps. A night at the opera, or something simpler, a vineyard dinner. Maybe pizza, the way it should be made. Just father and son."

Trevor managed a polite smile. "I'll think about it."

"Good." Antonio's eyes gleamed as though the plans were already finalized. He squeezed Trevor's shoulder once before striding from the suite, his guards falling in step behind.

When the door clicked shut, he was left alone in silence.

Trevor sank back into his chair, the pressure easing. His steak was half-eaten and his wine glass sat nearly full. While he still didn't know the specifics of what Antonio manufactured, he knew with bone-deep certainty it wasn't good. He'd never accept the future he had offered.

* * *

Claire

Claire returned to an interrogation of her own. The disappointed look she got from Colin rivaled the ones her dad used to give. She knew they were right, she had been reckless. She had risked the mission, her cover, and her safety. But even as they lectured her, she couldn't stop thinking about that kiss in the alley. His body pinning hers to the wall, his lips on top of hers. It rattled her in ways she hadn't expected.

She realized too late they had asked her a question.

"Sorry—what?" She asked, her cheeks warming a little.

Kane watched from a video chat on the laptop as Colin repeated himself, "We saw most of it, but what happened in the alley? Did you talk to him?"

A few minutes after she had slipped out, Kane had awoken and seen Trevor on the cameras. He called Colin and together they tracked him on CCTV, only to see Claire appear seconds later. Colin wanted to rush out after her but Kane had convinced him otherwise. They needed to be sure she wasn't followed before they blew both their covers. Colin wanted to protest, instinctively trying to protect Claire. However, he reluctantly agreed, pacing the small room until she had returned.

The cameras had shown her disappear into the alley and return a few minutes later. Even with the feed in black and white they could tell she was shaken. Thirty seconds after she reappeared, Trevor had come running out too, searching.

"No, there was no talking." Claire said timidly.

Kane's brows lifted in understanding. Colin needed a second before he muttered, "Ohh... yeah. I guess that was... inevitable."

The silence stretched before Kane broke it, "We should read him in. Find out what he knows. If he doesn't know anything, well then he deserves to know that his bio dad is kind of a dick and if he does know something it could help us. We know he's still got feelings for Claire, so it's not like he's going to turn on her."

"Even if he tried, what would he say? That she's Claire Huntington? Hale isn't stupid, he's probably going to figure it out soon if he hasn't already." Colin looked down at her, "Claire?"

Looking between both men, she fiddled with her bracelet absently and then wordlessly nodded. This is what she had wanted, to tell him everything, but now that it was happening she worried how Trevor would react. Would he hate her for letting him think she had died?

A few hours later Claire and Colin sat at a nearby café outside the Palazzo d'Oro. Claire was sipping on a caffè americano with a book propped in her hand. Colin pretended to be busy on a business call, an empty espresso cup before him. To passersby, they looked like a young couple. His arm draped casually over her shoulders, his hand resting on her arm.

They watched as Antonio was escorted out of the hotel by his bodyguards and into a waiting black SUV. Kane was glued to the CCTV feeds, taking screenshots of plates and faces, while logging every detail. He had patched the bug feed into their comms so they had heard the entire lunch.

The plan was simple, now all they had to do was wait to make sure all of Antonio's men had left. When Kane was satisfied that Trevor was indeed alone, he spoofed the hotel's front desk phone number and rang up to Trevor's suite.

"Good afternoon, Signore Bennett," Kane said, his Italian accent was decent enough though his pronunciation of "Bennett" betrayed his American roots. "This is the front desk following up on your stay. If you'd like to experience more of the neighborhood, I'd recommend the café just across the street. It has excellent coffee and a very fine view if you look out your window now."

Trevor appeared moments later at the window of his suite. His brow furrowed until he spotted Claire. She knew he would have seen Colin's arm around her, and jealousy would've stabbed him through. So she tilted her head back just slightly, a subtle *come-*

here gesture— casual to anyone else but unmistakable to him.

The call ended and Trevor vanished from the window. Claire rose, murmuring to Colin. "Meet you back at the apartment?" He nodded, still talking into his phone. She leaned down, kissed his cheek quickly for show, then walked away.

She moved slowly to the corner of the street, despite the anticipation of being close to Trevor again making her want to run. When he emerged from the hotel doors she made sure to catch his eye and then crossed to the far sidewalk, knowing he'd follow. Colin waited, watched, and walked behind Trevor making sure no one else had tailed them.

When Colin gave the all clear, she slowed near a corner, pretending to check her phone until Trevor caught up. She didn't look at him or hold his hand, wanting to appear as strangers just in case.

But after crossing, she whispered, "There's nothing going on between Colin and me. Our aliases are married. He's like a brother." She watched his body for a reaction but only saw a soldier's posture—his guard was up. "I'll explain everything. Just... not here."

He was mad—she'd expected him to be—but going from feeling his kiss hours ago to the distance she felt now made her chest ache in a way it hadn't since the day her parents died. When she stumbled on a loose stone, Colin's hand twitched toward her before he caught himself. Old instincts were hard to break, even now.

They reached the safe house a few blocks later. "Here," Claire subtly held out a key for him. "Third floor, apartment A. Go ahead, I'll be up in a minute."

Claire pulled out her phone once more, pretending to text. While she looked at her phone, Trevor went inside. She waited a minute before she heard Kane speak through the earpiece, "He's in."

Colin had caught up with her, and together they walked around to a back entrance.

Inside, Trevor waited in the middle of the room, awkward

with the key still in his hand. Taking the key Colin muttered that he'd give them some privacy, disappearing into a bedroom.

The tiny safe house apartment felt even smaller as the conversation loomed, Claire couldn't avoid it any longer. Adjoined to the kitchenette was a small tv area that included a loveseat just big enough for two. She sat down and patted the seat next to her for Trevor to join. He sat, looking uncomfortable and stiff. Tucking her feet under her, she reached out, wanting to take his hand she stopped just shy. Instead, she took a steadying breath...

"Wait," Trevor twisted so he faced her, his jaw tight as he searched her face. He swallowed hard, trying to keep his composure. "Before you say anything, I need you to know—I'm hurt, and confused, and honestly, I feel betrayed. You let me think you were dead for *seven years*. But none of that changes the fact that I've loved you every second you were gone. I just need to understand why you did it."

A wave of relief flooded her—he still loved her. Despite his anger and her betrayal, he wanted to understand.
"I'm so sorry that I hurt you, and your family," she said softly. "I want you to know that I didn't feel like I had a choice. I had to keep you safe."

His brows furrowed as he tried to take in her words.
"Safe from what?"
Piece by piece, Claire told him the truth—what really happened with the car wreck, finding Hugh, and the choice she'd made. She told him that if he'd known, he would have been in danger. She spoke slowly and clearly, even though every instinct pushed her to rush through it. When she told him about her time at the CIA and what they had found in the recent weeks, she searched his face. Unsure of how he felt she just needed a clue. The bombing, her aliases and the information on the Italian mob came next.

When she finished, it felt like a stone had been lifted from her chest. The only thing she kept from him was Antonio's true occupation.

She waited for Trevor to react—yell, argue, ask questions—

but he just sat there, processing.

After a long minute, Trevor finally spoke. "I'm really sorry for the way your parents died, and for everything you've seen and been through, but..." He took a slow breath, choosing his words carefully. "I still don't understand why you couldn't tell me you were alive. I would have kept your secret."

"Oh, I know you would've." She reached out and placed her hand over his. "But I also know you well enough to know you wouldn't have just let me go. You would've found a way to me—putting yourself in danger and throwing away your plans."

"You're right. I would've found you, no matter what." He rubbed the back of his neck, his voice quieter now, as if he was thinking out loud. "And if I had to make that choice... I probably would've done the same."

Claire felt a sting behind her eyes. He understood. "There's one more thing."

He threaded his fingers through hers. "Okay."

She couldn't look at him yet, unsure how he'd react when he heard about Antonio. Instead, she closed her eyes and focused on the warmth of his skin against hers while she spoke.

"The Italian mob—the one behind my parents' deaths..." Her throat tightened. "Antonio is the head of it."

She braced herself for him to pull away, to recoil, to deny it. But he didn't.

"I know," he said quietly. "Not all of it, but enough. The way he talks, the way people behave around him—no one good has that kind of power." His hand tightened slightly around hers. "That means my biological father killed your parents..."

"Yeah. We think my dad was onto Director Hale, and my mom and I... it was cleaner to take us all out." She chewed her lip. "So you can't stay. You have to go back to Tennessee and forget about me—and his offer."

Trevor blinked. "How do you know about his offer?"

Looking down at her wrist, she fiddled with her bracelet and answered quietly."Last night, when we ran into one another, I had just planted bugs in your suite. We heard your entire lunch."

"You bugged my suite?" His voice wasn't angry—just tired, laced with disbelief.

Claire nodded. "We didn't know it was yours at the time. Antonio had it booked under his alias, so we just knew it was going to be someone important."

He stared at her for a long beat, then exhaled through his nose. "Makes sense."

"You're not mad?" she asked carefully.

"No," he said quietly. "Just trying to figure out where the lines are between who you were... and who you had to become."

"I promise, I'm still me." She reached up to touch his cheek, but the stretch pulled at the wound on her shoulder. She hissed involuntarily and touched the spot.

"Are you alright?" The confusion and hurt vanished, replaced by worry. He went into medic mode, reaching for her shoulder, then paused. "Can I look?"

Claire nodded, turning her back to him. Easing her jacket off her shoulders and down her arms, he tossed it aside. Visible beyond her tank top strap was the taped gauze.

"I'm fine," she said as he pulled back the gauze, his army medic training taking over. She hadn't changed the dressing in hours; the wound looked worse off.

"Fine, huh?" he muttered under his breath, inspecting the stitches.

"I was a little reckless in my haste to get down the dumbwaiter shaft last night."

"You got this trying to get away from me?" He spoke slowly, the hurt in his voice was unmistakable.

She turned to face him, her tone firm. "It was my fault. I should have used the door, not the dumbwaiter."

He sat in silence for a beat, then rose and crossed to the first-aid kit on the table. Without a word, he grabbed new gauze and ointment, then came back to redress her wound.

Despite his silence, she knew him and knew he was still worried. "Trev, I'm okay. I've sustained a lot worse falling from the uneven bars."

Hearing her use his old nickname made him smile "So where do we go from here?"

"You go home. Tell Antonio that while you enjoyed meeting him, you're focused on med school. You keep your distance from him… and from me. When it's over, if you still want me to—I'll come find you."

She still wanted a life with him, in any way he'd let her—but part of her feared that, given time, his understanding might turn into resentment.

"I know I'm still processing everything, but I just got you back. I'm not going months without talking to you again."

Claire smiled softly. "We can't risk talking—especially not now that we know you're biologically related to him. You're already too close."

"Claire, I'm not an eighteen-year-old boy anymore. I'm a trained soldier. You're my family—let me help you."

"She's got all the help she needs." Colin stepped out of the bedroom, his gaze locked on Trevor. "I get it—you want to protect her. But the truth is, you'd only distract her, make her more vulnerable. If Antonio found out about the two of you, he'd use it. You'd be leveraged against each other. I've got her back. This is what she and I were trained for."

Claire watched Trevor's shoulders sag, the fight leaving him. He knew Colin was right. For now, he'd have to trust that this man could protect the woman he loved.

Before anyone could speak, Colin's phone rang. He answered and immediately put Kane on speaker. "Uhh… we've got a problem."

Claire straightened. "What? Do they know—"

"No. It's not Antonio or his men." Kane's voice softened, uncharacteristically careful he went on, "Trevor… Addie's in the hospital, she collapsed."

Trevor's blood turned to ice.

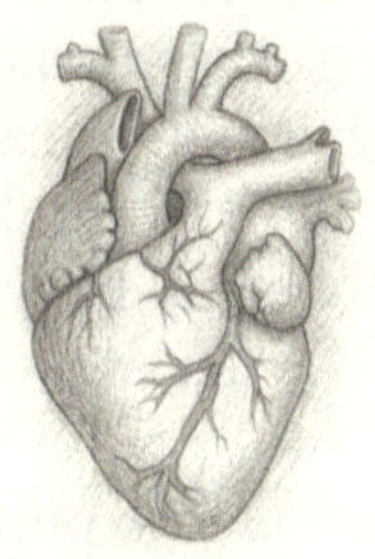

17
The Line I Swore I'd Never Cross

Trevor rushed back to the hotel to gather his belongings and was out the door hailing a taxi before 3:00 pm. Kane had booked him on the first available flight—one remaining seat, departing at 4:00 p.m.

In the cab, he distracted himself from the rapidly closing time window and called his mom. She was tearful and shaken, but Addie was stable and undergoing tests. As always, his sister was cheerful—maintaining her spirited attitude and cracking a few jokes. He let Alexis know he was on his way to the airport and he'd come to the hospital as soon as he landed.

It was close, but by some miracle Trevor reached his gate just before they closed the aircraft door. He'd never been more grateful for his habit of packing light—his duffel fit easily in the overhead, letting him skip bag check altogether. At security he was ushered through a fast-track line, which saved him precious minutes.

His adrenaline was still pumping even after the plane was in the air. He didn't feel himself calming down until he was able to get up from his middle seat and go to the bathroom to splash some cold water on his face. Taking deep breaths, he focused on lowering his heart rate—a technique he had learned in the Army.

When he returned to his seat, he turned on his phone's Wi-Fi and messaged Antonio, explaining there was an emergency and he was needed back in Tennessee. He added that, while he was grateful for the chance to meet and had enjoyed his time in Rome, his heart was set on becoming a doctor—and he wouldn't be taking over Antonio's business. He felt the darkness that had lingered since their lunch lift off him.

Sending one more text before putting his phone away, he let his parents know his ETA. Alexis had said she would text him if there were any changes or news so he didn't ask for an update.

Between the tense lunch, his tangled emotions over Claire, and now his sister's illness, he was beyond drained. All he wanted to do was turn off his mind and stare blankly at a movie for the duration of his flight. Unfortunately, the flight felt like it lasted twenty hours instead of seven. When he landed, Trevor drove straight to the hospital, not even stopping for gas, despite his car's low tank.

The sharp smell of antiseptic hit Trevor as soon as he pushed through the hospital's double doors. Fluorescent lights buzzed overhead, a constant hum that set his teeth on edge. His anxiety doubled the closer to his sister he got. He had arrived an hour before visitation would end and wouldn't have much time with his family.

He found his mother in the pediatric intensive care unit; she sat with Addie in a private room. Alexis's hair was pulled into her typical messy knot, one hand gripping a styrofoam cup of coffee that had long gone cold, while the other held Addie's hand. Alexis stared off into the distance, her eyes red and swollen from crying, while Addie lay in the bed sleeping, she looked impossibly small among all the wires and tubing. Her freckles stood out stark against pale skin and blonde hair.

Trevor quietly entered her room, careful not to wake his sister.

When Alexis heard him at the door she looked up, her face cracked with relief before her eyes brimmed over with tears. She stood and wrapped her first-born in her arms, holding him tight.

Alexis peeked down at Addie and then led him out into the hallway so they could speak normally.

"She collapsed in the backyard," she whispered, just as Trevor saw his dad, Grant, coming down the hall. "One second she was chasing the dog, the next she was just... down. Grant did CPR until the ambulance came."

Trevor's stomach flipped. "How is she? Have they diagnosed her?"

Grant reached them and immediately hugged his son, holding him a few seconds longer than usual. The contact with his real dad steadied him—reminding Trevor what a true father-son bond was supposed to feel like.

Grant nodded, answering his son's questions. "It's restrictive cardiomyopathy—RCM. Basically, her heart—"

"—is unable to relax, which means it's struggling to pump properly. How advanced is it?" He paused, struggling to ask the next part. "Will she need a transplant?" Trevor was already familiar with many conditions. He had started reading medical textbooks and journals when he was thirteen. He used to read while Claire practiced in the barn gym, always telling her about the most interesting facts. On days he wasn't with Claire, Trevor would help Grant at the veterinary office, often observing cases or assisting the vet techs.

Grant nodded and continued, "It's rare to find it at her age, usually kids are younger but her case is pretty advanced. They placed an intra-aortic balloon earlier today to give her more time but ultimately, she needs a transplant."

Trevor's own heart felt like it wasn't working. *She's so young, so active. How could this happen to her of all people?*

Alexis found her voice, "They've already started her on the right meds. Then in a few days, they want to place a mechanical pump to help her heart keep up. An LVAD." Tears balanced in her eyes, not quite falling yet, "Her cardiologist has already put her on the transplant list. But the chances..."

Alexis knew the LVAD surgery would give them valuable time they needed to find Addie a heart. But she also understood the reality of the situation—it wasn't a cure. Unable to speak anymore she broke into sobs and fell into her husband's embrace. Relying on him to help her find strength.

Grant stroked her hair as he finished Alexis's sentence. "The chances of finding a heart in time aren't good. Kids' hearts are rare."

Trevor's stomach dropped. His chest hollowed out. His sister was dying—unless she got a new heart. She's only ten.

"How long?"

"Once she gets the LVAD, they think she'll have a few months but they can't say for certain." Grant held back his own tears. He wanted to break down as he had earlier in the men's restroom, but in front of his family he was steady and strong.

Alexis's sobs were being muffled by Grant's clothing as they all just stood together in desperate, uncomfortable silence.

Trevor swallowed hard, staring at his little sister through the glass window in the door—ten years old, with scraped knees and a half-finished puzzle waiting at home. *She hasn't even started her life yet.* He'd spent years learning how to keep people alive in combat zones, and yet there was nothing he could do for his sister except stand there and beg fate to spare her.

He leaned into the doorframe, his voice low, speaking more to himself than to his parents. "She'll get one. She has to."

Begging wouldn't be enough, though. Not when time was already running out.

When visiting hours were over Trevor took his mom home while Grant stayed with Addie. Alexis insisted he stayed as he understood more medically than she did.

When they got home Alexis kissed her son and immediately excused herself to her room. Trevor knew she just needed space to process everything, she always did her thinking in the shower.

He heard the water turn on minutes later as he helped himself to a little bit of food before bed. As he ate he searched online medical journals for anything he could on RCM. It wasn't that he didn't trust Addie's doctors, it was more that research was the only thing he could think to do. It made him feel like he was helping instead of just waiting.

After eating Trevor got ready for bed. He didn't need to check on the animals as Grant had asked a tech to do so. With the house locked up, Trevor felt like he could go to bed, but he barely slept—again. Every time he closed his eyes, he saw Addie lying pale and small in that hospital bed, tubes webbing across her body like she was a fragile machine instead of a child. Sometimes Claire would appear in the hospital hallway, but before she could say or do anything, she'd vanish into the dark. By morning, his chest ached with the helplessness of it all.

Then, after filling up his tank with gas, he drove Alexis back to the hospital. The silence between them was heavy, but companionable. She clutched a box of freshly made cookies like it was a lifeline. Chocolate chips and heath bar chunks, Addie's favorite. Alexis had insisted on making a box for the nurses, setting a few aside for Addie—but only after getting the all-clear that she could eat and didn't have to fast.

Grant had texted updates through the night: Addie had woken briefly, confused and tired, but still cracking jokes and asking about the animals.

When Trevor pulled into the hospital parking lot, his phone buzzed from the cup holder. The number was unfamiliar.

I hear Addie is sick. Call me. I can help.

Trevor's stomach dropped. He didn't need to guess who it was—there was only one person who'd send a text from an anonymous number.

He shoved the phone into his pocket. He wouldn't give Antonio any attention, not yet.

Later that morning, Alexis sat at Addie's bedside. Her daughter was awake, with a little more color in her cheeks than the night before. Along with the cookies, Alexis had brought a backpack full of board games, coloring books, and chapter books to keep Addie entertained. Alexis was currently losing at a round of *Candy Land*. She was stuck in the Peppermint Forest while Addie bounced her pink character toward the Candy Castle.

Trevor had played a few rounds but needed to stretch his legs. Wandering into the hallway, he lingered by the vending machines—pretending to study the options—while his ears caught every word from two residents at the nurses' station.

"...low probability of a match anytime soon. She's so sweet and bubbly. Her mom brought cookies."

"The LVAD will buy some time, but at this stage—her prognosis isn't good without a transplant."

Trevor's throat went dry. They weren't wrong, and he knew all of this already—but hearing even the residents talk about it only confirmed how low the chances really were.

He walked away before they noticed him listening, heading for a deserted stairwell. His phone was already in his hand before he realized it.

Pulling up the text from Antonio, he hit "call" before he knew fully what he was doing.

Placing the phone to his ear, he hoped he'd get enough reception in this stairwell.

The line connected after only a single ring.

"Mio figlio." Antonio's slithery smooth voice filled Trevor's ear. "I'm sorry such a terrible thing is happening to your sister. I am sad you missed pizza lessons and that you did not call me directly to let me know you couldn't make it. I suppose you had little time though."

Trevor's grip on the phone tightened, he wasn't in the mood for pleasantries. "You said you could help."

"Yes, I know many people from my line of work, people who could... move your sister to the top of the list. Get your sister what she needs. And when she is stable, you could come back to Rome."

Trevor's chest burned. He understood what Antonio wasn't saying. He'd not just have to *come back* to Rome but *stay there*. His manipulation wasn't subtle—but what if this is the only way she gets a heart?

"She's ten years old," he bit out. "Don't you dare use her like this!"

Antonio chuckled softly. "I don't need to use her. I'm offering you a solution. You're a smart boy, you've understood from little detail what it is my business does. You know how important family is in our... community. Come back to Italy. Learn from me. Your sister lives and I get my heir."

"I just retired from the Army a few weeks ago, and you think I'm going to join your illegal... community?" He spat the word like it tasted of bleach.

"Morals are for the innocent, *mio figlio*. You haven't been innocent since you joined the Army. Wouldn't it be worth it to save your sister's life?" When Trevor didn't answer, Antonio continued, "You know, you remind me of myself at your age. Strong. Determined. Don't waste that loyalty on a system that will let your sister die."

Trevor pressed a hand to his eyes, fury boiling over. "Go to hell."

He hung up.

But hours later, as he sat at Addie's bedside and listened to the machines track every fragile beat of her heart, Antonio's words gnawed at him.

A solution.

Maybe the only one.

Trevor sat with Addie through the afternoon, his hand curled around hers. She was so tiny, his fingers brushed the edge of the tape that held the IV in. She stirred once. Her lips dry, whispering his name before falling back into a restless sleep.

Around 7 the nurse came in to check her vitals. Trevor took the opportunity to step out, telling his parents he needed air, then wandering down to the hospital courtyard.

The summer evening was cooling off, the scent of impending rain sharp in the air. A few people passed by on their way out, some laughing, some crying. He leaned against a brick wall and stared at the glow of the pediatric wing above him, a lump tightening his throat.

He was very aware of his phone in his pocket. Heavy. Almost burning from the indecision.

Antonio's words replayed like poison in his head.

Come to Italy. Learn from me. And your sister lives.

Trevor swore under his breath, pressing both hands into his hair, his army cut officially grown out. He hated himself for even considering it—but how could he sit here, doing nothing, while Addie's time slipped away?

He stayed there until the stars came out, wrestling with himself. The stars reminded him of her freckles. He couldn't just wait while he watched her waste away.

By the time he went back inside, one truth had settled cold in his chest: if the only way to save his sister was to step into Antonio's world, he might not have a choice. He hated even considering it, but the truth was sharper than guilt: if Addie died while he clung to morals, he'd never forgive himself. Maybe innocence had left him long ago. Maybe Antonio was right.

18
Terms and Conditions

Claire sat in the back of a town car outside the Rome airport, waiting for their private plane.

Trevor had left the day before, and she couldn't focus on anything but Addie—her condition, and the way he'd gone. After Colin hung up with Kane, Trevor had turned to leave—he was short on time, with a flight to catch. But after two steps, he'd turned back and pressed a brief, breathless kiss to her lips.

Claire touched her bottom lip, thinking about it. It hadn't been passionate or planned—just a desperate press of lips that felt like both *goodbye* and *wait for me*. After that, he was gone before any words could be exchanged.

She didn't know where they stood, and that uncertainty was its own kind of agony. So was knowing that Addie was sick— and that she couldn't do anything to help. She remembered the day Addie was born and had loved her like a sister since. Kane had promised to update them when he had time, but he'd been slammed. She fiddled absently with her bracelet, her mind spinning through every possible scenario.

With Trevor gone, his hotel suite would be cleaned and given to the next guest. The bugs they had planted had yet to be found. Kane had a program monitoring them, ready to alert him if any of the keywords were said—Antonio, Trevor, delivery, weapons. So for now it was back to their hideaway in the States.

The town car was cool—and provided an easy getaway if need be. The windows were fogged from the difference in temperature outside, and Claire watched as Colin paced back and forth in the balmy heat. He had his burner phone pressed to his ear with his other hand rubbing at the back of his neck, tension written all over his face.

Her own burner phone rang. Answering, she put it on speaker—only two people had this number, and she was looking at one of them.

Kane spoke, voice low but heavy. "I've got an update on Addie."

Claire sat up straighter.

"It's not good," Kane said. He didn't sugarcoat it. "I pulled her hospital records. She's been diagnosed with restrictive cardiomyopathy. Her case is advanced and she'll need a transplant. They placed a balloon to buy some time."

The words were like a gut punch. Her eyes threatened to flood as images of Addie swarmed in her mind. The last time Claire had seen Addie she had only been three. Addie grinning with flour on her nose at the bakery and running around with the dogs in nothing but a pull up, played like a movie.

"If she gets a transplant, will she live?" she asked, her voice catching.

"Most likely, they've got her on the transplant list. But there's always a small chance her body rejects it." Kane continued carefully. "That being said, her odds of getting a heart aren't good. Pediatric hearts are rare. They plan to do surgery and give her an LVAD that might keep her stable for a few months."

Claire bit her lip so hard she tasted copper. Every instinct in her screamed to hang up and call Trevor. She wanted to tell him he wasn't alone in this, that she was here. She'd fly to Tennessee and be with them. But she couldn't. The risk was too high—not just for her, but for all of them. One slip, and they could end up being used as pawns or worse, collateral damage.

Colin ended his call and slid into the back seat, catching the tail end of Kane's words. He didn't speak, just rested his elbows on his knees, staring at the floor mats. The silence stretched, thick with grief and helplessness.

Claire finally broke it. "Addie's strong," she murmured, more to herself than anyone else. "If anyone is strong enough to hold on until a heart comes, it's her."

A few beeps sounded on Kane's end. "I've got to go, but she may be just fine, we just don't know yet."

The line went dead and Claire looked up at Colin. "What's up with you? You looked tense out there." She needed a distraction and Colin's issues would be a good one.

He exhaled and slumped over feeling defeated, "That was my divorce lawyer. My ex is filing to revoke my visitation. She already has full custody because of the distance."

"She knows about the bombing?"

"Yeah, I have a call with Ethan scheduled in thirty minutes." He checked his watch. "My lawyer sent me an email this morning to call him, he wanted to give me a heads up before the call today."

Claire slid closer, giving her friend a side hug. "I promise we will get this sorted."

"I know. It's not like the framing will be hard to dispute, once we get the evidence. I just don't want it to affect my relationship with my son, if he believes it or thinks I don't want him..." Colin couldn't finish the thought, it was too difficult.

Fifteen minutes later the charter jet had landed and was getting ready to welcome them on board. Unlike last time they were the only passengers flying and getting back into the States would be more difficult than getting into Rome had been. Instead of landing at the small airport that they had left from, the plan was to land on a private airstrip in the Outer Banks and take a small boat back to Galesville. Landing at a private airstrip didn't eliminate customs, but the onsite passport check was visually inspected only. And that, their faux passports would hold up to.

Claire stepped out of the car and into the heat. The air smelled like jet fuel and sweat as she walked, bag in hand, to the plane. They had returned to the Palazzo that morning to check out and retrieve the Mischinoffs' belongings. Still dressed like Alexandra, she wore a pleated cream satin skirt and navy linen blazer. The skirt danced between her legs as she walked to the plane. Colin and the driver of the town car brought the remaining bags to the plane for them to be loaded into the cargo.

When Colin finally boarded, Claire was already buckled in at the table. The jet was a super-midsize and featured several wide leather armchairs, two of which faced a table, as well as a sofa, which would allow an adult to lie flat. On each of the pillowed headrests a circular logo was embroidered. He didn't recognize it, and he didn't want to ask—Kane's dark web connections had set this up. A skinny wooden bar ran in between the seats and the curved walls of the plane with cupholders, magazine slots, and private fold out tables.

Checking the time on his phone, he noted that he had ten minutes until his video call with Ethan. Grabbing a pair of water bottles from a mini-fridge, Colin handed one to Claire as he sat down across from her.

The captain popped his head out of the cockpit and let them know that they would be taking off momentarily, while his copilot began closing the aircraft door. Due to the secrecy of the flight and the limited number of passengers the only staff on the plane were the pilots. Colin and Claire didn't need to be waited on hand and foot and honestly preferred privacy.

Colin's phone began buzzing on the table as they leveled out and reached cruising altitude. Kane had built a one-way bridge—Ethan could reach Colin, but nothing could be tracked either way. It was still a risk. But losing his son without a word felt worse. Flooded with a mix of excitement and relief, Colin answered the video call.

"Hey Buddy!" Ethan filled the screen, tanned from living outdoors. He looked like a mini version of Colin. No matter what kind of day Colin was having, seeing his son could always make it brighter.

"Wow, Dad... you look different. Your hair is dark and you

have a beard. I thought you didn't like to have a beard?" At eleven, Ethan still often spoke without thinking.

Chuckling, loving his son's bluntness, Colin nodded, "I do. I hate facial hair."

Claire tried not to listen, but it was hard with Colin so close. The conversation between Colin and his son made her chuckle inside. He did hate his facial hair and she often found him scratching and pulling at it when he thought no one was looking. Watching him with Ethan, Claire's chest ached. He couldn't risk seeing his son, just as she couldn't risk seeing Trevor again.

"I had to grow it out for work." Colin continued.

His mini-me's eyebrows furrowed in confusion, "I thought you weren't working right now."

"Why wouldn't I be working?" Colin's heart started to race. He'd texted with Ethan, but he hadn't mentioned the bombing—or the fugitive label.

Frozen for a second, Ethan didn't respond. His face was an open book, especially to his father, and he confirmed Colin's fears when he spoke. "I saw the news, Mom said I shouldn't tell you that I saw it. But you didn't do it, right Dad? You help people, you wouldn't set a bomb."

Colin didn't think his pulse could climb any higher. Nausea rolled through him as his anxiety spiked. He made sure to speak very clearly, so his son had no doubt, "No. I didn't set a bomb. The video is fake and I'm working on fixing things."

"That's what I thought, I tried telling Mom that but she—" The image blurred as it was pulled from Ethan's hand.

Lauren's face came into focus, the woman he had fallen madly in love with in a matter of seconds. Her long blonde hair was curled in bouncy waves and her moss green eyes bore into the phone with an anger and hurt that twisted something sharp in Colin's chest.

"Colin." The one word was sharp, quick and yet it had all the years of pain wrapped up into two syllables. He missed the way she used to say his name when they had been happy, like it was a song all on its own.

"Hi, Lauren." He still loved his ex-wife, as much if not more, than he knew Claire loved Trevor. Seeing her face was a gift and a painful gut punch all at the same time.

"I don't think you should be texting or calling Ethan right now."

Claire's internal rage burned like a sister wanting to defend her big brother. She didn't know Lauren, but in Claire's eyes she had no right to keep a father from talking to his son, not when they wanted to talk to each other.

He had been expecting her words but it didn't soften the pain he felt with the statement. "I didn't do it, Lauren. And the number is encrypted. Ethan isn't in any danger talking to me."

The background changed as she walked away so Ethan couldn't hear them. She dropped her voice into a whisper. "I didn't say you did it. I think it's safer for our son's emotional state for you to not call until you get it sorted."

"His emotional state?" Colin couldn't help but think that sounded like his ex in-laws talking— not Lauren, "Wouldn't it be more upsetting for him to not hear from me? This way he can see I'm fine and I can reassure him I'm working it out."

"No, let him focus on school and soccer until it's over." She sighed, "Look, I know you love him, Colin, but love doesn't erase what he's seeing on the news. Right now, he needs stability. I'm just trying to make sure he's okay. We agreed to put him first."

She had been happy before the job transfer to the CIA. At first Colin had thought it was just the move and having to leave her New York friends behind. But he quickly learned how much more there was to it.

They had only been in D.C. four months before she started to share how much she hated the late nights, the extra stress of security and all the last minute trips chasing bad guys. He had promised it was just temporary and once he had been there a while he could get better assignments. Trying to give her something exciting to do, that's when he suggested they start house hunting. After two months of searching they found the recently renovated historical townhome he still owned. Lauren had decorated the place making it a homey mix of modern and vintage. But it wasn't enough, fifteen months after moving into the townhome she left, taking their six year old with her. She moved out of state to be closer to her parents and Colin was forced to only see the love of his life and son on weekend trips.

"Just," he spoke softly, taking a breath and centering his thoughts, "Just give me a few weeks. I'm going to get it sorted and then everything will go back to normal. I promise."

"Fine, two weeks. But if anything happens or Ethan gets stressed and upset by the situation you've gotten yourself into—phone privileges will be revoked and I'll be filing to remove your visitation rights too."

"Lauren please…" He tried to argue but she was already handing the phone back to Ethan, telling him they had ten minutes and then he had to start his homework.

Colin forced a smile, hiding everything but calm for his son's sake. They spoke for as long as Lauren would let them, talking about everything from soccer to girls and his favorite books. He had always been a big reader and Colin made a mental note to send him the latest book in a series he was gushing about.

The ten minutes went by far too quickly and Colin wished, not for the first time, that he had left the CIA and followed them. The thought was often fleeting and he didn't know if he really would have ever done it. But right now, with everything going on, the thought didn't leave him as quickly as it used to. Maybe once his name was cleared and this was all over, he would leave the CIA for good.

When the call ended, Colin set the phone face down on the table. He slumped back in the large leather chair, his face neutral, but Claire knew him well enough to see his sadness behind the mask. She didn't say anything though—she knew what it cost to keep someone you loved at arm's length. Masking the pain was sometimes the only way to get through the day.

* * *

Trevor

Trevor felt like he was also wearing a mask—but his was

for Addie's sake. She was awake, lounging in her hospital bed, watching *Tangled* for the thousandth time. She had just finished debating the benefits of having a chameleon as a pet with Alexis. Grant sat on the small loveseat beside Trevor. He'd begun shopping for chameleon habitats the minute Addie asked. Trevor knew they'd have a new pet waiting when she got home in a few weeks, despite Alexis's reservations and the new puppy they had just adopted. Dodger, the pit bull mix Addie had fallen in love with, was currently at a two-week training camp. The trainers sent updates and videos daily for Addie to see. Trevor's childhood had been filled with pets, and he loved that his sisters' had them too—no matter how long she had left.

The movie was just finishing when Dr. Nnadi, Addie's cardiologist, knocked and stepped inside. Trevor guessed he was slightly older than his parents—he was a tall Black man with dark brown eyes and a kind, knowledgeable demeanor. As he stepped in, he used the hand sanitizer by the door, filling the room with the sharp scent of alcohol.

"How are you doing today, Addie?" he asked as he removed his stethoscope from around his neck and listened to her heart.

"I'd be better if my mom would let me get a chameleon." The sass was there, but she delivered it sweetly.

"I said we'd talk about it." Alexis shook her head and smirked at her daughter, deep down, she knew that she'd give in. Addie was a very helpful kid—always did her homework and took good care of the animals they rehabilitated that weren't even hers. And now with her illness, Alexis just wanted to give her the world even more. If you couldn't spoil a sick kid, when could you?

"You're sounding a bit better today," Dr. Nnadi said, referring to her heart. "All of your tests came back and we can move forward with placing the LVAD tomorrow. We've already gone over it, but do you have any more questions for me?"

"Will you be doing my surgery?" Addie asked in a quiet voice, suddenly a little shy. Trevor knew she was nervous, she'd told him so that morning, but she didn't want her parents to know. She was always putting on a brave face.

"No, that would be Dr. Patel. You are so special—you have two doctors. He is your cardiothoracic surgeon and I'm your pediatric cardiologist. All three of us together are the dream team! But I promise I'll be in the room with you when it happens, of course you'll be asleep, so won't see me."

"Okay. I met Dr. Patel earlier—he seems like he knows what he's doing." All the adults chuckled a little.

"I promise he does know what he's doing. I wouldn't let him near you if he wasn't a really, *really* good doctor." Addie just nodded in response, biting her lip a little and letting the nerves seep through. "I promise to take good care of you. No need to worry. If that's it, I'll see you all tomorrow. Addie—no eating or drinking after the nurses tell you, okay?"

"Okay."

The doctor turned to leave the room as Trevor stood and followed him out.

"I actually have a few questions I wanted to ask, just not in front of Addie."

"Of course—Trevor, right? Your parents have already given me permission to share any information about your sister's case with you. Shoot." He lifted a hand, signaling Trevor to start.

"What's the probability she'll get a heart in time?"

"Oh, right down to the hardest one. Unfortunately, I can't give you an exact answer. With her condition and severity, she's a 1A status on the transplant list. Meaning she's high up on it. Statistically, 1A cases get a heart within three months about fifty percent of the time. However, your sister has an O-negative blood type, which means she can only receive a heart from someone who was also O-negative. It limits the options a little."

Trevor appreciated the doctor's blunt honesty..

"But you only think the LVAD buys her a few months." Trevor knew all of this but it was important to hear it from her doctor.

"We can't say exactly how long it'll give her. We hope closer to six months, but realistically we are looking at two to four months."

Trevor was quiet, taking in all of the information, hearing it from a professional left him feeling cold, deflated and defeated. All of the information the doctor was sharing was lining up with what he had read.

Dr. Nnadi could see Trevor's defeat all over his face. "Your parents said you're going to medical school in the fall, yes?" He nodded. "So you are familiar with medicine enough that you know we will do everything we can and sometimes new techniques or treatments show up out of nowhere. Don't give up hope and make sure to share that hope with your sister. Kids always do better when they're under less stress."

He patted Trevor on the back once and continued on, "I've got another patient to check in on. But if you have any more questions, let me know."

With that Dr. Nnadi walked back to the nurses' station and began reading a chart, presumably belonging to his next patient.

Trevor texted his parents he was going to get coffee and asked if anyone wanted anything. His mom asked for a decaf and his dad a bag of chips. Setting off for the cafeteria Trevor couldn't help but let the numbers run through his head.

Two to four months…. Fifty percent chance… less because she's O-negative…

Was it really a coin flip—for his sister's life? She was ten and it came down to a flip of a coin! He knew he should trust the list as much as his parents did but he couldn't, not with this. Trevor had spent years being trained to *do*—to not trust the system, but move anyway. Tilt the game in your favor. He couldn't just sit by and wait. While he now knew Claire was alive, he still had lost her, he still felt the ache and pain for seven years without her. He wasn't about to go through all of that again, not with his sister. Claire had vanished to protect the people she loved; maybe this was his version of that—doing whatever it took, no matter the cost.

On his way down to the cafeteria he entered the stairwell and dialled the number.

When Trevor heard the call connect, he didn't wait for a hello. "Can you guarantee that she'll get the heart?"

"Mio figlio, no hello?" Antonio's voice was sickly sweet.

In addition to the medical research over the last few days, Trevor had also been researching his biological father. If he was going to consider it he had to know exactly what he was getting into— down to every last detail.

"Hello. Can you guarantee that she'll get a heart?" Trevor didn't have the energy for too many pleasantries but he knew if he didn't play along, his father wouldn't give him what he wanted either.

"Guarantee? No. But a man in my position can shift the odds. The list is not always as... impartial as they say. There are hospitals, coordinators, surgeons—people who listen when I speak. A file moves higher. A call gets made. A donor that might have gone to another child, suddenly—it is Addie's heart."

Trevor gripped the phone tighter and stopped mid-staircase. "You're saying you can rig the system."

Antonio chuckled softly. "Call it what you like. I call it using influence. You've worn the uniform, you know the world isn't fair. Some live, some die. Would you rather your sister's fate be decided by chance? Or by a father who can tilt the board?"

Trevor's pulse hammered in his throat. "And the price?"

"You already know." Antonio's voice softened, almost paternal. "Come to Italy. Learn my world. You think the military taught you discipline, loyalty, sacrifice? With me, you'll learn what true power means—and you'll use it to protect the ones you love."

Trevor closed his eyes, images of Addie's future played through his head. Dodger, a chameleon, first dates, prom, college, becoming a vet like their dad. Then an image of a small child sized coffin.

Antonio pressed, "Fifty percent, Trevor. That's the number they gave you, isn't it? You know better than most what fifty-fifty means. Would you gamble with your sister's life? Or will you do something?"

Trevor's knuckles whitened around the phone. Fifty percent. The number replayed in his mind like a roulette wheel. Heads or tails? Life or death?

He'd gambled before—in combat zones where the odds had been worse, when it was only his life on the line. But this wasn't his life. This was Addie's. His ten-year-old sister who had never asked for any of this, who still drew crooked horses in her notebooks and begged him to braid her hair.

"I shouldn't even be listening to you," Trevor said hoarsely, though he didn't hang up. His throat burned. "You're a criminal, you sell weapons and you don't care to whom."

"I am, and yet," Antonio said smoothly, "you called back. Because you know the truth, Trevor. I am her only hope, I can help."

Trevor slammed a fist against the stair railing, his pulse ragged. He hated the man—hated his voice, hated the manipulation in every syllable. But more than hate, there was fear. A cold, hollow terror of standing by and watching Addie fade because he chose himself over her.

Antonio's voice softened, intimate, almost tender. "This isn't about me. It's about her. Every day wasted is a day closer to losing her. Say you'll come back, and I will make sure she gets what she needs. Do as I ask and you won't have to bury your sister."

Trevor pressed the heel of his hand to his eyes, fighting the tension headache this man was giving him.

His voice cracked when he finally spoke. "If I do this... if I come to learn from you... you'll get her moved up on the list as soon as possible?"

Antonio didn't hesitate. "I will, as soon as you're back in Rome."

"Fine, I'll come."

The line went dead, leaving Trevor alone with the silence of his decision. He slumped to sit on a step, feeling the cold stair beneath him. His phone dropped into his lap as the stairwell tilted and spun. He had just sold himself to the devil, but if it meant Addie lived, he'd pay the price.

19
A Shot In the Dark

Tossing the last of his clothes into his bag, Trevor went through his mental checklist: clothes, passport, phone, Swiss Army knife, wallet. With everything accounted for he clasped the cold metal zipper, closing his bag. When he scanned the room, his eyes landed on the photograph of him and Claire, staring back at him. He desperately wanted to take it with him, but he couldn't let Antonio know about their past. He wasn't sure what Antonio knew about Claire, or that she was alive. To him, she could have just been a minor inconvenience that he swatted, like a fly buzzing at his head. Trevor refused to give him more leverage than he already had.

He did take his leather jacket—the one she had picked out. A small piece of her with him. Trevor hoped that he would be able to go just long enough for Addie to get her heart, and then find an excuse to leave. Though he feared that if he tried to leave, Antonio would stop him—one way or another. Trevor's first priority was to do everything in his power to keep those he loved safe and alive, including Claire. Then he would worry about himself.

As he loaded his bags into the car, Trevor's phone buzzed. Grant had sent a text in the family group chat:

On my way.

Alexis had stayed at the hospital the night before, insisting that Grant get a shower and a decent night's rest. He gave in knowing his wife wouldn't let it go. On his way into the hospital this morning, he took the opportunity to pop into his vet clinic and make sure everything was going smoothly in his absence. He would've now been headed to the hospital.

Addie's LVAD surgery was scheduled for 10:00 a.m. and would take the most of the day. Trevor had promised her he would be there when she woke up, but he would have to duck out as soon as he could after that. Antonio needed him in D.C. tonight to *run an errand for him.* He was only given the time of his flight and told that a car would be waiting for him. Antonio would text him the rest later today.

After spending the night in D.C., Trevor would fly back to Rome for an indefinite stay.

Pulling out of the driveway, he glanced up at the house in the rearview mirror. A ray of sun broke through the morning clouds and lit the house like a painting. He didn't know when he would get to see it again. It felt a lot like when he had left for basic training right after Claire's funeral. Back then he'd been running from grief; now he was walking toward it—because she had once chosen the hard road to protect him, and he finally understood why.

Taking the long way out of town, Trevor drove past Claire's old house, pulling over just for a second so he could reminisce. He could almost see her on the porch swing, coffee in hand, while their kids played in the yard, laughter floating through the air. The picture hurt in that clean, necessary way—like alcohol on a wound. He let it burn, then let it go.

The drive to the hospital felt unusually long today; the sense of danger looming over him the closer he got to leaving for D.C. He warred internally with his fight-or-flight telling him to go home and unpack. Addie would get the heart; she would be fine. But just like all the times he had walked into combat before, he used logic to override his desire to flee.

Pulling into the hospital lot, he parked, leaving his bags in the trunk. When Trevor arrived at Addie's room in the pediatric ICU, she was sitting up in bed. Looking the same as she had the day before, pale and weak but determined. Alexis was brushing her hair while Grant sat on the sofa.

"Trevor! Finally, can you please braid my hair? Mom never does it right." Addie looked back at her mom and gave her a sheepish grin, "Sorry."

Alexis just laughed and handed her son the hairbrush and elastic hair tie as she stepped aside. She'd never been good at braiding anything but dough. Addie's blonde hair was so fine she could never get it to stay willingly in a braid. Trevor on the other hand seemed to have a knack for braiding hair. Sitting down on the sofa next to Grant, she leaned into her husband, enjoying the bond her children had.

"One or two?" Trevor asked as he finished running the brush through Addie's hair.

"Just one, but a French one."

Trevor proceeded to separate her soft hair into sections. Normally, it smelled like strawberries, but today all he could smell was the scent of a generic, clean hospital shampoo. He began twisting and picking up hair as needed, trying his best to tune out the constant beeping of the machines. Sometimes he caught himself counting her heartbeats along with the monitor. When he was done she had a perfectly styled braid.

Touching her hair, Addie smiled and looked up at her big brother, "How did you learn to do that again?"

He chuckled, "A friend taught me, when she learned I was getting a little sister, she said I would need to know how to braid hair."

Addie didn't seem to remember Claire; after all, she was only three when Claire *died*. "Is it that girl in all the photos in your room?"

"Yeah, her name is... was Claire."

Alexis and Grant exchanged glances at one another. Trevor didn't usually talk about her so willingly.

Dr. Patel and Dr. Nnadi poked their heads in the door, letting the sharp smell of antiseptic waft in from the hallway. It was time for Addie's surgery prep. After going over the details and having all of the consent forms signed, the operating room staff came in to take Addie back.

Hugging her dad and brother, Grant reassured her she was just going to take a little nap and see them all soon. Alexis was going to go back with Addie and would be by her side while she fell asleep from the anesthesia meds. Trevor didn't want to let go of his baby sister; he knew he'd see her again after the surgery, but this felt more like a goodbye rather than a see-you-soon. Reluctantly letting her go, Trevor gave her a kiss on the forehead and watched as the nurses wheeled her out the door with Alexis by her side.

Trevor knew this was it. He needed to tell his parents about going back to Italy. His stomach twisted in on itself, and he decided he'd procrastinate by getting coffee for everyone while he waited for his mom to come back.

"I'm going to go get coffee; I'll be back," Trevor said as he turned to leave the room.

"What's going on, Trevor?" Grant was calm, but he had noticed his son felt off—more than he would expect if it were just the surgery bothering him. Trevor looked back at him with a questioning gaze. "I'm your dad; I know when something is bothering you. You've been holding tension in your neck since yesterday afternoon. What's going on?"

Trevor rubbed at the base of his neck. It was stiff and painful. "I should wait for Mom to get back." Grant just gave him a look—one he'd gotten many times as a teenager. *No, spill.* Sighing, he knew it wasn't an option. "I'm going back to Italy."

Grant recoiled in surprise and confusion. "Why would you do that?"

Sinking down onto the sofa he let it all spill out. "I got a text from Antonio. He said he could help, that he can get Addie the heart, but only if I go back to Rome and learn from him."

"Learn what from him?" Grant felt the need to start pacing, but he fought it and sat down next to his son instead, clenching the armrest of the sofa.

"His business." Trevor's voice cracked as he spoke, the words not wanting to come free.

Grant was quiet for a long moment. The weight of those two words—*his business*—hung between them like a noose waiting to tighten.

"Trevor..." Grant's voice was low, steady, but edged with fear. "You don't owe that man anything. Not your time, not your life. And you sure as hell don't need to get your hands dirty for him."

Trevor rubbed both palms over his face. "You don't understand, Dad. It's not about me. If this is what it takes for Addie, if this is the price, I'll pay it."

"Addie wouldn't want that." Grant leaned forward, trying to catch Trevor's gaze. "And neither would your mother. I definitely don't."

Trevor swallowed hard. The words pressed against his chest, hot and desperate: *I've already lost Claire once. I can't lose Addie too*. His throat closed around her name, and for a second he almost said it out loud. He almost told Grant the impossible truth, that Claire was alive, that she'd found him again, that he wasn't just protecting Addie but he was also trying to protect Claire.

But then her voice echoed in his head, sharp and certain: *No one can know; it could put them in danger*.

He clenched his fists, forcing the words back down. "There's... someone else I need to protect," he admitted instead, staring at the floor. "Someone I can't let him touch."

Grant frowned. "Who, Trevor? Who are you talking about?"

Trevor's jaw tightened. He shook his head once, sharply. "It doesn't matter. Just... trust me, okay? I can't tell you anymore."

The silence stretched. Grant studied him, suspicion and worry mingling in his eyes, but before he could press again the door opened.

Alexis slipped back inside, her face pale and drawn from holding herself together in front of Addie. She glanced between them immediately, sensing the tension like a storm cloud still crackling in the air.

"What's going on?" she asked, looking from Grant to Trevor.

"I'm going back to Italy," Trevor said slowly.

"What? Now? Addie's sick and you're leaving the country again?" Alexis was baffled—the son she knew would never leave his sister, especially when she was so sick.

Trevor's eyes pleaded with his mom not to be upset with him as Grant spoke, explaining to Alexis what Antonio had promised.

"For how long? What about med school? Trevor, I know you probably want to get to know Antonio; he's your biological father but he's not a good guy. There's some stuff we haven't told you..." Alexis began to ramble, panic setting in.

Trevor cut her off, speaking calmly and moving over so that his mom could sit down between him and Grant. "Mom, stop. I know Antonio isn't a good guy." He took her hands in his. "And I don't want to get to know him. I'm only going to... to get the heart for Addie." He decided not to let it slip that he was also protecting Claire. "I don't know about med school yet. I still want to go but if this isn't all resolved in time, then I'll defer. I hope I can go and just stay a few weeks and then come back."

While Trevor spoke the truth—he did hope he could find some way to go to medical school, but he didn't really think it was going to happen. At least not for a long time.

"Trevor, you don't know everything." Alexis took a steadying breath and looked over her shoulder at Grant. He nodded and she turned back to her son, "Do you remember your dad's friend, Kyle?"

"Of course I remember Kyle. He was the best man at your wedding,   and he's the police chief two towns over." He was unsure of what Kyle had to do with this.

"When you left for Italy, I had a gut feeling that something wasn't... right. So, we asked Kyle to look into Antonio. Trevor... he's suspected of being the head of a crime family. We didn't hear back until you were already on your flight home. We were going to tell you when Addie was doing a bit better."

Trevor looked between his parents. "I know. I had the same feeling when I was there. I didn't know everything when I got home, but I knew I wanted nothing to do with him. I've done my research since then."

Grant spoke up for the first time since Alexis came into the room. "If you want nothing to do with him, then don't go."

"Dad, I have to. He promised…"

Cutting him off, Alexis spoke, "I have no doubt he probably has people he can bribe to get her higher on the list, but she doesn't need that. She'll get the heart; we just have to trust the process."

"I can't do that, Mom." Trevor stood up now. "I can't just sit and wait for her to maybe get a heart. Not when I can do something to raise those odds. I… I'm not going to sit back and watch another person I love die."

His parents stood like they were both about to argue, but Trevor spoke first. "I know you won't agree; I don't think you ever will, and I understand that. But I'm going. I won't sit by and let her die. If she gets worse, I'll come back. He can't keep me from her. I'll do my best to keep you guys updated, but I'm… I'm going to try not to talk to you too often. I want to keep you as far away from this as possible. Please just trust me, I'm a trained soldier, I can take care of myself."

Looking at him and then each other, Alexis and Grant knew that arguing was useless. Trevor had already made up his mind, and much like Alexis, he was stubborn as a mule.

"Fine, we clearly can't change your mind. But you have to call once a week at minimum. I want daily texts so we know you're okay, and as soon as Addie has the heart, we're talking about how to get you home." Grant was adamant.

"Daily texts aren't keeping you at an arms distance," Trevor protested.

"I don't care; it can be as simple as 'I'm okay.' But we need daily texts, or I'm following you to Italy." Trevor knew his dad wasn't asking for that much.

"Please don't follow me. It would only put you in danger." He just got questioning expressions from his parents, waiting for him to agree. "Fine, daily texts."

"Good." Grant sat back down on the sofa and just like that, the conversation was finished as far as he was concerned.

Alexis leaned in close to her son. "You know he will follow you, so don't miss a day. You're his child, he would do anything to protect you."

"I know." Trevor hugged his mom, not wanting to let go. He hadn't realized how much he needed contact until he felt her body against his. Hugging his mom had always felt soft, like hugging your favorite pillow, and sturdy at the same time, like she could slay any dragon in her path. At that moment he was a little kid again, just wanting to let his parents make it all go away.

Five long hours passed before Addie's doctors came to her room. She was in recovery and doing well. The surgery went as planned and she should be able to go home in two weeks—barring any complications. She'll need to restrict strenuous activity—definitely no chasing the dogs. Alexis was then escorted down to sit with Addie until she fully woke up and was able to be brought back to her room.

An hour later, Addie was being pushed on a hospital gurney down the hall to her room, the hallway echoing with her complaints about how hungry she was. Alexis suggested a bowl of ice cream, since her tummy was still okay after the popsicle she'd had in recovery. Addie agreed with enthusiasm as she was pushed through the door. Her eyes lit up at the sight of her dad and brother.

Once the nurses had reconnected her monitors, Grant and Trevor approached, giving light hugs and kisses. Trevor felt a wave of relief seeing his sister had more color in her cheeks, despite having just come out of surgery.

Vanilla ice cream was ordered for everyone through room service. When it arrived, it was already nearing 5 p.m., and Trevor had to leave soon. As hard as his discussion with his parents had been, telling Addie he had to leave again, was even more difficult. He told her how much he loved her and that he had to go to help someone else that he loved. Addie surprised him when she smiled and told him, with startling maturity, that she would be ok and she understood. She told him not to worry about her and that she would be okay. Trevor wondered absently when it was that his sister had grown into a young woman.

With tears welling up in his eyes he gave his sister a kiss on the forehead and told her to be good, before turning to his mom. She wrapped her arms around him in a bone-crushing hug, whispering in his ear to be careful and come home soon.

When he left the room, Trevor had a knot in his stomach, fearing that this could be the last time he saw any of his family. Grant escorted him down to his car and helped him retrieve his bags, moving them to a taxi's trunk.

Closing the liftgate, Trevor turned and handed his dad his keys. He was surprised to see tears in his dad's eyes. Hugging him before speaking, "I'll be okay, Dad."

"I just thought you were done going into war zones." Grant sniffled, trying to hold back his tears.

"Yeah, me too.." Pulling back so Trevor could look his dad in the eyes, "I want you to know, *you* are my dad. Antonio... he isn't you."

Tears streamed down Grant's face, "I love you, son. I know I'm not a soldier but if you need me, I'll be on the next flight out." "Deal."

With one more hug Trevor stepped back and got into the taxi. He told himself he wouldn't cry; his sister was stable and he could handle himself. Closing his eyes and taking a deep breath he steadied himself and turned on his soldier's demeanor. Knowing what was likely to come, he couldn't help but see the parallels between his choices and Claire's. For the first time, he let the feeling of betrayal go fully.

* * *

When Trevor landed at the D.C. airport and turned his phone on, he had a text from Antonio.

Short Term parking, section B, row 2, stall 29.

This was it. He was officially stepping into Antonio's world again. The entire way to baggage claim and then the car Trevor was hyper-aware of his surroundings and everyone that entered or exited his vicinity. He felt like he had when he was in Afghanistan for the first time, except right now he was unarmed. His firearm was at home in a lockbox. When Antonio had texted to tell him he was stopping in D.C., he mentioned a gun would be waiting for him in the car, along with the items he was delivering.

Trevor wasn't naive; he knew what *the items* probably were: weapons—guns and ammunition. He had debated about removing the firing pins or putting glue in the chamber, making the guns useless, but decided against it. Knowing that if it got back to Antonio he had done so, he'd not only be putting Addie's heart at risk but his own life too. Antonio may be his father, but Trevor didn't doubt that he'd punish a betrayal.

The keys were tucked in the wheel well when Trevor reached the dark SUV. The smell of gasoline and oil permeated the air around him as he lifted his bags into the rear seats. The trunk was already full with two metal cases. He decided not to inspect the trunk here. Too many eyes and cameras.

Sliding into the driver's seat, Trevor checked the center console. There was a gun, already assembled. Pulling the cold, weighted metal into his lap as discreetly as he could, Trevor disassembled it, making sure it would work if needed. Once it was put back together he checked the ammunition and engaged the safety and tucked it at his right side. He felt a little bit of relief, knowing he at least now had a way of defending himself, if it came to that.

Turning the car on, a set of coordinates were already programmed into the GPS. The drive would take him forty minutes and looked to be in the middle of nowhere. Every instinct told him he was walking into danger, but he pushed them aside and followed the robotic instructions.

When Trevor got to the location he was told to pull into a deserted parking lot in front of a dilapidated gas station. He hadn't seen another car in ten minutes and his instincts were screaming at full volume to turn around. Ignoring them he put the car in park. He had reasoned with himself the whole way here, that if Antonio had wanted him dead, he had easier ways to do it. The people he was meeting however, he knew nothing about.

Trevor sat in the car waiting until he saw another set of headlights. His hand instinctively closed around the handle of the gun, keeping it low and out of sight.

The driver of the other car brought it to a stop and flashed their lights twice. The first part of the signal that had been relayed to him. Now the buyer just had to give the correct response. Two large men got out of the other car and walked into the headlights of the SUV. Even in the lights, it was too dark to see details of the men's faces. Trevor rolled down the window and called out his line. "Nice night for a drive, huh?"

"Would be nicer if we were in Tuscany," the driver called back.

Trevor got out of the car at that, "Walk to the trunk." He wouldn't turn his back on them, instead following them after they passed by. He kept the gun in his right hand but pointed at the ground. Opening the trunk with his left hand he gestured for them to open the cases. The smaller of the two men stepped forward as the driver watched Trevor intensely.

Before the case was even open, sirens screamed down the highway coming right toward them.

"You called the cops?" The driver raised his gun, pointing it right at Trevor.

In a second, Trevor had his gun raised and pointed back, "No, I didn't." He was normally very calm in combat situations but here right now, he was on the wrong side of the law, and his heart knew it. It was ramming against his ribs.

Two cop cars squealed to a stop blocking the only entrance to the lot. The sharp sound of gunfire immediately reverberated through the air. Trevor ducked instinctively, dropping back behind his SUV hidden from view. He hadn't fired—so who had?

Bullets began pinging off the SUV on the far side. The cops were shooting at *them*. No warning or telling them to put down their weapons... just gun fire.

Trevor felt it then, a warmth spreading down his leg, followed by a shooting pain on his left outer thigh. Daring to look down, his jeans were soaked through with blood. In the dark it looked more like oil than blood.

The sirens and flashing lights were making it hard for him to think as his head began to spin. He slumped against the car, sliding to the ground. Ricocheting bullets sounded like they were right next to him. A haze washed over his vision. He looked around watching as the driver and passenger fired back at the cops.

The sharp pain was getting more intense with every second, in all the years he had been active duty he'd never been shot. Once he had taken some shrapnel to the back, which hurt like hell, but never anything like this. This was worse. The ping of the bullets began to fade, sounding a million miles away.

With his last few seconds of consciousness he assessed the damage to his leg, the bullet hadn't hit the femoral artery. That was good. Feeling the back of his leg he found another hole. A through-and-through. Two wounds meant more blood loss, he needed a hospital as soon as possible. But he couldn't keep his eyes open any longer. His whole body felt like it weighed a thousand pounds, his eyelids drooping, even as he fought to stay awake with everything he had. As his eyelids fell, so did the world around him. His final thought was her name... Claire.

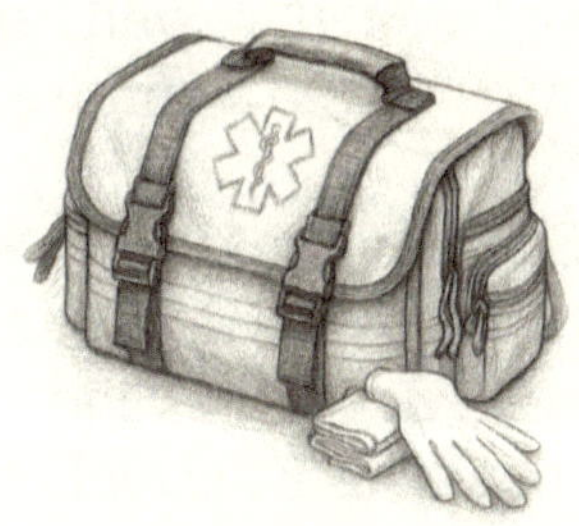

20
One Last Goodbye

The glow of passing headlights flickered across Claire's face as Colin steered the old minivan down a long, empty highway. The stretch of asphalt seemed endless, carved through dark fields and scattered boxelder trees. Wind rushed through a gap in Colin's window, carrying the smell of damp earth and diesel.

She kept her eyes locked on the small blinking dot on Kane's tablet, balanced between them on the console.

The signal from Trevor's phone.

When his flight information had tripped Kane's system hours earlier, Claire's chest had gone tight. He was here—but he was supposed to be with Addie in Tennessee, not thirty minutes from her. Kane had worked fast, tracing the SUV through traffic cameras and pinging towers. Now they were close—too close to slow down.

"He hasn't moved in ten minutes," Colin muttered, glancing at the screen. His jaw flexed, knuckles whitening around the steering wheel. He didn't dare say what he was thinking; this wasn't good. He knew Claire was already thinking it too—that Trevor was either hurt, or his phone was no longer with him.

Claire said nothing. Every nerve in her body screamed that something was wrong. He wasn't even supposed to be here, let alone going back to Italy. Antonio had obviously promised him something—something big enough to pull him back.

The rhythmic, sharp cracks of gunfire split the night. Distant, but clear.

"Kill the lights," Claire insisted.

Colin's hand darted to the switch, plunging them into darkness. The minivan sped down the road until, just beyond a cluster of trees, red and blue lights flashed up ahead.

Claire leaned forward, straining to make out the details. A deserted gas station loomed like a skeleton in the night, its rusted sign groaning in the wind. The two cop cars turned their lights off and sped out of the parking lot and back toward downtown D.C.

Only two cars were left in the parking lot, the black SUV that Trevor had been driving and a beat-up dark blue car that looked like they had driven it straight from the dump.

Two men straightened to standing, lifting a slumped figure into the SUV. Trevor.

Her heart seized. He was barely conscious, head lolling forward as his legs dragged.

Colin slowed the minivan down so he didn't draw attention, the closer they got the more Claire could see. Blood streaked the denim of his thigh.

Rolling down her window, she could hear their voices carrying across the air.

"He's bleeding out—Antonio'll kill us if he dies," The larger of the two men said as they dropped Trevor's limp form on the back seat. He lay on his right side, with the bottom half of his long legs hanging out of the door. At least they hadn't laid him on his wound.

"Then we'll dump him at a hospital. Let them patch him up."

"No, we deal with the cases first—"

"Are you out of your mind? Look at him! We may not work for Antonio, but if he finds out his son died and we could have done something to help him, it's our heads."

"Okay, what if we tried to help him but the cops just injured him too badly for us to do anything. Something so bad the hospital couldn't save him either."

Claire's fingers curled around the grip of her handgun, and before she even realized it, the hard plastic of the van's door handle was in the other, pulling it back. There was no time for debate, they were going to kill him.

"Claire," Colin warned softly, catching her movement out of the corner of his eye.

"They're going to kill him, and he won't survive if he doesn't get help soon," her voice was low and firm—the kind of tone that brokered no argument.

Two heartbeats passed. Then she finished opening the door and stepped out into the crisp night air. The slight scent of gunpowder floated on the air toward her, fueling her need to protect Trevor.

The men were still arguing when she raised her weapon. One precise squeeze of the trigger—and the first man dropped.

The second spun around, looking for where the shot had come from, his mouth opening in alarm, but she was hidden in the blackness of shadows. Her follow-up shot hit before he could do anything else. He crumpled beside his partner, the echo of gunfire rolling away into the empty fields.

Claire held her aim for a beat longer, then lowered the gun. "Clear."

As soon as Claire had climbed inside and the minivan door had clicked shut, Colin sped off down the road toward Trevor. When they entered the parking lot, she was out of the minivan before it had even come to a complete stop.

Trevor was slumped over on the back seat of the SUV, completely unconscious. Climbing up into the cab, she checked his pulse, catching the unmistakable metallic scent of blood. His skin was clammy beneath her fingertips, the pulse faint but steady. She let out a deep breath when she found it easily. Relief broke the walls she had been holding up as tears began rolling down her cheeks.

Examining his leg, she found both wounds. From the

location on his outer thigh, she knew it had missed bone and the femoral artery. It was a soft tissue wound, he wouldn't need surgery. Pressing her hands to his leg, one on either side, she asked Colin to bring over the first-aid bag. He was already halfway to her, bag in hand.

Setting it on the floor by the back seat, he began to open it, pulling out gloves and gauze. They're dead. I checked for a pulse," Colin said, jerking his head toward the gunmen.

Claire ignored him. She knew they would be—her aim was excellent. She should feel bad—she had taken two lives. But right now, she was completely consumed with saving Trevor. "It's through-and-through—opposite side of the artery."

He slipped on gloves and grabbed the trauma shears. Colin leaned in and began cutting away the denim. This gave them a better view and the ability to dress it properly. Grabbing some more gauze, he used it to put pressure on either side. Claire slowly slid her hands out of the way as Colin put his hands in place—a practiced technique to maintain pressure on the wound. The warmth of Trevor's blood seeped through the gauze, slicking Colin's gloved hands.

Trevor groaned from the pressure on his leg, still unconscious. The sound tore at her. All of her training told her to detach—but she couldn't with him. They would need to administer some pain meds before he woke up.

Using a towel from the bag, Claire wiped the blood from her hands and struggled to pull on gloves—a tricky feat with her skin still tacky. Grabbing the elastic wrap, she and Colin worked together to keep continuous pressure and wrap the bandage around his leg.

Finally, removing a vial from a padded pouch, she injected a local anesthetic into his leg. They could give him real pain medications when they returned to the safe house.

When the wound was properly dressed, Claire finally let out the breath she hadn't realized she had been holding. Looking up at her face for the first time since exiting the car, Colin saw her tear-stained cheeks.

"He's going to be okay. If it had been Ethan, I'd have done the same."

"I know." Claire gave a shallow nod. "Let's move him and get this scene taken care of."

"I'll move him. You keep your gloves on, just in case you need to apply more pressure." Colin jumped down from the SUV and removed his gloves.

When he was ready, Claire helped raise Trevor's torso, sliding him gently toward Colin. Being careful not to grab his wounded leg, Colin hoisted him over his shoulders in a fireman's carry, easily picking him up. She ran ahead, opened the sliding back door of their stolen van, and helped maneuver Trevor into place.

Gathering up their belongings, Colin moved the first aid bag to the minivan where Claire could reach it, just in case she needed it while they drove. After also transferring Trevor's bags to the trunk, Colin looked at the SUV's open liftgate. His gaze snagged on the two black-and-silver cases. Fury building inside of him. He didn't need to say it aloud—Claire knew why he was staring. She had seen the cases and assumed they were full of weapons. Illegal weapons.

They couldn't risk the stolen weapons falling into the wrong hands, but they couldn't take them either. The firearm or cases could have been wired with trackers. Besides, the SUV was too new—its own built-in GPS could give them away. And it wasn't exactly inconspicuous, not with an entire side riddled with bullet holes.

"We can't take the car," Colin said flatly. "And we can't leave it—it'll have Trevor's DNA and fingerprints. Plus, the weapons need to be turned in somehow."

Claire's mind raced, but when she looked down at Trevor, his breathing was even and color finally was returning to his face. She had to protect him at any cost. Nodding once, she told him to do the only thing they could, "Burn it."

It was exactly what Colin had been thinking. He moved like the special agent he was—quick, efficient, and without flourish. He dropped down to the pavement and looked under the car. Near the rear axle was the base of the gas tank. In some cases, models had a drain at the base, but they weren't so lucky.

He was going to have to make a hole; make it look accidental to avoid questions. With older cars, road debris or rust could plausibly punch a hole in a tank. Because the car was brand new, he'd have to make it look like a rogue bullet had punctured the tank. Covering his hands with the edges of his long sleeves, Colin picked up one of the dead assailants' weapons. Walking around to the side with the bullet holes, he aimed low enough to pierce the car's trim and gas tank. When the sharp smell of fresh gasoline filled the air, he knew he'd hit it. A puddle of fuel was now leaking onto the pavement.

Claire watched from the back seat of the old minivan as he worked, keeping one hand on Trevor's chest, needing that contact. His large frame took up the entire rear bench seat, forcing Claire to perch on the center console between the front seats.

At that moment, she remembered to disable another possible tracker. Trevor's phone. Running her hands over his pockets, she searched for it. She finally found it tucked into the jacket she had chosen for him. Removing the battery from his phone so it couldn't be traced, she tossed both pieces onto the front passenger seat, out of the way.

While she worked, Claire kept glancing at the two men lying on the cracked asphalt. She had killed them. She felt guilt for their families, shame for resorting to violence so quickly, relief that Trevor was safe—and finally, grief for the small piece of herself she'd lost when she pulled the trigger.

Tossing the gun into the open trunk of the SUV, Colin walked back to the minivan and grabbed a matchbook he had seen. With it tucked into his fist, he closed the sliding door and liftgate before jumping into the driver's seat. Turning the car on, he rolled down his window, the gasoline smell burning their throats. His heart hammered as he struck a match and tossed it at the fuel puddle. When the fire caught, heat washed over them, painting their faces orange and gold.

Colin hit the gas, careful not to leave tire tracks as they sped away. Claire watched out the rear window as a fireball stretched high into the night sky. The metal hissed as car paint blistered and smoke began to curl. She slid down to the floor of the van, keeping one of her hands on Trevor's chest to stabilize him. Her throat closed as visions of her parents' car going up in flames flooded her memory. "I'll call it in," she said, her voice small.

"I got it." Colin already had his burner phone in hand, dialing. He used a thick Southern accent, deliberately speaking with a slight panic in his voice, and gave the operator the details. The report was simple: a vehicle fire at the gas station. When he ended the call, he placed his phone into the cupholder and made a mental note to have Kane remove all traces from the burner when they got back. The call couldn't be traced back to him with the program Kane was running all calls through—the signal would bounce around endlessly, never giving an exact location.

The sounds of plastic and metal warping filled the night as they drove away. When he knew Claire's attention was on Trevor, Colin casually moved his hand from where it rested to the front passenger seat, grabbing the phone. He pocketed it, tucking it into the inner lining of his hiking jacket. He planned to hand it to Kane for cloning later, a secret they'd keep from Claire for now.

Keeping their lights low, they drove off into the night as the shadows swallowed everything around them. When they passed behind a cluster of trees, the glow of the now blazing flames looked like a tiny campfire amongst all the wild brush.

When they arrived at the safe house, Trevor's breathing was still regular and his bleeding was under control. Kane rushed out of the house in a huff, reminding Claire of her father, that one time she'd come home past curfew. His hands were on his hips as she and Colin exited the van. "Do you really think you should have brought him here? What if he tells them where we are? Or has a tracker on him?"

Claire stared at him, flabbergasted. "He would never put me in danger," she said, sharp and unyielding. "And if we don't irrigate that wound and get him antibiotics soon, he'll die of sepsis." Kane's scowl didn't change. "If he goes, I go… Please just trust me, he won't put us in danger."

Colin didn't disagree with Kane but he also had seen in person the way Trevor looked at Claire. He knew without a doubt Trevor would never put her in danger, but that didn't mean he trusted him. The weight of the phone felt like a boulder in his pocket—one that Claire may notice at any moment.

"Kane, it's okay. We've taken precautions. Claire, why don't you go inside and get the saline solution ready to clean his wound? Kane, give me a hand with Trevor."

Claire walked away before Kane had the chance to say anything. She was grateful, it seemed someone understood. But when she was out of earshot Colin spoke again, low so that if Trevor were awake he wouldn't hear. "I don't fully trust him either," he said, passing Kane the phone before pulling Trevor's limp form closer. Kane's eyebrows raised in surprise when he saw the phone.   "Will you clone it? I've seen how much he loves her, but we need to make sure he doesn't accidentally let anything slip."

"I'll get it done." Kane closed the minivan door after Colin lifted Trevor over his shoulder and walked toward the house.

Claire had just finished sterilizing the table in the formal dining room and laying out towels when Colin entered. As he lay Trevor down, she braced his back and head, making sure to put a decorative pillow from the sofa under his head.

The window that had been smashed was now properly boarded up from both sides, but even with the window covered, this room was still slightly cooler in the evenings.

"He'll come around, right?" Instead of fiddling with her bracelet like she normally did when she was nervous, Claire slipped her hand into Trevor's.

"Yeah. He gets it; he's just being… persnickety." Colin smiled when Claire chuckled under her breath. "He just wants to make sure we're all safe and nothing goes wrong. He and I don't know Trevor like you do, that's all. Kane understands, though."

Claire nodded and sighed as they began to work together, cleaning Trevor's leg. They started by cutting away the rest of his pant leg, then cleaning the skin of excess blood and debris. Claire popped a bottle of sterile saline and began pouring it over his wound. The salt water hissed as she squeezed the bottle and then dripped against the towels as it fell off his leg.

When the bottle was empty they used gauze to dry the skin. Because of the nature of his wound, it would need to be able to heal from the inside out, so they couldn't stitch the openings. Colin and Kane had previously worked together to stock up with everything medical that they might need, including antibiotics. Even after using a few supplies on Claire's still-healing shoulder, they had plenty to spare.

They were beginning to rewrap the leg with a clean dressing when Trevor started to rouse.

"Trevor? Trev, it's Claire, you're safe. We are just wrapping your leg." Despite her adrenaline dialing up, she spoke clearly and slowly. She wanted desperately to drop the bandage and move closer to his head. But she needed to finish.

He settled again, long enough for the wrap to be finished. Colin gathered up the used first-aid supplies when they were done and exited the room, giving Claire a moment alone with Trevor. After removing her gloves, she sat delicately on the edge of the table and placed her hand on Trevor's chest.

"Trev?"

"Claire?" Trevor's voice was gravelly and hoarse. He groaned and touched his leg. The numbing would have taken effect by now, but the muscle around it was bound to be sore. Then, taking in a sharp breath, he quickly sat up, wrapping her in one arm and pulling her close, while his other hand searched the table for a gun.

His quick movement surprised her, but she was trained not to react. "Hey, it's okay," she said, placing her closest hand on top of the one searching for a gun. "You're safe. No one is shooting. You're safe."

He took a deep breath and looked around the room slowly. His grip on her didn't relax until he'd taken it all in. "Where are we?"

"Our safe house near D.C.," she said. "Colin and I came looking for you when we were alerted to your name on the flight manifest. I was worried. We found you unconscious. Two men were talking about killing you. They're gone now." She let a moment of silence pass before she asked the question she feared she already knew the answer to. "Are you going back to Rome to join Antonio?"

Trevor's expression was grim when he nodded. "Addie needs a heart transplant. Antonio said he could make it happen. The chances she'll get it without him are only fifty-fifty."

Claire's stomach dropped. She understood—hadn't she already proven tonight that she'd do the unthinkable for someone she loved?

"I understand now, why you did it, why you let me think you were dead," he said quietly.

"Sometimes there's... just no other option," she whispered.

Trevor pressed his lips to hers, a sweet and tender moment full of understanding. He tightened his arm around her, instinctively trying to pull her closer—then wincing as his leg reminded him.

"Your leg—and we're not alone," she murmured, gesturing with her head toward the living room, where Kane and Colin could probably hear every word.

He had nearly forgotten about his leg and the slight throbbing he felt radiating down to his foot and up to his hip. "How is my leg?"

"It's going to be really painful and take some diligent daily cleaning, but it'll be okay. It's a through-and-through, so we didn't stitch you up, but the bleeding is under control. You've had some numbing, but no antibiotics yet—we only have oral ones, so we had to wait until you were conscious. You've been out of it for about an hour."

A knock reverberated around the room, causing both of them to look up at Colin in the doorway. "Sorry to interrupt. Here is your phone. We removed the battery for safety," he said, passing over both items.

"Thanks. I should get out of your hair." Trevor let go of Claire and shifted toward the edge of the table. She protested, and when he put weight on his leg, a sharp shot of pain overwhelmed his nervous system.

Catching him around the torso, she took some of his weight. "You need to rest." She glared at Colin when he didn't immediately back her up.

With a sigh, Colin reluctantly agreed with her, offering to help Trevor up to Claire's room for the night—but only on one condition: he'd have to leave early in the morning. Trevor agreed, he too wanted to do everything they could to keep their hideaway safe.

Thanking Colin with a smile, she ducked into the kitchen to retrieve the oral antibiotics and then followed the boys upstairs.

When she got upstairs, Trevor was sitting on the edge of her bed while Colin was just leaving for his own room. Claire closed the door to her room, walking to him with a glass of water and the pills. Handing them over, he took them without preamble. When handing the water back to her, he let his hand linger on hers. He couldn't get enough of her touch. His pulse was increasing every second; whether it was from the pain or her nearness, he wasn't sure.

She placed his cup on the wooden bedside table before backing up a step. A nervous energy hit her like a tidal wave. He was lying in her bed and they'd be alone for more than fifteen minutes for the first time in seven years. She was used to facing down armed men, sprinting across rooftops, and disarming bombs—but this? Being here with him, alone, after all this time? That was nerve-racking.

"You should rest," she said softly. "Is there—"

"I don't want to sleep." Trevor's voice was hoarse, threaded with emotion. "Come here," he said, stretching out his hand toward her.

Claire's breath stalled. He looked at her like he used to, with so much love it was all-consuming. If she stood there any longer, she didn't know what she would do—break down into tears from relief, hold on to him and never let go, or let the lust that was growing with every second burn up all of her nerves and take over. "Why don't I go get you some pain meds?"

She turned away from him, stepping toward the door when he stood on his good leg and reached for her hand. Claire felt so hot at that moment she was surprised he didn't recoil—like he'd just touched a hot iron.

A little unsteady, he pulled on her hand, encouraging her to turn back to him. "You saved my life, you know."
"Always. Plus, I owed you for lying," she whispered, her stomach and heart leaping. She was so overwhelmed with emotions now, she didn't know what she was feeling anymore.

"No," he rasped. "You don't owe me a damn thing." His fingers touching her cheek. She couldn't help pressing a quick kiss to his mouth. "If this is the last safe moment we get…I'm not wasting it."

Then he kissed her, slow and deliberate, like he needed to memorize the feel of her. His other hand wrapped around her waist and pulled her against him. Her lips were as soft as he had remembered. The smell of vanilla shampoo she had always loved wafted around them every time her head moved.

Letting herself give in to her deepest desires, she traced his body the way she'd dreamed about so many times. He radiated heat as she traced the ridges of his abs. He had always been fit, but now he was sculpted. Every kiss grew with intensity and passion.

When Trevor fell back against the bed, Claire broke the kiss, ready to catch him, ease him down. But he had already caught himself with his hand and was lowering to a sitting position. "You really do need to rest. I'll just go—"

"Don't you dare. I can kiss you and rest at the same time," Trevor said, scooting back on the bed so his back rested against the pillows again. "See, I'm resting—now come here."

Claire smirked when he used the hand on her waist to pull her against the bed.

She was very aware of his injured leg and sat down gingerly next to him, balancing on the edge of the mattress. Trevor shook his head and pulled her on top of him in a swift and graceful movement. He guided her legs so she was kneeling, straddling him. She made sure to keep all her weight shifted to his right side. Then, sliding one hand into her hair and the other beneath her, he pulled her close and pressed his lips to hers again. This time, he didn't start slow—he needed her... all of her.

They had never been together like this before. As his hands fell lower to her hips and found the edge of her t-shirt, he broke the kiss to ask, "Can I?"

"Please," Claire said breathlessly.

Trevor removed her shirt, tossing it to the floor. Pulling on the hem of his shirt he raised his arms, allowing her to slide his shirt off too. His dogtags hanging around his neck caught her eye. A physical reminder of everything he had been through without her.

He broke her train of thought when he leaned in to kiss her neck, the feeling of his mouth on her skin was overwhelming in the best way. He trailed down, kissing her collarbone as she ran her fingers through his hair. With his hands caressing her ribcage as he went, he stopped when his hands brushed over a raised scar. Pulling back he looked at her right ribcage, running his fingers over it again gently, a sad look on his face.

"I got it in the crash." She said, watching his face.

Leaning down he kissed it, gently, softly before continuing as low as he could without bending before returning to kiss her lips again. Trevor whispered into Claire's ear, "I love you. One day, I *will* marry you and we *will* have a life together."

Claire felt her heart swell with love. Her eyes burned as tears welled up. Maybe she could still have the life they'd always dreamed of. She pulled back, needing to look into his blue-green eyes. "I love you too."

Slamming his lips back down on hers, he poured everything he was feeling into the kiss. They both knew that their future was going to have to wait and it was going to be a long, torturous one. But at least they would have this night to think of. They'd love one another as much—and as many times—as they could until sunrise.

The bedroom door didn't open again until the first rays of

sunlight were bouncing off the ocean waves and into the window. Neither Claire nor Trevor had slept a wink, having savored every second they had together.

21
What the Fire Left Behind

By late morning, Claire slid into the driver's seat while Colin helped Trevor limp toward the van. Trevor needed to get to stop at a pharmacy before heading to the airport for his flight to Italy. Colin had offered to drive him, but Claire insisted. She wanted every last minute with him she could steal.

Trevor lay down across the back seat, keeping out of sight. The old minivan smelled faintly musty, its worn carpet stained by time. When he bent his knees to fit, pain stabbed through his thigh. His vision pinched at the edges for a second. Even with the pain meds, a deep, sharp pain knifed through him every time he tensed his leg. Trevor dreaded the physical therapy he knew he would need to get his leg back to normal.

In the meantime, Kane had hacked a pharmacy system and placed a request for antibiotics, pain meds, and a crutch to get Trevor through the next few days. When Claire had asked him to send in the order, Kane had only grunted in response—he was still a little testy about having Trevor there in the first place.

As she drove, she felt his fingertips brush the back of her arm. "Yes?"

"Nothing... you're just too far away."

Claire chuckled under her breath. "We were touching for six

hours straight. That wasn't enough for you?" she teased, reaching her hand back behind the seat and intertwining her fingers with his.

"Nope. Not even close." She could hear the cheeky smile in his voice.

They spent the rest of the drive hand-in-hand, talking about Addie. He had called just before they left to get an update from his mom. Addie was still sleeping but doing well. All of her vitals were holding steady and the doctors were still anticipating her going home in two weeks.

It was only about fifteen minutes to the next town over. When Claire pulled into the parking lot of the small mom-and-pop pharmacy, she went in alone. They were determined to keep Trevor's face off any digital camera feeds, knowing that Antonio was going to have questions about what happened and where Trevor had been all night. A link back to Claire would only put him in more danger.

Once Claire got what they needed, she pulled the minivan back onto the main road. Every few minutes, she checked the mirror, cataloging plates—no tail in sight. When she turned onto a narrow highway, sunlight flickered through the trees and across the windows. The faint hum of tires on asphalt mixed with Trevor's quiet chatter from the back seat.

When they reached a long stretch of road without cameras or stoplights, she eased the minivan onto the shoulder and parked. A small green-and-white sign marked mile 156 on the two-lane highway. They were a few minutes early for Trevor's scheduled taxi.

Claire stepped out and scanned the treeline—no trail cams, no utility boxes. Clear. Moving to the trunk, she tucked the meds and a few wound-care items into his backpack before unloading his bags. When she finished, she rounded the minivan to meet Trevor, who was adjusting the crutch to his height. His jaw flexed as he shifted his weight—too fast—and the wound lit up, hot and deep.

Sitting on the bench seat sideways, he stretched his injured leg out the door in front of him before setting the crutch aside.

The light rustling of leaves floated in the air as he watched the woman he loved approach.

"All set?" Claire asked as Trevor grabbed her hand and pulled her to stand between his legs.

"No. You forgot something," he said, catching her wrist and drawing her close, tilting his face up to meet her lips.

The kiss wasn't nearly long enough for either of them, but his ride was coming and she needed to be out of sight when the taxi arrived. "I would never forget to kiss you goodbye." She pulled an old flip phone from her back pocket, handing it to him before speaking again, "It's old, but the number is clean and it works. All of our burner numbers are programmed into it. But you can only use it once—after that, ditch it. And it's got a password on it, the date of the last day we saw each other before everything happened."

"So I shouldn't just call when I'm missing you?" Trevor smirked, taking the phone and zipping it into his jacket pocket.

Claire just smiled and rolled her eyes at him. "As much as I would love that, maybe save it for an emergency."

"Deal."

"Promise me you'll get out if it gets too dangerous," she said. "I know you can handle yourself, but if we ever want a future, we both have to survive."

"Okay, but only if you promise the same thing," he said. A part of him knew she'd never be able to promise that, not if it meant walking away from getting justice for her parents. But it made him feel better to hear her say it.

"I promise I'll do everything I can to come back to you safely."

He stood, keeping his weight on his good leg and tucking the crutch under his left arm. Then, cupping her face with both hands, he kissed her like it could make everything go away—they could go back to lying in one another's arms for the rest of the day. The soft skin of her neck felt like velvet beneath his fingers. Her lips were demanding and intoxicating enough to drive him mad.

They forced themselves to separate. The taxi would be here

any moment. Trevor grabbed his jacket and hobbled back to his belongings. Before rounding the van, she called out to him. "Trev, I love you."

"I love you too."

Claire slid into the driver's seat and drove down the road to a turnoff, where the car would be hidden enough that she could still see Trevor through the trees. They'd picked the spot after finding it on satellite maps that morning. When the taxi appeared a minute later, the driver exited and helped Trevor. The driver, a middle-aged man with kind eyes, helped him settle into the car before loading the bags.

When the taxi pulled away, Claire waited two minutes before exiting her hiding spot and driving back to the safe house. She knew Kane was tracking the taxi and would call if anything went awry—but unease still twisted in her gut as she drove the minivan down the tree-lined highway.

* * *

Trevor

When the plane landed in Rome, Trevor stretched his back while being careful not to move his leg too much. He was grateful that he had packed a set of loose sweatpants that didn't put pressure on his leg. Just in case Antonio wanted to see the evidence, he had made sure to keep the destroyed jeans from the night before. He wasn't naïve. Despite being his biological son, Antonio didn't trust anyone.

Trevor maneuvered through the airport in a daze, his mind bouncing between thoughts of Claire, the pain in his leg, and what he was going to tell Antonio. At baggage claim, a young couple offered to assist him with his bags. His leg was throbbing, and he had no idea how he was going to use his crutch and push a baggage cart, so when they offered, he accepted the help. Each step sent a sick, bright jolt up his hip, and he had to stop twice just to breathe through it. When they exited customs, he was once again picked up by the same driver from the week before.

He thanked the couple as his driver took the cart, and then limped out into the early morning. The sun was just rising, creating a pink and orange sky. Sliding into the car, Trevor noticed his driver shot off a text message before beginning to load his bags. He fully expected it to be a message to Antonio about his leg.

Sure enough, when the driver got into the car, he spoke in a thick Italian accent and gestured to his leg. "Signore, doctor?"

Shaking his head, Trevor answered, "No."

Not waiting for a response, he turned his head and looked out the window. Instead of driving into the city center, like they had a week ago, the car veered off onto a different highway after leaving the terminal. Circling the city, they passed by large country estates, farmland, and wineries before pulling up to what could only be called a palace—or a compound.

Turning onto a long, square cobblestone driveway, the car came to a stop in front of a wrought-iron gate. Waving a key fob, the gate opened and the car bounced down the drive between two stone fences that had been overtaken by winding wisteria branches. When the narrow driveway opened into a circular roundabout, Trevor could see a butler waiting with two servants at his side.

The car came to a stop after turning around a central stone-carved flower planter in the middle of the driveway. All around him was greenery, historical stone, and an old-world luxury that didn't exist in the States. Trevor noticed the cameras strategically placed around the grounds as they drove.

Exiting the car, he grabbed his jacket, making sure to keep his new phone safe. But when he stepped out of the car, he struggled with the foot of his crutch on the cobblestones. He nearly lost his balance before the butler rushed to his aid. White-hot pain flashed and his stomach rolled, but he locked it down before it showed on his face. Trevor was exhausted from staying awake all night with Claire the night before, and despite having slept a little on the plane, it hadn't been enough. With the throbbing in his leg, combined with his exhaustion, he was excited to get to his room.

Domenico, the butler, introduced himself and apologized that Antonio wasn't there to greet Trevor himself. He had stepped away for an urgent meeting and should be home in a few hours. In the meantime, he suggested that Trevor get settled. The servants would bring his bags up to his room. Domenico was an older Italian gentleman, about the same age as Trevor's grandparents; he had a wide nose and dark, thick eyebrows that contrasted with his white hair. Entering through a large set of double doors, he also explained that traditionally a tour was given. However, it might be best if that waited until he wasn't limping.

Inside, the villa had renovations and modern touches mixed with the classic Italian Renaissance architecture. The rooms were grand with high ceilings and stone floors. Unlike outside, there were no cameras that Trevor could see. The home was beautiful, breathtaking, but there was a sense of unease in the air. Like, if the walls could talk, they'd have seen some awful things.

At the bottom of the stairs, they paused so Domenico could point out the dining room, formal living room, and his father's office. Anytime someone called Antonio his "father," Trevor felt his jaw tense instinctively. He would have to work on not reacting when they did.

The stairs took him longer than he would have liked to admit, but Trevor pushed through, refusing to stop when Domenico suggested it.

"You're as stubborn as your father," Domenico said. The comment made Trevor tense again. He knew it was meant kindly, but the words still scraped.

To the right at the top of the stairs, and two doors down, was Trevor's room, a large room that looked like it was meant more as a master bedroom than a secondary. The opulence reminded him of the Palazzo d'Oro, and he briefly wondered why anyone would want to live in such grandeur all the time.

When they reached the bed, the butler helped him ease down onto the edge. Trevor lay his jacket next to him on the bed and shifted himself back so he was supported. Without being asked, Domenico placed the crutch between the bed and the nightstand so that Trevor could still reach it if need be. "Sir, may I get you anything while you settle in?"

"No, thank you." He could already feel his eyes growing

heavy with sleep. It felt like he had only blinked, but when he opened his eyes again, the butler was gone. Letting his eyes fall again, he was almost asleep when he realized he needed to hide his new phone. Unzipping his pocket, he removed it from his jacket and looked around the room. A large wooden wardrobe stood tall across from the bed, and a wooden desk sat beneath a large picture window to his right. Deciding it would be best to separate the battery and the phone, Trevor got up and hobbled to the desk.

His mother was a big fan of vintage chairs, and he knew from watching her reupholster one that they often had a webbing made from canvas on the underside. Gently lifting the chair and glancing underneath, he noted that this one had the webbing. It was close enough together that he could slip the flat battery between the weave. But before slipping the battery inside, he made sure he could get his fingers in far enough to pull it back out again. He could. Pushing it up into the webbing, then making sure it was flat and undetectable, he returned the chair to where it was.

Next he limped over to the wardrobe, a tall free-standing unit with hanging space above and two drawers beneath. He did his best not to swear or grunt from pain as he got onto his knees, feeling the bottom of the lower drawer. It was a fully closed unit, meaning there was an enclosed space behind the drawers where he could hide the phone. The drawers didn't come out easily, but if tilted at just the right angle, he was able to get the top one out.

He was just opening the phone to remove the SIM card when he heard creaking out in the hallway. Was it just the house settling or were they coming to deliver his bags? He held his breath, waiting. But when no knock came, he continued, a little faster now. After removing the SIM card he placed the phone down behind the bottom drawer, then replaced the top one.

He didn't need to think much about where he would hide the SIM card. Inside his leather jacket, the inside chest pocket had a small hole leading into the enclosed cavity between the lining and the leather. The hole was just big enough to slip the card into. When he had bought the jacket, the lining had seen better years, with many holes in it, but a few years ago he had decided to have the lining replaced. He thought the hole had come from a sharp pen tip he had placed in there and forgotten about.

Practically collapsing on the bed, Trevor fell into a deep sleep.

Sudden knocking at the door woke him. A quick glance at his military watch told him that he had gotten about three hours of sleep. When the knock came again, Trevor called out, "Come in."

Domenico opened the door. "Your father would like to see you."

Trevor knew he shouldn't make Antonio wait, not after everything that happened the night before with the guns. He didn't know for sure what had happened with the cops, but he knew something was off. His memory was hazy—being shot would do that—but he was sure the cops fired first. What kind of cops did that? The dirty or fake kind.

Grabbing his crutch, Trevor followed Domenico out of his room and down the hall to the main staircase. He felt much sturdier on his feet since he'd gotten some sleep, but the pain was building again; he'd need meds soon. With help, he made it down the stairs and to the imposing office doors. After knocking, Domenico stepped back and waited for an answer. When Antonio called out to enter, he simply opened the door for Trevor and then disappeared, letting the door close softly behind him. The older man's presence had calmed him slightly, and without him now, he felt his nerves begin to race.

Instinctively, he stood tall and stared ahead, his soldier training ingrained in every movement. When Antonio looked up from behind his imposing desk, he showed no surprise at his son's condition. A second man stood to Antonio's left, as if they had been going over some maps. The man was broad and imposing with a thinning head of hair and dark eyes.

"Sit. Are you going to tell me what happened?" Antonio was all business.

Trevor knew exactly what he was referring to: the shooting, the guns, and the two dead men. But the question was: could he lie to Antonio? If he lied and Antonio found out, he might not get Addie the heart. But if he told him the truth, that Claire had rescued him, Antonio would have questions that could put her in danger, and Trevor had no idea how much Antonio actually knew. Admitting about Claire's presence last night could also put Addie's heart at risk, if Antonio thought he was conspiring with a CIA agent. He had to protect them both, he had to lie.

Before he could give him any details, though, a brief knock reverberated through the large wooden doors, and an older man with a hospital bag stepped through. Rising, Antonio welcomed the man in with a gesture.

"Good, Vittorio. Trevor, this is Dr. Mancini. He's going to look at your leg."

Confused, Trevor looked at the doctor, who strode across the room and set his bag on Antonio's desk like he'd been here a hundred times. "Please remove your trousers." His accent was thick, and he looked so old that Trevor wasn't sure the doctor should even be practicing.

"Trevor." Antonio's tone was demanding, leaving no room for arguing. Instead of sitting back down, he remained standing, occasionally taking a few steps like an interrogator might.

He stood on his good leg, using the armchair for support. He pulled the elastic band of his sweatpants over his hips and let them drop. He freed only his left foot, leaving the fabric pooled around his good ankle, and lowered himself back into the chair, careful not to let the wound touch the upholstery.

Dr. Mancini finished pulling on gloves, then began to unwrap and examine Trevor's wound. It was sore and still very fresh, but there wasn't much blood and no sign of infection.

"Now tell me what happened, Trevor."

This was it—he had to lie. One lie to protect the woman he loved and the heart his sister needed.

He winced in pain as the doctor probed at his leg. When he did, the man at Antonio's desk smiled, seemingly enjoying his pain. Trevor ignored him, doing his best to think straight despite the pain. He spoke as he would to a commanding officer. "Yes, sir... I was showing the two buyers the delivery when the police pulled into the lot... and opened fire on us. I was hit in the leg... and lost consciousness. When I passed out... the others were exchanging fire with the police."

When the doctor poured saline onto a piece of gauze and touched his leg again, he nearly doubled over from the pain. His hands gripped the armrests hard enough to make the wood creak, but he kept talking, "After I came to, the men were dead... and the cases were empty. The police were gone."

"Did you leave behind evidence that could be traced?" There was no sign of Antonio even pretending to be worried about his son. Trevor knew he only cared about himself, but this felt like torture.

"No, I lit the car on fire... stole an old car that was left in the parking lot."

"Did you go to the hospital?" Antonio's eyebrows dipped.

The doctor pressed clean gauze into his leg and began to redress it.

"No... I didn't want a record. I treated it myself." Trevor met Antonio's eyes. He looked satisfied—whether with the answers or the pain, Trevor wasn't sure.

Removing his gloves, Dr. Mancini simply nodded at Antonio and began packing his bag.

"You can put your trousers back on. What did you do with the car?" Antonio's voice shifted. Where it was cold before, now he sounded almost parental. He walked around to his desk chair and finally sat. As he relaxed into the high-back chair, the imposing man took a step back, as to respect his boss.

Trevor slowly bent over, retrieved his pants, and with great effort managed to slip his foot back in and pull them up. Neither man moved to help him—compassion had no place in this room. "I ditched it in a bad neighborhood this morning and caught a taxi to the airport." Through all the pain caused by the examination, he had almost forgotten to be nervous. But now that it was done—now that his lie was out there—he felt relieved.

He was only just getting to sit down again when Antonio called out for his butler. "Domenico." He popped through the door so fast he had to have been waiting just outside. "Please escort my son back to his room; he needs to rest. And get him all of the supplies he'll need to take care of his wound." Domenico was already helping Trevor find his footing when Antonio continued, "Dinner is at 7:00 p.m. sharp, Trevor. I expect you there." With that, he waved them all off and went back to papers he had strewn across his desk.

Addressing the other man in the room as the doors closed, Trevor heard Antonio say his name."Enrico, let's get back to it—"

When Trevor returned to his room, he gripped the door handle and noticed the locks were on the outside of the door, not the inside. It could have been a mistake, but something in him didn't think so.

He found his bags placed in the corner, and a neat box of organized medical supplies had already been placed on his desk. Domenico left him to rest, telling him that he would return to assist him in finding something appropriate to wear for dinner.

It had only been a few hours, and already he felt like a prisoner—one who had been interrogated and tortured. Deciding he couldn't do this for too long, he'd play the dutiful son long enough to save Addie—and then he'd help Claire burn Antonio's empire to the ground.

22
Unmasked

Kane's fingers flew across the keyboard at lightning speed. Despite being up all night, adrenaline gave him a second—or maybe fourth—wind. Energy drink cans littered his desk; he was normally a tea-and-coffee drinker, but this tiny town was deprived of any decent choices. He'd rather drink the battery acid than suffer through bad coffee or tea.

It had been nearly two weeks since they had fled their apartments and he was beginning to get very frustrated. While he'd found the doctored reports and altered case files inside the CIA servers, getting anything that proved Hale's involvement was another story. Hale had moved the real evidence behind segmented vaults, rotating keys, and MFA tokens Kane didn't have—and every time Kane pushed too hard, the system pushed back: rate limits, dead drops, and honeytraps designed to flag whoever was snooping. He had barely left this dump of an abandoned house in that time, and the lack of evidence was starting to become an affront to his skills.

He'd get so close, and then the trail vanished—wiped. Kane suspected Hale had hired a second hacker to scrub every trace of wrongdoing. Until last night he had been one step behind the other hacker... for two weeks. The few things he had gotten his hands on—altered bank records, doctored files and a few cryptic text messages—didn't prove anything, not on their own.

If he could clear their names and take down Hale, they could have the full power of the CIA behind them to take down Antonio. However, Hale's footprints—digital and physical—the day of the bombing were clean. Too clean. But being squeaky clean wasn't a crime.

Last night he had decided to look into a few former associates of Antonio's, and one name stood out, Vincent DeRossi. He'd been born in Italy and lived there his whole life, working under Antonio—until he was just done. CIA records showed he had emigrated to Canada and then they mysteriously ended. When Kane took Vincent's old mugshot and ran it through facial recognition software, he got a cluster of potential matches—most garbage, a few plausible. It took an hour of image cleanup, lighting correction, and cross-referencing travel patterns before one result stopped being noise: Vince Gibson.

Vincent had entered the U.S. under the alias Vince Gibson a week before Max and Louisa's deaths—and stayed for two weeks. Over the last seven years, he'd crossed the border more than fifty times, always flying into D.C. and leaving from another city. Once Kane looked into hotel records for his alias, everything began to unravel.

Focusing on that first week that Vincent was in the country, Kane found not only hotel stays in D.C. and Chicago but also a video on a private social media page. The footage started on a young couple walking the streets of D.C. If you watched long enough, the camera turned—and behind the couple was a clear shot of both Vincent and Hale *together*. They were standing in an alley, deep in conversation.

Kane ran the clip through noise reduction, then muted the foreground audio. He pulled up the waveform and scrubbed until a phrase almost surfaced out of the static—fragmented, warped, the consonants chewed up. He had to run it through three passes and still couldn't swear it would hold up in court... but if you listen closely, watching their mouths, the words were unmistakable: "—

make sure they're actually dead."

The camera caught a flash of a thick white envelope passing between them.

He was just finishing enhancing the video's background audio when Colin came down the safe house stairs. "Have you moved since last night?"

Colin stepped closer when Kane didn't answer. Over his shoulder, he could see the video footage, zoomed in on Hale and Vincent. Instead of answering, Kane simply hit play.

Hale looked around the dirty alley; paranoid, he leaned in and spoke quietly, "I need it done quickly, today or tomorrow, and make sure they're actually dead. I don't know what evidence Max has on me."

It was not as obvious, but a flash of the white envelope passed between their hands.

"I need the full names and what about the kid?" Vincent was the opposite of Director Hale; he was calm, confident and focused on counting his money in the envelope.

Hale sighed as he shifted his body back and forth, "Max, Louisa, and Claire Huntington. I don't know what the kid knows or if Max has left anything for her, so get rid of her too. And make it look like an accident. I don't need an investigation."

"I will message you when it's done."

Hale nodded and scurried out of the frame just before the video ended.

They watched in stunned silence. Kane's grin widened slowly, disbelief and triumph warred in his face. Colin's jaw clenched. For the first time in weeks the future felt like something they might actually reach.

Kane leaned back in his chair, a beaming smile spreading across his face. "I got his ass," Kane said, then his grin faded. "And I probably tripped something doing it. If Hale's watching for this file, he'll know someone found it."

"Yes, but we need to also have proof that we didn't set the bomb. If we are clear, it'll hold more weight. And if they don't take it seriously enough, Hale could get away before they finish even analyzing it. Where are we on that?"

"Kill joy." Kane said under his breath. He sighed, sat up and swiveled around in his chair to look at Colin, "Dead in the water. The real footage is gone. Everything has been scrubbed. Unless we can figure out who set the bomb and find evidence on their side that exonerates us."

Colin sighed and rubbed his hand down his face. "Okay, I need coffee. Let me think on it."

The hot water was just finishing coming to a boil when footsteps sounded above, and Claire appeared at the top of the stairs a few seconds later. "Morning." She called out descending the steps.

The aroma of instant coffee overwhelmed the room as she took in their demeanors. Colin stood stoic as he stirred two mugs, his mind clearly somewhere else. While Kane stared blankly at his screen, it was eerie and unsettling. She'd never seen him just stare.

"What happened?" she asked, looking between them, concern filling her voice. Her heart began to race as anxiety flooded her veins, all of the worst-case scenarios filling her head.

Colin walked toward her, sipping on his coffee and holding a mug out for her. When he saw the look on her face, he spoke, "Everyone is okay. We found a video you need to see, but we have a problem with the bombing evidence."

Her pulse began to slow as he explained. "What's the problem?"

"There is none." Kane's voice was thick with irritation. He hadn't bothered to turn around when he spoke; he just stared at the computer screens, his arms folded across his chest. In that moment he reminded Claire of a teenage girl, pouting when she didn't get her way.

"Ignore him, he's feeling defeated." Walking toward Kane's back, Colin patted him on the shoulder, "Replay the video."

Claire watched the computer screen fill with movement as Marcus Hale stood talking to the shooter from the crash. Her hands went clammy, she felt her stomach twist making her nauseous. That face was burned into her brain and had fueled her nightmares for months after the crash. Part of her wanted to smash the computer screen; the other half wanted to crumble to the floor in sobs. That was the man who had killed her parents.

For a moment, the safe house dissolved. She was back in twisted metal and glass, the smell of blood, hearing her own screams—then hearing nothing at all but the ringing in her skull. The old, familiar urge rose in her throat like bile: *Run.*

She forced air into her lungs. Forced her hands to unclench. If she fell apart now, Hale still won.

This was it. They finally had what she'd bled for. And instead of triumph, all she felt was rage—because it had taken seven years for the truth to crawl into the light.

And they still needed to prove their innocence and take down Antonio. It took Claire a moment to realize Kane was talking—to hear him through the ringing and the rage.

"—everything regarding the bombing is gone. Hale's got someone else scrubbing every bit of evidence against him." Colin was calm as he spoke. "We just need to think of this from a different angle. Hale would have hired someone to do it. Who are the possible bombers we know of that have the skill level to do this?"

Getting comfortable, the three of them began thinking through all their old cases, looking into anyone who was skilled enough to create the bomb that had gone off.

Two hours later, Kane paced the room. Claire watched from her position on the floor as she stretched, all this tension had her feeling tight. Sitting at the kitchen table, Colin had a list in front of him. It was filled with names that they had brainstormed, but as each one was looked up, they were all quickly ruled out.

"What about Silas Ward?" Colin said, resting his head into his hand. He was resisting the urge to doodle.

"Isn't he serving life?" Kane questioned.

"Yeah, but it's worth it to double check."

Kane groaned deeply, plopping into his swivel chair so hard it bounced a little. Typing *Silas Ward* into the CIA database, the computer searched. After what felt like an eternity of the *spinning wheel of death*, an error message appeared on the screen.

NO RECORD

He recoiled in confusion and tried again. Same result. Hale had scrubbed the record.

Colin and Claire came to peek over his shoulder. "There's no record of him in our database."

"Try a public one." Claire suggested.

"Won't he have scrubbed the public database too?" Colin asked.

"Maybe not." Kane said, while pulling up another screen, going to the official government site for incarcerations. "Wiping public databases is loud. It leaves audit trails, triggers integrity alerts, and would get DHS and half the cybersecurity world crawling all over what he's trying to hide."

This time, when his name was typed into the search bar, records appeared in seconds—records that stated he was released *four* weeks ago.

"It's him. I remember when Hale arrested him personally and he could easily have copied the schematics." Colin was invigorated now. "He was notorious for keeping records; I'm surprised Hale would hire him. He must have been desperate. Kane, look up what you can on him and see if you can find his digital records."

"Already on it." Kane's fingers moved faster than Claire had thought possible.

Leaving Kane to do his thing, Claire and Colin went for a run, needing to work off some excess energy. Though they stuck to the fields and trails, both still made sure to wear hats and glasses, covering their faces. They were so close, they couldn't risk getting recognized now.

Colin scratched his jaw as they ran. "I can't wait to shave this stupid thing." His beard had filled in, growing to a solid quarter inch in length.

"It looks good on you, but I know it's itchy." As they ran Claire felt the soft late-summer breeze on her cheeks. If she closed her eyes, it almost felt like the world could come to a stop, and just for a minute, she'd have peace.

"It is. I've never been a big facial hair guy. I think Kane misses his though."

Claire laughed, her breathing steady. "I bet he does, he's not a fan of change. I really think you guys will be clear soon. You could go home. Shave."

He stopped in his tracks. "You won't go back?"

Claire stopped next to him, smiling halfway. "I don't know, it depends on the CIA. I lied, they may not want me back. They have grounds to arrest me."

"True, but you're helping bring down a mole. I think they'd look past it." Colin could be such an optimist; Claire loved it, but she also knew the truth. She'd probably serve a few years for fraud before she could really put this all behind her.

She smiled, wanting to let him have hope for the both of them. "Race you back to the house?" She took off sprinting before the suggestion had even processed in Colin's brain. He followed behind her. A few times he almost caught up to her, but she was fast, and over fifteen years of running every day would do that to you.

"Come on, old man," Claire yelled back at Colin as she rounded the corner of the house, running for the front door.

"Who are you calling old? I'm only a few years your senior!" Colin came to a skidding stop a few feet from Claire when they heard a "hell yeah" reverberate throughout the safe house.

Breaking back into a run, they burst through the front doors to find Kane standing, fists in the air, in front of his computer. They had come in so fast the front door had bounced back, nearly hitting Colin in the shoulder.

"I'm in!" Kane said, sitting back down and motioning to his computer. "I couldn't get into it the old fashion way because he had redundancies galore. So instead, I worked around it and piggybacked on one of his legacy devices—"

"What did you find?" Colin said, impatiently.

"Ugh, You really ruin my buzz sometimes Abs." Kane groaned but moved with his explanation. "You were right, Colin.

I was able to get into his cloud. He had everything backed up—recorded phone conversations, bank statements with the deposits highlighted; he even had the schematics sent to him from Hale's email."

The computer screen was filled with all the evidence they could need, proving Hale had hired Silas to bomb the National Monument.

Kane double clicked, raising up a minimized video, "He even had this—"

Hitting play, the video came to life. It was the original undoctored surveillance footage, showing Silas setting the bomb.

"So now what, are you going to take it in directly, or send it digitally?" Claire knew this was it, she might be separating from her friends for good. She'd be truly alone again—she had let herself get used to having a team, one that knew everything. People who she trusted with her life to have her back and this might be it.

"We send it digitally. If we wait to drive in, we could get caught on CCTV or Hale could get wind and see us coming." Colin made the decision for them.

"Agreed." Kane typed out an encrypted transfer of files directly to the Director of the CIA and FBI. He attached everything they had that proved their innocence, and Marcus Hale's guilt. The evidence didn't directly expose Claire's identity but she had no doubt they'd figure it out... if they hadn't already.

Kane hit send. For the first time in weeks, silence filled the safe house—like the calm before a storm.

23
The Reckoning

Twenty-four hours—the delayed silence was torture. Then an email arrived with a single line of instructions and a list of conditions: call in for a secure video chat, confirm identities on camera, and understand until further notice—they were still suspects.

On a secure, untraceable line, the three of them readied themselves to answer any and all questions. Before the video would connect, each of them had to show their ID badges for scanning, complete facial recognition, and enter their eighteen-digit passcodes.

When the video call finally connected, the Director of the Agency, DCI Leon, sat behind his desk with the Directors of HR and Legal, Smith and Jansen, across from him. The camera, mounted high on the wall to Leon's left, caught them all in frame.

Director Jansen began by asking each of them to recite their names and badge numbers for the record. Then she stated that the video was being recorded and that anything they said could be used against them. Claire's gut twisted as Kane and Colin recited their credentials. When it was her turn, she recited her badge number and then paused, almost saying her real name instead of her alias, Georgia Anderson.

"When did you first suspect Director Hale of being a mole?" DCI Leon was tall, his dark facial hair worn in a thick mustache. Usually polite, today he was all strict formality.

"Thirteen days ago, sir. I found the first altered files and looped in Officers Anderson and Bhatt. My access record should confirm that—unless it's been tampered with." Colin was clear and confident with his words, but Claire saw the truth as he fiddled with his watch just out of the camera's view.

She and Colin stood behind Kane's chair, carefully filling the frame and leaving nothing visible that could give their location away.

"Why didn't you come directly to me when you found this, Officer Davenport?"

Colin had met the DCI before and he considered for a moment why he hadn't gone to him with his suspicions. When he spoke, he was as honest as he could be. "I didn't want to accuse anyone without proof. We didn't know for sure until the night of the bombing," Colin said, voice even, but his hand restless on his watch. "Officer Anderson and I were on our way in the next morning with the evidence we had when we heard about it. After that, we knew we needed more. We had to prove we didn't plant the device before you'd believe us."

It went on for twenty more minutes, each one of them grilled for answers. It surprised all three of them when DCI Leon turned to each of the other directors and raised an eyebrow. They each nodded in turn before he returned his attention to the video call.

"We have enough to bring you in," Leon said. "Techs have been working overnight to verify your evidence. They were able to do so successfully. You have been cleared of the bombing. However, given the way you handled it—instead of coming directly to me—you will all be on probation. You will not be in charge and you will not improvise. Because you all had exemplary records before this incident, we are choosing to give you a faster return."

"Teams are already being assembled to move out and pick up Hale. Officers Davenport and Anderson, you may join the team breaching his home. Officer Davis is your team lead. Hale's not come in yet today. His phone and CCTV have him at home. Officer Bhatt, you may assist from your lab. If you're not here by 1200 hours, they'll roll out without you. We can't risk Hale getting wind of this."

Colin looked at his watch, "Yes, sir, we can be there."

"Good. You will be armed," Leon said. "Sidearms only. If you fire without authorization—you're done. Bhatt your screen will be monitored and watched by Officer Carmicheal."

"Yes, sir." They chorused.

The video call ended without another word.

Grabbing their badges, shoes, and keys, the team ran for the minivan. They would make it, but only just. Adrenaline flooded their veins as they climbed into the minivan and peeled out of the driveway, Colin behind the wheel.

They were already a few minutes down the road when Colin's eyes widened. Turning to Claire, he spoke, "Should you be going in? We should have said you were injured or unavailable. What if they know who you are? They'll arrest you on the spot."

Realization ran into Claire like a freight train. She didn't know what to say. They hadn't given any indication that they did know, but bringing her in under false pretenses would be something the CIA would do.

Kane spoke before anyone else could. "Give me a minute— I'll use my backdoor and see if anyone has reported anything that could indicate that they know."

The only sound that could be heard for two tense minutes was the whir of the engine and the hum of the tires on asphalt. Above them, the sky was clear and sunny, but dark clouds were gathering ahead—a storm rolling in like an omen.

Typing away on his phone, Kane finally said, "It looks like you're clear, at least for now. But you'll need to be careful. If anyone says anything, get out. Disappear. We'll find you."

She looked down at the soft leather bracelet around her wrist, grounding herself. She was so close now. She shouldn't risk arrest—but she couldn't miss seeing the look on Hale's smug face when the cuffs clicked shut. He may not have hit the car or pulled the physical trigger but he had set everything in motion. He was responsible for her parent's deaths. Marcus Hale had been her father's colleague—and he had still ordered them killed like cattle at a slaughter. She wasn't about to miss this.

"I'll be careful."

"We need a code word. If anyone hears or sees anything, we say it and you run." Colin's hands were gripping the wheel tight enough that his knuckles appeared white.

"Sushi," Kane said, like they had already discussed it.

Claire looked back at him from the front passenger seat, raising her eyebrows. "Why sushi?"

"Because I'm hungry, but also because if I see anything, I can ask an intern to order me sushi and it won't seem like I'm tipping you off."

It made perfect sense: Kane often ordered sushi for lunch, and it was a clear, distinct word. "Okay, sushi it is."

They pulled into headquarters, with only minutes to get suited up and get out to the van. Once they were through security, Kane wordlessly raised a hand with a stiff wave as he veered off toward the elevators.

When Claire and Colin entered the loading dock, the DCI was waiting with three six-person teams ready to load up. They were given vests and comms to put on before being given weapons. Every other officer was holding their long arm rifles, already suited up, and waiting. Claire could feel their eyes on her, silently judging.

"Officers," DCI Leon nodded as they raced toward the open van doors. Claire couldn't read the older man—if he knew who she was, he gave no sign.

The vans loaded in seconds. Static hissed in their earpieces as Kane came through.

"Welcome to my funhouse! Today, we capture the lion tamer. Can everyone hear me?"

Someone cleared their throat behind Kane's shoulder. "Yes, Carmichael. Why don't you sit down and learn some things." Kane's sass was clear even from floors away.

Claire caught Colin's eye, they both knew how much Officer Carmicheal aggravated Kane, but he needed to be professional, they were on probation after all.

A chorus of mumbled 'yeses' and snickers echoed through the comms as engines roared to life in unison. The sound was a low, coordinated growl that vibrated through the van's metal hull. The convoy peeled out of headquarters and onto the highway, sirens off and lights dark. The sky hung heavy with gray clouds, pressing low over the city as they cut through traffic, every second stretching thin.

Claire sat beside Colin on one of the back benches, eyes fixed on the route displayed on the GPS—Hale's address glowing like a target. Her pulse drummed in rhythm with another officer's foot tapping. The quiet before an arrest always felt like a storm building, but this was more; Hale had been one of their own. Claire could feel the weight of this moment pressing down like a barbell as they turned into Hale's neighborhood.

Marcus Hale's home was modern, large, and full of windows. The irony wasn't lost on Claire—there was so much glass for a man full of secrets. The convoy stopped, blocking the street. Armed officers filed out in formation. Six rounded the mansion's left side, with two peeling off at each door they passed. Officers from the second van went around the right side leaving three at the garage. Finally, Colin and Claire followed Officer Davis toward the front of the house.

Kane's voice rang out through the comms. "His phone signal has him in the kitchen on the north side of the house, main level."

"On my mark, breach!" Davis's voice rang out as another officer smashed the door with a battering ram. The wood splintered around the frame as it swung free, and the rest of the team surged forward. Echoes of other doors around the house could be heard flying open and hitting walls.

Firearms raised and ready, Davis signaled two officers toward the dining room on the left and three more up the stairs. Claire tapped his shoulder to tell him he was clear to move ahead.

Despite their heavy gear, they moved like shadows—silent,

precise. Davis was first into the expansive kitchen, taking the right side, while Claire and Colin took the left. She'd expected Hale to be at the kitchen table, calmly sipping a cappuccino—or fighting his way out. But neither happened. He simply wasn't there.

"Clear," echoed again and again, each call stripping away the last of Claire's adrenaline. Hale wasn't here. Defeat filled the home as the sky opened up and began dumping rain.

"Kane, start searching CCTV. He's not here." Davis's jaw tightened and his fists clenched.

Claire walked around the kitchen, spotting Hale's phone plugged into a charger against the back of the counter. Either he had forgotten it when he fled, or he had deliberately left it as a false beacon to give him more time to get away. She didn't dare touch it; a forensics team would collect it.

"What about his cars? Are any missing from the garage?" Another team leader asked over the comms.

A quick response from another officer. "No, both are here."

"There are empty hangers in the closet."

"I've got an open and empty safe in the office." Officers from around the house added in what they were seeing. It was obvious he had run.

Someone had tipped him off, and if Claire had to bet on it—he was already gone.

Kane didn't find anything on CCTV. It was like Hale had vanished.

* * *

Kane

Back at headquarters, Kane sat in the dim glow of his monitors, a pen in his mouth, as he chewed absently on the cap. Every monitor had a different system searching for Hale: facial recognition, passport, credit-card usage. His disappearance didn't make sense; the timing was too perfect. Someone inside had tipped him off, and Kane intended to find out who.

Officer Carmicheal was breathing down his neck, as if she couldn't see the monitors—each one the size of a tv.

He'd been combing through the CIA's internal comm logs

for hours when a string of archived messages caught his eye. They were encrypted using an old clearance cipher—the kind only senior analysts or high-level assistants had access to. He bypassed the firewall and began to decrypt it.

The signature popped up first: K33N-VK.

Kane frowned, leaning closer. Valerie Keene.

The messages popped up next. Weeks of them between Valerie and Hale, starting years ago. They'd discussed which files to alter, who needed to be "redacted," and meetings with so-called "foreign ambassadors." The code was thinly veiled—'foreign ambassadors' clearly meant mob members, and 'redacted' referred to eliminating someone or erasing their records. There was money, too. Hale had wired deposits into an offshore account under the alias *Florence Howard.*

Kane exhaled sharply through his nose. Kane's first instinct was to curse loud enough to shake the building, but he bit it back just in time. Glancing back over his shoulder at his warden, he gave her a grimace.

Looking back at his monitor, he pulled up Valerie's other computer logs and found more encrypted interactions—this time with the username 'E.Cross/IT-Intern.' An intern's account. One that shouldn't even have access to classified storage. He cracked open the audit records, scrolling through the timestamps.

"Evan Cross," Kane muttered aloud, recognition hitting. "The kid from records management."

Evan's profile was spotless—no red flags, no disciplinary actions, not even a late login. But there it was: he'd 'redacted' half a dozen of Hale's encrypted folders the morning after the bombing—the same ones that had vanished from the database. Including Silas Ward's file.

Kane's jaw tightened, forgetting he was chewing on the pen until the plastic cracked. It was possible Evan hadn't known what was going on—he'd been used. The intern's digital signature was all over the deletion protocols, but the access command had originated from Valerie's terminal. She'd told him what to do, feeding him false orders under Hale's authority. He probably thought he was helping, a special assignment.

"Damn," he whispered, this time not caring if Carmicheal heard him.

Pushing back from his desk, he grabbed his tablet and stormed down the hall toward the elevators, his babysitter close on his heels. She was asking him questions in her whiny high pitched tone but he ignored her. He had to show this to the DCI ASAP. The soles of his shoes smacked against the concrete floors as he did his best to walk calmly. He'd seen Valerie at her desk earlier and didn't want to alert her that he'd uncovered the messages.

Stepping into the elevator, he turned, Carmichael only just getting through the closing doors in time. Looking past her at the last minute to see if Valerie was still at her desk. Still there. She was either arrogant enough to think they wouldn't catch her—or she had something big to leverage.

Exiting the elevator, Kane strolled past the secretary, not stopping when she spoke.

Stopping short halfway down the hall, he turned, nearly causing his ball and chain to run into him. "I'm going to the DCI's office obviously. You can see me from here. Why don't you wait." He smiled sweetly, turning on his heel before returning to his mission.

To his surprise she did as he requested.

His fist was in the air, ready to knock when a voice filtered through the heavy wooden door.

"—Anderson's real identity is confirmed," a familiar voice said from inside. It was DCI Leon.

Kane froze.

"Georgia Anderson is an alias," Leon continued. "Her name is Claire Huntington. She's not to leave the building once she returns."

Kane's pulse spiked; the words ringing in his ears like a gunshot.

For a second, the world narrowed to the sound of his own pulse. Then, with quiet precision, he stepped back and forced his breathing steady. Kane had to warn her.

Pulling his comm from his pocket, he slid it in and whispered, "Sushi."

* * *

Claire

Static crackled softly in Claire's earpiece as she swept the last hallway of Hale's mansion. The steady rhythm of rain against the windows echoed through the quiet rooms. The sky had grown darker with each passing hour. She paused at a framed photograph: Hale shaking a senator's hand. The familiar twist of anger rose in her chest.

She couldn't help thinking her father could have done all of this—become a director, met with senators, led a department, and made a difference—if Hale hadn't murdered him.

They'd been stuck here for hours when she should have been out hunting Hale. But they had to wait while forensics got what they needed. While she tamped down her anger and impatience, the faint hum of comm chatter broke through. It was Kane's voice. Calm. Too calm.

"Sushi."

With that single word, her anger switched to panic. She turned instinctively toward Colin across the hall; he was already looking at her.

She didn't speak. She didn't dare. But with that shared look, she knew he had heard it too.

Without a sound, Claire unclipped her comm from her ear, letting the tiny device fall into her palm. The metallic click of her vest buckles followed—soft, deliberate—before she set both pieces on a hall table, along with her sidearm. Her chest tightened, the weight of understanding pressing down like lead. They knew who she was.

She looked back at her partner one last time. Colin's lips pressed into a firm line, a near-invisible nod—*go.*

And she did.

They were on the top floor, so Claire slipped out a balcony door into the storm. The wind sliced at her face. Propelling off the railing like a vaulter, she somersaulted twice, landing on the lawn below. The wet ground squelched with every step as she ran across the slick grass. The world blurred as lightning streaked through the sky. Thunder chased her as her boots hit the edge of the trees that lined Hale's property. Mud splattered up her legs as she disappeared into the dark tangle of trees and brush.

Branches scratched her arms. She knew she had a head start; it would take a moment before anyone realized she was gone. But she didn't look back; she just kept putting one foot in front of the other. Hale was gone, and now she was too.

Once again, Claire Huntington vanished into the night.

24
Leverage

Claire's boot popped free from the mud with a wet suction, sending a spray of brown across her pant leg. She was nearly back to the safe house. Rain had chased her the whole way, soaking her hair and jacket until both clung to her skin. Thank God for her boots—if she'd worn sneakers, every step would've squelched.

The woods behind Marcus Hale's property were dense but shallow. The last little bit of natural foliage that hadn't been bulldozed. She didn't waste time trying to disappear in them. After a few minutes of hard sprinting, she cut perpendicular to the road instead of heading straight toward it. Once she reached the main road, she waited in the trees until traffic thinned. She flagged down a local headed toward the highway and caught a ride.

When she saw a busy gas station, she asked the driver to pull over, then darted across to disappear within the large semitrucks. One of the semis stood out: a flatbed with a tarp she could easily disappear under. She waited until the driver finished refueling, his back turned, then dicked under the tarp. She rode it as long as she dared, then jumped off when the truck slowed for traffic and dashed for the nearest cluster of trees.

Lightning tore across the sky, followed by thunder that shook through her bones. She'd kept to the trees along the road, invisible to passing drivers, but now the quickest route back cut straight through an open field—in the middle of a lightning storm, fully exposed. The safest option was to stick to the trees, but she'd have to go miles farther east and double back. She couldn't afford to waste time.

She waited, counting the seconds between flash and impact.

The CIA might already know where they'd been hiding. If officers reached the house first, every trace of her would be catalogued, bagged, and logged. She needed her go bag and her backup weapon before they arrived. She'd try to make contact with Colin or Kane after that, but first she had to hide.

Her pulse thundered in her ears as she watched the roiling sky. When the timing was right, she ran. The ground was slick; mud clung treacherously to her boots. Twice she slid, catching herself before she went down. When she reached the far side, she ducked back under the trees—just in time to see lightning rip through the ground where she'd been seconds earlier. The ground smoked. That could have been her.

Branches clawed at her sleeves as she pushed through the brush toward the safe house. When the roofline appeared through the trees, she slowed. No tire tracks, no lights, no shadows moving inside. It looked clear. Still, her hand went automatically to her hip—only to find it empty. No sidearm. She'd left the CIA-issued weapon at Hale's and hadn't brought her backup.

Weaponless, she crept out of the woods, keeping low. The windows were dark. Everything looked untouched. Sprinting across the last few yards left her exposed, but she didn't have a choice. Circling the building, she stuck close to the wall of the house, listening for any movement, and checking her sightlines. Only when she was confident that she was alone did she slip inside, exhaling as the door shut behind her.

Mud streaked the hardwood as she ran for the stairs. She hadn't unpacked; grabbing her things took seconds. Hugh had taught her to live ready to leave at a moment's notice. She grabbed her backup firearm and tucked it into the back of her jeans. Her go bag slung over her shoulder, Claire was halfway back to the stairs when a floorboard creaked below.

She froze.

Every muscle locked.

Someone was in the house.

Holding her breath, she slipped her phone from her pocket and angled the screen like a mirror toward the stairwell.

Kane stood in the entryway, hands on his hips, glaring at the muddy footprints. "Seriously? I'm not cleaning this up, Claire."

Relief broke through her tense muscles so fast she laughed under her breath. Coming down a few steps, she met his eyes over the railing. "How did you get away?"

He gave her a look that screamed obvious. "I walked out. After telling the DCI that Valerie Keene and an intern were in on it."

Her brows furrowed. "What about Colin?"

"He's meeting us at the airstrip."

"Airstrip?"

"Grab our go bags," Kane said, already turning toward his worktable. "I'll explain in the car. We don't have time to dawdle."

He started packing his equipment with practiced efficiency, cords and hard drives vanishing into his bag. Over his shoulder, he added, "Take anything you don't want the CIA bagging into evidence. They're not far behind me. We've got,"—he checked his watch—"five minutes, give or take."

Claire didn't need to be told twice. She bolted down the hall, grabbing Colin's and Kane's bags, sweeping up anything personal. The rain beat harder against the windows, echoing her pulse.

They were out of time.

Kane was already halfway out the door when Claire caught up to him, the rain coming down in sheets as they sprinted toward the van. Tossing their bags in the trunk, they rounded the van— Kane taking the driver's side. The engine roared to life and tires spat mud as she slammed the door shut.

"Now tell me what's going on," she demanded.

Kane flicked his windshield wipers on. "While I was with the DCI, I got an alert." He tossed his burner phone at her, still streaked with raindrops. A photo filled the screen—Marcus Hale, grainy but unmistakable, stepping onto a private jet. "Caught on a private hangar camera forty minutes ago. Destination on the flight manifest—Rome."

Claire's pulse quickened. "Italy."

"Yep." Kane's mouth twisted into something between irritation and disbelief. "Apparently, he didn't waste any time running back to Antonio's territory. Leon said Colin and I had passed his little test and wanted us to prove ourselves by following him to Rome—said to bring Hale in by any means necessary. And of course he wanted us to take a baby sitter."

Claire's stomach knotted. "And you said?"

"I said no." Kane threw her a quick glance. "Told him we started this with you, and we're damn well going to finish it with you. He didn't like that answer."

She could almost picture the scene—Kane's stubborn defiance, the flash of the DCI's temper. "You walked out," she said quietly.

"Not before leaving a little parting gift." Satisfaction coloring his voice. "My service weapon and badge—right on Leon's desk. Last thing I saw before the elevator doors closed was Valerie Keene being cuffed. They had her against the wall while another officer cleaned out her desk into evidence bins. When they turned her toward interrogation, I caught her eye. She'd been trying to talk her way out of it, of course. But when she saw me, I waved."

Despite everything, Claire couldn't help the small, exhausted laugh that escaped her. "You're unbelievable."

"Yeah," Kane said, eyes fixed on the storm-dark road ahead. "But at least I'm consistent." A smirk tugging at his mouth.

The wipers beat faster as they turned onto the main road. Headlights cut through the rain, illuminating the narrow asphalt strip that wound toward the airfield. Somewhere out there, Hale was already in the sky, heading straight for the heart of the storm that had started all of this.

Claire gripped the handle of her go bag, her jaw set. "Then we're going after him."

Kane smirked, shifting gears. "Buckle up. Italy's waiting—and this time I get to go too!"

The minivan accelerated into the downpour, its taillights vanishing into the fog.

* * *

Trevor

By early afternoon, the fog over Rome had burned away. Trevor hobbled through the back garden toward the kitchen door, cane tapping against the stone. His Swiss Army knife bobbed against his uninjured hip. Over the past several days, he'd learned that unless Antonio summoned him for meals, he might as well be invisible.

When he did leave his room, he spent most of his time with the staff. Trevor had grown fond of the staff—especially Domenico and Alessia, the short, plump older woman who made all the meals. She was teaching him how to make pasta from scratch.

So far, the whole experience felt more like an odd imprisonment than an initiation into a criminal network. Mealtimes were spent answering Antonio's never-ending questions, many of which centered around delivery routes and where the US had troops stationed. Antonio was clearly expanding his empire, but when Trevor didn't have the answers Antonio would get irate, asking his son what he *did* know. Antonio's attitude, mixed with the unease circling in Trevor's stomach, meant that he never left his room without his knife—the only weapon he had.

Entering the kitchen, Trevor noticed the smell of lunch, hung thick in the air. He was about to ask Alessia what she was making when his name echoed through the manor.

"Trevor!" Antonio's voice cracked through the air like a whip.

When Trevor stepped into the office, the air felt heavier—static and tense.

A speakerphone blinked on the desk; Hale's voice came through, distorted by engine noise and aggravation. "...burned, Antonio. My company's hunting me. They found the cover-ups. I need help. You approached me and brought me into this—you owe me that much."

Antonio leaned back in his chair, one elbow on the armrest, the ghost of a smirk curling his lips. "I owe you? Interesting word—for a man who's happily accepted every paycheck I've offered. Your fancy life, that new home—it's all because of me."

"I covered up everything for you," Hale snapped. "I made sure the CIA didn't have evidence on you for years. You should be thanking me."

"You've been a good soldier," Antonio said smoothly, "but you knew the risks."

There was a pause, a hitch of breathing on the other end. Then Hale hissed, "If your man had taken care of Huntington's family properly, I wouldn't be in this mess. His daughter survived." Antonio's expression barely flickered. "You'll have to be more specific."

Trevor's whole body tensed as he listened. Antonio didn't even *remember* killing Max and Louisa.
"Max Huntington, he was another CIA officer who started to suspect I was a mole."

Antonio let the silence stretch before he gave a low, dismissive laugh. "Yes, his daughter—the gymnast. What was her name?" It took him several seconds to think of it, and Trevor had to bite his tongue to keep from screaming it at him. "Claire. A child exposed you?" He laughed, a true belly laugh this time.

"She's not a child anymore! She falsified her name and joined the agency. Two of our best officers are helping her. I guarantee she's coming for you too."

"Marcus, I'm not scared of a child. I'd like to see her try." His arrogance was on full display as he spoke; Antonio didn't notice as his son's face hardened. Trevor was struggling not to dive across the desk and tackle Antonio. Instead, he stood in the corner, fists tightening so hard his knuckles were white and his nails dug into his palms.

He should be afraid.

When the call ended, Antonio turned the phone off with

deliberate calm. "Hale is a sloppy fool. It was only a matter of time before his own company figured him out. He's useless to us now." Taking an expensive decanter off the bookshelf behind his desk, Antonio poured two glasses of red wine. Motioning for Trevor to come forward and sit down, he handed him a glass. "The men I do business with, they value intelligence and cleanliness. They also value family. This is why you're here. Continuity. Blood."

Trevor took the glass but didn't drink. "What men?"

Antonio's gaze flicked to the window, a predatory gleam in his eye. "I'm expanding. My new partners believe in family above all else—old bloodlines. They won't deal with a man who has no legacy."

It took Trevor a beat to realize what he meant. "You want me at the meetings."

"Yes—and at a gala next week. They need to see my heir." Antonio smiled thinly. "You will sit beside me, learn the names, the numbers. Show them that the Giordano line still has a future."

Trevor had known he'd be a pawn, but hearing it stated so plainly pissed him off more than he'd imagined it would. He focused on the weight of the glass in his hand, using it to ground himself. "And if I say no?"

Antonio chuckled softly. "Then perhaps your sister's doctors find themselves short on funding."

Trevor's stomach turned, but he didn't speak.

"You see, my boy," Antonio continued, swirling his wine, "every empire is built on leverage. Even family."

He didn't know the meaning of family—what he wanted was ownership. Control. Not love.

Antonio raised his glass, the crystal catching the light like a blade. Taking his son's silence as agreement, he continued. "Good. I knew we understood each other. I'll have Domenico bring up the files you need to learn. Our first meeting is the day after tomorrow. You're excused."

The dismissal hit like a slap, but Trevor only nodded. He wasn't ready to give Antonio the satisfaction of seeing fear.

Without hesitating, he rose, needing to get out as soon as he could. Before he reached the door Antonio spoke again. "One last thing—you'll need a few suits. The maids tell me you don't have any. My tailor will be here later today for a fitting. Don't be late."

Nodding once, Trevor left the room. As the door closed behind him, he finished processing Antonio's words. *The maids tell me...* They must have looked through his belongings. Had they found the phone? His pulse quickened; a faint ringing filled his ears as the realization settled in.

25
Access

Trevor's instinct was to sprint to his room—not that he could, with his leg still healing—but he forced himself to walk, slow and unbothered. Once the door finally clicked shut behind him, he went straight for the dresser. If the maids had searched anywhere, it would've been there.

He yanked open the top drawer and dropped to one knee, careful to keep strain off of his thigh. Reaching inside, his fingers closed on... nothing.

His heartbeat slammed against his ribs. *Where was it?* For a second, the room narrowed to the drawer and the sound of his own pulse. If someone had found it and given it to Antonio, Addie's heart could be gone along with the phone.

Pain flared through his thigh as he swept his hand side to side—until his fingertips brushed metal. The phone. Relief and panic collided in his chest. He pulled it free, exhaling shakily. Whether they'd found it or not, he couldn't risk leaving it in there any longer. It had already been several days, which was long enough.

He'd learned from watching his Army friends sneak contraband onto base that the best way to keep something hidden was to keep moving it.

Sliding the drawer back into place, he stood—and bit back a curse as sharp pain flared in his leg before melting into a dull, burning throb.

He sat on the edge of the bed, scanning the room for options. The phone wasn't exactly slim—it needed a larger hiding spot. His eyes drifted to the headboard.

Standing, he limped over to the headboard and ran a hand along the wood frame. The upholstered panel was tacked tight around the back, but a small gap at the corner caught his eye—it was just big enough. With care, he pried one tack loose, slid the phone inside the fabric lining, and pressed it deep into the padding. Replacing the tack was harder; his fingers trembled, the fine tip biting into his skin as he forced it back into the wood. But once it slid into place, the surface looked untouched.

Next, the battery.

He walked over toward the desk chair and was just about to lift it when a knock reverberated through the door. Trevor froze, then quickly sat at the desk, leaning his cane against it as he called out, "Come in."

His pulse hammered.

Domenico entered carrying a folder. "The documents your father would like you to review."

Trevor took the folder, placing it on his desk. "Thank you."

"Is there anything else I can get you, signor? Do you need assistance with your medical dressing today?"

Only then did Trevor realize he was absently kneading at the muscle around his wound. "No, I'm alright, I have what I need."

Domenico nodded and withdrew silently, closing the door with a soft click.

Letting out a sigh of relief, Trevor took a full minute to let his heart rate settle. When he was sure the coast was clear, he stood up and flipped the chair. He pried the battery free from between the strapping, then looked around the room for another hiding place.

The curtains.

A heavy brocade fabric over a gauzy one. The top brocade

casing was thick, and he remembered noticing a loose seam earlier in the week. If he stood on the chair, he might reach it.

Climbing onto the chair was risky—his balance was still off from the wound—but he had to try. Moving the chair closer to the base of the curtains he climbed up. Bracing his hand on the wall he put all his weight on his good leg. His fingertips could just graze the seam. The opening was small, but after slightly widening the hole, he slid the battery inside the hollow. It disappeared easily. Testing the curtain, he moved it back and forth making sure the battery wouldn't fall out when the fabric was drawn.

Satisfied, he climbed down and replaced the chair. Sitting, his eyes drifted to the folder, still on the desk where he had left it.

Opening it, a six-pack of mugshots filled the top page, names and titles neatly printed beneath. Under that were maps of shipping routes, spreadsheets of financials, and finally a list of weapon inventories. Antonio had just handed him everything the Italian government would need to dismantle his business. Names tied to accounts. Account numbers tied to shell companies. Route dates, port codes, and warehouse addresses—enough to trigger raids, seize assets, and put half of Antonio's inner circle in prison.

All Trevor had to do was send it.

He stared at the pages, his jaw tightening. Addie's heart was gone if he betrayed Antonio. For that alone, he couldn't risk turning it in. And how much of it was even real? Antonio could've filled the folder with lies just to see what he'd do. This was a test— one he had to pass.

Trevor studied for over an hour before he decided to take a break and change his bandages.

The next two days blurred together in a haze of studying, forced civility, and sleepless nights. Trevor memorized the names and faces in the file until they haunted his dreams. Every meal with Antonio was another test; every question, a probe for weakness—a measure of how much defiance still lingered beneath Trevor's polite façade. By the second evening, the constant strain had left him with a pounding headache, and his leg wasn't improving either. His only respite came from the brief texts he exchanged with his parents—simple check-ins to say he was fine and to get updates on his sister.   He still hadn't told them about his gunshot wound and didn't plan to; if he mentioned any injury, his dad would be on the next plane out. Addie was doing well and was still on track to go home the following week.

He was buttoning one of his new shirts the tailor had brought when a knock came at the door. Grabbing his suit jacket and cane, Trevor walked to the door, answering it.

Domenico was on the other side, in a formal suit of his own. "Your father is ready for you. The guests from the Rossetti family have arrived." He then turned on his heel and walked to the dining room, expecting Trevor to follow.

When they entered the dining room, Trevor immediately recognized the head of the Rossetti family—Lorenzo. Tall and broad-shouldered man in his mid-sixties, with crow's feet and a posture that rivaled a soldier's. He was the only man Trevor had seen interact with Antonio that didn't automatically submit to his authority.

Flanking Lorenzo were his two eldest sons, Matteo and Enzo. Matteo was the eldest. He was the pragmatic sort, always running the numbers and being the voice of reason. The complete opposite, Enzo, was a fiery young man, impulsive and yet oddly charming. He was everything Trevor imagined Antonio would have been like at that age. Both men were around Trevor's age and shared a similar stature to him.

He stood back, waiting until Antonio motioned toward him. Before this moment they had been speaking in Italian but when he introduced Trevor, Antonio switched to English. Explaining that Trevor was raised in the States—for safety purposes, of course. Not because he was an absentee father.

Lorenzo introduced each of his boys and shook Trevor's hand. There was an odd sense of warmth to the crime lord, one that almost disarmed him. Almost.

"Let's sit and drink." Antonio motioned to the table, a large ornate piece that sat twelve. Neither man was willing to give up power, so Lorenzo sat at one head of the table while Antonio claimed the other. Their sons sat in the seats that denoted legacy.

Domenico entered the room with a decanter of wine and began pouring each glass, starting at Antonio's seat. The power play between the two men didn't go unnoticed, but Trevor had trouble seeing past the pointless posturing of the two oldest men.

"What happened to your leg?" Enzo spoke for the first time in several minutes, breaking the polite small talk. His father sent him a look that shattered the warm exterior he had created, underneath it all he was deadly and dark.

Trevor answered despite the look, not seeing the point in hiding it. "A deal went bad. Wrong place, wrong time."

Enzo smirked, swirling his wine. "Or maybe the wrong man for the job."

Matteo shot his brother a warning look, but Antonio only laughed—a deep, practiced sound that filled the room. "My son's recovery has been... educational. He's learning the business the hard way."

Lorenzo's eyes flicked between father and son, the hint of a knowing smile tugging at the corner of his mouth. "Sometimes that's the only way worth learning," he said. His voice was low, gravelly, the kind that made every word sound deliberate. "Pain is the most natural lesson."

Antonio raised his glass in agreement, eager to steer the conversation toward business. "Now, I believe we have an arrangement to finalize."

Lorenzo nodded once, motioning for Matteo to slide a sleek leather folder across the table. Inside were maps, manifests, and lists of shipments—high-end firearms, smuggled tech, and narcotics disguised as medical supplies. "Our shipments have been running through Naples and then by cargo ship into the States," Lorenzo said. "But U.S. customs have been getting nosier. We need a cleaner point of entry."

Antonio leaned back in his chair, fingertips pressed together. "There's a port near Fort Raleigh—small, quiet, military-controlled. Half the docks are leased to civilian contractors. Easy to bury a shipment in their paperwork. I have... connections there."

The moment the name left Antonio's lips, Trevor's pulse quickened. Fort Raleigh. His old base. He knew that dock, knew the shifts, the offloading schedules, the exact blind spots the cameras didn't cover. And now he understood—Antonio hadn't wanted a son. He'd wanted access.

Trevor forced his face blank, though his knuckles whitened around the wineglass stem until it almost cracked.

Lorenzo's gaze slid toward him. "You were stationed there, sì?"

Trevor swallowed, then nodded once. "For four years."

"Then your father's proposal makes sense," Lorenzo said. "You know the rhythm, the people, the oversight. That kind of familiarity is... valuable." He exchanged a glance with Antonio that sent a spark of satisfaction across both their faces. "I have a shipment ready to leave tomorrow. If you can handle it, we'll discuss a regular schedule at the gala."

Antonio inclined his head in agreement. "Perfect. You'll see, Lorenzo, this partnership will outlive all of us."
The two men raised glasses, sealing the deal and making Trevor's stomach turn.

When everyone else drank, he obliged, not wanting to be rude. But his mind was busy, already running ahead. He was replaying every camera angle, every potential breach point at that dock—not as a conspirator, but as someone searching for a way to dismantle it all later.

A short time later, Lorenzo and his sons finally stood to leave, Enzo leaned close as they shook hands. "Next time, try not to get shot, *americano*," he said quietly, a razor-sharp grin spreading across his face.

Trevor met his eyes and smiled, thin and cold. "Next time, I won't give them the chance."

Enzo's smirk faltered for just a second before he turned to follow his father out. Lorenzo's voice echoed down the hallway, fading only when the heavy doors closed behind them. Antonio lingered at the table, the faintest look of satisfaction on his face— the look of a man who thought every piece was right where he wanted it.

For the first time since arriving in Rome, Trevor knew exactly what he was to his father—not a son, not even a pawn. An access badge.

He sat long after Antonio was gone, the only sound the faint tick of a clock, like a countdown. The scent of wine and expensive cologne clung to his clothes. Somewhere beyond these walls, Claire was out there, closer than either man realized. And if Antonio wanted to use him as a key to open doors, Trevor was going to make sure what awaited him behind the door wasn't friendly.

* * *

Claire

The late afternoon light bled gold over Rome, catching on car roofs and marble facades. From the cramped back seat of their rented sedan, Claire peered through the monocular and tinted window at the hotel across the street. Another dead end. The third hotel they'd staked out in two days—and still no sign of Hale. She was beginning to get incredibly frustrated. They'd all landed at the same airport, but once Hale left the grounds, he vanished—completely off the grid.

Four days in Rome, and he was still a ghost.

She lowered the scope, rubbing the bridge of her nose. Kane sat in the driver's seat, his laptop balanced on the console, a half-drunk espresso cooling by his elbow. He'd stopped swearing out loud after day two, but the quiet clicks of his keyboard had grown more violent by the hour. This wasn't the day out in the field that Kane had imagined when he had agreed to it. He was typing away on his laptop—which he could have done from the comfort of their safe house—searching CCTV and running it through facial recognition.

"Nothing?" she asked.

"Not unless you count a honeymooning couple from Texas," he muttered. "Which I don't."

Before she could reply, Colin's voice broke through their comms. "I might have something." He was back at their safe house, monitoring a feed they had aimed directly at Antonio's gated drive.

251

His home hadn't been hard to find, at least not for Kane.

Claire straightened. "Good, because we don't."

"A catering van just left the Giordano estate. No security escort or other vehicles. It's worth checking out."

Kane perked up. "You think Antonio is throwing himself a dinner party?"

"I think," Colin said, "if he's planning something, this company knows what it is. It may be a way to get close."

Claire exchanged a look with Kane. "Send us the address."

Kane had driven to their last location complaining about the traffic the entire way—claiming it was worse than DC traffic. And while he might be right, Claire preferred to avoid any road-rage incidents. So she motioned to Kane to move to the passenger seat before they left. He was perfectly happy to comply, closing his laptop and clambering over the console with the grace of a baby deer.

Thirty minutes later, they were parking the car.

The catering business was tucked into a narrow street in Trastevere, the kind of old-world neighborhood that was full of picturesque buildings the tourists liked to photograph. The air smelled of bread and rosemary. Claire had told Kane just to follow her lead and play along before they entered.

When they did Claire informed the pretty receptionist that they would like to speak to someone about having an event catered. Ducking the back, the young woman disappeared. Claire clocked the security camera above the door, the open ledger on the counter, the way the receptionist's eyes lingered on Kane's shoes. If this went sideways, they'd need a reason to leave without booking—or being remembered.

A woman in her fifties came out instead of the young receptionist. She had long flowing curly hair and emanated a true motherly energy.

The owner, Signora Petrelli, ushered them into a small office lined with floral sample menus and invoices. "Of course, of course," she said in accented English. "We specialize in discretion. Politicians, film stars, businessmen—we serve them all."

Sitting down in the wide cushioned chairs, Claire smiled politely and leaned into Kane affectionately. "Perfect. My husband and I are hosting a small vow renewal," she said, squeezing his arm with mock tenderness.

Kane choked on a laugh and quickly turned it into a cough—he hadn't been expecting the word *husband*. "Excuse me."

A loud timer beeped on Signora Petrelli's desk just as they were sitting down. She excused herself, bustling into the kitchen to remove a tray of biscotti from the oven. As soon as the office door closed, Kane's fingers flew across the unattended computer. He navigated through the scheduling software, scrolling past client lists and delivery routes until he froze.

Claire kept one eye on the hallway, already rehearsing a question about dietary restrictions if the woman came back too soon.

"Got it," he whispered. "Three days from now. Palazzo Bellavita. Hosts: Antonio Giordano and Lorenzo Rossetti."

Claire's stomach turned. "The Rossetti family. They're just as bad if not worse than Antonio."

The venue name alone implied armed security, vetted guest lists, and money loud enough to draw every power player in Rome. "Yeah," Kane said, eyes gleaming with excitement. "That's way bigger than a dinner party."

Footsteps clopped against the stone floor; Kane minimized the window and leaned back, pretending to admire a menu.

When the owner returned, Claire breezed through the obligatory conversation. The last thing she wanted was to seem memorable—or suspicious. She thanked the woman warmly, accepted a brochure, and guided Kane out the door before he could push their luck or open his mouth.

Once they were back in the car with the doors shut, Claire finally spoke. "Look up the venue. A name that fancy has to be a gala. And if it is, we are going to need invitations or be staff. We can't break in blind."

He typed away as she navigated back to their rental—an old farmhouse fifteen minutes from Antonio's estate. "You're right—it's gorgeous and ridiculously expensive. Only someone with a god complex or a trust fund could afford it." Kane grinned. "Guess we better find something to wear."

Claire's lips pressed into the ghost of a smile. "Then we better make sure we're on that list."

26
The Gilded Hour

Claire stippled foundation over Colin's new nose prosthetic, widening the tip and softening the bridge. This wasn't the first time either of them had worn prosthetics in the field, but Colin had never quite mastered applying them. When she finished, he was nearly unrecognizable. Between the dyed-black hair, the grown-out facial hair, and the altered nose, there was no way Marcus Hale would recognize him.

"Finished. You're good to go get dressed—just don't get makeup on your white dress shirt."

"Yes, ma'am." Colin smirked faintly. "Is Kane applying his own, or will you do his too?" He hadn't seen the tech genius in hours and could only guess what kind of chaos he was orchestrating elsewhere in the house.

"He said he could handle it." Claire began priming her skin, tapping lightly along her nose and cheekbones. "I can touch it up if he needs, but honestly, he's probably better at it than I am."

"True," Colin muttered as he walked out, rolling his shoulders like a man heading into battle with a tuxedo.

* * *

Two hours later, Claire was setting the last curl of her Old Hollywood waves. She had styled them so they cascaded down over one shoulder in a dramatic, sultry swoop. She was just misting them with hairspray when a knock sounded at the door.

"Come in," she called.

Colin entered holding a classic bow tie in his hands. "I never did learn how to do the special bow," he admitted, sheepish. "Mind helping?"

She glanced up and caught him staring—not at her, but studying her face, as if trying to place the woman in front of him. With her higher cheekbones, widened nose bridge, and sharply contoured features, she looked like a stranger.

A quiet laugh slipped out as she raised her brows. "Why do you think I know how to tie one?"

"Oh, I guess I just assumed—"

"I can do it." Kane's voice cut in as his door swung open.

He stepped into the hall, fully dressed in a black-tie waiter's uniform—crisp vest, flawless bow tie, and an air of theatrical superiority that was unmistakably Kane. Claire had been right—he'd masterfully applied his prosthetic, a subtle jawline enhancement making him look older.

Kane held out his hand for the fabric with mock impatience. He began artfully looping it around Colin's neck while he spoke. "I can't believe we finally get to go to a soirée and I have to be the waiter. I live for a good suit, and you"—he sighed dramatically— "look uncomfortable. You'd better turn on that charm, Abs, or you'll stick out like a sore thumb."

When he finished the bow tie, Kane gave Colin's chest a brisk pat and sauntered away down the hall without another word.

Colin glanced back at Claire, who was trying, and failing, to hide a laugh behind her hand. Shaking his head, he muttered, "Unbelievable," and disappeared into his room to grab his jacket.

Claire finished with a final mist of hairspray before stepping into her gown and heels. The gown was a deep forest-green satin, its thigh-high slit and halter neckline balanced by an elegant low cowl back that fell into a cascade of soft folds. Her gold stilettos were sleek, pointed, and delicately beaded—beautiful, but chosen carefully.

The first rule of a mission like this: *heels that come off fast and a dress that allows movement, in case she has to fight her way out.*

She slipped a vintage beaded clutch under her arm, took one last glance in the mirror, and headed downstairs for their briefing. Walking downstairs, she felt steady and focused mixed with a bundle of excitement. She was thrilled about the possibility of seeing Trevor. Even if they couldn't speak, she'd at least be able to put eyes on him. And the thought of finally getting her hands on Marcus Hale was... overwhelming.

Claire was the last one to arrive in the living room where Kane was distributing comms and IDs. Handing her the earpiece, she set it into her ear canal. It was a tiny, flesh-colored device that was imperceptible unless you looked directly into the ear. It was much smaller than they usually used—typically saved for occasions like this. The earpiece was very expensive and dreadfully uncomfortable.

When she was done, Kane handed her a stunning gold and pearl ring. If twisted, the pearl would swing wide to expose a small pin that was laced with a fast-acting sedative. One that would put a grown man to sleep in seconds—but it was only usable once. She had used these rings before but never one this glamorous. Sliding it onto her finger, it felt heavier than she had expected. Claire wasn't sure if that was the physical weight or the knowledge that this would be her only weapon—unless she improvised one.

They would have to pass through metal detectors on arrival. It would be ironic that the kings of arms dealing in southern Europe wanted a weapon-free gala—though she expected Antonio's men would smuggle theirs in anyways. He wouldn't be caught dead without a way to defend himself.

When Kane handed her the new identification, Claire tucked it into her clutch. But not before noticing how odd her photo looked. It wasn't that the photo was bad, it was just that it looked like she did now, with a new face shape. The driver's license was good enough for the evening but wouldn't stand up to a more critical interrogation. She would be impersonating Daphne

Brown, a British citizen who was the daughter of a wealthy English aristocrat known to have shady business dealings. The whole family was a little eccentric and rarely showed their faces. Claire had spent the last two days building her backstory and learning everything she could about the mysterious woman. From the few photos she'd found, she now looked like the woman's twin.

For Colin, Kane had created a new alias, Benjamin Frank, a young tech guru who had sold an app and made millions. He was now looking to "*diversify*" his portfolio.

Hacking the guest list was the last step. Both Benjamin and Daphne had been placed onto the guest list by Kane, but neither would stand out as someone who hadn't been invited.

While Claire and Colin got to socialize, Kane was stuck playing the waiter role. He would have loved to have worn a tux and mixed with the criminal elite, for pure entertainment of course, but being a waiter would allow him to go unnoticed when needed and slip away to monitor the cameras.

Handing Colin his own earpiece, Kane also gave him an expensive but modified wristwatch. It, too, had a sedative pin, this time hidden in the dial on the side.

Kane tucked his own forged ID into the inside pocket of his vest. "All right," he said, glancing between them. "Time to play nice with the devil and his guests."

Colin adjusted his cufflinks, smirking faintly. "Let's just hope the devil doesn't recognize us."

Claire gave a half smile as she double-checked the clasp of her clutch. "He won't. We don't even know if he knows what we look like. It's Hale we have to worry about. If he's there, he may recognize us even with our prosthetics."

"We'll handle him, if he shows his face."

They left the safe house in staggered intervals. Kane was first to leave so he arrived with all of the other wait staff. As soon as he arrived, he began helping to unload the food from various vans. Melting into a crowd of twenty other servers he wouldn't be noticed. If the woman from the catering office was here he hadn't seen her yet, and even if she was, his prosthetics made him look different enough.

When he had a chance, Kane excused himself to the restroom and used his smartphone to breach the Wi-Fi. Unexpectedly, the network pushed back immediately—segmented VLANs, rotating access keys, and a captive portal designed to kick unfamiliar devices every sixty seconds. Kane swore under his breath, rolling his shoulder as he spoofed a catering tablet ID and waited out the timer. One shot. If he tripped an alert, the entire system would lock him out.

He was in, but only barely.

Sitting in a stall, he mapped the venue's subnet—security cameras, access points, and the admin-tablet. If anyone else joined the network he should also be able to hack their device, cloning any information they had to share. If someone was careless enough to join the Wi-Fi he could literally hit a gold mine of information. When he was done, he flushed the toilet—for realism—and exited the bathroom, just another faceless waiter.

Thirty minutes later, Colin rolled out in a sleek black Maserati that suited his cover perfectly. He had a thing for cars, and relaxed into the seat as he hit the gas. The engine's rev made his soul sing as he took off toward the Palazzo Bellavita. In the passenger footwell sat a small leather briefcase filled with meaningless "business proposals" in case anyone got too curious. He gripped the leather steering wheel, pushing harder on the gas and savoring the purr of the magnificent car.

From a bathroom at the venue, Kane did a comms check. "My dazzling duo, can you hear me?" His voice crackled quietly through the line, faint music echoing in the background. "The security is heavy but predictable—metal detectors, bag scanner, the works. I'm currently tapping into the network and have complete control. Looks like the men of the hour are arriving now through the back entrance."

Claire's voice came next, steady and low. "Copy that."

Ten minutes later, Colin pulled up in front of the glittering building and handed his keys over to the valet. "Don't scratch her," he said, tossing the keys lightly.

Benjamin had been raised in California, so he made sure to drop his "t"s and merge his vowels where appropriate. With his briefcase in hand, he approached the metal detectors. He set the briefcase on the mini conveyor and stepped through the arch; the machine stayed silent.

Cleared, Colin was just stepping away from security when Claire's car pulled up. The gloved hand of an usher opened the back door of the sleek black town car that she rode in. As she swung her legs out, cool air swept across her right leg where it poked through the slit of her gown.

The venue was beautiful, an 18th-century palace with a long sweeping gravel driveway. Floodlights swept across manicured gardens and marble fountains, throwing shards of silver and gold over the courtyard. The palace itself glowed like a beacon with crystal chandeliers burning bright through tall arched windows. It truly belonged in a fairy tale. From the outside, you'd never know the men hosting tonight's gala had bloodstained hands.

Claire's pulse thrummed in her ears, half anticipation, half dread, as she walked up to the palace. This wasn't just another mission—they could apprehend Hale and get what they needed to take down Antonio. And on top of all that, the man she loved was standing in the middle of it—and he could easily become collateral damage.

The air outside was warm, filled with perfume, cigar smoke, and the low murmur of expensive laughter. Walking up the marble steps, she approached the grand doors flanked by guards in tuxedos.

"Benjamin Frank has been checked in," Kane murmured through the earpiece. "Daphne, you're up."

Claire smiled faintly, tucking her clutch under her arm as she approached security. After placing her clutch on the scanner, she stepped through the metal detector. Just beyond security was a stunning young woman checking in guests. Walking up to her, Claire silently handed her ID to the girl. Catching a glimpse beyond her, she could see the party up another set of stairs and through a grand archway.

"Miss Daphne." The hostess swung her arm wide, welcoming her to the gala as a very large man stepped aside, allowing Claire to pass.

Ascending a set of marble stairs, she took in the room. Marble walls lead to dome ceilings with sprawling frescos. A soft throat-clearing from the top of the stairs broke her gaze, looking up.

A handsome man stood at the top of the stairs—tall, in a tuxedo, slightly overgrown military haircut, and blue-green eyes that beamed down at her. Her heart sped up and suddenly all she could think about was ducking into a dark hallway with him.

Trevor.

He recognized her instantly—she'd only altered the shape of her face for tonight, and he'd already seen her with her red hair.

He was only there a second before his name was called. He gave her a brief smile and then slipped away. While he was still walking with a cane he barely put any weight on it. Claire noticed a slight limp with every step he took. She could see he was hurting— but only because she knew him. To anyone else, he would look like the confident son of an elite criminal.

The moment Claire stepped inside, the air shifted—warm, perfumed, and heavy with wealth. Crystal chandeliers spilled light across marble floors, where men in tuxedos and women in glittering gowns moved in elegant currents to the sound of a live string quartet. Every inch of the Palazzo Bellavita radiated opulence. Every smile looked rehearsed. A grand marble staircase led to an upper level with balconies that looked down on them.

Her eyes swept the room automatically—exits, guards, surveillance points. Two guards were stationed by the grand staircase, one by the mirrored doors leading to the courtyard. No visible weapons, but that didn't mean anything. These people didn't need guns to be dangerous, but neither did she.

Antonio was easy to spot, standing near the quartet with Lorenzo at his side. Between them, Trevor lingered, his posture was perfect, polite, but his eyes were distant. Claire's chest tightened. He didn't belong in this world, and yet here he was, trapped in it. She prayed that Addie would get her heart soon.

A movement across the room caught her attention. A couple turned toward the light, laughing quietly. For a heartbeat, she froze—her mother's laugh, her father's profile. Louisa's hand on Max's arm. The room tilted, her pulse jumping in her throat, and then reality snapped back. It wasn't them. It would never be them.

She drew a slow breath, steadying herself. She had no time for ghosts tonight. She was here to get her parents justice, not imagine them on the dance floor.

She lifted a champagne flute from a passing tray, forcing her hand not to tremble. The bubbles fizzed, catching the light, delicate and deceptive. Just like this place.

In the service hall, behind the hum of the kitchens, Kane was elbow-deep in a stack of serving trays, his waiter's vest already unbuttoned. The catering corridor buzzed with movement— chefs shouting orders, servers hustling between stations—but Kane looked perfectly at home. A tray balanced on his forearm, a disarming smile in place, and a small catering tablet tucked against his palm—one he had swiped.

It was time to begin the "fun" part of the evening: hacking any personal device that had logged onto the Wi-Fi. Dropping the tray onto a counter, he ducked around the corner into a shadowed nook where he could type in private. Clicking the tablet on, he began.

"Come on, sweetheart," he muttered under his breath, coaxing the tablet's security prompt to load. A few taps and a bypass later, he was inside the devices of everyone attached to the Wi-Fi. Lines of data began scrolling across the screen, the names of each device. The eldest Rossetti heirs, bodyguards, politicians— many of them probably had no idea their phones had automatically connected. He toggled between them, whistling quietly as he worked. First up, he'd check Matteo's phone. He was bound to have financial information given his position in the company. Searching it, Kane frowned. Matteo's phone was too clean—burner apps scrubbed, metadata stripped, message threads looping back on themselves. Someone had taught him how not to get caught.

"Okay," he murmured, "Enzo Rossetti... you're up." The younger of the two brothers, he was also the messy and reckless one. Kane decrypted the device, scanning its contents—invoices, yacht manifests, charity donations, all popped up. A gold mine of information. But nothing that incriminated Antonio specifically.

Searching Enzo's phone for "Antonio Giordano," he found... nothing.

Despite his frustration, he didn't want the other documents he'd found to go to waste. So Kane funneled the data into a secure channel, and started encrypting it. He was about to address it to the CIA—then he decided they didn't deserve the data. Instead he'd send it off to Interpol, hoping they might be able to do some good with it.

A notification flashed on his screen before he could send it: **Network scan in progress.** Kane stilled, breath shallow, as the progress bar crept forward. Kane finished encrypting it, hit send, and dropped the guest-device access a second before the scan completed. He kept the camera feeds live on his phone though. Viewing the cameras was safe and quiet. Hacking phones, on the other hand, was noisy and disruptive. He'd have to be done with the "fun" hacking.

Kane was about to return the tablet when his phone flagged movement in one of the rear cameras. A shadow slipped through a service corridor near the rear entrance. Not catering staff. Not a guest. Kane frowned and zoomed in closer, freezing the feed.

"Well, speak of the devil," he whispered, his pulse ticking up.   "Claire, Colin—heads up. Hale just gate-crashed your fairy tale."

Claire froze mid-step, the glass still balanced between her fingers. Across the ballroom, Colin had already lifted his head, scanning the room. The chandelier light caught the sharp edge of his jaw as his expression shifted—alert, controlled, dangerous.

"Where?" she whispered, eyes tracking the gilded archways along the upper level's balconies.

"Back service entrance, headed for the east corridor," Kane's voice came softly through her comm. "Cameras picked him up just a minute ago. He's alone and not on the guest list. Hence the back entrance, guess he didn't like being left out."

Her adrenaline spiked. "He's desperate. He knows the Agency's after him—he must need Antonio's help."

"I'm going to try and hack his phone," Kane muttered. "You should move. He's alone right now, but that won't last long. You've got maybe three minutes before someone notices he's not supposed to be here or he tries to approach Antonio. He's entering on the upper level now."

Claire resisted sprinting to the grand staircase. The man who had ordered her parents' deaths was standing under the same roof. She forced calm into her movements and scanned the upper balcony until she found him—Marcus Hale. Same rigid posture. The same self-satisfied calm that always made her skin crawl. His tuxedo was immaculate, his expression unreadable, as if he owned the room.

"I've got him," she murmured.

Colin's voice cut in immediately. "No. You stay focused on Antonio. I'll handle Hale."

Her jaw tensed. "You shouldn't go alone."

He looked at her across the ballroom, expression steady but unyielding. He was already nearing the base of the stairs. "We can't ignore Antonio. Let me get Hale."

There was no arguing with that. She gave a single, tight nod. "Be careful."

"Always am."

Colin turned, slipping into the flow of the crowd, his champagne glass placed on a waiter's tray as he angled toward the staircase. Claire forced her gaze away, back to Antonio.

She couldn't afford to get distracted. Not now.

The orchestra shifted into a slow waltz, the notes warm and familiar enough to make her heart ache. Claire began to circle the room's perimeter, eyes flicking between Antonio, Lorenzo, and the exits. She needed a moment alone with one of Antonio's men—any thread that could hint at any leverage or evidence she could use to take him down.

But before she could move closer, a familiar voice stopped her.

"Leaving without a dance?"

Her breath caught. Trevor stood in front of her, holding out his hand. The tuxedo fit him perfectly, but there was still a hint of the soldier beneath—the squared shoulders, the quiet readiness. His blue-green eyes met hers, steady and knowing.

"We shouldn't," she whispered. "There are too many eyes, and what if Antonio saw?"

He tilted his head slightly, a ghost of a smile playing on his lips. "He told me I needed to try to not look like a hostage. That I should ask someone to dance. It will be more alarming to him now, if you say no."

Claire exhaled through her nose, rolling her eyes just enough for him to see it. "And you just had to ask me. You're impossible."

He grinned softly. "You used to like that."

With a reluctant sigh, she placed her hand in his and let him draw her onto the dance floor. The moment he touched her, the room seemed to narrow, the noise fading into a low hum of violins and murmurs. He slipped one arm around her waist, the other braced lightly on his cane. Their movements were slow at first—controlled, almost mechanical—before easing into rhythm.

While the rest of the dancers glided in sweeping waltz patterns, they circled in spot, swaying to accommodate Trevor's leg.

Trevor's voice was low, meant for her alone. "I figured you'd be here tonight."

She met his gaze. "Yeah, well I've always loved a good party."

He looked at her with such pleading in his eyes. "I need you to hold off, whatever your plan is. Just give me a few more weeks."

"I know you think he can get Addie a heart, but if he could, why hasn't he already? You've been with him for over a week now. I bet the only time he's brought it up is to threaten you with it, right?" Her heart broke to say it out loud, if she thought Antonio could get Addie the heart, she would wait. But Claire had studied men like Antonio, at this point he'd never do anything about it. Trevor was simply blinded by hope, he couldn't see the truth.

For a moment, neither of them spoke. The soft fabric of his tux brushed against her arm, the heat of his hand steady on her waist. When he shifted his fingertips slipped off the edge of her dress, brushing the bare skin of her lower back. Her body responded, trying to melt into his touch. It took everything she had not to wrap her arms around him and drag his mouth to hers.

Instead, she leaned in, her lips barely moving. "I'm sorry. I know you feel helpless and this is the only thing you think you can do. If you really think he could still come through, ask him about it. If you still need more time, use the phone I gave you. I'll give you what I can."

He hesitated, his eyes flicked briefly toward Antonio's table.

"I should go." She knew she had hurt him, which was the last thing she wanted to do. But he was putting himself in unnecessary danger for something that she didn't think would ever happen. She believed Addie would get the heart, but Antonio wouldn't be the one to get it for her.

His hand tightened on her waist as she shifted her weight away from him.

"Finish the song." All traces of flirtation were gone from his voice. Her chest tightened as she nodded.

For a heartbeat, everything stilled—the world reduced to the slow circle of their dance and the familiar ache between them. When the song ended, Trevor released her like touching her hurt.

"Be careful," he said softly.

"You too."

She turned and walked off the dance floor, her nose beginning to tingle as she felt her eyes well up with tears. She wouldn't cry—not here, not now. Claire felt like she had just shot the man she loved—then ripped his heart out and stomped on it. She had taken his hope.

"You only told him the truth." Kane murmured, soft and kind.

"I know."

Claire scanned the room for one of Antonio's men, someone preferably slightly intoxicated but not incoherent, when static hissed through her comm.

A grunt tore through Claire's earpiece—followed by the sharp, unmistakable snap of fists hitting flesh.

Colin.

27
The Lion's Den

Colin slammed face-first into the wall, grunting as the impact drove the air from his lungs. Hale's forearm ground into the back of his neck, pinning him hard enough to send sparks across Colin's vision. Colin had followed him down from the balcony into a dark corridor, and the moment they were out of earshot, Hale turned, attacking fast.

The corridor was dark, lit only by a handful of wall sconces. The music from the ballroom seeped through the walls, distant and romantically ominous.

Pinned against the wall, Colin swept his foot low, knocking Hale's weight off balance. Hale shifted his hips and rode the move, barely giving an inch. Hale recovered fast—too fast. By the time Colin reset his stance, Hale was already squared up, breathing steady, eyes flat and calculating. With fists raised, the two men circled one another, waiting to see who would strike first. Hale was too impatient; he stepped forward, throwing a punch.

He swore under his breath, shaking out his hand once—barely slowing. If Colin hadn't ducked, the broken bone would've been in his face, not Hale's hand. He'd always been good at hand-to-hand, but ten months of sparring with Claire had honed him into something lethal.

"I'm not letting you take me in, Davenport." Hale spat his name like a curse.

"So what, you think Antonio is going to help you? You wouldn't be sneaking in the back if he was."

Hale cradled his hand, then shook it out and reset his stance. Colin swung first—his fist slamming into Hale's stomach before an elbow cracked down on his shoulder. Hale absorbed it and answered with a brutal hook that clipped Colin's jaw, lighting his skull on fire and stealing his balance. They traded strikes in tight, ugly bursts—forearms, ribs, throat—nothing was safe.

Kane found them on the cameras and directed Claire to the right hallway. When she arrived, Colin had tackled him, but Hale didn't stay down. Now Colin was on his back with his legs cinched around Hale's neck—fighting to keep the hold while Hale clawed at his knees and drove elbows into Colin's thigh. Colin popped the watch pin with his thumb—Hale's hand shot out to grab it. Colin jerked his wrist back, taking a hard knuckle to the ribs for it, then drove the pin into Hale's cheekbone. He fought it for one heartbeat—then his body went heavy and limp in Colin's grasp.

"You good?" Claire walked calmly toward the duo as Colin stood and brushed off his tux.

"Yeah, I'm going to have a few bruises but I'm fine."

Once she got closer, she could see more in the dim light. Colin had a split lip dripping blood, and the skin on his right knuckles was raw. He still looked better than their former director, who bled from a gash on his forehead, his face covered in blood.

"Kane, we need an extraction plan for these two. There's no way Colin can go back into that ballroom without drawing attention."

"Already on it."

With a plan in place Claire was sent to retrieve the Maserati keys from the valet as Kane directed Colin to the back entrance Hale had used to get in.

Avoiding the main ballroom, Claire moved quickly through the equally dim hallways until she made it back to the main staircase. When she exited the secluded hallway, she slowed her pace to a confident, controlled walk. Colin had given her the embossed leather claim ticket before she left him.

The valet didn't blink when she handed over the leather ticket. Moments later, the black Maserati purred to life at the curb. Kane guided her around to the back of the building. She waited, pretending to text, until the valet turned away. Then she eased the car around the back, careful not to rev the engine, keeping the noise to a minimum.

When she got around to the back Colin was waiting with Hale tossed over his shoulder. Together they loaded the unconscious man into the back seat of the sleek two-door car. When they were done, Colin handed Claire a set of zip tie handcuffs. Smiling, she leaned in and cuffed Marcus Hale's hands together, making them just a hair too tight.

For you, Mom and Dad. One down, one to go. Two if she could find Silas Ward, but for now Antonio was the priority.

She was turning to return to the gala as Colin got into the driver seat when Kane stopped her.

"Wait. Claire, you need to go with Colin." Kane's voice was full of urgency.

"What, why? I'm not done, Antonio—"

"The Italian police are here, Interpol too. I don't know what's going on, but you have to go."

"He's right, get in the car Claire." Colin's tone left no room for argument, though Claire hesitated a second before circling the car and climbing into the passenger seat. "Keep your head down."

"I'll stay, see if I can figure out what's going on."

Shouting could be heard through Kane's earpiece as he followed the other servers into the ballroom. Police in three different uniforms stormed the ballroom, heading straight for the hosts.

Colin stepped on the gas and peeled out of a back driveway before the police could stop them. They had to get Hale to the U.S. Embassy. It would have been easier to hand him over to Interpol or the local police but they didn't know where Hale had friends.

The car sped down the dark roadway. Claire's pulse was

pounding from the extraction and now from not knowing what was going on. "Kane, what's happening?"

"Hold on... I'm trying to get better eyes on the situation." She heard a door close and quiet murmurs from people around Kane as he melted into the crowd. "It looks like they're going straight for the hosts."

"Antonio?" Colin's focus was on the road but he was just as invested as Claire.

"No, they're putting cuffs on the Rossetti's."

Through the comms they could hear one of the Rossetti's resisting. "If you don't unhand me, I'll have your badge!"

"Shut up, Enzo."

"That's the Rossetti sons—Matteo and Enzo. Lorenzo's keeping quiet." Kane explained as he gave them a play by play of what was happening.

"It's just Lorenzo's family right? Trevor's not involved?" Claire didn't know exactly what Trevor had been doing this past week but she doubted he would have done anything illegal. At least not bad enough to get on Interpol's radar. She was gnawing on her lip as she awaited his response.

The street lights blurred past as they neared the embassy.

"No, Trevor's not involved. Neither is Antonio. I guess the agency worked a little faster than I thought." Kane said, more to himself.

"What do you mean?" Claire prodded.

"Well, dumb and dumber let their phones connect to the Wi-Fi. So... I took a peek and they had some incriminating evidence on their phones, so I forwarded it to Interpol. They must have thought they had enough to move."

The embassy was in sight now.

"Kane, we're approaching the gates now. Going dark," Colin said, then removed his earpiece. Claire followed suit. He stopped the car as two armed guards stepped into the drive. The American flag snapped above them in the wind.

"ID?" one of them called, already reaching for the radio. This was the secure entrance, for officials only.

Colin held up his CIA badge through the windshield. "Officer Davenport, I have a guest and a high-priority detainee for immediate handover."

The guard's tone shifted. "Copy that, sir. One moment."

Claire kept her head low as the radio crackled with confirmation. The gates rolled open. Colin glanced at her. "Stay in the car. Let me handle this."

She nodded, keeping her gaze fixed on Hale's unconscious body and away from prying eyes. A minute later, the vehicle rolled inside the compound, disappearing behind reinforced gates and U.S. seals. Behind them, the gates sealed. Across the city, another door was about to shut.

* * *

Trevor

Trevor watched as the Rossetti men were placed in handcuffs. He'd been standing beside Antonio and Lorenzo when the grand doors burst open and uniformed officers poured in from every direction. For a moment, he couldn't process what he was seeing. When he turned to Antonio, searching for a cue, the older man looked just as stunned—though his expression stayed carved in stone.

Officers converged on the three men at once, surrounding them to cut off any chance of escape. Lorenzo calmly extended his hand for the warrant. After scanning it, he sighed, turned his back to the officers, and held out his wrists without protest. Matteo followed his father's lead. He had been standing nearby, deep in conversation with a man Trevor didn't recognize. Enzo, however, had been draping himself over a woman in red and was now shouting at the police, his outrage drawing every eye in the room.

Within minutes, it was over. The men were read their rights and marched out of the ballroom, leaving behind nothing but the echo of chaos—gossip rising in their wake, Antonio's men closing ranks, and fury radiating off Antonio like heat from a forge.

Enrico took point—Antonio's right-hand man, his eyes sweeping the room like a weapon. The group closed around Antonio and moved him out with the precision of a protection detail. Enrico's gaze flicked once to Trevor—measuring, dismissing—before snapping back to the exits. There were no bullets or bombs, but the air was charged all the same. Trevor couldn't shake the feeling that he was walking into another kind of war zone.

The bulletproof town car sped down the Italian roads faster than was legal. Everything had happened so quickly that he had been yanked out of the headspace Claire's comment had put him in. "...if he could, why hasn't he already?" It had been echoing in his subconscious, building his anger and crushing his hope ever since she'd said it.

When they arrived back at Antonio's villa, Domenico was standing at the door holding it open, a tray of whiskey glasses balanced on one hand. Antonio, Enrico, and the others swept past him—grabbing a glass as they went—without so much as a glance in his direction. Led by Antonio, they filed into the office. Trevor hesitated in the hall, unsure whether to follow, until Domenico gestured him in.

Trevor hadn't spent much time with Enrico, but it had taken only a few minutes to realize he was just as bad as Antonio—ruthless, violent, and motivated solely by self-interest. The only thing that kept him from being Antonio's clear choice for a successor was his age; he was only a few years younger than Trevor's father.

The click of the door behind Trevor felt like a grenade pin hitting the floor as Antonio went off. He hurled his whiskey glass at the bookcase and swept everything from his desk in one furious motion. It was a tantrum—childish and violent.

Antonio's rage didn't burn — it detonated.

"You *idiots!*" he roared, shoving the contents of a drawer to the floor. "Do you have any idea what this means? Years of work—gone!" He slammed a fist down on the desk, the veins in his forearm straining like cables. "Lorenzo was supposed to be untouchable! How did they know?"

No one dared answer. The other men stood frozen in the corners, eyes fixed on the polished marble, each one hoping not to be noticed.

Antonio's breathing was heavy, uneven. He snatched a decanter off his bar and filled a glass with trembling fingers, the wine sloshing over the rim. Turning, he pointed the glass at Enrico. "You suggested them. You told me they were clean."

Enrico's jaw flexed, but his tone stayed calm, measured — the voice of a man who had survived too many tempers to flinch. "My contact in the police said they were clean. Someone inside the Rossetti circle must've talked."

Antonio stared at him for a long, dangerous moment. Then, to Trevor's shock, he laughed—a low, humorless sound that made the hair on Trevor's neck rise. "Someone always talks," he muttered, setting the glass down hard enough to crack it. "And when I find out who, I'll make sure they never speak again."

Enrico's gaze flicked briefly toward Trevor, a look that said everything words couldn't—*You're the new comer. If it was you, I'll find out—and you're dead.*

Trevor held his stare, matching it beat for beat. He wasn't sure which of them Antonio would shoot first if the wrong word slipped out, but one thing was certain—none of them would see it coming. Antonio's moods flipped like a switch, but one thing Trevor knew for certain: Antonio needed his help to get the shipment through the port.

Antonio's chest heaved as he braced both hands on the desk, head bowed. For a moment, the room was silent except for the faint crackle of a log in the fireplace and the drip of spilled wine sliding off the edge of the desk.

Then, just as abruptly as the storm had started, it broke. Antonio inhaled deeply through his nose, straightened his jacket, and smoothed his hair as though nothing had happened. The transformation was terrifyingly calm.

"Clean this up," he ordered flatly, gesturing to the shattered glass and scattered papers. His men scrambled to obey. Enrico lingered only long enough to make sure Trevor didn't move before stepping toward the door.

"Enrico," Antonio said without looking up. "Find out who

tipped the police. Quietly."

"Yes, boss." Enrico's voice was low, efficient. He glanced once more at Trevor as he passed—an unspoken warning, colder this time. Then he was gone, the door clicking shut behind him.

The silence that followed was worse than the shouting. Antonio's men crawled across the floor like ants searching for food.

Trevor stood there, pulse pounding, watching Antonio retrieve another glass from the cabinet as if they hadn't just witnessed a meltdown. Returning to his desk, Antonio stepped over one of his men as if he were an ottoman. Trevor couldn't keep it in anymore. Claire's comment still circulating in his head, he knew this might be his only chance. "You never answered my question."

With an annoyed sigh, Antonio looked up, brow arched. "Which one?"

"The one that actually matters." Trevor took a step forward, ignoring the ache in his leg. "Are you still getting Addie the heart?"

Antonio's expression didn't change, but his eyes sharpened—a predator focused on prey. "Of course I am. I gave you my word, didn't I?"

"Your word?" Trevor's voice cracked, anger breaking through his fear. "You promised me she'd get it. That she'd live."

Antonio set his glass down with deliberate care. "And she will, as long as you continue to do your part. You want her alive; I want order restored and my shipments in America. We both have motivation."

Trevor's hands curled into fists at his sides. "You said as soon as I was back in Rome, you'd make the call. I've been here for over a week."

Antonio smiled faintly, that cold, patient smile that meant he thought he was teaching a lesson. "I'll tell you what, *mio figlio*, you give me the information I need to get shipments through the port undetected, then I'll call."

"You just keep putting it off. You can't do it, can you?"

"You watch your tongue—" Antonio's temper began to rise again, threatening to spill over.

Trevor didn't back down this time.

His voice came out low, steady. "No."

Antonio froze mid-breath. "No?"

"I'm not helping you," Trevor said, the words solidifying into something stronger than fear. "Not until you make the call."

The silence stretched razor-thin. Antonio's jaw tightened, eyes narrowing to slits. The men cleaning the floor went still.

Then Antonio's smile returned—slow, serpentine. "Careful, mio figlio. That sounds an awful lot like defiance."

Trevor met his gaze without blinking. "Maybe it is."

Antonio leaned back, studying him like a lion considering whether or not to strike. "You forget who you're talking to."

"No," Trevor's voice was calm. "I know exactly who you are—I always have. Now, I see you're not as powerful as you want people to believe."

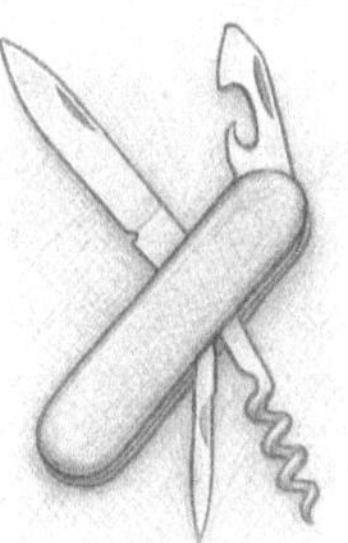

28
The Breaking Point

Antonio didn't move, but fury burned behind his eyes.
Trevor's words hung between them like a lit fuse—thin, trembling, and seconds from detonation.

I know exactly who you are—I always have.
Now I see you're not as powerful as you want people to believe.

For a heartbeat, Antonio simply stared. His eyes—dark, cold, calculating—shifted slightly, as though choosing where to land the first blow. The air in the office tightened; even the men cleaning glass had frozen mid-movement.
Then Antonio stepped around the desk.
Slowly.
Deliberately.
His shoes clicked on the wood floor, each step echoing in Trevor's chest like a countdown. Trevor's pulse hammered, but he didn't look away. He wouldn't. He was a soldier on a battlefield again, and he knew from experience—looking away got you shot.
Antonio stopped inches from him.
"Mio figlio," he murmured, voice unnervingly soft. "You're speaking about things you know nothing about."

Trevor swallowed, but he held his ground.

Antonio's jaw flexed—once, twice—before he lifted a hand as if to brush a speck of dust from Trevor's shoulder.

Instead, he clamped down—hard.

Trevor sucked in a breath as Antonio yanked him half a step closer, eyes burning with simmering fury.

"You don't realize, do you?" Antonio whispered. "You were valuable because you were my blood. The Rossettis valued blood. They're gone now. The only value you have left is your knowledge of that port."

His fingers tightened.

"I can get that knowledge in any way I choose."

Trevor braced for a punch—but the pain that followed was far worse.

Antonio's other hand shot down and clamped around Trevor's injured thigh like a vise, fingertips digging straight into the raw, still-healing flesh. Trevor dropped instantly, unable to bear weight as molten agony ripped through his leg and into his hip. It felt like being shot all over again. Warmth spread beneath his tux pants—blood through the gauze.

Clutching his leg, he refused to cry out. He wouldn't give Antonio the satisfaction.

Looking down at him, Antonio's voice was calm, almost bored. "A son who forgets his place must be reminded."

With a flick of his hand, two of the men who'd been clearing glass rushed over. They hauled Trevor up by the arms, dragging him across the floor before he could react. A trail of blood dotted the polished wood behind them.

Up the stairs. Down the hall. Into his room.

They tossed him inside. Trevor hit the floor on his hip, white-hot pain reverberating up his leg. The door slammed, the soft click of the lock sounded—final, absolute.

Finally alone, Trevor let out the guttural cry he'd been holding in since Antonio's fingers dug into his wound.

Moonlight spilled through the picture window—soft, serene, painfully at odds with the violence he'd just endured. It was the only light in the room, and it took a moment for his eyes to adjust to the dark.

His pant leg clung to him, heavy and soaked in blood. He needed his medical supplies. Pushing up to his knees he tried to stand. Unable to, Trevor collapsed and crawled—dragging his leg behind him as he army-crawled toward the desk and the box of medical supplies. His determination and sheer stubbornness were the only things that pushed him forward.

Propping himself against the desk, he fumbled open the pain meds. With no water, he swallowed them dry, forcing them down with saliva alone. Moonlight gave just enough light for his eyes to adjust.

Next, he shimmied his pants down over his hips—each movement causing more pain. When he exposed the wound, the bleeding was already beginning to slow, his body doing its best to clot the blood. He pulled on gloves and cleaned around the fresh bleed with alcohol wipes, pausing repeatedly as waves of dizziness and nausea rolled through him. When the area was clean, he tore open fresh gauze and pressed pads to either side of his thigh. Pain and nausea ripped through him with the pressure. Without lidocaine, all he could do was wait for the pills to kick in. Thirty agonizing minutes.

His teeth ground together as he held pressure until the bleeding finally stopped. He wrapped the thigh in layers of clean gauze, then slumped back, trying to breathe through the throbbing.

Trevor pictured what Antonio would see if he walked in now—blood streaked across the floor, Trevor slumped against the desk, pants halfway down his legs. The thought made his stomach twist. He hated giving Antonio even a glimpse of weakness. He gave himself another minute to recenter before he removed his shoes and stripped his pants the rest of the way off.

Bracing on the desk, he pushed himself upright, putting all of his weight on his good leg and the desk. Then he shoved the desk chair forward, using it like a makeshift crutch as he shuffled toward the bed. The chair feet screeched against the floor with every shove. He didn't care if he scratched the floor—he just needed the bed.

His cane was presumably still in the office where he had dropped it when he collapsed. The crutch Claire had gotten him waited by the bedside—he'd need it now more than ever.

Once he reached the bed he was able to sit down and slide his way up to the pillows. Pulling himself all the way onto his bed, he used a pillow to prop up his leg before stripping off his jacket. He was about to toss it aside when he thought of his cell phone in the breast pocket.

Checking the time, it was just after 10 p.m.—3 p.m. back home. Unlocking his phone, Trevor pulled up his dad's contact and took a steadying breath. Grant still didn't know about the original gunshot wound, and he couldn't hear pain in Trevor's voice tonight. If he did, his dad would be on the next plane out.

The phone only rang once before Grant's voice filled the silence, "Trevor, this is a nice surprise! It's late there. Is everything alright?"

"Yeah... yeah I'm good." His voice cracked a little on the first word. He swallowed hard and hoped it didn't give him away. "I just got some alone time and wanted to say hi."

"Okay, let me get your mom."

A soft shuffle, muffled voices and an audible change indicating he was now on speaker. Then Alexis came on, her tone bright and instantly soothing. "Hi, baby. We miss you."

Trevor used to hate the nickname but in this moment "baby" gave him a sense of comfort and home. Tonight, it felt like oxygen. "Hey. How is everything there? How's Addie?"

"We were actually going to text you tomorrow," Grant said, excitement bubbling under his words. "Addie's doing really well. They're discharging her tomorrow. It's a few days early. The doctors say she's doing remarkably well."

Trevor felt the weight lift. His sister was doing well. She's okay. Safe. Relief hit him so hard his vision blurred from unshed tears.

Then Alexis spoke—gently, carefully. "We were hoping that since she's doing so well... you might consider coming home."

Trevor went very still.

When he didn't answer, she continued softly. "You don't need to be there. Not anymore. Dr. Patel said she's doing so well with the LVAD that... she has longer than they originally thought. We have more time."

Trevor's heart swelled. *He could leave. He should leave.*

Claire's words echoed in his head again. *If he could... why hasn't he already?*

"Son?" Grant prompted quietly, breaking the echo.

"Yeah, sorry. I'm here." Trevor hadn't realized how long he'd been lost in thought.

Grant's tone deepened, steady, warm and fatherly. "Staying there... it's just putting you in danger. We don't need that man. You have a future here. Med school. Your family. We don't want you to jeopardize that. Wanting to help your sister is admirable—but you don't have to sacrifice yourself anymore."

The words hit harder than Antonio's grip.

Trevor stared into the darkness of his room, the sting in his leg pulsing like a reminder of exactly how unsafe he was. He wanted to go home. He needed to go home. Antonio proved that tonight.

"I'll be home as soon as I can." The truth of it nearly broke him. Relief rushed through his chest so sharply it released the tears that had filled his eyes. "I promise. I'm coming home."

After sending his love to Addie, Trevor said goodbye and hung up. It was too late to leave now, wasn't it? He noticed the sting in his leg was beginning to dull.

This might be the only chance he'd get to leave.

With the decision made, he grabbed his crutch and hobbled toward the wardrobe and his duffel bag. He moved quickly and efficiently, making sure to take only the belongings he had arrived with and leaving behind the new suits Antonio had provided. He didn't want any part of that man in his life. He did take the extra medical supplies, tossing them into his backpack.

Once his bags were packed the last thing he had to do was change, he couldn't exactly leave in a tuxedo shirt and his briefs.

Pulling on his loose sweat pants he found a t-shirt and replaced the button up with it. He was putting on his leather jacket when he remembered the burner phone.

He'd need to turn off his phone until he left the country, just to be safe, and he should let Claire know he's leaving. Without another thought he retrieved the battery from behind the headboard. Climbing onto the chair to retrieve the phone was harder now with the pain, but he managed to get it out without trouble.

Trevor dropped back onto the bed, breathing hard from the simple act of climbing. His leg throbbed with every heartbeat, but the burner phone was finally in his hand. He slid the battery in, listening for the quiet click. The screen stayed dark—perfect. He didn't want it on yet, not until he was away from the villa.

He shoved the flip phone into his jacket pocket, grabbed his crutch, and tossed his backpack and duffel onto his back. Crossing the room, his pulse had steadied into a grim, determined rhythm.

Leaving was the only option.

He paused with his hand on the doorknob.

Locked.

He hadn't expected anything else—he'd heard the lock click—but the sudden, unmoving resistance still made his stomach twist.

His leg burned with all of the movement from the last few minutes. Closing his eyes, he exhaled through his nose, steady and controlled, pushing the pain away and clearing his mind. He could do this.

He *had* to do this.

Trevor leaned into the crutch, dragged his duffel closer, and reached into the side pocket for the Swiss Army knife Grant had given him years ago. The weight of it felt grounding in his palm—a memory, a lifeline, a silent reminder of who his family was. Not Antonio.

Kneeling on his bad leg was out of the question, so he eased down onto his good knee and braced the crutch against the wall to keep himself upright. He slid out one of the thinner tools tucked inside the knife's handle.

He'd picked locks before, barracks doors with cheap latches, supply room padlocks with worn teeth. Dumb pranks from bored soldiers. This shouldn't be much different—just higher stakes.

He slid the thin tool into the lock and tested the tension. It was too small. He pulled it out and flipped to a different tool. This one fit. His hand shook as he lifted the pins, searching for one that would set. His injured leg throbbed beneath him, and the crutch wobbled threatening to slip if he shifted wrong.

Come on...

A faint click—and then nothing.

He twisted the tool, applied a little pressure—too much. The tool flexed, threatening to snap. He eased off, breathed through the burn in his thigh, and tried again.

Click.

Another.

Only one more. He steadied his hand and pushed the tool in a hair further.

Click. The final tumbler slipped into place with a soft metallic snap that sounded deafening in the silence—loud enough he froze, listening for footsteps.

Trevor exhaled shakily and eased the doorknob, cracking the door just enough to listen. Nothing—no footsteps, no voices, no guards.

For once, Antonio's arrogance benefited him. He folded the knife with shaking fingers and pocketed it.

He slipped into the hall and quietly closed the door. He gripped the crutch and kept his injured leg lifted as he moved as fast as he could down the corridor. Keeping the leg lifted felt like Antonio's hand digging into it all over again—but he bit down on the pain, refusing to stop. Putting weight on it would only slow him down.

The villa was dark and quiet—unnervingly so. Dim sconces offered just enough light, shadows stretching long across the tile floor. The men who'd dragged him upstairs were nowhere in sight.

Trevor took the stairs slowly, lowering his weight one step at a time. Halfway down, he had to stop and brace himself against the hand rail as dizziness crept back in, but he forced the wave down. He was almost out. He could see the foyer—

Voices.

Soft. Tense.

He descended the last few stairs, doing his best not to make a sound. Pausing at the foot of the stairs, his heart hammered. The office door was cracked open, light spilling into the hall. He inched closer, staying just out of sight.

Antonio.

And Enrico.

Their tones were hushed, edged not with anger, but with paranoia and calculation.

Trevor's breath hitched. He shouldn't listen. He should leave now, while he still could.

But then he heard it.

"...the shooting should have scared him straight," Enrico murmured. "If he's still thinking about being defiant, maybe he needs another reminder."

Trevor's blood ran cold.

He pressed himself tighter against the wall, pulse pounding so loud he was sure they'd hear.

Antonio's reply was low, measured.

Deadly.

"That won't be necessary. He knows his place now. He bleeds, he obeys. We arranged the shooting to cripple him—keep him focused on his own pain and not me. And as long as he gives me the port intel, I don't care if he crawls home afterward."

Enrico snorted. "I should have tortured the intel out of him when he arrived."

Trevor's vision tunneled. The room blurred. His grip tightened around the crutch until his knuckles went white.

They were talking about *him*.

About the night he was shot.

About *ordering* it.

Antonio's voice came again, cold as marble.

"And let the Rossettis' see him bloody and bruised? No. He's desperate to get what he wants, he knows his place now. He'll behave."

Trevor's stomach twisted. The world seemed to tilt beneath him. Every instinct screamed at him to run—but something stronger rooted him to the spot.

They had orchestrated the shooting. They had nearly killed him just to benefit their game.

And they would do whatever it took to get the intel—including coming after him.

They thought they could manipulate him—promise him his sister would live and then just let her die. Shoot him, and he'd just behave.

Antonio needed to be taken down. And Trevor—bleeding, exhausted, and limping—finally understood:

He wasn't going home.

Not yet.

29
Behind the Iron Gate

Trevor was still straining to hear more details when a chair scraped and footsteps moved closer to the door. He couldn't run—not with the condition of his leg. Even if he bolted now, he'd only make it up the first few stairs before the door flung open and he'd be caught in plain view. The only room close enough to duck into was the sitting room, but it had no exits. He'd be cornered instantly.

With no other option, Trevor took a few steps back into the formal sitting room. His leg screamed in protest as he forced himself to walk normally, fearing the crutch's rubber foot would make a noise on the tile floor. His gear made him bulky—backpack on one shoulder, duffel on the other—too big to vanish behind anything small. He needed a spot that could hide all of it. Taking the first option he saw, he wedged himself between an armchair and a towering Weeping Fig tree; the shadows and foliage swallowed him just enough to stay hidden.

He sucked in a sharp breath as Enrico stepped into the hallway.

The older man strode toward the foyer, passing only a few feet in front of Trevor's hiding spot. Trevor pressed himself tighter against the wall, his heartbeat thundering in his ears.

Enrico reached the front hall—then froze mid-step. He turned slowly, scanning the shadows.

Trevor's grip tightened around the crutch.

One more step and Trevor would be exposed—visible in Enrico's line of sight.

"Enrico." Antonio's voice cut through the silence.

The man pivoted sharply. "Boss?"

"Inside. Now," Antonio called from the office. "We're not finished."

Enrico hesitated—just long enough to make Trevor's blood run ice cold—then headed back the way he had come, his footsteps clacking sharply against the tile.

Trevor waited until the office door clicked shut before moving, every instinct screaming at him to run even though he couldn't. He tucked the crutch under his arm, slipped past the Fig tree and moved as fast as he could toward the stairs. Halfway up, he thought he heard voices drift closer to the door. Instead of stopping to look back, he kept his eyes forward and moved like bullets were flying behind him—if they caught him with his bags, bullets might actually fly.

At the top, he lifted his bad leg and pushed forward as fast as he dared, praying he didn't misstep and fall. He reached his room and ducked inside, adrenaline firing through every vein. He nearly slammed the door but caught himself, flipped the lock from the outside, and eased it shut.

His heartbeat didn't ease until he'd unpacked everything, returning the room to exactly how it had looked before—except for the burner phone clutched in his hand. He scanned the room for anything he could use to barricade the door. The wardrobe and desk were out, he couldn't lift them—too heavy—and if he slid them across the floor it would make too much noise. Similarly, the nightstands were topped in a thick slab of marble, also making them too heavy. The only possible option was the desk chair—but it was vintage, fragile and it creaked when he sat on it. If someone gave a quick push on the door, it would snap in half—easily. It wasn't worth it. Instead, Trevor grabbed his dog tags from his backpack, he hadn't worn them to the gala, and looped them gently around the door handle. If the handle moved, the tags would swing and clatter—just loud enough to wake him.

Crutch tucked under one arm, Trevor limped back to the bed. Leaving on his sweatpants he removed his leather jacket and settled into the soft cushions of the mattress. Placing a pillow beneath his leg he made sure to elevate it as best as he could. Even with the pain medication kicking in, his leg still burned—deep, sharp, and unmistakably nerve pain.

Leaning back, he debated calling Claire now. He needed her help, he couldn't do this alone. But he may only have one chance to call her and if she didn't pick up, he had no other way of getting in contact. His personal cellphone was too risky and could trace back to her location. He would have to wait. It was already the early hours of the morning, a few more hours and he'd be more likely to get through.

He tucked the burner phone into the waistband of his briefs and sank down into the bed. The last thing he managed to do before losing consciousness was to pull the covers over his torso and uninjured leg, burying the phone beneath layers of fabric.

Trevor woke with the first rays of sunlight shining across his bed. He hadn't gotten much sleep between the ache in his leg and his fear that someone might come through the door at any second. But he couldn't wait, he had a phone call to make.

Sitting up, he reached for his leather jacket on the end of his bed. The SIM card was still tucked into the cavity between the lining and the leather. Reaching into the inside breast pocket with the hole, he tipped the jacket sideways trying to get the tiny computer chip to reappear.

Nothing.

He pushed his fingers deeper into the hole, the threads biting into his skin. He still didn't feel it. Tilting his jacket he shook it, hoping to dislodge the tiny card. Still no luck. After a moment of debate, he accepted he had no choice—he'd have to make the hole bigger. It was only the lining and he had already paid for it to be replaced once, he could always do it again. Retrieving his knife out of his jacket pocket, where he'd put it the night before, Trevor pulled out the straight blade and sawed along the bottom inside of the pocket. The lining fabric gave way easily but when he got to the edges of the pocket fabric he still couldn't fit his hand all the way in.

Deciding to try one last time to get the SIM out before cutting the lining even more, he shook the jacket and felt the small device hit his fingers and then slide past into the cavity again. Taking a deep breath he tried again, tipping it back the opposite way. Finally, the tiny SIM dropped onto his fingertips and slid down to the palm of his hand.

Trevor exhaled shakily, closing his fist around the SIM like it was a lifeline.

Removing his phone from the waistband of his briefs, it left behind a red indent on his skin. Careful not to drop the SIM he removed the battery and slid the chip into its slot beneath. Snapping the battery and the back panel back into place, he held down the power button. The old screen flickered, glowed faintly, and then stabilized, fully powering on.

A clean, untraceable number. But he only had one chance, Claire had said he could only use it once before he had to toss it. This was it.

Trevor toggled over to the contact Kane had pre-programmed in.

He hesitated.

His hand trembled—from pain, fear, exhaustion, he wasn't sure—but he pressed CALL before he could overthink it.

The ring was soft; he waited, his heart beating in tandem with the seconds. Then Kane's voice filled the speaker, half a whisper, half panic.

"Trevor?! "

Relief slammed into his chest so hard his eyes stung.

"Yeah," Trevor breathed. "It's me."

He heard the chaotic scramble of Kane's feet on hardwood before he spoke again, "Claire, Colin—wake up, get in here. Now. Trevor's on the phone."

The rolling of wheels, and clacking from computer keys were followed by running feet growing louder and louder.

"Trevor? You okay?" Colin's voice was slightly groggy, but warm and full of concern.

And then Claire.

Wide awake. Sharp. Breathless. "Trev?"

Everything inside him softened at the sound of her voice.

"I'm here," he said quietly.

A beat of silence floated between them—heavy and fragile.

Then Kane whispered, "Alright, we're good. Talk to us."

Trevor swallowed, steeling himself.

"I want out," he said. "I'm done. I'm going home."

Claire sighed audibly; he could feel her relief through the phone.

"Wait, Trev... why now? It can't be because of what I said last night." Her voice tightened, he knew if he could see her right now, her mind would be running away with theories.

He glanced down at his bandaged thigh—at the dried blood staining the gauze—and forced his voice steady.

"Long story short—you were right. He's never going to follow through. And I'm just putting my life at risk being here. I overheard Antonio last night—he sent the cops that shot me. It was the plan to keep me... preoccupied."

The line went silent before all three voices erupted at once. He couldn't make out a single word. His pulse spiked as he glanced toward the closed door, irrationally certain someone might overhear their outrage even through the thin wood.

Trevor cut them off, voice low, controlled. "He never planned on helping Addie. It was leverage. He wants information about a port my platoon was stationed at for a while."

Claire's voice broke in—furious and scared and soft all at once.

"Trev... I'm so sorry."

He closed his eyes, letting the ache settle and her voice soothe his raw edges. He pictured her leaning against him—his arms around her—both of them somewhere safe.

"I'm going home as soon as I can, but he can't be allowed to get away with this. He needs to pay. I want to help you make him pay."

A pause.

"Your help could be useful, but you could be there a lot longer. That's not taking you out of harm's way." Colin's voice was steady and reasonable, and Trevor was ready to hear him out.

But then Claire spoke up, agitated and fiery. "What?! No. No, you're not going to be a mole. Do you know what happens to most moles and CI's? They're killed. You're going home."

Trevor pressed his palm over his eyes. "Even if there is something happening tonight? I could be done by this time tomorrow."

There was the faint sound of arguing before Kane cut in, interrupting Colin and Claire, "Tell us more."

"There's a meeting tonight. We were supposed to be meeting with the Rossetti's at 9, at the port Antonio uses most often, I don't know the name. What I do know is that Antonio's moving a huge shipment—weapons, ammo—and he wanted me to walk the new partners through how to get past U.S. port security."

"The port of Civitavecchia," Kane said. "There's been chatter for years about it, but no one could ever get eyes inside."

Colin spoke next, all business. "What's his plan now that the Rossetti's were arrested?"

"I don't know exactly, but I know he's pissed and not going to let all his planning go to waste. He needs the intel from me and then he'll move forward."

"Move forward with what? The shipment or getting rid of you?" Claire's voice was tight and unwavering. "You can't do this. The minute you give him the information he wants, you're as good as dead. He's already shot you once, how do you know he won't do it again?"

Trevor didn't know what to say. He waited for Kane or Colin to back him up, but the silence stretched uncomfortably until Colin finally broke it.

"Trevor, has he hurt you again?"

"I'm fine. He assaulted me last night, but I'm okay." He made sure to stress the word 'okay,' but he could still visualize Claire throwing her hands up in the air like she used to in the gym after a hard day.

Claire's voice went razor-sharp when she snapped. "And you still want to put yourself in this position?"

Trevor pressed his palm over his eyes."I do. For you, for me, for Addie, and for every other person he's hurt. He's got to be held accountable and I'm probably as close as anyone is ever going to get. It could all be over in less than 24 hours."

Colin added, "He's right. If we can get the intel, the whole network collapses."

Kane chimed in eagerly, "All we need is audio. A clean recording. Names, routes, quantities. That's enough to bury him."

Claire's voice was a whisper—trembling with anger and fear.

"Trevor, he already hurt you. He *shot* you. If he suspects anything—"

"He won't," Trevor lied gently. "He needs me. He thinks I'm scared enough to behave."

"You're not scared," Claire bit out. "You're injured."

Kane, oblivious to emotional nuance, muttered, "Okay, so we're voting? Because I vote in favor of the mole plan."

"Same," Colin said. "He's right. He's the only one who can get close."

"Kane, Colin, I swear to God—" Claire snapped.

Trevor cut in softly, "Claire. Please."

A long silence.

Her breath cracked.

Then, barely audible,

"If you die..." Her last word hung in the air, the weight heavier than the weight of the world.

He didn't know what to say. He knew the risks, and he wouldn't promise her something that he couldn't guarantee.

Claire exhaled shakily, defeated but still trembling with fight.

"Fine," she whispered. "We'll be there outside the

warehouse. Close enough to get you out if anything goes wrong."

He nodded, even though she couldn't see it.

Kane said quickly, "I'll prep a micro-cam and transmitter. Colin can get it to you through the garden gate."

Trevor steadied his breathing.

"Okay. Technically I've been locked in my room, so we should probably wait until after a meal. I can convince Domenico to let me take a walk after one. Antonio usually eats lunch at 1 pm sharp, can you get here by 1:30?"

"I'll be there," Colin assured him. "We won't get to speak again until it's over. Plant the device on someone besides yourself— someone who won't leave the room or get scanned. Antonio, if possible. If they suspect anything, they'll sweep you. But they'd never sweep him."

"Okay, do I need to turn it on?"

"No," Kane walked Trevor through the best places to hide the device, what it would look like, and how to attach it without it being seen.

When they were done, the call disconnected before Trevor even thought to say goodbye.

He sat in silence, processing everything, the phone bouncing in his trembling hands.

Trevor didn't know how this was going to end—but he was going to make sure Antonio paid.

And despite this burning leg pain, he sure as hell was going to try to make it back to Claire in one piece.

Before anything else, Trevor had to deal with the burner phone. His one call was used—now the phone had to disappear. Powering it down, he popped the back panel loose, slid out the SIM, and snapped it clean between his fingers. The battery followed. Then, using his pocketknife, he pried into the hinge until the flimsy plastic spine cracked in half. Only when the phone lay in three useless pieces on the bed did he finally breathe. No one was tracing this.

When his hands finally stopped shaking, he hid the pieces. If anyone found proof he'd contacted the outside... it was over.

The SIM card he wrapped inside the bloody gauze from the night before—disgusting enough that no one would dare sift through it. He stared at the battery and cracked shell, debating where else to hide them. He didn't want to repeat a spot but could only see places that were too obvious: the toilet tank, folded into clothing, or under the mattress.

The mattress made him pause. While under the mattress or in an obvious hole would be found quickly, what if he hid the hole in a seam? Pulling up the corner of the sheets, he looked at the pinched stitched edges. If he made a hole using his knife, one only just big enough it might just work. He opened his knife and slid the blade along the seam, making sure to only cut a hole just big enough to fit the broken pieces. When it was done he slid the pieces inside, as deep as he could get them, and replaced the sheets. It would have to do for now.

He then showered in the attached bathroom and redressed his wound. Testing his door handle afterward, he found it still locked. He wasn't sure if this made him feel safer—or more afraid.

Before returning to his bed, he removed his dog tags from the door handle, slipping them back around his neck and beneath his shirt.

By the time noon approached, his leg had settled into a relentless, pulsing ache—pinching when he shifted wrong, nagging when he stayed still. He did his best to ignore it. He had to. If he let himself linger on the pain, he'd crack before the meeting even began.

At 12:55 p.m., just as he predicted, there was a knock.

"Signor Trevor?" Domenico's soft voice called through the door. "Lunch is ready. I was told to bring you a tray."

Trevor's heart jumped. Perfect. He could convince Domenico to let him out for a walk.

He pulled himself upright on the bed, as the older man unlocked the door and stepped inside.

Domenico pushed in a cart topped with pasta, bread, and water. The scent of tomato, basil and garlic was normally mouthwatering, but today it turned his stomach—probably from pain and taking meds without food. As he approached the bed, Domenico paused, his eyes dropping to Trevor's leg.

"You are bleeding again?" Domenico murmured. His voice faltered as his eyes flicked to the doorway behind him, like he expected someone to barge through it at any second.

Trevor forced a stiff smile. "Just a rough night. I'll be fine."

Domenico hesitated longer than usual. His eyes flicking toward the doorway, then back to Trevor. A nervous tension crept into his posture, like the man was caught between a rock and a firing squad.

"Eat," Domenico said as he backed away. "You'll need your strength, later." He raised his eyebrows on the last part of the sentence. Trevor got the sense that he was trying to convey something he didn't dare speak.

He knew what was going on—of course he did. Trevor yet to find a single thing the man didn't notice.

Domenico reached the doorway and turned. As he pulled the door shut Trevor caught the shift in his expression. A flicker of unease. Of guilt?

When the door shut, the lock clicked—softer this time, slower, like Domenico was hesitating.

He hadn't eaten since last night, and knew he should at least try. Eating the bread first he then tried the pasta, but he only got two bites before his stomach rebelled. He pushed the cart away and checked his personal phone for the time, waiting as it crept closer and closer to half past.

When it was twenty minutes past he got up and used his crutch to hobble toward the door.

Knocking lightly on the inside of his own door, he knew Domenico wouldn't be far, ready to collect the dishes.

"Domenico?" Trevor called softly. "I'm finished."

A few beats of silence and then the lock clicked.

Domenico opened the door ready to take the cart, but when he saw it was still on the other side of the room his face tightened.

"Could I get some air? Just on the grounds? Please. Five minutes," Trevor used his eyes to plead, channeling the look his sister often gave their mom. "Only the garden. Nowhere else."

The older man's eyes darted back toward the staircase before softening. He nodded briskly and stepped aside, waving him on.

Trevor kept his weight on his good leg, and nodded. "Thank you."

He made his way down the hall, down the stairs, ignoring the spike of pain with each step. The villa was quiet—eerie quiet—it hummed with that pre-storm tension he now recognized as Antonio's moods shaping the whole building.

Out in the courtyard, sunlight hit him like a slap. Warm. Bright. Almost unreal.

Domenico followed a few paces behind, pretending not to watch him. But he was watching. Every step.

Trevor kept to the outer path of the garden, walking slowly along the hedge-lined walkway. His heart picked up when the wrought-iron side gate came into view, half-hidden behind climbing roses.

He didn't look at the fence. Didn't glance. Didn't break stride or move faster.

He made a slow lap of the courtyard, until he heard the faintest tap of a stone. He waited for a tackle, a yell or anything that would indicate Domenico had also heard. But nothing came.

It was a signal.

Trevor paused near the gate as if admiring a bush of roses. Down the path behind him, Domenico checked his watch.

Now.

Trevor shifted his weight and moved toward the gate. His leg throbbed hard enough his vision blurred, but he didn't stop. He'd only have seconds before Domenico was watching again. Planting his crutch quietly on the decorative gravel in the bed, he took one step closer to the gate.

Close enough now, he angled his body to block the house's view. Crouching—or trying to—he faked the motion of tying his shoe. Pain ripped down his thigh, nearly taking him out, but he forced himself lower.

A hand shot through the bars—fast.

Colin's.

Trevor reached instinctively, doing his best not to look at the tiny plastic case in Colin's hand. But instead of his fingers closing over the camera case he knocked it. The case landed in the gravel with a soft thunk.

Looking this time he grabbed it as fast as he could before looking back at his shoe and attempting to "retie" the laces.

Colin whispered urgently through the fence, "You good?"

Trevor gave the faintest nod.

Colin's voice dropped even lower. "Be careful. Claire's gonna kill both of us for this."

Trevor huffed a quiet breath—something almost like a laugh—then glanced behind him.

Domenico had turned.

He was heading in their direction. Fast.

Colin vanished from view in an instant—but Trevor heard a sharp hiss. Colin had caught his hand on a rose thorn, ripping open the top of his hand.

Trevor straightened too quickly, pain spearing his leg. He forced his face neutral and pretended to admire the climbing rose vine as Domenico approached. With the case still in his hand, he closed his fingers around it and slid the thin case under his watch strap—praying the cuff of his sleeve would cover any view of it.

"Time is up," Domenico said, voice tight and eyebrows drawn together.

Had he seen Colin?

Trevor swallowed. "Okay. Heading back."

Domenico didn't respond. He only stepped aside to let Trevor pass, his eyes darting once—just once—toward the gate. His face didn't read as angry, or suspicious—it was raw fear that filled Domenico's eyes.

Trevor saw it.

Then he limped past him, heart pounding up in his throat.

Tonight, everything would hinge on this.

Everything.

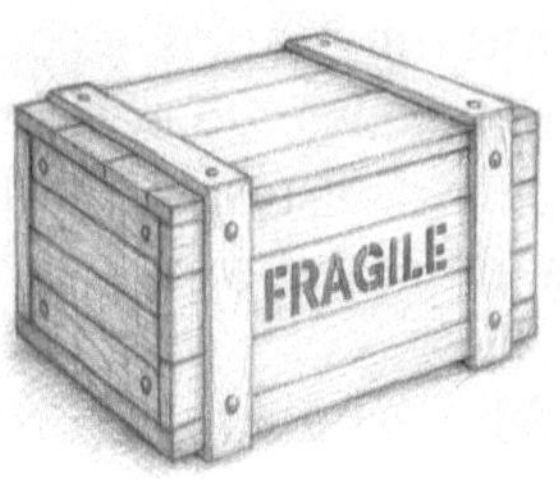

30
Trigger Point

When Domenico came to retrieve him earlier than planned, Trevor felt his blood pressure spike. He had just finished changing into jeans and a T-shirt, ready for tonight's trip to the docks. Grabbing his leather jacket from the bed, he felt the familiar weight of his Swiss Army knife settle against his right thigh—one of the few things that made him feel remotely armed.

Shrugging into his jacket he felt the outline of the micro-camera's case in his left pocket. He still wasn't sure how he was going to get it onto Antonio, but he'd figure it out. Kane had said the device was designed to slip into the grooves of a jacket button—so small it vanished unless someone swept it with a frequency wand.

Following Domenico down the stairs, Trevor listened to his crutch tap a steady rhythm against the tile. His leg felt marginally better after resting all day and taking pain meds an hour earlier, but every step reminded him that he was operating on borrowed strength. Halfway down, a second set of footsteps fell in behind them. One of the men who'd dragged him to his room the night before now flanked him silently.

Right. A babysitter. Insurance that Trevor didn't run—or try anything stupid.

His thoughts spiraled. *Was something changing? Was Antonio already adjusting the plan?* He could move the meeting. Cancel it. Force Trevor to give up the port information right here in the office. If that happened, Trevor would be trapped in this villa even longer... and he wasn't sure he could endure another night under this roof.

The whole place felt suffocating. Earlier, the villa's tension had been heavy enough to taste—everyone breathing shallow, terrified to disturb the air. Somehow it felt heavier now, thick and electric, the kind of atmosphere where a wrong breath might get someone killed.

Stepping into the cigar-scented office, Trevor found himself alone with Antonio and Enrico. They stood near the massive walnut desk, trading quick, sharp sentences in Italian. No greeting. No glance in his direction. Trevor glanced behind him, only to see the heavy double doors closed—Domenico gone, no buffer left.

He hovered awkwardly, unable to sit; the chairs were blocked, and he wasn't about to piss off Antonio by touching *his* chair. So he stood there, pain slowly blooming down his leg as the seconds dragged by.

While they were distracted, Trevor forced himself to breathe and scanned the room. Behind the desk, Antonio's suit jacket hung on a polished coat rack—freshly steamed, draped over a hanger, and perfectly positioned for exactly what Trevor needed to do.

He shifted his weight forward, ready to drift toward the coat rack and built-in bookcase behind it, when Antonio suddenly looked over. The sudden movement sent a jolt up his spine. Antonio's gaze was hard enough to cut a diamond.

"How was your day? Feeling better after your rough night?" He stressed the words *'rough night'* just enough to send panic slicing through Trevor's bloodstream.

Did Antonio know he'd tried to escape? Had Enrico seen him in the hall?

Trevor forced himself to keep breathing. He had to assume Antonio only meant Trevor's defiance from the night before.

"Yes, sir. I feel better. And... I apologize for my mood." He summoned the same tone he'd used with superior officers in the Army, though the apology caught in his throat like barbed wire.

A slow, sadistic smile curled across Antonio's face—the kind that terrified Trevor more than he'd ever admit.

"Good. And you're ready to share your information about the dock."

"Yes, sir. I'll tell you everything I know."

Antonio studied him for one long, dissecting beat — as if weighing the value of fear versus obedience. Whatever he saw, or whatever conclusion he reached, seemed to satisfy him. Because he dismissed Trevor with a flick of his fingers.

"*Bene*. Enrico. Wait a moment. We still have business." And just like that, Trevor was nothing more than furniture again. Antonio turned back to Enrico, resuming their rapid, clipped Italian argument without another glance at him.

Trevor released a breath he didn't realize he'd been holding.

Perfect. That was the opening he needed.

He moved carefully, using his crutch for balance, drifting toward the wall of bookcases as though browsing the spines. From there, he angled himself closer to the coat rack, heart pounding in his throat. The freshly steamed suit jacket hung exactly where he needed it.

Now all he had to do... was get the camera in place before anyone looked his way.

With the plastic case still in his pocket, he eased it open as quietly as he could. Nestled into a small piece of foam was the camera. He felt for the tiny indentation in the foam near the center where Kane had said it would be. Pressing his finger as hard as he could into the camera it clung to his skin. It was so small it felt like a tiny bead, instead of a high tech recording device. Turning his finger up so the camera wouldn't fall he slowly and carefully removed it from his pocket.

His heart beat faster than he had thought possible. He didn't know how anyone did this, he'd rather have faced ten deployments than ever do this again. Hyperaware of Antonio and Enrico, he checked them out of the corner of his eye before reaching toward the jacket. Their backs were still toward him, arrogantly oblivious to his actions.

Keeping his attention on the books—not on the jacket—Trevor pressed his fingertip into the ornate carved button on   Antonio's suit jacket. Rolling his finger he felt the device slip onto one of the buttons grooves. He held his finger there for an agonizing extra second to make sure it was securely in place. Moving his finger slowly he checked to make sure it didn't move. It held.

Trevor swallowed, stepping back from the coat rack with the most casual movement he could muster, pretending to study the rows of old leather-bound books. His pulse pounded in his ears. The micro-cam was in place. If he could get out of this room without being noticed, it would be a miracle.

Antonio and Enrico's voices rose—sharp, clipped, escalating. A disagreement. Good. The more distracted they were, the better.

Trevor kept his back to them, eyes skimming meaningless titles while forcing his breath slow and quiet. *Just look like you belong. Just look like you're killing time.*

A desk drawer slammed.

Trevor flinched before he could stop himself.

Both men paused.

For a terrifying heartbeat, the room went still.

Then Antonio exhaled sharply through his nose—the irritated dismissive sound he'd often used in response to Trevor. Muttering something to Enrico, he slipped the watch he had just retrieved from the drawer on and snapped the band closed. "Andiamo. We're late."

Trevor's stomach dropped.

Late. They were leaving. This was it. He prayed that Antonio didn't see the camera tucked in the grooves of the button.

He forced himself to turn naturally, leaning more on the crutch as he stepped away from the bookcase, his heartbeat hammering like a war drum.

When Antonio approached his jacket he reached out—

And stopped his hand mid-air.

"No," he muttered, almost to himself. "Not this one." He clicked his tongue in irritation. "Domenico!"

Trevor's blood turned to ice.

What did he mean, *not this one*? That was the one he had just bugged!

Footsteps hurried in from the hallway as the older man appeared in the doorway, bowing his head in a silent question.

Antonio gestured sharply. "Bring me the pinstripe. The black one. The one with the peak lapels. I'm not wearing this tonight."

Trevor's vision tunneled for a split second, as he felt the panic flooding his system.

Domenico nodded and disappeared down the hall.

Antonio's fingers brushed the button with the device—his thumb was so close he was practically touching the lens—but then he released the jacket entirely, letting it sway back against the coat rack.

"I don't like the shoulders on this one," Antonio said to no one in particular, already turning back toward his desk.

Trevor kept his expression blank, despite his pulse racing.

He hadn't seen it—thank God.

But if Antonio didn't wear that jacket... the camera would never get inside the warehouse.

And once Domenico returned with the new one, Trevor would have mere seconds to retrieve the device before Enrico or Antonio saw him near it again.

He steadied his breathing.

He had to move.

Now.

Before Domenico came back.

And before Antonio changed his mind again.

Antonio and Enrico's backs were to him once again as he re-approached the jacket.

Trevor angled toward the rack, pretending once more to browse the books—but every muscle in his body thrummed with a single thought:

Get the camera back before it's too late.

He brushed his finger over the button, feeling for the camera... but he couldn't find it.

He leaned closer—as close as he dared, without drawing attention—and he still couldn't see it.

Domenico returned, standing at the entrance to the office, holding the jacket out for Antonio to grab as he went by. Seeing him, the two men began to leave the office.

Trevor had seconds to get the camera. He couldn't ruin this, not like this.

Slipping his hand back into his pocket, he found his knife, flicking out the blade...

"Trevor, andiamo!" His heart stopped as the words left Antonio's mouth, cold and bitter.

But he hadn't looked up. Antonio hadn't seen him with his jacket again.

With two quick strokes, he sliced the stitching holding the metal button in place. Catching it in his other hand, Trevor tucked the button, knife, and camera into his jacket as he turned his body back toward the office door to leave.

Moving quickly to catch up, it wasn't until he reached the doorway when he noticed Domenico's eyes on him—questioning him silently and full of fear.

There was nothing he could do but move past the older man and pray he hadn't seen anything.

* * *

The drive to the docks took over an hour. Trevor had been relegated to the back of Antonio's SUV like a child. Climbing into the third row with his injured leg had been torture—burning and pulling with every movement. He knew getting out would be just as bad.

Trevor's "babysitter" from before was driving, with Enrico to his right in the passenger seat. Alone in the second row, Antonio sat behind Enrico, muttering rapid Italian into his phone, his tone clipped and furious. A second SUV followed with several more men, and Trevor knew they'd be meeting even more on site.

Trevor had the full rear compartment to himself—barely enough room for his six-foot frame. His knees brushed the seatbacks, and extending his injured leg was out of the question—there simply wasn't enough room. Every time they hit a bump, he tensed, worried he'd accidentally knee Antonio in the spine. The constant constricting of his muscles meant that his leg was killing him again. So much for the pain meds. But the isolation had given him one small advantage: a modicum of privacy. If he kept his hands low, worked slowly, and only glanced down occasionally, he had enough privacy to retrieve the camera. Once he had it in hand, he tucked the device back into its case before Antonio noticed.

Now came the real problem.

How the hell was he supposed to get it onto Antonio *again?*

Antonio's jacket hung on the back of the driver's seat, ready for him to slip into the moment they parked. He wouldn't have a single clean opportunity. Even if once they got out, if he somehow managed to reach Antonio, how was he supposed to place the camera somewhere with a clear view? And without Antonio feeling or seeing him place it?

It was impossible. And more than impossible—it was suicidal.

One idea continued to claw at Trevor's mind. His thumb brushed over the tiny camera case in his palm, slick with sweat despite how cold he felt.

Fine. If he couldn't get it on Antonio, then he had to place it on himself. They needed the video footage as evidence.

He looked down at his own jacket zipper; he had taken it off when they got to the car and laid it across the seat beside him. The metal pull tab was thick, solid, with a wide enough recession where the camera could sit almost unnoticed. It wouldn't be as invisible as he would like but it would have a clear view.

Trevor slid his jacket into his lap and returned his gaze out the window. Trevor pressed his fingertip against the button, slowly shifting his finger until he felt the camera. Pushing as hard as he could he felt the lens stick to his skin the way he had before. Slowly, carefully, he moved the bead-like device into the square recess of the zipper pull. The recess was a little too large and he worried it might fall out—but it caught on the little ridge of metal and held.

Good enough.

He closed the case and felt the panic rise again.

The case. The jacket button.

Both could expose him.

His mind raced while he scanned the dark interior—then saw the deep crease where the second-row seat met the carpeted floor. A perfect hiding spot.

Antonio's voice was rising in Italian—angry, impatient. If he saw him hiding something, everything would unravel.

Trevor worked fast.

He dropped the case silently onto the carpet and used his foot to guide it into the gap. Pushing with the toe of his good leg he wedged it deep into the crease until the metal edge vanished between the carpeting. The button went next, but it wouldn't fit—at least not as deep as the camera case. It was out of sight though and that would have to be good enough.

Trevor had a sudden thought. His Swiss Army knife.

His stomach twisted. If they patted him down—and they might—someone would feel it. They'd take it. They'd question why he had it. He clenched his fist while he debated it, his pulse hammering.

Going into that warehouse without a weapon?

He couldn't.

That was suicide.

He closed his eyes, forced a slow inhale, and left it alone in his jacket pocket. If they found it, he'd deal with it. If they didn't... it might save his life.

A sharp curse from Antonio broke through the tension. The SUV slowed, then lurched as they turned off the main road. The air outside changed—colder, foggier. The docks.

Trevor braced himself with both hands as the SUV rolled over the uneven pavement leading into the lot. His leg throbbed with every bump, sweat trickling down his spine from the effort of holding himself still.

Enrico turned in his seat, checking him through narrowed eyes.

"Stay close," he warned. "Don't try anything stupid."

Trevor didn't answer. He didn't know what to say.

The SUV rolled to a stop, the other one just behind them. The doors opened.

When the doors opened, the temperature hit him. The summer day had turned into a cool coastal evening, thick with fog. Shadows shifted outside—flashlights, movement, the metallic echo of chains clinking against stacked shipping containers.

Trevor swallowed hard, adjusted his grip on his crutch, and prepared to move.

Getting out of the SUV was going to hurt like hell, but that was the least of his problems now.

Antonio hung up his phone and got out of the SUV without saying a word to anyone. Someone else had reached in and grabbed his jacket off the seat back before shaking it out and holding it for him to slide his arms into. Trevor took the moment to shift forward, giving himself more room to put on his own jacket. It was warm and offered a bit of comfort in this terrifying moment. He zipped it shut not only to keep away the chill but also to put the micro-cam at a better height for video.

When someone finally lifted the seat lever to move the seat so Trevor could get out, it had been so long it was as if they had almost forgotten him. If they hadn't needed his information, he probably would have been left in the car deliberately.

The seat back in front of him folded down so he could climb over. Raising his left leg to go over first, his injured leg burned with the use of his muscle. Straddling the seat he brought his good leg around and placed his crutch in front of him before dropping down onto his feet. The crutch took a good deal of his weight and dug into his armpit when he landed.

They had parked next to a warehouse with two docks extending to Trevor's left. Boats of all sizes were visible in the distance, but the closest were freighters stacked high with shipping containers.

Walking forward away from the car, he approached a group of Antonio's men. Antonio was speaking in hushed tones before he approached. Two men peeled off leaving the group and going around the back of the building. A slap of suspicion hit him, but he didn't have time to process it before someone approached with a wand in hand.

* * *

Claire

The SUV felt unusually small tonight, and the frigid air didn't help—she felt like she was sitting in a fridge. Kane was set up with his laptop on his lap in the backseat, while Colin sat to her left in the driver's seat. She had hated this plan from the beginning. She could see the strategic value, but it wasn't worth putting Trevor's life in danger—again.

She watched as two black SUVs entered the docks. Her heart hammered, and she couldn't decide if she wanted Trevor to be in one or not. Maybe they had left him at home—but if they had, what kind of condition would he be in? There was nothing Claire could do but wait and see.

With her handgun secured in her leg holster, and a rifle laying across her lap, she waited for any excuse to move. If she didn't do something soon her nerves might eat her alive. She hadn't noticed she was twisting her bracelet, working it back and forth around her wrist. Claire didn't dare touch the rifle, knowing she wouldn't be able to stop herself from shooting—even if it was premature.

"I've got the signal," Kane said, interrupting Claire's internal spiral.

For a moment, the only sound in the car was Kane's fingers speeding across the keys. "Oh, shit." Claire's heart stopped as the words left Kane's lips.

"What?" She turned sharply, grabbing his laptop so she could see the footage on his screen. He hated when someone touched his laptop; she'd apologize later.

On screen was a view from the back seat of Antonio's SUV,

and just in the corner of the frame was a younger man's hands holding a crutch. "It's on him. Trevor's wearing the bug."

Claire froze, her mind whirling with ways to fix this mess and get Trevor out safely. Taking his laptop back with a huff, Kane sat back and began typing again. "Yeah. It's on Trevor."

She finally moved, looking over at Colin. He had been quiet, watching her for a reaction. "Don't, Claire. Give him a chance. It's only a problem if they use a frequency wand on him. Don't panic yet."

Claire felt rage beginning to bubble; if it were Lauren, she knew he'd feel the same way. But instead of starting an argument she turned her attention back to the scene outside and muttered under her breath. "I'm not going to panic. I'm going to shoot."

They had parked their SUV several hundred feet away in a dark, unlit patch of asphalt. It was a good spot, but they had no way of knowing where Antonio's men would park. As a result, they weren't in the best location to protect Trevor and wouldn't be able to fire from the car without significant luck—and the fog clearing.

"T's out of the car and approaching Antonio's men." Kane's eyes were glued on the screen, hands posed and ready to begin a keystroke at any moment.

Claire felt the air in the car change before she heard anything. Kane's fingers began typing again, faster than Claire had known he could type. "What's going on?"

Colin placed his hand on her shoulder, not soft or comforting but restrictive—meant to make her wait and think before acting.

"They're going to wand him." Kane didn't stop typing; his fingers flying.

Claire pushed Colin's hand aside and opened the car door before anyone could stop her. She was already out of the car and running, keeping her body low and switching off the safety, when she heard Colin's door open and his footsteps following behind her. Up ahead was a concrete barrier, still nicely shadowed in the dark. The cold air bit at her skin despite her black fleece jacket being zipped all the way up. When she got to the barrier Claire dropped to her knees and balanced the tip of the rifle on top of the concrete.

When Colin finally caught up to her, his expression said it all—clenched jaw, mouth pinched and eyes narrowed. She only looked at him for a second before returning her eyes back to Trevor and leaning into the scope to get a better look.

"Kane, is there anything you can do? Claire's about to go Rambo on them." Colin hissed into the com.

"I'm almost there, I'm turning it off remotely. The only problem is I might not get it back online."

Antonio's man lifted the wand, dragging it down the sides of Trevor's pants.

Claire gripped the trigger ready to shoot the man with the frequency wand if she had to. Taking a deep breath she steadied herself. The fog made it harder to see, but they were closer now. She had the scope, and Trevor stood in the center of the warehouse's floodlights.

The wand was scanning over Trevor's torso now raising toward his neck and the top of his zipper.

Three inches.

Two inches.

"Done. It's off." The tapping of Kane's fingers stopped abruptly as he let out the breath he had been holding.

The wand passed over the zipper pull and didn't signal. Trevor was clear.

Still Claire kept looking through the scope waiting. Her attention was on Trevor but just beyond him she saw Antonio, his lip twitching ever so slightly as nothing set off the wand.

Colin didn't dare say a word. He hadn't seen her this uncontrolled—reckless—emotionally driven. Even the night they found Trevor in D.C. she had more control. She was a grenade with the pin hanging halfway out.

Trevor and the men walked into the building when she noticed his gate. Trevor was limping harder. She had known he was injured, known Antonio had assaulted him again, but seeing his visible pain fed the flames that were building in her gut.

When the door closed, Claire felt the weight of Colin's hand on the rifle's nose. "He's inside, this won't help you anymore." He spoke calmly. She instantly recognized the tactic from their de-escalation training, but before she could react Kane's urgent voice cut in.

"Ugh, I have another issue. I can get the audio back but the video, it's not working."

Together, Colin and Claire raced back to their vehicle, each running for a rear passenger door. When she whipped the back door open, Kane jumped a little. It was visual evidence that she needed to calm down. Yes, this was serious. And yes, that was Trevor inside. But emotional officers got people killed.

Taking a deep breath she reengaged the safety on the rifle and laid it over the center console as she climbed in and shut the door. Sitting next to Kane she could see his open laptop screen. Colin shut his door on the other side of Kane, squishing the three of them together like sardines.

Kane let out a groan and huffed as he scooted forward so he could get enough elbow room to still type.

Looking at his screen was like trying to read Latin. She prided herself on being decent with a computer but the gibberish coding flying across his screen was something she'd never understand. In the box where the video should be, it was simply black. But the audio was coming through clearly—and it would have to be enough.

Antonio spoke again, his voice low and deliberate—asking Trevor to walk them through the layout. The cameras. The blind spots.

Trevor answered calmly, his tone even, measured. Too measured.

Claire held her breath, fingers digging into the door handle. She prayed he was telling the truth, it wasn't worth his life if they suspected he was lying now.

The questions kept coming. Not rapid-fire—worse, slow and precise. Paperwork. Dock classifications. Packaging requirements.

It blurred together in Claire's mind—technical language, with details stacking on top of one another until all she could hear was Trevor's voice and the faint, relentless pressure behind Antonio's.

Time stretched.

And then—

Antonio's voice changed. He went from measured and probing to icy and lethal in a split second. The flip was so visceral it felt like it reached into Claire's blood—freezing it in her veins.

Claire did her best to listen carefully, not getting worked up when she realized they never set up a safe word. A word Trevor could have used to get her attention. Something to say 'I need help now, get me out.' She tried telling herself that he is a trained soldier, he's intelligent, he can think on his feet. But she felt her fire beginning to burn hotter, her worry eating away at the restraint she had put it under.

Trevor's voice wavered—just slightly—

Then a shot rang out.

She heard it outside first, with it echoing through the computer half a second later.

Shouting and more shots followed, but she barely heard them—she was already running for the building—her handgun drawn. She hadn't waited for Colin. She didn't stop to think. She just took off, not even closing the car door.

31
The Price of Survival

He'd just finished walking them through how to conceal the contraband inside the crates—what to move, what to rearrange, what inspectors rarely checked. Moments ago, Enrico had been pacing behind Antonio, restless. Now he stood completely still.

Something was coming. Trevor could feel it crawling up his spine.

He glanced at the men scattered around the warehouse— some had been pretending to work, others not to listen. Now every single one of them had gone still.

Trevor swallowed hard.

Antonio flicked two fingers—wordless. Sharp.

Several men peeled away instantly, heading toward the private office at the back of the warehouse. Boots moved fast across the concrete. A door opened—and something heavy was dragged free.

Then Antonio spoke.

"Thank you for sharing that information..." His tone was frigid, polished—wrong. "...but I wonder if you're sharing *everything* with us."

Trevor's pulse spiked. He knew it. Antonio knew something was off.

"Is there anything else you would like to share with us?" Antonio asked softly, almost inviting.

Trevor opened his mouth. "I'm not sure—"

The office door slammed open.

Two guards emerged, dragging Domenico between them.

His face was battered—one eye swollen shut, with blood running down from a split brow.

Trevor's words died in his throat.

"Domenico wasn't eager to talk either... but he's become quite *forthcoming* in the last fifteen minutes. Hiding in the sitting room. Planting something on my jacket. Your strange behavior in the courtyard this morning."

Trevor's mouth went dry. He didn't know how to respond— even if he could have.

"I just need to know if you're telling me the truth about the port cameras." As Antonio spoke, Enrico drew his gun and cocked it.

Trevor had expected the firearm to be pointed at him, but instead Enrico raised it and pointed directly at Domenico's slumped form. Domenico had been so kind to Trevor over these past few weeks. He had been the one of the only two people who had shown Trevor any kindness while in Antonio's home.

"I'm telling you the truth."

Enrico pulled the trigger—after angling it down so the bullet ricocheted off the concrete near Domenico's feet, missing one of the men that held Domenico up by only millimeters.

This time, panic flooded his voice, "Don't—please. I'm telling the truth. I haven't lied."

Enrico fired again, this time directly at the older man's feet. The bullet struck the floor and hit something metal, a loud ping reverberating through the open space.

"I didn't lie."

"You lied, admit it."

Both men shouted over one another, as Enrico lifted the gun higher, aiming for Domenico's chest. Trevor looked around, desperate for anyone to stop this. No one moved, they were terrified, and probably thinking the same thing—*if Antonio's willing to hurt Domenico, I could be next*. Trevor was going to have to end this madness himself.

Trevor released his crutch and hurled himself at Enrico slamming into him with every ounce of anger that had been building up for weeks. The two of them fell to the floor in a twisting heap of limbs. A stray bullet shattered the overhead lights, spraying glass over them.

Trevor's leg screamed in pain as he drove a knee up between Enrico's legs, using his momentary distraction as a way to get ahold of the gun. He tried to ignore his body's warning system— and the fresh warmth spreading down his leg. Once he had the gun securely in his hand with the nose facing away from him he flipped Enrico so that he was on top pinning him to the floor. It didn't last. Antonio's number two bucked and fought back.

Trevor barely registered Antonio shouting, trying to regain control of him. He ignored the vile man, as long as he wasn't shooting at him, Antonio wasn't his direct concern. He was surprised when he heard another set of fists and a body crumpling to the floor. Between blows, Trevor caught a glimpse of Domenico—standing over one of the collapsed guards. The gun that had been secured at his guard's hip was now in his hand, pointing down at the groaning man.

Had he just regained consciousness... or had he never been out at all?

Enrico took the brief moment Trevor was distracted to elbow him in the head followed by a knee in the gut. The gun in Trevor's hand went flying, before it landed and slid under a wood pallet yards away.

Another shot rang out, pinging off of the warehouse wall. Followed by another and another.

The room froze—every head snapping toward the older man who had just *shot at his boss*. Domenico was shooting at Antonio.

The icy spell broke, every man running for an exit as Antonio dodged another bullet. His designer shoes skidded on the concrete, sending him sprawling as he dove behind a crate.

Antonio scrambled to his hands and knees as the warehouse erupted into chaos.

* * *

Claire

Claire's feet pounded the pavement as the fog devoured her the closer she got to the warehouse. Trevor was in trouble and he needed her. She had already drawn her gun, holding it in both hands as she ran, muzzle down. More gunshots cracked through the air the closer she got.

She was only feet from the door when it burst open and men poured out into the night, scattering in every direction. If she hadn't been terrified for Trevor, the sight might've made her smile. Antonio had lost control of his men.

Fighting through the stampede, Claire shoved her way inside.

Chaos greeted her.

The overhead lights were dim, several shattered, glass glittering across the concrete. One flickered above, swinging on a damaged chain. Trevor was on the ground wrestling with a man she recognized from CIA files—Enrico. Several of the men who hadn't yet fled scrambled to grab weapons before fleeing. Not one of them made a move to help Antonio, who cowered behind a crate.

Claire swept the room—locking eyes with Domenico. He looked her over: her stance, her ready weapon, the unmistakable CIA precision in her posture. She saw the exact moment he made his decision.

Survival.

He wanted no part of whatever Antonio had coming.

Without a word, he turned and ran, disappearing into the fog.

She had one second to choose: help Trevor—or chase Antonio?

Trevor, despite everything, had the upper hand—pinning Enrico, adrenaline and desperation giving him strength he shouldn't have had. And Colin was seconds behind her; he'd never let her go in alone.

So she ran.

Claire was so close—*this was it*. The man who orchestrated her parents' deaths was finally within reach.

Antonio was fast, but she was faster, and his Italian leather shoes were slick on the floor. He stumbled twice, nearly falling. Reaching the far warehouse door, closest to the water's edge, he shoved it open and vanished into the night. Claire burst through just after him.

He was heading for the docks—only a few yards away.

She didn't think, she just ran.

Wind ripped against her, the fog thick as smoke, but she could hear his feet running down the metal gangway onto the dock. Without thinking she ran, desperate to not let him go. She caught him halfway down the narrow dock. Boats lined both sides, poised for a getaway.

"Antonio, stop." She kept her gun trained on his center mass.

He skidded to a halt. Didn't turn. Then a low laugh rolled out of him, the sound thick with mockery. When he finally faced her, he lifted his arms as if greeting a guest.

"The gymnast." His smile sharpened. "Let me guess—you're working with my insolent son—"

"He's not your son. He might have half your DNA, but he's not yours." She stepped closer, rage burning through her. Antonio laughed—truly laughed—and it poured gasoline on her fury.

"You're in love with him. So what? You're going to kill me the way I killed your parents? Shoot me the way I shot Trevor?"

He was baiting her—wanting to blind her with rage. He wanted her to make a mistake.

"You'd like that," she said, breathing steadily now. "You'd love to haunt me from the grave. But no. You're going to stand trial. You're going to rot behind bars while your organization collapses. Though honestly, there's not much left."

His expression twisted with fury, but he said nothing.

"What? No retort?" she taunted. "Did I silence the ever-charming Antonio Giordano?"

A beat. Then her voice dropped, sharp and commanding. "Lay down on your stomach. Cross your ankles. Hands behind your head. Now."

He didn't move.

A slow, dark smile crept across his face. The dock was narrow—barely a yard wide. He reached to the side, grabbing a pike pole from a hook Claire hadn't seen.

Before she could fire, he swung.

The pointed metal end sliced toward her head. She dodged back by inches. The sudden movement threw her balance off; she fired a reflexive shot and missed as he twisted away.

Antonio lunged, driving the pole at her chest. She blocked with her forearm—pain ripping open a cut she didn't dare stop to look at.

He dropped the pole and lunged again, this time grabbing for her gun.

She saw it coming—just barely—and fired a second time. The bullet caught him in the side. A flesh wound, but enough to slow him down. He clutched his side and dropped to a knee. The metallic scent of blood mixed with the salty ocean air.

Claire shoved him down and moved around to grab his hands behind his back—but Antonio swung upward, the back of his hand smacking into her wrist. Her gun flew out of her grip, hit the water with a splash, and sank.

It surprised her but she refocused immediately, anticipating his next move.

He was already pushing to his feet.

Claire dropped low and swung her foot out, cracking into his ankles with her leg. He hit the dock flat on his back with a brutal thud. The impact forced the air from his lungs; he wheezed, coughing and rolling to his side.

Before he could get up, Claire grabbed the pike pole off the dock and leveled the pointed end at him.

"Don't move." Her voice shook with fury. Her restraint—already fraying—snapped one thread further.

She pressed the pole into his back, forcing him onto his stomach. One of his arms ended up pinned beneath him; the other lay at his side. She kicked his feet apart and barked, "Cross them."

He obeyed with a growl of defiance.

Claire planted her boot between his shoulder blades and tossed the pike pole down the dock, far out of reach. Dropping to a knee, she straddled his hips and grabbed for his free arm, wrenching it behind him. She leaned forward, reaching under him for the trapped arm—as Antonio twisted.

He rolled beneath her with a surge of desperate strength and drove a knife upward.

The blade drove into her abdomen.

Claire choked on a breath, a sound caught somewhere between shock and pain as she toppled sideways. Her hand clamped instinctively around the ornate handle jutting from her stomach—training the only thing keeping her from yanking it free.

The world tilted, blurred. Sound muffled. She couldn't hear the sirens screaming in the distance.

Antonio pushed himself upright, panting, clutching his own bleeding side.

He leaned close and hissed into her ear, "I barely remember your parents' deaths. And you will never haunt me. I hope Trevor finds you and you die in his arms. Punishment for betraying me." He stood, glanced once over his shoulder, and fled into the night.

Claire forced air into her lungs. Every breath lit her nerves on fire.

"Colin...? Kane...?" Her voice rasped out through the comm. "Are you there?"

Static crackled back. Words she couldn't understand. Her vision pulsed black at the edges.

Claire's fingers slipped from the knife handle and fell against her chest.

Her eyes closed—but instinct pulled her hand along her wrist.

She had almost forgotten about the burning on her left arm when she reached for her bracelet. She wanted to be as close to

Trevor—as she could in her last moments. But her fingertips only brushed bare skin. It was gone.

She blinked hard, forcing her eyes open, fighting gravity. The world swayed. She scanned the dock—the fog, the shadows, the slick boards—until—

There.

Her bracelet lay several feet away, leather untied, abandoned in the center of the dock.

Supporting the knife with one trembling hand so it wouldn't shift, she angled her body and pushed with her heels, inching forward. Pain knifed through her abdomen. She gritted her teeth and reached—

Too far.

She stretched again—twisting, dragging herself another few inches. Her fingers skimmed the leather once—unable to close around it. Stretching just a bit more...

Her fingers closed around the leather.

The second she secured the strip of leather, her body gave out. Claire slumped to the dock, consciousness slipping away.

The world faded to black with Trevor's bracelet cradled in her outstretched hand.

* * *

Trevor

Trevor's eyes followed Claire as she burst through the west door. Fog and salty air blew through the door as if she had been consumed. Trevor was still on top of Enrico when the man's fists slammed into his arm—his elbow buckling. Enrico twisted, flipping Trevor onto his back and pressed a forearm into his throat.

Enrico's move took Trevor by surprise but his body responded with instinct and not panic. Trevor hooked Enrico's arm, yanked it toward his torso, then swung his legs up around the man's neck, forcing the other arm straight. Then he squeezed his thighs together as hard as he could. He would have ignored the pain if there had been any, but his adrenaline was pumping so hard through his veins that he no longer felt it.

The warehouse exploded with noise as the doors burst open.

Officers flooded in from every direction, their weapons drawn. Men and women in black tactical uniforms surged forward, converging on the few remaining members of Antonio's crew still rifling through crates.

One officer closest to Trevor had his rifle trained on him but held position, motionless, waiting for orders.

Enrico went limp in Trevor's hold, blacking out just as Colin entered the building. His weapon was drawn but pointed at the floor, his eyes sweeping the room as he took in the mayhem.

Trevor released Enrico, shoving away from the man's limp form and raising both hands.

"Colin. She went out that door."

Colin's eyes darted to the exit. "You good?" He was already moving toward it.

"Yeah."

"Good. He's with me." Colin signaled to the other officers, then jerked his chin at Trevor. "Come on."

Trevor didn't hesitate. He pushed to his feet, taking off in Colin's direction. When he was within arms reach, Colin removed a second firearm from his back waistband and held it out to him. Taking it Trevor fell in line behind Colin moving together as a unit, despite never training together. Three more officers trailed behind.

Sirens wailed in the distance, growing louder.

"Who are they?" Trevor asked as they neared the exit.

"Interpol," Colin replied. "I called them in for backup this morning. More are out front rounding up anyone who tried to run. Ambulance is on its way... Claire doesn't know I called them. She went after Antonio didn't she?"

"Yeah."

Together the group exited the doors carefully, checking both sides before exposing themselves. The fog was thicker now— swallowing the docks in shifting walls of white. They scanned both directions. Then a boat engine roared through the fog. They ran toward the sound.

With their guns raised they all slowly advanced down the ramp in a tight formation. When their feet hit the bobbing concrete float, a figure appeared through the fog. Prone, unmoving and small.

Trevor's heart jumped to his throat, he couldn't tell if it was a man or a woman. Moving strategically but quickly they grew closer. Colin kept his gun trained ahead, ready to fire, should anyone attack as the men behind him cleared each ship.

When they were only a few yards away Trevor could finally see clearly.

It was Claire.

Her body lay twisted, arm outstretched, reaching for something he couldn't see.

It barely registered to Trevor that Colin was radioing in, confirming that they had found Claire. She was down. Trevor was desperate to sprint ahead, but he swallowed the instinct—if Antonio was nearby, a bullet would drop him before he could reach her. He forced his muscles to obey, to move slowly and controlled behind Colin.

When they finally reached her, Colin stayed forward, his weapon raised and scanning the dock. Trevor dropped to his knees, checking for a pulse.

"Pulse is thready... and weak." He barely got the words out. "She's got a penetrating abdominal wound and a laceration to the left forearm."

Without thinking he stripped off his jacket, removed his shirt, and used it to apply pressure around the knife. Blood soaking through, warm against his hands, it contrasted with the cold air that bit at his skin.

He couldn't lose her—not again.

The sirens mixed with the soft slap of the waves as Colin took a few more steps toward the purr of a boat engine. Colin shifted forward, his instincts telling him to advance with the other officers. To find Antonio and make him pay for what he had done to Claire, Trevor and the Huntingtons. But he couldn't leave her side, he couldn't leave Claire.

"Where are those medics?" Colin called out into his com, ever the leader.

Trevor considered lifting her up and carrying her toward the ambulance, but if the knife shifted, it could kill her. He forced himself to not panic and stay still.

Silhouettes finally approached through the fog—medics sprinting down the gangway.

Trevor looked down at Claire's face for the first time—she was so peaceful he could have sworn she was asleep—until the sticky warmth of her blood slid through his fingers.

Keeping pressure on her wound, he leaned in as close as he could, his voice trembling. "Hang on, Claire. Just hang on for me."

Tears spilled down his cheeks before he realized he was crying.

A roar from the other end of the dock cut through the air. The Interpol officers on the dock shouted as the boat engine revved, fading as it sped away. Shots rang out, sharp and distant. Trevor instinctively threw himself over Claire, shielding her with his body. His dog tags brushed her cheek as he did.

An officer at the docks edge confirmed: the suspect was in the wind. Antonio was gone.

Moments later, Trevor felt Colin's hand on his shoulder, silently urging him to move away. Two medics were already kneeling on either side of Claire, stabilizing the knife for transport.

Logically, Trevor knew he was in the way. Allowing them to take control sparked even more panic in his chest. The lack of control, of trusting someone else with her life, made him want to argue.

He couldn't let go—not completely. So he shifted back, giving them space, but kept a hold of her outstretched hand.

Only then did he notice her hand was clasped around something. When he gently opened her fingers, he found the leather bracelet he'd made for her.

Before he could do anything with it, a medic slid her hand from his. The bracelet slipped from her grasp, falling to the dock as they rolled her onto a backboard and then lifted her to the stretcher.

It felt like the world around him sped up as the medics took off with Claire. Trevor couldn't make his body move fast enough. Desperately trying to catch up, he grabbed her bracelet off the dock floor and stumbled after them.

Between his sobbing, his adrenaline fading and the pain setting in, Trevor couldn't keep up. By the time he reached the asphalt, the ambulance doors were already closing.

His last glimpse of Claire was her blood-covered body, the knife still protruding from her abdomen.

Trevor's legs gave out. He collapsed onto the hard pavement—shirtless, shaking, and covered in blood. Sobs racked him, raw and broken.

He was losing her all over again.

Clutching the bracelet in his fist, he held it like it was the only thing tethering him to the world. Maybe if he gripped it hard enough, she couldn't die. He refused to let her go.

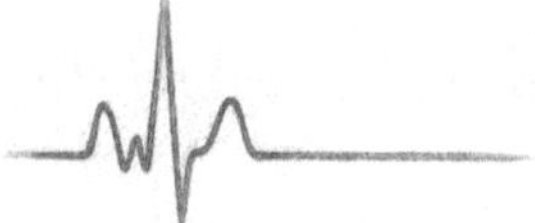

32
Into the Shadows

The pressure on her abdomen and hand was the first thing Claire noticed when she came to. No pain—just a heavy, insistent weight. The rhythmic chirp of a monitor and the sharp scent of antiseptic crept into her awareness. When she finally opened her eyes, it was Trevor she saw first—slumped in a recliner, asleep. His hand gripped hers like a lifeline while his other hand clutched her bracelet.

The room was dim, lit only by under-cabinet LEDs and the harsh fluorescent glow that spilled in from the hallway. She barely had time to register any of it before sleep dragged her under again.

When she awoke several hours later, the room was warm and bright—even through her eyelids. Trevor's hand still held hers, his thumb idly brushing along her knuckles as if reassuring himself she was real.

"Claire?" His voice was gravelly, like it was the first sound he'd made all morning.

Slowly opening her eyes, she let the world come into focus. Trevor's face appeared—unshaven, exhausted, and yet his eyes still shone with hope.

"Hey," she whispered. Her throat was dry and raw. Already reclined, she fumbled for the button to raise the bed.

"Are you okay? Any pain?" His voice was thick with worry but warm with relief. Standing, he helped her adjust to a more comfortable position.

She winced as she readjusted her hips slightly, but the pain stayed manageable.

"Here, you'll probably need water," he said, holding out a small Styrofoam cup and straw.

Taking a sip, the water coated her throat, relieving the sandpaper feeling.

"Let me get the nurse—they'll want to check your wounds." He started to back away, but she grabbed his hand again, squeezing it.

She shook her head and set the cup on her bedside tray. "No, just give me a minute."

Tugging lightly on his arm, she encouraged him to sit on her bed. She shifted her legs to make room, but this time a deep, sharp pain sliced through her middle. Grabbing her side, she let out a hiss.

"I'm getting the nurse." Trevor's face tightened, pained at the sound she made. He turned to grab his crutch—

"No, no. Sit. I'm fine," she said, breathing through a wave of nausea. She felt Trevor's hand touch her cheek as he brushed a stray lock of hair out of her face. She'd braided her hair last night, but it had begun to come apart, strands falling everywhere.

Leaning into his touch, Claire smiled, relieved to see his face again. She'd never admit it, but she'd worried she'd failed when Antonio stabbed her. She hadn't thought she would wake up.

She wanted to know what had happened last night, but looking at the man she loved, she needed his touch even more. Grabbing onto the sweatshirt he wore, she pulled him in, reveling in the feeling of his lips on hers. He braced himself against the bed with one hand while the other slid around the back of her neck.

When she broke the kiss, Claire eased back and tugged Trevor closer. He sat on the edge of the mattress, keeping his weight angled away from her abdomen. She leaned into him carefully, mindful of her stitches, and rested her head against his chest. It puled—sharp and brief—but his arms closing around her made the sting worth it. Breathing him in, her body finally loosened. In his arms, she was home.

After a few quiet moments, she reluctantly shifted back, taking the pressure off her stomach wound. "We're quite the injured pair, aren't we? How's your leg?"

"I'm fine. I have a fresh dressing, and I've been resting it."

"Good. Now, tell me what happened after I passed out."

Sighing, he took her hand again—careful of her bandaged arm and the tenderness in her abdomen. "Colin and I found you. I put pressure on your abdomen while Colin and his team searched—"

"—his team? Do you mean Kane?"

Trevor froze, caught mid-sentence, his eyes wide. "Oh. Yeah. You didn't know... Colin called in Interpol as backup. They were waiting on standby down the street."

Claire was conflicted—part of her felt betrayed, and part of her understood. She had gone rogue last night, and Colin knew her well enough to know her feelings for Trevor would have clouded her judgement.

Waiting for her reaction, Trevor didn't speak; he just looked uncomfortable.

"Okay, keep going. What happened with Antonio?"

Trevor was about to answer when a knock tapped on the door—soft, as if not to wake her if she'd still been asleep.

Colin poked his head in, exhaustion etched across his features—but relief lit his eyes when he saw Claire awake. He stepped fully into the room, holding coffee cups in both hands, followed by Kane, carrying a cup of his own.

"Morning sleepyhead," Kane said, smiling. He was wide awake, almost buzzing, unlike the other two.

"Morning," Claire said in return, smiling at her honorary brothers.

Colin approached the bed and handed one of the cups to Trevor. Claire gave him a puzzled look; he was never one to drink much other than water.

"I need the caffeine," he said in response to her gaze.

She nodded and turned her attention back to her friends. "Trevor was just about to tell me what happened with Antonio and Interpol." She gave a pointed look to Colin.

He grimaced in return, taking a sip of his coffee and turning his head.

Claire turned her attention back to Trevor as he shifted on the edge of the mattress, still holding her hand. He took a deep breath before he spoke. "Antonio got away," he said quietly. "By the time Colin and I reached the dock, he was already on a boat. Between the thick fog and low light... we couldn't see a damn thing until after he was gone."

Colin exhaled through his nose, setting his coffee on her tray. "Interpol has teams out now. An arrest warrant's been issued, but he's in the wind. The boat he stole was found docked in Bari about two hours ago. No sign of him since."

Kane plopped onto the recliner Trevor had been asleep in. "I've put a freeze on all his accounts and facial recognition is scanning all transit locations for his ugly mug."

Claire's stomach tightened—not painfully, but with anger. Antonio slipping away now felt like a cruel joke.

"What about his men?" she asked.

Colin nodded. "Most who didn't flee were arrested. They were processed through Interpol. Officers are still combing the area looking for Domenico and anyone else that got away. But they did get Enrico in custody." His eyes shone sympathetically. "He'll answer for a lot."

Kane added, "Interpol's lead officer will want your statement. Probably today, if you're up for it."

Claire groaned softly—not from pain, but from annoyance. "Yeah."

"And... the CIA hasn't been notified yet," Colin said carefully, shoulders tense. "Interpol made sure you're listed as a Jane Doe in the hospital's system for privacy. But it won't take long before the CIA finds you."

She saw Trevor's jaw flex; she didn't have to ask how he felt about the CIA. He had only just gotten her back, now she could be going away for fraud. She squeezed his hand, trying to reassure him.

Claire fixed Colin with a tired but understanding look. "I know. And... about Interpol—"

Colin winced. "Claire, I should've told you. When Trevor called, the scale of the operation doubled—we couldn't risk not having backup."

She softened. "You were right to call them. I'm not mad."

His relief was instantaneous, visible in the way his posture eased and he nodded once.

Before anyone could speak again, a knock sounded and the door swung open. A doctor in dark blue scrubs entered, flipping through a chart as she approached the bed. She was in her forties with long chestnut curly hair and had an air about her that told Claire she was probably top of her med school class.

Following behind the doctor was a petite nurse wearing light blue scrubs and a cheerful smile. Her ID badge was attached to her scrubs with a rhinestoned daisy clip and read: Isabella.

"Good morning," the doctor said with a warm professional smile and a thick Italian accent. "I'm Dr. Ferrara. Let's take a look at your injuries."

Trevor reluctantly released her hand and scooted back so the doctor had access, while Kane and Colin shifted to the far side of the room.

After placing her chart on the table, the doctor sterilized her hands and put on gloves, while the nurse removed a package from the drawers behind the bed, placing it near Dr. Ferrara on the side of the mattress.

The doctor lifted Claire's gown just enough to remove her dressing so she could see the incision. "You were very fortunate. The knife missed all major organs." Her hands were practiced, gentle, but even the light pressure made Claire's breath hitch. "There was significant bleeding, and the blunt-force trauma around the wound caused bruising of the abdominal wall. You'll be sore."

Dr. Ferrara motioned for Claire's left arm and peeled back the gauze, revealing a neat row of stitches. "You were lucky here too—it was a clean laceration. No nerve damage. The stitches will dissolve when it's healed. We are just keeping an eye on both areas for any kind of redness or swelling which would indicate an infection."

"How long until she's back to her full strength?" Trevor asked, voice tight, as if he already hated the answer.

"Four to six weeks for full recovery," Dr. Ferrara replied. "But she'll be able to move around on her own in a few days. No heavy lifting for at least two weeks and absolutely no strenuous activity. You'll need to be medically cleared before returning to duty."

Claire raised a brow playfully at Trevor, who sputtered, "I wasn't referring to that!"

Dr. Ferrara continued, stepping back and removing her gloves. "Your stitches look clean. No sign of infection. Isabella will redress both sites now and continue to monitor your vitals. You should be able to be discharged tomorrow as long as nothing changes."

She stepped aside and switched places with the nurse. Isabella opened a fresh packet of supplies and, like a seasoned pro, redressed both Claire's abdomen and left arm.

"I'll be back for afternoon rounds. Rest, Ms... ah—Doe." She nodded politely, then left the room, taking the chart with her.

Trevor hovered near Claire's shoulder again, instinctively reaching for her hand now that there was room again. Isabella was just finishing up when Colin's phone rang and he excused himself into the hallway.

After taking and notating Claire's vitals, the nurse said she would be back soon, then cleaned up and slipped out. Kane reclaimed his spot on the recliner while Trevor scooted closer to her again. Kane was entertaining her with his commentary on Antonio's men, describing some of them as guys whose collective IQ couldn't power a nightlight and the rest were discount henchmen at best.

Five minutes later, Kane was describing Enrico as pacing around the holding cell like a Roomba with anger issues, when Colin reentered the room with an even larger smile on his face.

"What's with you? Did you finally learn that you could contour your abs to make them look bigger?" Kane gave Colin a smirk and a wink.

"No, could you show me how you do it?" Colin teased back.

Claire had been taking a sip of her water when he spoke—she nearly snorted her water and ended up having to grab her stomach when she laughed.

"The call was the lead officer, they wanted an update on Claire. I let them know you were awake and could give your statement sometime today."

"That's what made you so giddy?" Kane deadpanned.

"No," Colin rolled his eyes at Kane. "I checked my email after that and found an email from my lawyer. The news ran a story two nights ago that cleared our names with the bombing and because of that, Lauren has agreed not to file the paperwork requesting that the court remove my visitation rights. She's willing to talk about Ethan coming to stay with me for two weeks in D.C."

"That's wonderful!"

"That's great."

Kane and Claire chorused together. Trevor didn't know anything about Ethan and looked a little confused; Colin was briefly explaining his situation to him when Kane's phone vibrated. This time it wasn't a call; it was an alert.

FACIAL RECOGNITION CONFIRMED flashed across his screen.

"Shit," Kane sprung up from his place in the recliner. "They're here. CIA's in the building—it looks like six officers coming from several entrances."

"Did you hack the hospital cameras?" Colin asked.

"Of course I did."

Claire's pulse-ox alarm chirped, as her heart rate spiked. They didn't have time to think, just move.

Trevor jumped up and began turning off the monitors and

removing the leads.

Taking the lead Colin spoke up first. "Wait. Claire, are you sure you want to run? I'll support you, but you need to be sure."

She tried to think, but her head was spinning. "I... I don't know... Antonio is still out there but..." Trailing off she looked up at Trevor, her heart broke when she did. She wanted desperately to be home with him, but she had come so far, she couldn't give up now.

Trevor stopped just before he removed her IV. He held her gaze unwaveringly. "It's okay. You need to finish it, for your parents, for you too... But this time I'm coming with you."

"What? No." She didn't think her pulse could spike any higher. "You can't, you have med school and you need to go home for Addie. She needs you."

"No, I'm not leaving you now. Addie is doing okay with the LVAD. I can help you." He placed both hands on either side of her face.

She loved that he wanted to help her, but she had to protect him. She'd always protect him. She leaned into his hand, turning her head and kissing his palm before speaking. "If you do, you'll have helped a fugitive. Your career as a doctor could be over before it's even begun. I need you to go home, take care of Addie, start your degree. I'll be home before you know it."

Claire could see how much he hated the idea.

"Fine, *but* you can't go alone." Trevor's voice left no room for argument, he dropped his hands from her face and resumed removing her IV, peeling back the adhesive bandage that held it in.

"I can't expect them to come with me. Th—"

"I'll go." All of the spunk was gone from Kane's demeanor. "Colin, you can't go—you're just getting things sorted with Ethan. I resigned before we left, and it'll be easier if you have someone who can make IDs on the fly. Plus I want to get Antonio as much as you do now. You're my family. He tried to kill you."

"Careful, you're starting to sound like me." Colin added in. "I'll still help, I can be your man on the inside. Keep them off your tail for a while, but you'll have to come in eventually."

"Okay."

"Alright, Kane, go do whatever you have to at the nurses' station computer to keep them from noticing her monitors have been turned off. I'll go get a set of scrubs, a mask and a surgical cap. She'll need to blend in to get past the team downstairs. When I get back, Trevor, you'll help her get changed and get the rest of those monitors off so they don't draw attention. Then I need to make a phone call."

Claire knew Colin had been thinking this through for hours. She wouldn't be surprised if her go bag was stashed somewhere nearby.

Kane and Colin both disappeared out of the door before she could say anything. Trevor's hands worked swiftly placing a cotton ball where he'd just slipped out her IV. Holding it there, he wrapped her hand with a bit of tape to keep it in place.

"You look like you're already at home, Dr. Bennett," she quipped, watching him move like he belonged here. His leg didn't seem to slow him—focus overriding pain.

He let out a light laugh. "Now, miss, that sounds a bit like a come-on, and my girlfriend might not like that so much."

"Girlfriend?" She had loved hearing him call her that when they were teens, but now it sounded even better.

"Eh, girlfriend, future fiancé, future wife... What do you call someone who is just yours? Labels don't matter, you just... belong to each other." He had finished removing all of the wires and tubes and was beginning to untie her hospital gown.

"I don't know, they all sound like good titles to me."

A quick, efficient knock sounded at the door. Colin slipped in, his hand shielding his eyes just in case. Without a word he tossed the stack of clothing on the end of her hospital bed and retreated back to the hallway.

"Good, because I don't want you going and getting another boyfriend while you're on the run."

She chuckled as he slid her hospital gown forward and replaced it with a scrub top. "I promise no other boyfriends. I'm only yours."

Pulling the shirt down at the hem, careful not to touch her stomach, Trevor took the second to lean in and place a passionate kiss on her lips. She threaded her hands through his hair, pulling him into her.

They moved together like seven years had never passed, their lips fitting perfectly against one another.

Trevor was the one to pull apart first, reaching for the pants. Keeping his injured leg straight, he lifted each of her feet, sliding the pants over them and up so all she had to do was stand. When she did he lifted the pants over her hips and tied a bow at the front.

Handing her the hat, Trevor went to retrieve the bag of her belongings near the base of the recliner. While she tucked her hair up into the surgical cap, he lifted her feet one at a time and slid her socks and boots from the night before on.

"One more thing," Trevor pulled out her bracelet from his pocket—tying it back where it belonged, around her wrist. "I love you."

"I love you, too." Claire said, giving him one last peck on the lips as Colin and Kane came back into the room, their backs turned for her privacy.

"Ready?" Colin asked over his shoulder.

"Yeah." Claire stood up, taking it slow. Trevor put his hands out to stabilize her but while she took his hand, she still leaned most of her body weight against the bed.

Turning around, Claire noticed Kane had also tossed on scrubs and a cap.

"Kane has an access badge that will get you down the staff elevator next to the parking garage. I've already arranged a car; your go bags are in the trunk. Make contact when you can."

"We will," Claire wrapped her arms around Colin. "Who got the go bags and the car?"

"Interpol's lead officer. This was one of the biggest busts of his career; he owed me a favor since I brought him in. I had one of their officers grab our stuff last night while you were in surgery and the rest of their team was searching Antonio's place. They brought our bags here since they had to do the same with Trevor's stuff. I just had them drop off a car and move your two bags into a getaway car."

"Thank you, you've had my back since day one."

"I always will."

"We've got to go; the team is on their way up," Kane said, looking down at his phone screen.

"Okay, Trevor, let's go, we need plausible deniability. Time to get coffee." Colin turned to Kane, "Talk soon."

Kane nodded, and the two of them clapped each other on the back before Colin walked to the door. Trevor grabbed his crutch and turned to Kane.

"Please take care of her." His eyes were so desperate, Claire wanted to just throw her hands up and say he could come. But she kept her resolve. He deserved to become a doctor not a fugitive.

"I will." Kane promised.

Leaning down for one last quick kiss, Trevor's lips met Claire's. She savored each of the two seconds the kiss lasted—it was nowhere near long enough but would have to be enough for now.

Colin and Trevor were out the door and moving as quickly as they could while still trying to look casual down the hall toward the set of public elevators. A minute later, when Trevor and Colin had gotten onto an elevator, Kane and Claire pulled their masks over their noses and mouths and made their way in the opposite direction toward the staff-only elevator. Claire tried to walk on her own, but dizziness rolled through her in waves. Kane adjusted instantly, taking just enough of her weight to steady her without drawing attention. She leaned into him, using his arm to help brace against her weight.

Kane swiped the key card and called the elevator. As they waited, Claire fought to keep her anxiety from running wild. The elevator dinged at their floor—but it wasn't the staff one.

The public one opened at the other end of the hallway, and three men stepped from the elevator. Out of the corner of her eye she saw the men, dressed in plain clothes with defined muscles and moving like an armed unit. She would have recognized them from a mile away—CIA officers. They briefly checked the room numbers on the walls and began making their way quickly down to Claire's room.

Without knocking, the three men shoved her door open, drawing their weapons as they did so.

Finally, her elevator arrived. The doors slid open agonizingly slowly. Staying as calm as she could, Claire and Kane walked forward onto the elevator. Just as the doors began to close, they heard a few choice swear words echoing down the hallway. They had found her empty bed.

Beginning to move, the elevator descended to the ground floor. Looking at his phone again, Kane confirmed that Colin and Trevor had made it to the coffee cart and were on camera. They'd be safe from prosecution.

When the elevator car arrived at the ground floor, the doors opened just as slowly. Without moving too quickly, the pair walked like coworkers heading home for the evening, despite being dressed ready for the operating room. One of the first rules to blending in was looking like you belonged and behaving like it.

They were only a few yards from the door when Claire heard a set of American accents, speaking to a pair of nurses. Taking a deep breath, she straightened and immediately regretted it—her abdomen pulling tight—but she forced herself upright, refusing to give herself away.

Kane waved the badge once more at the end of the hallway. The door clicked, and they descended down the stairs slowly into the staff parking garage. As soon as the door shut behind them, Claire let out a sigh of relief. They weren't home free yet, but she didn't have to stay as rigidly upright as she had upstairs.

The car wasn't far: a dark blue Fiat hatchback with tinted windows. Clean, unremarkable, forgettable—the kind of car that would disappear seamlessly into traffic.

Kane helped Claire slide into the passenger seat, reclining it to a comfortable position. As he walked around the car, she glanced back at the doorway they'd just come through—imagining Trevor bursting through after her, insisting he was coming. Logically, she wanted him to go home and continue with his plans—but now that she had seen him, touched him, leaving again was even harder than ever. Her heart ached for him.

As Kane dropped into the driver's seat, he started the engine and pulled out of the garage, using the key card one last time to raise the barrier. He eased the car onto the street, merging into traffic. They were finally clear.

Claire Huntington was vanishing again—becoming someone new, slipping into the shadows to hunt for justice. For her parents. For herself. For Trevor. The difference was she wasn't walking into the dark alone. She had a partner at her side and a family to fight her way back to. No one mourned a ghost that didn't exist. This time, it wasn't Claire who feared the mob. It was Antonio Giordano who should fear the *gymnast*.

Epilogue

Six Weeks Later

Trevor pulled up to the 1950s-style diner, his car packed to the brim with everything he'd need for medical school. He'd also snagged a few things from Claire's old house—items he knew she'd loved. It was the first time he'd stepped inside her home since she left for that competition seven years ago.

The drive from his home town to D.C. was long—seven and a half hours—and he was excited to see Colin again. Trevor was only passing through on his way to Baltimore. He was scheduled to start at Johns Hopkins in two weeks and wanted to get settled in his new apartment, but after everything they'd been through, he couldn't not stop to see Colin.

The red-and-white sign above the roadside diner read *Betty's*. Through the window, he spotted Colin, sitting in a booth, studying the menu. He was clean-shaven and had dyed his hair back to its natural light brown. If they hadn't been texting for the last six weeks, Trevor might not have recognized him at first glance.

Getting out of his Jeep, Trevor locked the doors and headed inside. The moment he stepped through the entrance, Colin stood and greeted him with a hug and a pat on the back. It was good to see a familiar face—one who knew everything that happened in Italy. Trevor still wasn't cleared to tell his parents the whole truth.

After Claire and Kane disappeared, the CIA officers found Trevor and Colin in the coffee shop on the hospital's ground floor. Their alibi held up well enough, and they were released. Trevor returned to his home to begin physical therapy and spend time with his family before school. His leg had healed on the surface. Therapy was painful, but it was helping. He still walked with a slight limp, but could stand for several hours and even run short distances.

Colin had returned to D.C. and was welcomed back at the agency—but only after convincing Director Leon that, with a mole inside and Hale's knowledge of the system, the only way to apprehend him was to go dark. Delivering Hale into custody so quickly didn't hurt either. Colin still wasn't sure who he trusted at Langley, or how long he wanted to stay, but he knew one thing for certain: he'd stay until Claire didn't need him anymore—and Antonio was behind bars.

They ordered their meals and traded small talk while they waited. Colin was taking the next week off to spend with Ethan. He planned to take him camping, show him around D.C., and take him to a Nationals baseball game.

Trevor shared how well Addie was doing on the LVAD. Her doctors were optimistic she'd get a heart in time, as she'd already moved up the list with each successful transplant ahead of her. Keeping her from overexerting herself was practically a full-time job for his parents—especially now that Dodger, her pit bull puppy, and Rainbow, her chameleon, had joined the family. To Addie's dismay, the two pets did not get along, and Grant continually reminded her that chameleons did not ride on dogs' backs. Trevor made his dad promise that if she ever managed it anyway, he'd get video proof. In the meantime, she'd taught Dodger to play dead. She had a dark sense of humor for a ten-year-old.

When the conversation shifted to international updates, Colin had to be careful about what he could share. But Trevor had earned the right to know what he could. Antonio was still in the wind. No credible movement. Every reported sighting was useless by the time they followed up. What had been found were the bodies of Vincent DeRossi and Silas Ward. They suspected Valerie Keene murdered Silas days after the bombing, but there wasn't enough evidence to convict. Vincent had been killed in a hit-and-run during one of his rare trips to the States. Again, Hale or Valerie were likely suspects, but the proof wasn't there. His body had been identified as a John Doe until the CIA found him.

When their burgers were finished, they leaned back into the booth relaxing. Conversation drifted to Claire—careful to avoid her real name or a known alias. Instead, they called her *Mary Lou*. Trevor had chosen the nickname in honor of one of Claire's favorite gymnasts, Mary Lou Retton. Neither of them heard from Mary Lou or her partner in a few days. Colin usually received encrypted emails; Trevor got postcards. He suspected they were never mailed from where they were purchased, and none included a return address. The messages were brief—just enough to say they were alive, and that she was healing. Claire had written that she was recovering well and regaining strength after the stabbing. When their drinks were empty and dessert finished, they paid their checks and stepped outside into the bright August heat. After one more hug, they promised not to let too much time pass before their next meet-up, then headed for their cars.

Reaching his Jeep, Trevor hit the unlock button and opened the door. What sat on the driver's seat stopped him cold—a stack of letters tied neatly together. They were written on different types of paper, in various pens and inks, each page unique. But they all shared one unmistakable thing: Claire's handwriting. He'd know it anywhere.

Trevor twisted around, scanning the parking lot for any sign she was still nearby. When he saw nothing, he sighed and slid into his seat. Pulling the top letter free, he realized it was written on the back of a train ticket—dated the night her parents died. He read slowly, then the next letter, then the next.

Claire watched from a cluster of trees as Trevor discovered

her letters and began reading. She saw his face fall, soften, break—though she couldn't tell which letter he was reading, she knew the first one was brutal. His hair had grown out since she last saw him, brushing the tops of his ears, looking so much like the boy she'd first fallen in love with. Her chest tightened. She wished she could run her hands through it, touch him again. But she had to stay away—for his safety. Being seen with a fugitive could destroy his future.

She double-checked that the code breaker she'd used to get into his car was back in her backpack, then zipped it shut. She couldn't linger—not with CIA surveillance this thick. Pulling her baseball cap lower over her now-black hair, adjusting it until the brim kissed her sunglasses, she took one last look at the man she loved. Then she melted back into the trees.

A few minutes later, after a short hike, she stepped into the truck stop where Kane waited with the car. Tossing her backpack into the back seat, Claire slid behind the wheel.

"Perfect timing—I found Antonio. We've got to get back to the airfield." Kane didn't even look up from his tablet as he spoke.

"Where?"

"London. England."

Bonus Content

November 22, 2018

Trev,

Morning my love. It's the first Thanksgiving without you and my parents. It feels strange without any of you. Hugh is surprisingly good at cooking so I know the meal will be good. He even asked my favorite dish that my mom used to make. So he's giving the sweet potato casserole a go. I wish I was with you today too, that I could see you and your family. Your parents would like Hugh. He is a bit rough on the outside, but he softens once you get to know him. He told me I shouldn't be writing to you. I know he has a point but I need to have something. Even if you'll never read these, I need to feel like I'm communicating with you. I try not to write to you too often. Otherwise, I'd end up with a box full of letters. I couldn't hide those as easily.

Writing to you, knowing you'll probably never read my letters, hurts. But not writing hurts more.

Love,
C.

December 12, 2020

Trev,

I can't believe you're about to deploy. I've been keeping up with your unit's activity. I'm excited for you but also a little worried. Please be safe. I know you probably won't end up on the front lines, but I still worry. I always will.

I've been following your family too. Addie is getting so big! I can't believe she's already five. I bet she's doing really well with school and is everyone's best friend. She was always way more outgoing than both of us. Your mom looks good too. I miss her baking so much, so when she set up shipping around the US, I may have ordered a few goodies. I know I shouldn't have but no one makes brownies like she does. I used a P.O. Box and my alias so it should all be safe. I hope the vet's office is doing well too. I can't see much, but I check in on social media frequently. Scout looks good too, I miss her cuddles.

I miss you. I miss talking to someone who understands me so easily. I desperately want to be able to tell you about my day and what's new with me, but even more so I want to be able to hear about your day and everything you've learned.

Oh, I saw photos of you in uniform. You look steady. Older. It fits you. I'm sorry. I know losing me played a part in how fast you aged. I hate that I did that to you. I like the haircut, it's sexy. But I won't lie, I prefer your longer hair. I miss the way it never quite behaved and fell into your eyes at the end of the day. That version of you still feels like home to me.

I wonder what your mornings will be like in Kuwait. What the air will feel like when you step outside. I suppose it'll be a little like it is here. Mild and warm with cold evenings. I don't know why I think about things like that. I guess it helps make the distance feel smaller. Like even though we are apart, we are still together in a way.

I love you,
C.

July 6, 2023

Trevor,
One of my friends got engaged tonight. It was a total surprise to everyone. She's been with this guy for a year and a half and he's really sweet. He's a good guy. He even looks a little bit like you. I'm excited for her. I can't believe I'm at the age when our friends are getting engaged. Until everything happened, I thought we'd be engaged by now. I guess life doesn't always go the way we planned.

I hope that we still get that future one day, but it's been so long sometimes I feel this will never end. You may not even be single if this ever ends. I want you to find love again, you deserve that. But selfishly I want you for myself too. Maybe you've already found someone and you're thinking about proposing to her. I don't know.

C.

Italian Terms & Phrases

Americano
American. In this context, it is used in a derogatory or dismissive manner.

Bene
Well, Good, or Okay.

Caffè
Coffee.

Caffè Americano
An espresso-based drink made by adding hot water to espresso.

Cappuccino
An Italian coffee drink made with equal parts espresso, steamed milk, and milk foam.

Mio figlio
My son.

Palazzo
A large, stately building or palace.

Palazzo Bellavita
Palace of beautiful life. The fictional event venue the gala takes place.

Palazzo d'Oro
Golden Palace. The fictional hotel where Trevor stays during his first trip to Rome.

Port of Civitavecchia
A real port often referred to as the Port of Rome; the main port used for goods entering or exiting Rome.

Rossetti
A fictional crime family. The head of the family is Lorenzo; his two sons are Matteo and Enzo.

Sì
Yes.

Signora/Signore
Lady/Sir. A respectful way to address a woman or man.

Trastevere
A neighborhood in Rome known for its bohemian atmosphere and centuries-old working-class roots.

Villa
A large private country house or estate, often luxurious.

About the Author

Rachel lives in Utah, where she balances writing, fashion design, and motherhood. *Leave It All Behind* is her debut novel.

For over a decade, Rachel has founded and managed Rachel Elizabeth Bridal, a luxury design house specializing in wedding gowns, custom bridal gowns, and bridal accessories. She has worked with hundreds of brides, telling stories through silhouette, fabric, and texture.

Rachel has always had a passion for writing. She has been developing this story for more than ten years, and is thrilled to finally share it with readers. While she can't pinpoint a single moment of inspiration, Leave It All Behind is the result of a collision between her favorite genres: romance, crime and mystery.

Rachel writes because she believes every person carries a story worth telling. She believes there is beauty even in the hardest life moments, and is drawn to the quiet truths we uncover through the stories we read—whether they change us profoundly or simply teach us something small about ourselves.

You can connect with Rachel online for updates on future books and behind-the-scenes glimpses into her creative world, including news about Book 2 and the continuation of Claire and Trevor's story.